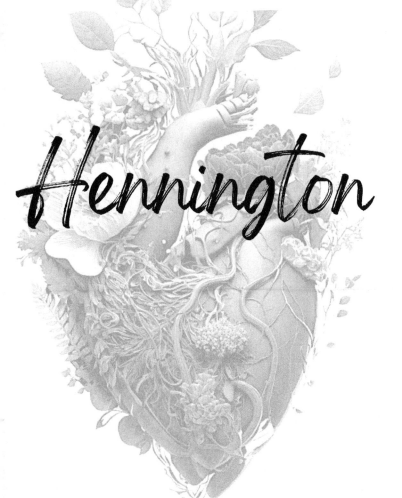

Hennington

Hennington
Jenn Jackson

First edition: 2023
ISBN 978-1-7381957-0-1 (paperback)
ISBN 978-1-7381957-1-8 (ebook)

Graphics by Canva
Edited by Samantha Gove
Cover Image from Depositphotos

To my husband.
Our love story is my favourite.

Note from the Author

Even though this is a dark contemporary adult romance with a happy ending, it's still one dark and twisted ride. Our characters go through some rough and dark situations and end up a little broken, with bumps, bruises and scars.

Just like us.

Yes, this is a work of fiction, but I've tried to keep this story based in reality, and that means that not everything is wrapped up in a pink bow with sunshine and rainbows. We don't always get out of situations unscathed. Sometimes, we struggle, and things don't turn out how we hoped they would or how we'd wanted them to. But that doesn't mean it wasn't an exciting journey.

Content Warning

This is an 18+ book, with many possible triggers and themes that could be disturbing and upsetting to some readers, such as stalking, kidnapping, abuse, sexual assault, torture, death of a family member, feelings of isolations and inadequacy, infertility, animal cruelty, thoughts of suicide, and child abuse.

Hennington

JENN JACKSON

Prologue

Adeline

Alex rolled off me, a small dribble of his release falling from the tip of his softening penis onto my naked thigh, and reached for the remote. Sex to TV in less than three seconds.

I'd love to say that this was new, or shockingly different, post-coital behaviour, but it wasn't. That was pretty much what happened whenever we had sex. Well, that wasn't true. It was what happened after sex for maybe the past year and a half. Before that, well, it wasn't fireworks, but it was good. You could tell there was intimacy and feelings involved. Now, it was like he couldn't get it in (or out of) me fast enough.

I knew that our marriage had been going down the shitter for a while now, but this was solidifying it for me. Sex had become a routine, like eating breakfast, brushing your teeth or locking the doors before you went to bed. Alex would look at me, look at his watch and simply say, "Come on," before he would grab my hand and take me up to bed, quickly pulling off his clothes like it was a race. The lube, which was necessary as there was zero foreplay, was left on his bedside table for easy access and bing, bang, boom, we were having sex. Or more like *he* was having sex…and I was the hole he was having sex with.

He flipped through the channels until he found the baseball game he didn't want to miss tonight while I lay there wondering if he even noticed that I hadn't come…and hadn't in a very long time.

I got out of bed, threw on my nightshirt, put my long strawberry-blonde hair up into a messy bun on the top of my head, and went back out to clean up the house. It was only 7pm, and the remnants of dinner were still on the stove, dishes needed to be done and Lucy, our golden retriever, was sitting by the back door wanting to be let out. I still had stuff to do before I could call it a night.

But as I put away the leftovers and started on the dishes, I got to thinking that tonight was different. Yes, it was different from the sex and intimacy that Alex and I used to have, but it was even different from the sex we more recently had, too. And the more I thought about it, I came to the realization that not a word was said, there was very little eye contact, and he didn't even kiss me. My husband, the man I was married to for seven years, didn't even touch his lips to mine while he was inside me.

The whole interaction just felt completely awkward and forced, as if it was something we *needed* to do to prove we still wanted each other versus the yearning, passion and desire that used to fuel our lovemaking. If I were honest, it hadn't felt good at all. It had felt like we were strangers having sex that neither of us actually wanted to have.

I never would have imagined Alex's touch feeling awkward or forced, but it had. I hadn't *wanted* him to touch me. I hadn't *wanted* to have sex with him. It shocked me to admit that I didn't *want* contact or intimacy from my husband anymore. We had clearly been growing distant for some time, but I never thought I would have gotten to the point where his touch made me uncomfortable.

I realized he had stopped giving me a kiss when he came home from work, and he had stopped saying "I love you" when he left in the morning, too. We barely talked about our days anymore; instead, just ate dinner in silence in front of the TV, and then he'd read the paper on his tablet, and I would clean up and feed Lucy. He did his thing, and I did mine. Two separate lives living under one roof. There were no shared interests, no shared hobbies, and, as of late, no shared life. There were no more sly touches when he walked past me, no more swats on the butt while I was doing the dishes, no more cuddles at night. I honestly didn't remember the last time he looked at me with lustful eyes. I was starting to feel undesirable, insufficient and insignificant. Something I never thought I would feel with Alex.

We used to be so happy, always on the go, making memories and laughing together all the time, but when I thought about it, I couldn't remember the last time I was really, truly happy. I couldn't remember the last time we were partners, making memories and enjoying life together. There was no more meaningful time with each other. Sure, we'd sit in the same room at dinner and together when the TV was on at night, but just because we sat in the same room didn't mean we were spending time together.

My life had become a repetitive routine of waking, working, cooking, sleeping, with no sprinkling of joy or life to be seen. We were no longer the Addy and Alex we once were.

All those small things were suddenly adding up. All the little changes I hadn't noticed came to light. It was a subtle change, but it was there. He was still the person I was closest to and cared about the most in the world, but it was like our entire relationship had suddenly flipped on its axis, and he was no longer my North Star. He no longer felt like home. There was a wall that wasn't there before. We had slipped into a roommate zone. It was a revelation, and not a good one, or one I could ignore.

I put down the pot I was scrubbing and made my way to the bedroom. The chores could wait.

We had met at 26, were married at 28, and here I was at 35. Alex and I used to know everything about each other, but suddenly, it felt awkward being in the same room with him. This no longer felt right. *We* no longer felt right.

I walked in, sat on my side of the bed and just waited. I ventured a look at him and saw the man I fell in love with. He was the first person to ever love me.

I remembered the first time I saw his soft, emotion-filled brown eyes. The first time I ran my fingers through his thick, floppy black hair that was now down to his shoulders. The first time I kissed his beautiful mouth that always hitched to the left when he smiled his charming, crooked smile.

But the man I first fell in love with was nowhere to be found. Now, his eyes were glued to the TV on our dresser, his body was tense, his jaw clenched, and it was as if he was purposefully trying to avoid eye contact. The old Alex would have pulled me into his arms and held me while he watched the game. But not now. Not this Alex. And I knew, instantly, that he felt it, too.

We couldn't live like this anymore. It had taken us over a year to get to this point. A painful year of constant fighting, biting our tongues, and just going through the motions. We had pulled so far away from each other; it was as if we were no longer invested in the life we created together. Our marriage had flatlined, and it needed life support, but we were both tired of trying to make it work when we both knew that what we had wasn't working anymore and couldn't be what it once was.

I turned back to the TV, knowing if I looked at him any longer, I wouldn't be able to keep it together. I steadied my voice and said the three words that had taken me a very long time to finally say.

"Are we done?" And as simple as those three words were, his "I think so" was just as easy.

And just like that, my marriage was over.

Chapter 1

8 months later

You've got to be fucking kidding me!

I stared at the flashing red and blue lights in my rear-view mirror as the cop signalled for me to pull over. This was just what I needed. It was only Wednesday and had already been the week from hell, and now I was getting pulled over just two houses down from my front door. Frickin' unbelievable.

Monday, I received a layoff notice from work due to a company buyout, and because I had just started the job two years ago when Alex and I moved to Hennington, the "last in, first out" rule applied. It was a job I could do in my sleep, completely thank-less and think-less. I was an assistant at a small legal divorce firm. *Ironic, isn't it – starting a job at a divorce firm just before I filed for my own divorce.*

Basically, the job was to answer phones, send out mail, book appointments, and set up and clean up meeting rooms. *I didn't work my ass off at university and get an English degree for this.* I wanted to be a writer, but writing didn't pay the bills. And although Alex's job working for the city as an urban planner was great, it hadn't been enough to support both of us in the new house. I had needed something to keep me busy, something to bring in extra income to be able to travel and have fun. Plus, I had wanted to work. I had wanted to contribute to society, wanted to know that I didn't need to rely on Alex for everything. But now, I had a measly severance package, no job as of Friday and knew pretty much no one in this town…aside from Alex.

We had thought that moving to a small town that was quieter would have been great, and it was, except that when you moved to a place where you knew no one, it was hard to make friends as an adult, especially when you worked all day in a tiny 5-person office where you're the youngest one by at least 15 years.

Now, here I was on my way home to a quiet, almost empty house, with no husband, no dog – since he got Lucy in the divorce - to finish packing up the rest of my life. Selling the house as part of the divorce was the easiest decision for both of us. Not only had neither of us wanted the memories that went along with the house, but neither of us could have

That was one thing I hated about books. They could be a wonderful escape to a world you never knew and could let you live out your dreams and fantasies, but apparently, they could also slap you across the face with the truth of your own life and force you to face the ugly parts of yourself head-on.

I didn't want to disappear, not really. I just didn't want to…I don't know, deal with life? Be an adult? Start over? Be vulnerable? All of the above? And the worst of all, the only person I could talk to about it was Alex. The only person I could complain to or go to for advice was the person who was in the exact same boat I was in but was also the person I was trying to separate from. And now, living in the house by myself, not even having Lucy to talk to, talking out loud and screaming out to the Universe had become a frequent outlet.

But this was reality. This was the hard truth about being an adult. You didn't always like where you were in life, you didn't always have someone to lean on, and sometimes you had to pull up your big-girl pants and face what you didn't want to.

I got up off my air mattress, put my Kindle away, and went back out into my empty home. I still had work to do, and it was time I faced that reality and not allow myself to disappear in my despair.

Chapter 2

It was my last night in the house, and everything was already packed and moved to my new place. Tomorrow morning, I would pack up the air mattress I'd been sleeping on for the past week, put on the outfit that I left unpacked and be gone from here forever. Thankfully, the housing market was crazy, even out in the small towns. We were in a "sellers-market," and the buyers ended up paying far above the asking price, allowing us to sell the house for WAY more than what we paid for it. It was a great investment that left me feeling okay with not having a job at the moment, but in all honesty, that money mostly went into the down payment on my new home.

My phone dinged while I was wiping down the inside of the fridge and throwing out the old takeout flyers that were still stuck to the outside.

Alex: Happy last night in the house. Look outside.

I went to the front door, and there, in its brown bagged glory, was my favourite Chinese food. Alex was in his car across the street and waved.

With a large smile on my face, I quickly slipped on my black ballet flats and ran across the street to his driver-side window.

"What are you doing here?" I asked with a smile as soon as he rolled the window down. The crooked smile that Alex gave me still had the power to squeeze my heart. "Why don't you come in?"

"Nah," he drawled, "I've already said goodbye to the house, and I don't want to make your last night harder with me sticking around."

"Are you sure? I honestly don't mind."

"It's okay, Addy." He placed his hand on top of mine, which was resting on the window frame of his door. "But you enjoy your crappy, heartburn-inducing Chinese food."

We stared at each other for a beat before he gave me another small, crooked smile. "Love you, Adds."

"Love you, too."

I ran back into the house and grabbed the Chinese food from the front stoop before I headed into the kitchen and dug into my Cantonese Chow Mein.

Alex was a good man, a damn good man, but he wasn't the man for me. That's not to say that he was perfect because he was not, but neither was I. No one was. But the Alex I married was not the same Alex I divorced.

There were times when my life with Alex wasn't so good. There was the time he forgot to pick me up from work when my car was at the shop, the time he told me he had settled for me because he was tired of dating around, there were times when he got mad that meals weren't made for him when he got home, or he couldn't find clean work pants because I hadn't washed them for him. The worst was the time when we got into such a bad fight he ended up punching a hole in the drywall in the garage.

But I knew I wasn't the perfect wife either. I would get mad at Alex over the stupidest things. He would say something, and I would take it personally, even though it wasn't meant that way. I would hassle him because he was tired after work, and I wanted to do something. And let's not forget all the times when I would get mad at him because he left his laundry on the bedroom floor and didn't put them in the hamper, but he was out mowing the lawn, trimming the hedges and picking up the dog poop in the backyard.

Alex was no angel, but neither was I. We were both flawed and, truthfully, annoyed each other and started the same amount of arguments and fights. No one was to blame for our marriage falling apart. It had run its course and had to inevitably come to an end. We had a successful marriage. It was just shorter than we thought it would be.

And, like this house, my life now felt empty. My best friend was gone, the person I spent every day with for the past seven years. I didn't know who I was without him.

On top of that, my parents and I weren't on speaking terms anymore. They were very religious people and didn't believe in divorce. They thought I was giving up, that I was too greedy and selfish and said some horrible things that they couldn't take back, not that they would ever want to. They said I had made a promise when I got married, and by divorcing Alex, I was breaking that promise and going back on my word. My happiness didn't matter in the eyes of the church. I had broken my promise to God, and for that, they couldn't forgive me.

But it was time for a fresh start, time to hit the reset button on my life. How often did people have that chance? And as crappy and miserable as it was just having gone through a divorce, a buyout at work, family abandonment, and house loss, I had the chance to start over. A chance to reshape how I wanted my life to be.

I had already made one huge change this week after the divorce was finalized; I was officially in the process of legally going back to my old last name. I would no longer be Adeline Adams, the wife of Alexander Adams. In six to eight weeks, I would once again be a Peters. I had already started calling myself Adeline Peters again, making a clear cut from the Adams life I once had.

"Addy Adams" had always made me feel like a 12-year-old cartoon character. People had always said they liked it, but it didn't feel like a strong, powerful name, something that I was proud to call myself. *That should have been my first warning that the marriage was doomed.*

I didn't want to be a Peters again either, and I didn't even know if I should technically call myself one since I was disowned by my Peters family. Going back to the Peters name felt fake. I wasn't a Peters anymore, anyway. Not in the eyes of my family, at least. Adeline Ruth Peters, the name I was born with. The name I would once again (reluctantly) embrace, even if it didn't embrace me back.

As I labelled some of the final boxes, I thought about who I was now. This was the first time in my life I was just...me. My identity had always been valued in relation to others; I was my parents' daughter, or I was Alex's wife. And even in those rare situations where I was just "Addy Peters," I was always being compared to others. I was never just good enough being me.

I was the daughter who wasn't enough for my parents. I wasn't smart enough, wasn't pretty enough, wasn't friendly enough, wasn't helpful enough, wasn't ambitious enough, was too lazy because I would have rather curled up with a book than go pear picking for my family's farm.

Addy Peters, the friend, was the forgotten one. I was the one who was overlooked and, when seen, was criticized. Somehow, I had been called too loud, too opinionated, too 'in your face,' too withdrawn, too quiet, and too shy all at once. I was too much and yet never enough.

Addy Peters, the girlfriend, was the one the guys kissed once but never dated. The one they said was "too emotional," "a bad kisser," "boring," and "a prude." I was the kind of girl guys were friends with. They didn't date. And if they did date, I was the dirty little secret who they dated behind closed doors. I wasn't good enough or hot enough for them to be seen with me in public.

And now I was back to Adeline Peters, the adult. By society's standards, at this age, I *should* have been settled, financially secure, had a friend and a family base, a secure job, a place to live, and be confident in who I was. I should have been good enough for *myself*, but somehow, never being enough to others had made it that I was not good enough in my own eyes. I was a bad friend, a bad wife, a forgettable employee, and a disappointing daughter.

Instead of spiralling down another Sand Trap of despair, focusing on my husband-less, child-less, job-less, friend-less, family-less life, I taped another box shut and moved on to the next task. All I saw now was a blank slate. Some people would have seen it as an opportunity, an adventure. I saw it as similar to being dropped in the middle of a field, no buildings, people, or life in sight, just vast, flat lands and emptiness. And instead of searching to find your way home when you didn't even know what home looked like anymore, I was looking for a plot of land to start over.

A place where I could carve my own spot in the earth, claim it as mine, and build my life how I wanted it to be.

I had to take this moment in life for what it was. People got divorced, people lost their jobs, people faced hardship all the time, and they moved on. They persevered. I knew it would be hard, but I had to do it. I had to get over myself and my struggles and put one foot in front of the other. I had no other option. I either had to get over it or give up, and over the past eight months that Alex and I had been separated, I had learned that I was all I had. I was the only person I could rely on and the one who had to get everything done. I couldn't give up. As hard as it was, I had to swallow my sorrow and self-pity and stand up for myself.

Chapter 3

My new home was the ground floor unit of a tri-plex on the opposite side of Hennington. I still loved the small-town life, and my new home was small, simple and seemed perfect.

It was an older building, originally built in the 1950s, but had clearly been kept up with. It looked like the last renovation was done in the late 1990s, with the countertops, cupboards and bathroom vanity all needing to be brought up to date. But they all served their purpose and were all still in great shape. I didn't pick the house because it was stylish but because it was comfortable and affordable since I still hadn't found a new job and was living off my savings from the sale of the old house.

The place was small, no more than 800 square feet, but it was just me now, and it was really all I needed. It was a cute 2-bedroom with huge windows, lots of storage space and beautiful original hardwood floors. It had loads of character with deep window sills, original lighting fixtures and tons of natural light. I was excited to move in… until I woke up on moving day.

If the dark skies weren't an indicator that today was going to be harder than necessary, the torrential downpour certainly was. This felt personal and fit my mood.

"Fuck," I whispered as I sat in my car, staring at my new front door. I was parked in the driveway, my hatch full of boxes that needed to be unpacked, the final load from the house, and zero motivation to take this final step. Five boxes, one suitcase and a duffle bag, that's all I had left, but with the rain, it felt like a monumental task.

I grabbed the keys out of my purse and sprinted up the steps to the front door, making sure it was unlocked before I grabbed a box.

My door was the one on the right; the person who lived upstairs had their door to the left of the shared porch, and there was someone who lived below, with their door at the side of the complex.

It was a strange arrangement. According to the real estate agent, the complex belonged to some bachelor who rented out the upstairs and basement units but lived on the main floor. He recently bought another tri-plex and was moving into that one, but didn't want to let this one go. In order to get the down payment, he sold the main floor unit to me but kept the other two as rentals. Strange, but worked in my favour.

I let myself into my new home, did a quick look around and darted back out to the car to start unloading. I hadn't even managed to get the first box unloaded before I slipped on the wet steps, crashed down onto the porch and dropped my box labelled "Kitchen FRAGILE." The sound of smashed plates broke through the sound of rain. *Of course.*

Tears burned behind my eyes, but I refused to let them fall. I set the box down on the porch and brushed off the rain and dirt on my hands before I went to lift the box up again.

Two things happened at once: one – the door to the left opened, allowing my new neighbour, or at least I assumed the blond man staring at me was my neighbour, to see me on my hands and knees trying to pick the box back up in the pouring rain, and two – the bottom of the box fell out. Completely fell apart, and the contents inside fell through the bottom like the cardboard was a wet Kleenex. If I thought all my dishes were broken before, oh, how I was mistaken.

"Oh, shit!"

The voice beside me barely even registered as I dropped the box and looked down at the porcelain graveyard that was once my kitchen set. Not a single plate, dinner or side, was saved.

"Let me help."

I turned to look at the source of the voice and finally took in the man standing beside me. Although he was now wet because of the rain, he still quickly claimed my attention. He was probably in his late 20s, at least 6 feet tall, blond, light eyes, and surprisingly looked like the Cincinnati Bangles Quarterback Joe Burrows. How the hell I retained information about the Bangles QB, I'll never know. I was not a sports fan, but Alex was, and we watched football religiously on Sunday nights. I guess some things must have stuck.

"I'm Kyle," he said as he knelt down beside me and started to help me gather up the broken pieces. "I'm guessing you're my new neighbour?"

"Yup," I sighed, trying not to let my current depressive state taint the introduction. I held out my hand to shake his. "I'm Addy."

I quickly started picking up the large pieces and throwing them into a pile in the corner of the porch. It was still pouring, and the box they originally came in was pretty much non-existent anymore. When the rain finally stopped, I would clean everything up properly, but for right now, I just wanted to clear the path so I could finish unpacking and get out of these wet clothes. "Talk about a good first impression, huh?"

Kyle laughed as he added pieces to my pile. "Meh, I've had worse. I'll take the chance to help a pretty lady in need any day."

I chuckled under my breath before a piece of plate slipped out of my grip and sliced my palm.

"Shit!" I looked at my hand, which was quickly spilling blood down my fingers. I needed to get it wrapped, but of course, I had no idea where my first aid kit or even my dish towels were. "Do you have any gauze?"

Kyle looked over, seeing my hand clutched to my chest and blood now running down the outside of my jacket and jackknifed to his feet. "Oh, damn. Yeah, I have stuff upstairs."

He ran back into his place as I went into mine, purposefully leaving the door cracked so he could just come in. A knock came on the door not 30 seconds later before Kyle called my name and came in. He found me in the kitchen, running my palm under the faucet.

"Here," he said as he threw a red box and a bunch of towels on the counter. "Wrap your hand while I find a Band-Aid or something. How bad is it?" I pulled my hand away from under the water to see how much it was still bleeding. It looked like it was slowing a bit, but a long cut was clear on my palm.

"It's not too deep and not bleeding as bad anymore."

Gently, he took my hand in both of his and looked at the wound. If I were in a movie, this would have been the perfect "meet-cute" and the start of a love story. As it was, it was now thundering and lightning outside, the wind was howling, we were both sopping wet, soaking the floors. I had nowhere to sit as all my furniture was still wrapped from the movers, and boxes were all over the house. This wasn't the start of something romantic; this was my life in chaos.

Kyle cleaned my wound with Polysporin and applied gauze and medical tape.

"You're good at this," I remarked as he gently tore off the last bit of tape.

"Thanks. I used to play football and got injured all the time." He looked up at me and quirked a little smirk.

I cleaned up the kitchen as Kyle went back outside and began bringing in the rest of my boxes. I told him multiple times he didn't have to since he was clearly on his way out when he ran into me on the porch, but he insisted. "If I'm gone, and you fall again, who's going to help you? Plus, I'm almost out of gauze. I can't risk it." *Okay, I know I'm rusty, but this guy is definitely on the flirty end.*

Before I had the floors dried with the towels he brought over, all the boxes were in the hallway, and my duffle and suitcase were in the guest room.

"I don't know how I can thank you. You really didn't need to help, but I really appreciate it."

"Well," he began as he gathered up his now wet towels and the first aid kit, "you could join me for dinner."

"As sweet as your offer is," I said, "I'm soaked, have a house to unpack, and you were on your way out." Kyle's face instantly started to drop. *Way to make nice with the new neighbour, Addy.* "But, what about a rain check? How about you come over tomorrow for pizza and beer as a thanks for all the help?"

The smile instantly returned to Kyle's lips, which I realized I was staring at, and he enthusiastically agreed.

"It's a date," he winked as he made his way to the door. "See you tomorrow."

It felt weird having a guy wink at me when I was just newly divorced. I was just being friendly. I didn't want to jump into anything…although a rebound might be good to get out of the way and out of my system. Kyle was cute and seemed really sweet, but would a rebound with the guy who lived upstairs be a horrible idea?

Oh, who was I kidding? He was probably just trying to be nice and break the tension. Guys didn't flirt with someone like me. I had slept with two people in my entire life, and it wasn't for lack of trying. I slept with one guy in my final year of university, and it was a huge mistake. If I had known it was a "one and done" situation, I would have walked away, no matter how good a kisser he was. After that, I had the biggest dry spell in history until five years later when I met Alex at a pub when I was out for Nicole's birthday and ended up marrying him. I knew better than to read too much into Kyle's winks and his flirty banter, but maybe it was time for the new me to take some risks and see where life took me.

Chapter 4

I couldn't sleep.

It was the first night in my new house, and all I felt was loneliness. I had been alone in the old house after Alex and I separated, but this felt different. This felt like a new low. My life had officially started over. I had no husband, no friends, and I couldn't even take comfort in my new home since it wasn't a home yet; it was still just a house. I had no memories here; my life was still all packed up in brown boxes.

All my possessions, everything that meant something to me, ended up in eleven cardboard boxes. Eleven. My entire life and identity fit into eleven boxes. That was all that I was. I was only worth eleven boxes.

The sinking ache in my chest that had been present on and off all day came back and settled right between my ribs.

The more I accepted that this was my new reality in my new house and the more my Sand Trap spiralled, the lower I sank into the ache.

My Sand Trap had turned into a black hole in my chest, a dark pit where there was no light, no shadow, no sound, no warmth…just vast…nothingness. A deep emptiness where a feeling of numbness and "the end" seemed to live, and I was the fish on the end of the line that the unknown demon fisherman was slowly reeling in. With every feeling of despair, every thought of loneliness, every hurtful word I remembered, every pitiful look or moment I was ignored or forgotten, I got pulled a little bit closer to the nothingness, closer *into* the pit of nothingness.

My Sand Trap wasn't just my brain going over and over details of conversations and emotions anymore. It had become a literal sinking quicksand trap where I was being pulled down deeper and deeper into the darkness, and I was starting to become afraid of what would happen when I inevitably got pulled into the nothingness, and the nothingness finally took over.

Would my emotions shut off? Would my hopes and dreams be a thing of the past? Would I turn into one of those people who were like robots, going through the motions of life without even seeing it? Would I become a shell of myself? Would I care about anything, even life itself?

And the scary part was that I didn't know if that would be a bad thing.

I *yearned* for the freedom to not care what other people thought. I *wanted* a life where I didn't always feel like I was lacking or not enough. The attraction to the nothingness felt peaceful, almost as if giving up on myself and not caring about moving on would be a relief from the constant pressure that had been dragging me down my entire life.

But if I longed for the nothingness, what would be the point? What would have been the point of getting a divorce and wanting to start over? What would be the point of moving into a new home so I could start fresh? What would be the point of making friends with Kyle, who genuinely seemed nice and was, truthfully, cute and on my mind? If I fell into the nothingness, I wouldn't have cared that I was unhappy in my marriage, and I would have stayed with Alex.

But I wanted more. I wanted more than nothing.

Kyle could be more.

The thought made me stare harder at my bedroom ceiling where I imagined Kyle would be. I assumed all our units had the same layout, and if so, Kyle's bedroom would be right on top of mine. I listened closely but didn't hear anything. *At least he's not a snorer.*

It had been nice meeting Kyle today, although it had been under shitty conditions. I looked at the Band-Aid on my hand and remembered how gentle Kyle was. He had been nice, and if nothing else, I knew I had a caring neighbour just above me. A neighbour who kept stealing glances at me and who was very obviously flirty. And truth be told, I liked it. It wasn't something I was used to, and I didn't know how to react to it, but it felt nice being noticed.

What I felt for Kyle was definitely not *nothing*. It was most definitely something that I couldn't let the black hole take away. I didn't want to be detached and oblivious to the world around me. I wanted to feel. I wanted to have emotions and sly looks and tender touches.

I wanted it all. I wanted to live an exciting and happy life.

But until I got my life in order, I'd have to live vicariously through an outlet, so I sat up in bed, fluffed up my pillows behind me and grabbed my Kindle. I pulled up my favourite book, which I had read more times than I could count, and went along with Dakota as she put her three men in their places and set off on an adventure through the deadly terrain of the Superstition Mountains.

Dinner the next day with Kyle was easy and relaxing. He was once again flirty, but I was starting to think that was just his personality. I had managed to set up the living room before he came over, so we chilled on the couch, a football game playing on the TV in the background, and ate while getting to know a bit about each other. We talked about my move, where I moved from, and if I had any plans for the holidays, which were still roughly a month and a half away. Halloween had just passed three days earlier.

"Actually, this will be my first Christmas alone ever," I began, not wanting to delve too much into my divorce, but I could feel the "relationship status" question on the horizon. "My ex and I are newly divorced, so it's just me this year."

There was a shift in Kyle's eyes, and I couldn't tell if it was pity over my divorce or curiosity over my single status. One thing for sure, though, was that his smile instantly disappeared.

"It's okay. You don't have to be sad for me," I said. "I'm actually looking forward to a quiet Christmas without having to drive around and see family."

"You're not visiting any family either?"

"Nope," I said, letting the P pop at the end, trying the keep the conversation as light as possible. I took a drink of my beer before I continued. "We don't really talk. They're super religious and were completely against me getting a divorce. They won't accept the fact that I," I actually had to use air quotes here so Kyle didn't think these were my thoughts, "'broke my promise to God' as they put it, no matter how unhappy I was in my marriage. God came before me and my happiness."

The air grew thick and awkward between us. That was one thing I was always known for: no filter. I always just said what was on my mind, and in times like now, I wish I knew how to shut up.

"So," I jumped in, begging for a change in topic, "tell me about you."

"Well," Kyle started, a smirk coming back to his lips, which I couldn't take my eyes off of, "I'm 27, single, work as a data programmer, am single, love pizza, beer and football, and am single." We both chuckled at his emphasis on his single status.

He continued to talk about himself, dropping little facts here and there. He worked from home most days doing his techie web-based thing (to be honest, it was way over my head), grew up in Toronto, moved to Hennington about two years ago for a girl he thought he was going to marry, was an only child, and was big into sports.

It was so easy to carry on the conversation. He was smooth, scootching closer to me when he came back to the couch with another beer for each of us, constantly made me laugh with his stories but made sure that I had the chance to talk as well. His hands would sometimes touch my arm or my thigh when he was really animated about something like his team getting a touchdown when we paused our conversation to watch a bit of the game.

By the time the game was over, it was clear that Kyle was a huge flirt and that this hot 27-year-old was flirting with my 35-year-old, divorced ass. *Does that make me a cougar that I like it and want more?*

"Well, I'm going to head up," he nodded his head to his unit upstairs, "but thanks for a great night." He leaned down and pressed a sweet, soft kiss to my cheek as I walked him to the door. "Next game at my place?"

With one final wink, he walked out the door and made his way up to his unit. The gentle sound of his footsteps followed him, and it was a nice reminder that although it was just me down here, I wasn't really alone. A new friend was definitely welcome.

Chapter 5

"So, how's the unpacking going?"

I flopped down on the couch, careful to keep my paint-covered hands off the furniture as I carefully held the phone up to my ear, trying not to get paint from my hands on it.

"It's freaking exhausting, and I haven't even unpacked yet. I'm still painting the place, but there's so much shit. It's just moving boxes from one room to another at this point so I can paint," I sighed to Alex. "I didn't think I had this much crap."

He laughed in my ear, and it made me miss him deeply.

"Addy," he chuckled into the phone, "we had more crap than we knew what to do with. The old house was packed, and now you've moved into a smaller place."

"Yeah, but the majority of that crap was your work and baseball stuff."

"Plus, your library of books."

"Hey," I protested with a smile, "don't knock the books. There may be many, but they don't take up too much room. Unlike your signed bats and balls or your *hundreds* of vintage vinyl records that are in display cases and have been untouched for years."

"Yeah, but we had fun dancing to those vintage vinyl records."

The air grew thick over the phone, remembering the old days when Alex and I would dance to the sound of his old records playing throughout the house. More often than not, in the early days, those dances turned into naked, horizontal dancing.

"Yes," I admitted, "we did."

Alex cleared his throat, clearly on the same walk down memory lane that I was on. "So, what room are you painting?"

"I finished painting the bathroom yesterday and have now moved on to the office. It's taking longer than I expected, and now I'm stressed over how long the kitchen will take."

"Well, why didn't you ask for help?"

"Because it's not your problem, Alex. We're divorced. My problems are no longer your problems."

"Yes, but we're still friends. Friends can ask each other for help when they need it. You don't have to be Super Addy all the time." *Super Addy…I haven't felt like her in a long time.* "Why don't I come over tomorrow, and I can help you paint the kitchen," Alex offered, "and I can help set up the bedroom set and kitchen table and anything else that requires more than one set of hands."

"You don't have to do that," I protested. "I can figure it out."

"Or," he interrupted, "you can stop being stubborn and accept the help I'm offering."

With a sigh, I accepted Alex's help. It wasn't that I didn't want it; it was that I didn't know how I would feel being so close to him again. You never forgot your first love, and sometimes just the phone calls made me miss him and want to start things over again, maybe give us a second chance.

I missed him so damn much. The old him. The Alex who had swept me off my feet, who would sweep me up in his arms to dance with me when a good song came on, or who would randomly decide that we needed a date night and would take me out to our favourite restaurant. I also missed the hot and sweaty Alex, who had a fine ass in the tight baseball pants he wore for his rec league, or his naked chest that would glisten and heave when he exerted himself and tried to fix things around the house.

My heart and my hoo-ha missed him so much, but that Alex didn't exist anymore, and it was a battle my brain always won in the end.

A knock on my door broke me out of my lusting and heartbreak.

"Someone's at my door," I told Alex as I carefully got up off the couch, "but I'll see you tomorrow? I'll text you the address."

We said our goodbyes as I went and answered the door.

"Wow," Kyle said from the open doorway as his eyes swept over my body, "um, I'm…uh…" he broke off, cleared his throat and swept his hand over the back of his neck, averting his eyes to the ground. I looked down at myself and noticed, to my horror, that I answered the door in my tight bike shorts, a loose tank top and an old, worn-out sports bra. But it wasn't my clothing that made me turn around and furiously blush. It was the fact that one of my boobs had popped out of the sports bra.

I had always been heavy-chested, and when I laid down, gravity became an evil bitch and moved them around. I hadn't even noticed that when I was lying on the couch, one had popped out the top of my sports bra and my *very* low-cut tank top, saying hello to the world.

Luckily, it wasn't my whole breast, but just the top and my nipple that had waved to Kyle.

"I'm so sorry," I said as I shoved my breast back in place.

Kyle cleared his throat twice before he lifted his eyes and answered me. "No worries, I barely saw anything." The smirk he gave me told me he was lying and had gotten a full, unobstructed, front-row view of my nip slip. "I was going to see if you wanted some help, and then maybe I'd order some subs for dinner. Did you maybe want to join me? I know I said dinner at my place next time, but I thought you could probably use a hand."

With Alex's words about not always having to be "Super Addy" still rolling around in my head, my knee-jerk reaction to say, "That's okay, you don't have to," turned into a grateful acceptance of help.

Kyle ran upstairs to change into some painting clothes while I ran to the bedroom, ripped my old, clearly unsupportive sports bra off and threw it in the trash. I grabbed a newer one and made sure the girls were secure before putting back on my paint-covered top and going to let Kyle in.

It was hard to ignore the smirk that played on Kyle's lips or the way he was standing sideways, looking at the driveway when I opened the door.

"All clear?" he asked with a chuckle as he slowly turned his head to peek at me.

"Yes, you jerk," I laughed as I felt my cheeks turn pink. "All body parts are back in their proper upright and locked positions."

"Well, damn," he muttered as he walked past me and kissed my flaming cheek. "So, what are we painting?"

"The spare room," I said as he followed me down the hall. "It's going to be my office, so I was hoping to paint it and get some bookshelves assembled today."

"Well, I'm all yours." Kyle stood in the doorway to my office and took in the tarped floor and the cans, brushes and rollers sitting in the back corner. "Where do you want me to start?"

"Would you rather tape the baseboards and ceiling and then do the edging or paint the walls?" I held up a roll of painter's tape in one hand and the paint roller in the other. Unsurprisingly, he grabbed the roller and made his way to the tray that already had paint in it but was covered with plastic wrap to keep it from drying out.

We quickly got to work on our respective tasks. It wasn't even two minutes after I got down on the floor to tape and edge the baseboards that I heard something fall onto the floor, and Kyle mumble a soft "shit." I turned around just in time to see him turn away from me and look at the paint roller he dropped on the tarp.

"Everything okay…" I asked as Kyle seemed to remember himself and quickly picked up the roller.

"Uh…yeah, just got distracted there for a second." He quickly rolled the roller into the tray of paint and started painting the wall. If I hadn't known better, I would have sworn the back of his neck looked flushed.

"So, what else are you fixing in the house?" Kyle asked as he worked the deep wine-red paint over the ugly beige wall.

"Pretty much everything," I huffed as I grabbed another length of painter's tape and lined it up against the wall and floorboards. "It's all cosmetic, though. Paint, re-stain the hardwood floors, and maybe try and do something with the kitchen cabinets. The house itself is solid. It just doesn't look pretty."

"Everything looks damn good from where I'm standing," Kyle said as he looked down at me, his chest expanding as he took a deep breath. There was no misinterpreting his double meaning.

"Kyle…" I laughed awkwardly as I lowered my butt to the floor and sat on my legs.

"I know, I know…sorry," he said as he turned back to the wall and continued to paint. "But you can't blame me. You're bent over there, kneeling on the ground with your ass in the air, taping the floorboards…it's a nice view, and I'm only human."

"Well, thank you," I blushed, trying to accept the compliment for what it was. "And no need to apologize. It's nice being told I look good."

"Addy," he gritted through his teeth, "you look more than good. You're beautiful. Add to that how nice you are, the nip slip before, and now watching your ass in the air as you work…just…" He made a noise between a growl, a moan and 'mmmmmm,' and the sound went straight to my core.

Over the next half an hour, I kept feeling Kyle look at me. I would slyly look behind me and catch Kyle checking out my ass before he saw me looking and turned back around. The flirty banter continued as we worked side by side until I felt something cold and wet move over my ass and up my back. On instinct, I rolled away from the feeling and noticed Kyle standing right behind me with the paint roller in his hand.

"You didn't," I screamed as I quickly got to my feet and saw the red ass mark on the tarp. I turned my head and saw that a dark red line ran all the way up my back.

"Sorry, Addy, but it was just too tempting." His laugh proved that he wasn't sorry in the least. "Your ass was just there calling to me while you were bent over edging the baseboards. I couldn't help myself."

I grabbed the roller from his hand before he could stop me and rolled a wide stripe on his left cheek. "Yeah," I laughed, "I'm sorry too. Your face was calling to me."

"Give me that," he chuckled as he reached for the roller in my hand, but I held it away. He followed me around the room before he finally gave up the chase, grabbed me around the waist and rubbed his wet, paint-covered cheek against the side of my face.

"KYLE," I yelled as the paint transferred from his cheek to mine, but I couldn't help my smile. This was fun.

Kyle was fun, and if the way he was still holding onto my waist was any indication, he wanted to have more fun.

With a gentle, paint-covered finger, he pushed a piece of hair behind my ear, purposefully running his finger along the shell of my ear until he cupped my jaw. His thumb ran over my cheek as his eyes danced between mine and my mouth. As he leaned in closer, he ran his thumb over my bottom lip. Instinctively, my tongue poked out before I brought my bottom lip into my mouth, biting it softly. His thumb against my lip had tingled, and that wasn't the only place the tingles had started.

Slowly, he leaned down and rubbed his nose against mine before he finally met my lips in a kiss. His hand on my face held me in place as he took my bottom lip between his and kissed me with an urgency that was unmistakable.

His other arm was still wrapped around my waist and harshly pulled me closer to his body. As his kiss turned more forceful and his hands held me tighter, I began to panic and pulled away. This was my first kiss since Alex, and I was immediately in my head, worrying about where Kyle clearly wanted this to go.

Instantly, his shoulders slumped in disappointment. I wasn't ready for hot and heavy and desperate passion yet. I wasn't even sure I was ready to test the waters I was currently swimming in.

I stepped out of his hold before we got carried away and put the roller back in the tray, but when I stepped back up to face him again, my heart stopped. There he stood, not two feet away, using the bottom of his shirt to try and wipe the paint that was quickly drying off his cheek. My eyes couldn't help but take in his body as he lifted his shirt even higher to get some paint that was on his ear, revealing more of his abdomen and chest. His body was all muscle and smooth skin, damp with sweat from painting the room.

My body temperature instantly went up. Damn. Kyle may act like a child, but his body was definitely that of a man.

Chapter 6

Between unpacking, painting the bathroom, kitchen, master and spare bedrooms and setting up my new house how I wanted it, the next few weeks passed by in a blur.

Thursday nights had turned into PBF nights with Kyle: pizza, beer and football. For the past three weeks, he knocked on my door at 7 p.m. with four beers in hand and pizza delivery already on its way. It was never a discussion between us that Thursday nights were reserved for each other, but it was nice to have a new friend in my life, even if he was a bit presumptuous that he thought I'd be sitting and waiting for him every Thursday night.

We never really discussed the kiss that happened when we were painting my office. I think he got the point the next day when he came knocking on my door, and as soon as I opened it, he pushed me against my foyer wall and started licking, biting and groping me. Before I realized what was happening, his tongue was in my mouth, his one hand was gripping my hair, and the other hand was pushing up under my shirt. I immediately turned my head and tried to push him away. When he finally got the hint – after calling his name and telling him to stop twice – he apologized for going overboard and said he had been thinking about me all night and was just really happy to see me. I understood what he was saying, but his lack of control and the force he was using was an instant red flag.

After that, the flirting never stopped but never really went further. There were sly touches, lingering looks and a kiss on the cheek at the end of the night, but that was it. When he was sweet, I felt like I was a teenager again, waiting for the boy to make the move. Last night, he even pulled the "yawn and put your arm over her shoulder" move. This was the Kyle I liked and wanted to get to know better, not the aggressive man who came in and forced his desire on me. This was the Kyle that I could see myself being with. I cuddled into his side as we watched his beloved Cleveland Browns win. Kyle was over the moon as he had some money on the game, and tonight, he insisted on taking me out to celebrate. Apparently, I was his "good luck charm."

"A dive bar? Really?" I took in the small *Ape Hangers* sign above a non-descript door with surprise. We were tucked away in the back corner of the parking lot that all the shops on Main Street shared. I'd never noticed this little piece of small-town rebellion before, even though I passed it all the time to come to the market. The little gathering of motorcycles in the corner should have been a dead giveaway.

"Trust me," Kyle smirked as he opened the door for me and let me in, "they play the best classic rock and have cheap drinks. Plus, it's the only real bar in town."

It was true. Small town Hennington didn't have any bars as far as I knew, except for the small one inside the restaurant three doors down. But *Ape Hangers* was a true bar. As we walked into the small hole in the wall, I was surprised at how big it actually was. There were a dozen small tables scattered around, a couple pool tables, and a small stage that looked like it was for live bands but was currently being occupied by a woman in a leather bikini top and black leather chaps (and thankfully underwear underneath) dancing away to Aerosmith. The entire opposite side of the space was taken up by the bar.

We snagged a table in the back corner, away from the girl drunkenly dancing on the stage, and Kyle grabbed a couple of beers. He had learned early that when I said I liked beer, it was one type and one type only: Corona with extra lime. And like the friend he was, he came back with three extra lime slices in a glass for me.

"Cheers," I toasted as Kyle sat across from me with those intense eyes again. "To your beloved Browns. May they make you loads of money and keep me in free beer."

"Oh, trust me," Kyle chuckled with an evil grin, "if my bets keep paying out like last night, I'll be set for life."

He pulled out his wallet and set it on the table between us. The black leather bowed with the amount of bills that were stuffed in there. And by their brownish-yellow colour, it was easy to see that they were all hundreds.

"Holy shit," I coughed, almost spitting my beer in his face. "You got all that last night on one bet?"

"Sweetness," he purred, "this is just what they gave me in cash. Only a fraction of what I actually won. The rest went straight into my account. You should see it all. We could go swimming in the pile of money, it was so much. It's a heap of money we can have sex on. And it's all thanks to you. My little good luck charm. I'm so loaded I don't know what to buy first. I can buy you someone to paint your place for you, Sweets. I have people-buying money." He leaned over the table to press a kiss against my lips before he clinked his bottle against mine again and downed the whole thing in one go.

I couldn't wrap my mind around what I'd just heard. I ignored him calling me "Sweetness" for the moment, as that was a whole other issue. He had to have had at least a couple grand sitting in his wallet, and that was just a little bit of what he won? And then to whip it out to show it off? There was being happy and proud of your accomplishments or sharing good news, but that wasn't what Kyle was being. He was being cocky and smug. The couple of times that Kyle and I had hung out, he was confident, sure, but wasn't so high on himself. The fact that he whipped his wallet out to show me his winnings and said that he had enough money to "buy people" didn't sit well with me.

Nor did the fact that even though he had scooted his chair closer to mine, had his hand on my thigh and had just kissed me, his eyes kept finding the girl dancing on stage and the hot bartender on the other side of the room. His eyes moved between the two of them before coming back to settle on me. It seemed my initial assessment was correct. Kyle was a flirt, and it wasn't just me he was interested in. At the rate of his wandering eyes, it looked like he was interested in anything with long legs and short shorts.

"Thanks for coming out with me to celebrate," Kyle said as we walked the four blocks home. "It means a lot." He put his hands on my hips and pulled me to the inside of the sidewalk so he could be on the roadside. "Wouldn't want you to trip and fall into the road."

"Thanks." The smile I gave Kyle was genuine. Although he had been more...boastful...than I would have been in the same situation, I guess I wasn't really in a place to judge someone's happiness. I may not be as "in your face" when I celebrated good things, but it didn't make Kyle a bad guy. It just made him a happy, showy person. Maybe it was an age thing.

But in the end, it really didn't matter. I had fun with Kyle tonight. He had introduced me to a new, fun bar in town, and we laughed most of the night away. And he even pulled me up onstage to dance when STYX came on. And although, yes, he did keep eyeing the dancer and the bartender, he never abandoned me for them. He looked at me with the same interest as he did them. There was no extended lingering at the bar when he got the drinks, and he didn't go up to the dancer and start dancing with her like some of the guys did.

I was starting to think that I was judging Kyle too harshly. I felt old compared to him, already married and divorced, but he was still having fun in his twenties. I couldn't judge him for that, especially since he was starting to make me feel younger and more carefree.

Kyle was growing on me.

"I had a lot of fun tonight," I told him as we turned onto our street. "Thanks for taking me out."

"Adeline," he smiled as he kissed the top of my hand, which was linked with his, "it was my pleasure." He gave my fingers a little squeeze as we walked up the driveway. "In fact, would you want to go out for dinner sometime this week?"

"Kyle," I teased, "are you asking me out on a date?"

The sincerity on his face as we stopped in front of our doorways gave me little butterflies. "Yeah, Addy, I am."

Was I ready to date? Was I ready for my first date after my divorce to be with Kyle? He was fun to be around, but did I want to date him? But then again, was tonight a date? Regardless of what it was, I had fun. When Kyle and I had our Thursday pizza, beer and football nights, I had fun. I enjoyed being around him, even if there were some personality differences between us.

"Okay," I smiled up at him, "I'd like that."

The smile I got back was huge. "Does tomorrow night work?" he asked excitedly.

"Tomorrow night works perfect," I smiled back.

Kyle leaned down and gave me a slow, gentle kiss before he said his goodnight and went up to his unit. I was actually excited for this date. I didn't know if I had feelings for Kyle, but I liked hanging out with him. Maybe tonight's bravado was just a fluke because he was so excited. I guess I'll find out tomorrow.

Chapter 7

Rollies was one of the two non-fast-food restaurants we had in town. The other was a ma-and-pa diner that made amazing homemade soups and sandwiches, but *Rollies* was where you went for dinner. It was a nice place that wasn't too fancy but served good food and had a relaxed environment. The booth we sat in was on the bar side of the restaurant and was right along the front window that looked out onto Main Street. It was perfect for people-watching.

Kyle had been sweet when he knocked on my door to pick me up. He actually brought me a tiny pot of beautiful, deep burgundy chrysanthemums. He was trying, and that was all I could ask for. The arrogant, showy Kyle from last night was nowhere to be seen. He was funny and relaxed, and the conversation was easy. It just seemed like two friends hanging out.

But as the dinner went on, and the more beers he ordered, the more "Sweetness," "Sweets," and "You're so hot" came out. Whenever I bent down to eat my meal, I would notice his eyes would go straight down my top. Moments later, I could feel his foot moving up my leg, trying to play footsie with me underneath the table.

"Kyle," I warned as I pulled my leg back. Normally, I wouldn't have minded, but this was a family restaurant, and Kyle wasn't being discrete at all.

"You're so sexy!" The table beside us looked over at how loud Kyle was. "Fuck, look at your rack! I can't wait to suck your nipples."

"Kyle!" I scolded. "Keep your voice down."

"Your ex is a moron for divorcing you. When I finally get to fuck you, I'm never letting you go."

"Kyle, enough!" I said as I turned and apologized to the table beside us for the interruption.

"What?!" Kyle barked back. "It's true. You're hot."

"Can we get the cheque please?" I asked as the waitress came by to see what the ruckus was.

"But I'm not done," Kyle whined as I finished my one glass of wine, and Kyle held up his fifth schooner, which was still half full.

"You're being inappropriate and loud," I told him, trying to be as quiet and non-confrontational as possible.

"Oh, come on, Sweets, let loose, have a little fun."

"I was having fun, but maybe you've had enough to drink. You're causing a scene."

"Why do you have to be so uptight and judgemental? I'm just having a couple beers with my hot neighbour."

Maybe the bravado was all because of his drinking. He was never like this when we had our pizza, beer and football nights, but that was only two beers each over the span of a football game. He'd already had five schooners in the 45-minute dinner so far. Maybe he just couldn't hold his alcohol…or had a drinking problem.

Whatever the reason, I didn't want to sit here causing a scene, especially in front of the nice family with two young kids who were sitting at the table beside us. I grabbed two twenties out of my wallet and put them on the table before I grabbed my purse and jacket.

"Thank you for the date, Kyle, but I think we've both had enough for the night. I'll see you later."

I heard him yell out, "PRUDE!" as I walked to the front of the restaurant, apologized to the hostess and walked home. Apparently, I had to rethink my earlier judgment of Kyle. He was too unpredictable, and I couldn't figure out who he was. One minute, he was kind and sweet, but the next, he objectified me and called me a prude. One thing was for sure. Kyle needed to grow up.

Rollies was just a couple doors down from *Ape Hangers*, so the walk home was quick and pretty, as the streets were already decorated for Christmas. The street lamps had small wreaths over the old-fashioned glass lights, the storefronts had winter scenes painted in their windows, and the town had decorated the clock tower with beautiful white lights that lit up the structure. The streets and sidewalks were cleared and salted, but I still had to pay attention to where I was going as the snow started to lightly fall. I took a quick glance at the huge nativity scene the town had erected beside the clock tower before I got to my street.

But as I got to the corner, I could see my house and noticed someone standing on my front stoop, trying to peer into my front window. I paused on the corner and watched the man pound on my front door, jiggle the handle and then peer into my front window again.

"KYLE! Man, let me in!" The guy was looking for Kyle and was not too happy about it from the looks of things. I slowly made my way closer to home, somewhat relieved that it wasn't some random person trying to break into my house. "Come on, man! I'm freezing my balls off out here."

I walked up my driveway with caution as I couldn't tell if this man was drunk, high, or mentally unstable, yelling as loud as he was.

"Ummmm, Kyle's not home," I said as I stopped at the end of the walkway, leaving plenty of space between me and the stranger. "You're actually pounding on my door. Kyle's is the one on the left."

The man turned with a quick jerk, clearly surprised to be caught off guard. He wobbled a bit and had to shift his feet to keep his balance. The man was clearly drunk – much like Kyle had been when I left him at the restaurant. Makes sense that these two inappropriate, inebriated idiots would be friends.

"What?" the man asked, not understanding what was going on.

"Kyle's unit is the door on the left. That's my unit you're trying to break into."

He turned back to look at the door and then turned his head to the left, clearly seeing the other door for the first time. He looked back and forth a couple times before he shuffled over to Kyle's door and proceeded to knock on it.

"KYLE! Open the fucking door, man!"

I grabbed my keys out of my purse and made my way onto the front porch. "He's not home," I told him again, just wanting him to leave at this point. "He's at *Rollies* having a couple drinks if you need him."

The guy's face transformed into pure excitement, and without a single word, he ran and jumped off the front porch and booked it down the driveway.

Before he could turn around and try to get into my house again, I let myself in, closed and locked the door behind me. But once inside, the silence and emptiness of my home brought on a wave of loneliness. Out of nowhere, I had an urgent need to talk to Alex.

Addy: Hey

I put my phone on the kitchen table as I took a bottle of beer out of the fridge. Just as I was popping the cap, my phone chimed with an incoming text.

Alex: Hey, Adds. What's up?

Addy: Not much. Just got home from a really shitty date.

I plopped down on my couch, my beer in hand, and turned on the TV. Telling Alex that I was on a date felt weird, but when he first started back on the dating scene, he told me so that it wouldn't be awkward if I saw him on a date around town. I actually appreciated the thoughtfulness of it, to be honest.

Alex: That sucks. Why was it shitty?

Addy: We were at *Rollies,* and the guy got drunk and was really loud and inappropriate.

Alex: Oh shit, what did he say?

Addy: Oh, just stupid stuff about how hot I was, how I had nice jugs, and he couldn't wait to fuck me. Mind you, this was all said at a super loud volume with a family of 4 right beside us.

Alex: Bahahahaha! Well…at least the guy was telling you the truth. You are hot, and you do have nice jugs lol 😊

Addy: You only say that because you're a boob man.

Alex: No, I'm saying that because you have lovely tatas.

Addy: You always did have an unhealthy obsession with my breasts.

Alex: Hey, I lost them in the divorce, too.

Addy: They're part of me lol. It's not like they're children where you can get them for a weekend.

Alex: Maybe that can be arranged?

I paused. *Is he serious? He wants to arrange time to spend with my breasts? No, he's got to just be playing along.*

Deep down, I knew he was joking, but the thought of his hands on me again lit a small fire in my stomach. Fuck, I was starting to get butterflies by just thinking of the possibility. I did miss him. I missed his hands and his lips and being held by him. But was he missing me? Was he being silly or serious?

I stared at the message for a minute, my thoughts running over all the possible scenarios that could happen if I responded the way I wanted to. I eventually took a deep breath and bit the bullet.

Addy: Is that something you'd want? Some time with the twins?

I was nervous. It felt strange being all flirty with Alex. It had just started out as a fun conversation, but for some reason, now it felt more intense. It felt more real. I wanted to see where this went. Unfortunately, I didn't know what he was thinking and if this was freaking him out.

Alex: Don't go there, Addy. It's been a long time since I've seen my girls. I miss them terribly.

My heart was racing in my chest. He was flirting right back. Was he wanting this, too? I took a big breath before I replied with a question I knew I shouldn't have asked.

Addy: How terribly?

The three dots immediately started, then stopped, then started again.

Alex: Bad enough that just thinking about them is stirring up feelings I don't want to have.

Addy: And what are these feelings making you want to do?

A good three minutes passed without a response from Alex. I knew I shouldn't have gone there. I knew I shouldn't have pushed him. We were divorced. We shouldn't be flirting and talking like this. I had gone too far. With regret in my stomach, I turned off the TV, chugged the rest of my beer and started to get ready for bed. I was making bad calls all over the place today and just needed this day to be over with.

DING

My notification went off just as I was throwing my last make-up remover wipe in the trash. Alex had responded, but did I want to see what he wrote? Did I want to be lectured by him for pushing the boundaries of our divorce and friendship? *God, why am I such an idiot?*

I turned off all the lights and double-checked the locks before I climbed into bed. With a deep breath, I picked up my phone and checked Alex's message.

Alex: They're making me want to come over to your place, rip off your shirt and suck your beautiful, hard nipples into my mouth while you run your fingers through my hair and moan my name …

I was stunned. That was NOT the response I was expecting from Alex. He was the controlled one, the one who made the mature, smart decisions. He wasn't the one who took risks or made rash decisions. But here he was, sexting with me.

And I liked it.

I had to figure out how to respond. This was new territory for us. I had to be careful here, or we risked losing the fragile friendship we still clung to. But if he was willing to open up and be honest…

Addy: And then what?

Alex: Are you really wanting to go there, Addy?

My response was immediate and true.

Addy: Yes. What do you want to do to me, Alex?

Chapter 8

Christmas was always a time I both loved and hated. I loved the snow, the decorations, the spirit of giving and being just the tiniest bit kinder to everyone. However, I hated the commercialism, the pressure to get "the right" gift for someone and how it was all about being with the ones you loved. And for someone like me who didn't have anyone to love, let alone someone who loved me back, it was a bit lonely.

Alex: Happy Tree Hunting Day

Alex and I continued to text on and off. I was afraid after our sexting encounter that it would change our relationship, but it didn't. We both just acted like it had never happened. But truth be told, it had been hot, and I had ended up writhing around in the sheets before I had to take matters into my own hands…literally. We haven't ventured into the sexting situation again, but he would randomly text to see how I was doing and check in. Just like now.

December 1st had always been our Christmas tree day. We would go to a tree farm and cut down a real tree, bring it back to the house and start to decorate. There were no Christmas movies, no Christmas decorations and no Christmas music in the house until December 1st, and then it was as if the house threw up Christmas after that. And today was December 1st, our traditional Tree Hunting Day.

Alex: Still planning on going out and grabbing a tree this year?

Addy: I haven't decided, actually.

Alex: What do you mean you haven't decided. You freakin love Christmas, Addy. Why WOULDN'T you be getting a tree?

Addy: I don't know. I would typically start decorating the house today, pull out my old Christmas CDs and movies and … well, you know what I was like. But this year, I don't know if that's something I want to do.

Alex: Is it because you're alone?

Wow, leave it to Alex to hit the nail on the head. He was never this observant when we were married, but he knew me well.

Addy: Maybe?

Alex: How about I come pick you up, and we go together. Just because we're not married anymore doesn't mean that we can't still do things together.

A tear came to my eye while reading Alex's message. I did miss him; he was my best friend, and it was hard having the main person in my life not be there anymore. Yes, we had separated before the divorce papers were signed, and yes, Alex had moved out, and I had been living alone in our old house before moving here, but the pain didn't go away. I had just become numb to it.

Addy: Thanks, but that's okay. If I decide I want to do this, I think I need to do it on my own.

Alex took a while before he responded. The text message went to READ, and the three dots appeared, showing he was typing and then stopped and began typing again. Knowing him, there was something he wanted to say but didn't know how to say it. I knew that I just had to be patient.

Alex: Okay, but I miss you, so if you want the company, let me know. I'll drop my plans and be right over.

Addy: Thank you, but that's not needed. We can get together over the holidays when you have a couple days off.

Most people would think it was strange the way that Alex and I stayed connected after our divorce, especially since there were no kids involved to force our continued communication, but Alex was still my person, my comfort. We still spoke all the time, and I didn't see that ending anytime soon. We still loved each other; we just weren't in love anymore.

Alex: Sounds good. Let me know if you change your mind.

Addy: Will do.

Alex: So, besides being unsure how you're going to celebrate Christmas this year, how is everything else going? Are you all unpacked? How's work going?

Shortly after I moved in, I put an ad in the local paper that I was looking for freelance remote administrative and writing work, offering to help with document creation, data entry and proofing of documents. *Thank God for that English degree.* Amazingly, I got a couple responses within the first couple of days. I was asked to edit an article for a special Christmas Newsletter the local paper was publishing, helped the new wellness centre create a press release for their grand opening, was asked to manage data entry for someone who made jewelry in their garage and sold it online and at the local Sunday flee market (but who apparently was horrible with numbers and had no idea if she'd made any money in the two years she had been doing this), and was asked by a ma-and-pa bakery if I could write a blurb for the paper since they were closing their doors after 55 years.

Addy: House is about 75% done. I have some boxes in the spare room, but the house is livable as is,

so I'm not rushing. Work is okay. The only repeat I've had was Cindy. She's the one who sells the jewelry, and she asked if she could keep me on weekly to run her sales numbers. Haven't heard anything back from anyone else, and no new requests.

Alex: Well, at least Cindy will be providing you with a little spending money for the holidays. And don't give up; you have money from the house and the little coming in. Maybe now is the time to focus on you and that book you've been saying you wanted to write for the past 10 years.

Alex and I chatted a bit more before I tossed my phone on the couch beside me and looked out the large front window at the snow lightly falling. The desire in me to Christmas-up the place was strong and was eventually strong enough to get me out of my lonely Christmas funk.

Before I lost my nerve, I put on the same ugly Christmas sweater I wore every year on Tree Hunting Day, put on my warm winter boots and bundled up for my adventure. The first adventure and tradition I would now face alone.

I stood at the back of my SUV and let out a dejected sigh. The sad, pathetic little tree I found at the tree lot was bundled in the back and already looked a bit limp. The selection was poor this year, and of course, I didn't have a saw with me to cut a fresh one down, so I had to pick from the pre-cut trees the lot had.

"Hey, hot stuff!" I looked up and rolled my eyes as Kyle sauntered down the porch to meet me at my vehicle. "I was just coming to see if you were up for a road trip." Kyle, for being the cute and friendly neighbour that he was, was starting to become the creepy, clingy guy who wouldn't take the hint and who I couldn't avoid.

After our disaster of a date at *Rollies,* I told Kyle that I wasn't ready to date but that I still wanted to be friends. Truth was, I didn't know what to do with him. Sometimes, he was sweet and fun to be around and made me laugh, but other times was pushy, immature and inappropriate. His terms of endearment, if you could call "Sweetness," "hot stuff," "honey buns," "sexy lady," and my least favourite, "hotty with a body" terms of endearment, had replaced my name every time we saw each other. He was acting more and more like a frat boy, and I was really starting to feel like the 8-year age difference between us was more like a 20-year difference. He was always just dropping by or at my door when I came home. He even just let himself in without knocking the other day when I was getting out of the shower. He had come over uninvited every single day since we went to *Rollies* two weeks ago.

His flirty nature was becoming over-friendly, with his hugs now including a butt squeeze. I had already managed to put a pause on the Thursday Night Football routine, stating that I was taking an online class Thursday nights, which was a complete lie. I had asked him a couple times to just text instead of coming down if he wanted to know if I was free, and as politely as I could, stepped away when he went in for the hug and overly wet kiss on the cheek. But it didn't seem like he got the hint…or just didn't want to.

But I was still trying to be the polite neighbour. He still lived above me and, truthfully, could turn my quiet oasis into party central if he wanted to. We had to live in close proximity, so politeness won out. Plus, I didn't really want to push away the only friend I seemed to have besides Alex. There were always growing pains in every new friendship, where you didn't know what the other person's boundaries were or what their values, beliefs and maturity level were. I was hoping that the more I learned about Kyle, the more he would learn about me, and we could hopefully find a happy medium where friendship lived. I at least had to try.

"Hey, Kyle," I said, "good timing. You wouldn't be interested in hauling a Christmas tree into my place, would you?"

He laughed and easily picked up the little 3-foot fir tree and followed me to the door. "It would be my pleasure, milady."

"So, what are you up to? What road trip?"

"I'm heading to Toronto. I left some stuff at a buddy's place there, so I'm going to go down and grab it and then maybe have a drink. I was just going to go for a couple of hours."

Kyle put the tree down in the living room while I hung up my jacket and put my hat and mitts in my winter accessory basket.

"It'll be fun," he continued, "and I'd love the company of a foxy lady. Plus, my buddy owes me some money from a bet he lost, so I can collect and take you out for dinner. We can have a re-do of our date."

"Well, I'm flattered," I pretended to smile and dug out the Christmas tree stand from the back of my storage closet, "but I have a full day of Christma-fying to do today."

"Christma-fying?" he laughed. "Making up our own words now?"

"It's my decorating day. December 1st is always the day I do my tree and decorations. I know it sounds like a lame excuse, but it's tradition and the first one I'm doing on my own."

"Well, did you want some help? I wasn't going to leave for another couple of hours, so I'd be happy to lend a hand."

"Thanks, but I think I need to do this on my own."

After Kyle wished me luck, and I reminded him not to have too much fun if he went out partying and to make good choices, I went about decorating the tree.

In the bin of ornaments, I found a book ornament Alex had gotten me since I was an avid reader, a Star Wars bobble I had gotten him since it was his favourite movie, a little dog paw with "LUCY" in the middle, and a snowflake with a year in the middle so we'd never forget our first Christmas together. But when I found a wedding bell decoration from the year Alex and I got married, my chest got tight at the memories. I could feel the emotions bubbling up as I thought about our wedding, how handsome he was in his suit, the tears he had in his eyes as I walked down the aisle to him and the sweet kiss he gave me when we were pronounced man and wife. I had to stop before I broke down. The memories were flooding in and pulling me down into another Sand Trap. Clearly, the tree was enough agony for one day. I could decorate more tomorrow.

I hated that I was struggling so much at just being me and being by myself. I always thought that I was a strong woman, that I was independent and self-reliant, but I felt lost somehow. Truthfully, it didn't matter if I was now alone. I was still the same person. I could do this. I was a kind, funny, sarcastic, sweet, intelligent, charismatic, and somewhat independent woman.

But if decorating the Christmas tree was this hard and pulled me into one of my Sand Traps, I could only imagine what Christmas day, my birthday or our anniversary would do to me.

Chapter 9

Weak. There was no denying that's what I was.

It had been a week since I decorated the Christmas tree and officially a month since I moved in. I had struggled every day last week. Every time I decorated the house a little more or did something that reminded me of how different my life now was.

On December 2nd, I put on "Home Alone" while I finished decorating the house and ended up crying on the couch and going through half a box of Kleenex by the end since it reminded me of when Alex and I dressed up as Harry and Marv for his work Christmas party. Kyle ended up coming down because he could hear me crying through the floor. I tried to pull myself together quickly when I felt his hands sliding down my body and felt his lips brush a kiss on the top of my head as he consoled me in a hug. When I pulled away, he wiped my tears away with a gentle touch, which was sweet, and I started to think that maybe I was judging Kyle too harshly. That thought vanished when he pulled me tight into his body, the bulge in his pants pressing into my stomach, and he tried to pull my face into a kiss. I turned my head, and I politely asked him to leave after that.

The next day, I was out getting groceries and saw a perfect gift for Alex's 10-year-old nephew, Philip, before I remembered that I didn't have an Adams family anymore and didn't need to get his parents or nephews gifts. I shed a few embarrassing tears in the toy department but managed to pull it together pretty quickly.

Yesterday, I received a Christmas card from my ex-in-laws telling me how much they missed me and still loved me and that they would always view me as their daughter-in-law. I sniffled and got emotional but refused to let the tears that gathered in my eyes actually fall.

I was getting better, but I knew I still had work to do to fully embrace this life I'd chosen. I still had work to do on me to get out of this funk. Life wasn't over just because my marriage was. I was 35, still relatively young and had a full life just waiting for me. My happiness didn't depend on my marital status. *God, we're not living in the Bridgerton era, Addy.*

I was determined that in this new life, I could build a new me. So, I made a list. A list of 10 things that I wanted to accomplish in my first year of being on my own that would make me happy. They were simple things, but things I was doing for myself and made me think about what I wanted out of life.

I went to my spare room and spent a good hour coming up with the list on my computer. If I typed it out and printed it out, I couldn't ignore it and give up on it as easily as I did on New Year's resolutions.

1 – make new friends who I can call upon, not just acquaintances

2 – try a new sport/outdoor activity

3 – Set aside an hour a week completely dedicated to my writing

4 – find a job I'm excited to go to each morning

5 – learn to make 5 new dishes from scratch (Lasagna – should be easy enough, an apple pie – crust and all, the rice paper pork rolls from my favourite Thai place – will save me money as well, my great aunts cabbage rolls, and the perfect thin crêpe)

6 – lose 20lbs so my clothes fit better, and I'm more confident in my tighter stuff

7 – buy a plant and keep it alive for the whole year

8 – start a self-reflection journal so I'm more aware of how I'm feeling and what is making me feel that way

9 – volunteer one day a week (ideally at an animal shelter if they're taking new volunteers)
10 – look into becoming a foster parent or adoption

Number 10 was the hardest by far to put into writing, but I had always wanted to be a mother. Alex and I had tried for years, not using any form of birth control since a month before our wedding. But as the months went by, and then the years, we knew something was wrong. And after countless invasive tests and fertility specialists, we found out that I wasn't able to have kids. They stressed that it wasn't impossible but that it would be extremely difficult for me to ever get pregnant naturally, and the older I got, the more the odds drastically plummeted. By the time women turned 30, the odds of getting pregnant naturally each month dropped to roughly 20%, and that was *without* taking my fertility issues into account.

Eventually, we just gave up. I stopped tracking my ovulations, stopped the supplements and the special fertility lube the specialist had given us and stopped the special diet I was on.

Now that I was on my own, I had to look at my options. I didn't want a sperm donor, and there weren't any penises knocking on my door besides Kyle, and that was a BIG no. I didn't care if the child was mine or not; I just wanted to help take care of someone, help someone in need. Help someone not feel as alone as I feel right now.

Christmas morning came before I was mentally prepared, but as I woke up, I was surprised to realize I felt okay. I could do this.

This year, there was no husband to spend it with, no in-laws to welcome me with open arms, and, of course, I was no longer welcome in my parents' home. I didn't know if I would ever be welcome back into my family, but I was coming to terms with that. It was unfair to expect me to be someone I was not, and as an adult, I had the right to be me and not have to pretend to be the person my family *wished* I was.

I felt independent and, although sad and lonely, somehow lighter this morning than I had this past month. I had a Christmas day to myself where I didn't have to run around making a huge family meal for everyone or drive hours upon hours to see people. Christmas was about spending time with the ones you loved, and this year, I was working on loving my new self, so there was no better way to spend the day than with me.

I got dressed in my cozy emerald green sweater and black leggings, fuzzy socks, and tried to figure out how I was going to spend my day. This was the chance to start a new tradition for me, and the possibilities were endless.

But first thing was first, I turned on all the Christmas lights I had put up. There was the Christmas tree, the lights around the front window, all the electric candles I had placed around and the light-up garland that surrounded the door frames and the fireplace mantle. The lights lit up the house and looked ethereal against the snow that was lightly falling outside.

I turned the radio on to the Christmas station and bopped away to "I Want a Hippopotamus for Christmas" as I pulled out all the ingredients to make some butterscotch chip cookies. I was planning on giving a tin to Kyle as a Merry Christmas and a thanks for being my friend, as well as to the guy who lived below me, even though I hadn't met him yet. When I asked Kyle about our downstairs neighbour, he scoffed a bit, saying that the guy was "a piece of work" and kept really strange hours.

My doorbell rang as I put my first batch of cookies in the oven, and I was shocked to open my door to Lucy, my old golden retriever, wearing a big bow around her neck, and Alex standing there with a gift bag in his hand.

"Merry Christmas," he sang as Lucy pushed her way in. Alex had been to my place before when I needed help putting the bedframe and kitchen table back together, so I shouldn't have been surprised to see him, but I was shocked, in a wonderful way.

"What are you doing here?" I asked as I stared at him in awe.

"I'm on my way to my parents' and thought I'd quickly stop by if that's okay."

"Oh my God," I opened the door wider to let him in. "Of course it is. Come in."

Alex threw his jacket over the arm of the couch and put the bag he was holding under the tree.

"Wow," he said, looking around the living room, "you've done a lot with the place."

"Well, doing Cindy's accounting work doesn't take up much of my time, so…"

Alex smirked as he walked towards me with his arms open wide. "Come here."

He pulled me into a tight hug, instantly making me melt into his body. "Merry Christmas, Addy," he whispered against the side of my head.

"Merry Christmas." My lips were in the crook of his neck, and they inadvertently moved against his skin as I said the words.

He pulled back slightly, his arms still wrapped around me and gazed into my eyes. Alex and I had only *officially* done one backslide since we separated – I didn't count the sexting night since there was no actual sex, although it was mentioned in great, GREAT detail. Ironically, the real backslide happened the night we signed the divorce papers and then went out for a drink afterwards. One drink led to two, which led to four, which led him back into my bed.

And the way he was looking at me now, it would be so easy to make another "mistake," and the strangest part was, I wasn't opposed to it.

Alex's eyes danced between mine and my lips before we both leaned forward and closed the gap. His soft lips, which were so warm and familiar, pressed into mine for only a second or two before his tongue ran across my lower lip, and our mouths opened.

God, I missed this. The way he held me, the possessiveness in his kiss. I never noticed it when we were together, but right now, I just wanted to delve deeper into him.

The rough moan that escaped my mouth only encouraged him more, making his hand slide into my hair, tilting my head in order for him to kiss me deeper. I clung to his shirt as I pulled him closer, our tongues dancing with each other as his other hand slid under my sweater.

A shiver ran up my spine, and my hands moved up his shoulders and around his neck to hold him closer. Our bodies were pressed against each other from head to toe as we made out like teenagers. I couldn't get enough of him, and we were both breathing heavily as our lips crashed together.

We were completely lost in each other, all mouth and tongue and hands grabbing. I hadn't even noticed that we had moved down the hallway until both his hands went under my ass cheeks, and he lifted me up, grinding his hardening erection against me and pressing my back against the wall.

"Alex," I moaned as his lips found the weak spot just under my left ear, making goosebumps erupt all over my skin and my body shiver, "I...."

The oven timer went off, breaking off what I was going to say. To be honest, I didn't know *what* I was going to say. I think we need to stop? I need you? I miss you? I need you to make me come? I think you should go? I want to give us another shot?

Alex lowered me back to the floor, both of us trying to catch our breath as the oven continued to buzz in the kitchen. We stared into each other's eyes, but not a word was said.

I quickly ran into the kitchen, turned off the timer and set the pan of cookies on the cooling rack before putting the second batch in the oven and once again setting the timer. *Oh fuck! I'm in BIG trouble.*

Chapter 10

My lips still tingled from Alex's kiss. He hadn't kissed me that way in years, and I didn't know what to do with it. Leaning over the counter, I put my head in my hands and closed my eyes. I just needed a minute. But before the minute was up, I felt a hand softly run up my back.

"Addy...I'm sorry."

I stood up straight and looked Alex in the eye. I wanted to kiss him again. God, did I want to feel his lips and hands on me again, but I knew it was wrong. I couldn't go back there. I wasn't strong enough. But his lips, soft and pink and warm and wet...I needed them. Just one more time.

I put my hand on his hard chest, instantly remembering what his skin felt like, the solid chest under warm skin, the tickling of chest hair that I loved to play with. I rose up on my toes and tenderly pressed my lips to his one last time.

This has to be the last time. It only lasted a second, but I absorbed as much of it as I could.

"It's okay," I confessed as I pulled away. "I miss us, too."

"Maybe this wasn't the best idea." I cocked my head, wondering if he meant the kiss, being alone with me or coming to see me at all. "Maybe I shouldn't have come over."

I nodded. "Maybe." We had seen each other since the divorce and spoke all the time, but maybe we weren't strong enough to stay away. It was strange; we didn't have this attraction and *need* when we were together, but now, it took all my strength not to drag him to the bedroom and christen my new house.

"I brought you something, though." He led me out to the living room and grabbed the gift he put under the tree. We both sat on the couch as I looked inside the small, sparkly gold gift bag. As soon as I pulled the gift out, I broke out in laughter. "I thought it would be appropriate for you to add to the collection."

I ran to the tree and grabbed the small silver box I had for him. He opened it up and started howling with laughter. We had gotten each other the exact same gift. A new Christmas ornament. It was a flat white square ornament that looked like a scroll of paper and had "Divorced and Loving it" with the year and a picture at the bottom. Mine was a picture of a wine glass, and on Alex's was a picture of a beer stein.

I put mine on the tree, right beside the wedding bell ornament from the year we got married. Those two would always go side by side from now on.

After Alex left, with a kiss on the cheek this time, I went about the kitchen and finished putting the cookies in festive tins. Just as I was putting my coat on to deliver the baked goods, there was a knock on my front door.

"Hey," I smiled at Kyle. "Merry Christmas."

"Who was that?" He scowled as he pushed his way in like he lived here.

"Who was who?" I asked, shocked by his demeanour. I had never seen Kyle angry before, and right now, he looked like he had caught his girlfriend cheating on him.

"The guy…" he seethed, "the guy who just left with the stupid dog with the stupid bow around its stupid neck."

"Alex?" I was completely lost. "That's my ex. Why are you so upset?"

"Why was he here?"

"Kyle – "

"Are you back together with him?" He cut me off and cupped my cheeks in his hands. I was still holding the cookie tins, so I couldn't push him away. "Please tell me you didn't take him back. Please, Addy." His entire demeanour went from pissed to worried. He was almost panicked that I went back to my ex.

"No," I reassured him, trying to de-escalate the situation so that I could somehow get control of what was going on. "We're not back together. He just came over to wish me a Merry Christmas."

Kyle visibly relaxed, gentling his hold on my cheeks and eventually letting me go.

"But we are still friends, Kyle, and it's my right to see him. Why are you so worried and angry?"

I had managed to move our conversation from the entryway, where I was trapped between the wall and the closet with an upset Kyle, to the living room, where I at least had space to take a step back and put the cookie tins down.

"Sorry," he exhaled, barely getting the word out on the breath. "I'm sorry. I saw the car and then saw him leaving, and it's not even 10 in the morning, and I know you were having a hard time, this being your first Christmas alone and all, and I was just worried he'd taken advantage of you."

Well...crap. If that was true, that was very sweet and caring of him, but by how possessive he was when he knocked on the door, it seemed to be jealousy and not concern that he was feeling. Kyle was smooth. His touches and looks and friendly banter made it seem like he was staking a claim on me, but he never actually did anything that said, "You're mine." His hugs and cheek kisses were over-friendly for my taste but could be seen as just a personality trait. He would easily pass off as a caring friend looking out for the single woman who moved in below him. *Clever bastard. I'll have to keep a closer eye on him and his "concern."*

"Thanks for worrying about me and checking in, but it's not necessary." *Or wanted*, I thought. "You don't need to worry about me, Kyle. I can take care of myself."

He just looked at me as if he was trying to figure something out, like he wasn't sure if he should believe me or not.

"Here," I quickly said, pushing one of the cookie tins towards him, "Merry Christmas."

"Thanks," he lifted the lid to look inside. The cookies were still somewhat warm, and the smell of butterscotch drifted out of the container. He just stared at the cookies for a moment before he closed the lid, said a quick "Merry Christmas," and left back to his unit. Was he touched that I made him cookies, or was he disappointed that the tin didn't hold an invitation to my bedroom? That man was so confusing, and, in all honesty, I didn't even want to bother trying to figure him out.

I grabbed the second tin and made my way to the door of my basement neighbour. I knew he kept strange hours, but I heard noises coming from his unit from time to time, so I knew someone was there. But after waiting a couple minutes and knocking twice, I just left the tin by his door. I had written him a card saying *"From your upstairs neighbour.*

Hopefully we can meet soon. Merry Christmas. From Adeline" and taped it to the top of the tin. Hopefully, this olive branch would invite him to introduce himself. If not, I would just be happy that he was a quiet neighbour who wasn't nosy and clingy like the guy upstairs.

Chapter 11

It was a dreary morning. It had been raining all day. All the snow that had fallen on Christmas day, just two days ago, was now gone, leaving nothing but the brown and gray slushy mess everywhere. It was constantly cold and damp in my place, no matter how warm a shower I took or how much I turned up the thermostat.

It was after another hot and steamy shower that I noticed water on my bathroom floor when I stepped over to the sink to brush my teeth. As the water ran over my toothbrush, my feet almost instantly felt wet, and I noticed water coming out from the bottom of the vanity cabinet, trickling through the cabinet doors.

Quickly turning off the tap, I crouched down and opened the doors to see water leaking out of the elbow joint under the sink and water running to the edge of the cabinet and onto the floor.

"Just great," I mumbled as I tried tightening the elbow joint by hand. I didn't know a lot about home repairs. Heck, I knew very little in the grand scheme of things, but I was someone who always tried to do something myself before asking for help. Unfortunately, the elbow was wet from the leak and too wide for me to get a solid grip on it. I needed a wrench or something to get a good hold and tighten the joint up, and, of course, I didn't have the type of tool I would need. I didn't think the screwdriver set, the drill or the hammer I had would help in this situation.

I hastily got dressed, threw a towel on the puddle on the floor to soak up the water, and went over to Kyle's door to ask if he had any tools.

"Nah, sorry, Sweets. I don't really have any tools, but you should check with G.I. JOE."

"Who's G.I. JOE?"

"He's the guy who lives downstairs. You still haven't met him?" At the shake of my head, he continued. "He's probably out in the garage working out or something, but he has tools."

I thanked Kyle, not wanting to stay and chat as it was windy and damp out. Plus, I had noticed his eyes start to wander down the centre of my open jacket. He ran his tongue over his lips and then, as if remembering I was actually a person and not just a picture he could ogle, snapped his eyes back up to me and gave me a crude smirk that I was sure he thought was sexy.

I walked out to the back parking lot, trying to ignore the chill the look in Kyle's eyes gave me, and made my way to the detached double-car garage that was in the corner. I always just thought it was a garage for property maintenance (lawnmower, weed whacker, snow blower, etc.) or storage, but as I walked up, I could hear music blaring from inside. The main doors were closed, but the side door was cracked, thankfully not forcing me to pound on the door to get the attention of whoever was inside.

As I pulled the door open a bit more, I was completely shocked to find a full gym in there. I didn't recognize the majority of the stuff I saw. There were metal contraptions standing up everywhere, different-shaped bars and loads of plates and weights scattered all over the floor. The music was blaring, and as I looked around, slowly sneaking inside, my eyes landed on the only person in there, and I was granted a clear view right up the man's shorts.

There, laying on his back, bench pressing what looked like an obscene amount of weight, was a huge, buff, sweaty man grunting away…with a huge bulge in his shorts. The sight in front of me was shocking, like looking at an accident on the side of the road: it was hard to look away. If I wasn't wary of walking up to a stranger and asking to borrow something before, I sure as hell was paranoid now. This man was the definition of intimidating, and he hadn't even sat up and shown me his face yet.

And just as I thought that he re-racked the bar and sat up. *Holy hell, he's hot, and hot in an intense good-God-don't-blush-or-fumble-your-words, hot.* He reached down and took a deep draw from a water bottle before he faced forward, noticing me.

Grabbing his phone, he hit a button, and the volume of the music automatically went down while I just stood there, staring at him, completely intimidated by his size. I couldn't look away. He was only wearing shorts and runners, no shirt, and it showed off his massive body that was hard, dusted with hair, shiny with sweat, and decorated with tattoos. This was a real man. He wasn't ripped like the men on TV with the six-packs and bulging muscles clearly attained through steroids. He was just a completely solid, hard-all-over body of muscle. He was a fucking brick wall. His chest and arms were so wide it made me think that the reason he wasn't wearing a shirt was because he was too muscular for one. His shoulders and arms would obliterate any shirt sleeve it met.

"Hi…" he panted as he took another drink of water, "can I help you?"

I shook my head, trying really hard to get my mind out of the gutter and my eyes off his body. *Frig, his bicep is bigger than my thigh.* Maybe if I wasn't just standing at the garage door, staring at this freakin Adonis, I wouldn't seem like such a weirdo.

"Ummm, Kyle said I should talk to you about borrowing a tool?"

"And you are…." He smirked as he grabbed a towel from beside him and wiped the sweat off his face.

"Oh my gosh," I mumbled as I slowly approached him. "I'm Adeline. I moved in last month."

"Conner," he said as he stuck his hand out for me to shake. "I live in the basement." His hand was huge and sweaty, but I honestly didn't mind. It was kind of expected, given the weight he was lifting.

As he stood up from the bench and towered over me, I quickly stepped back out of his way, not wanting to interrupt what he was doing more than I already had. I did notice, however, the smirk that played on his lips as he gave me a once-over. I also couldn't help but notice the flush that I could feel spreading over my cheeks.

Conner moved to the other end of the gym, grabbed a huge blue band off the wall and came back over to the bench to wrap it around the leg. It looked like a massive rubber band, and it seemed to be rubber or something resistant as he began to pull it across his chest.

"So, what can I do for you, Adeline?" He stood facing me, a smirk still on his lips, and crossed his left arm over to his right hip, the band held in his left hand, and pulled his arm out until his left arm was straight out to the side and the band was stretched tight across his chest. He did that move five times before he turned around and did the same with the other arm. Turning back around, his eyes returned to mine.

"I was just wondering if I could borrow a wrench or something? I have a pipe leaking, and Kyle said I should check with you about borrowing a tool."

God, this guy was making me nervous. Besides his amazing body, he had a gorgeous face. He had a strong, wide jaw, dark hazel eyes that were either navy blue or dark gray, a beautiful mouth with a large, plump bottom lip that I had an instant need to bite, a close-shaved head that showed dark hair on top and a bit of grey on the sides, and neatly trimmed facial hair.

"Did he now?" There was a definite difference in his tone once Kyle was brought into the conversation.

"If it's not too much trouble? I tried tightening it by hand, but the pipe was too thick and wet, and I just couldn't get a solid, tight grip on it. I just need to get a better squeeze on it so I can yank it a bit tighter."

Okay, even to me, that sounded dirty. And by the sexy smile playing on Conner's lips, I knew he was thinking the same thing.

"Sure, Adeline," he almost purred, wiping his body down with a towel and walking towards me, "you can use my tool anytime you want." It didn't escape my notice that he said tool singular and not tools plural. *God, kill me now.*

I followed Conner out of the gym once he grabbed his hoodie and threw it on. We went over to the old red truck that I saw in the parking lot from time to time, and he rooted through the metal toolbox that was attached to the bed of the truck.

"Lead the way," he smiled as he locked the box back up. He held some tools, some rubber circles and a tube of something in his hand and started walking to the front of the building.

"Wait," I panicked, not wanting to be even more of a pain in the ass for disrupting his workout, "I didn't mean for you to do it when I asked. I can do it myself. I just needed to borrow a wrench or something."

"Adeline…" he started, but I interrupted him.

"Addy is fine," I hurried.

"Addy," he smiled, and damn, it was a nice smile, "I don't mind helping. I have no doubt you could do it yourself, but if you have a leaky pipe, it's usually an overtightened joint, a loose or damaged washer, a cracked pipe or something more than just a loose connector. I have the stuff in my truck to fix it, so don't worry about it. Look at it as a thank you for the best cookies I've ever had."

Okay, now my cheeks were blushing for sure, and I couldn't stop my smile.

"Best cookies you've ever had, huh?" I teased as I let him in the front door.

"I ate the whole tin in one sitting," he admitted as he stepped in after me and looked around. "Bathroom this way?" he asked, heading down the hall.

We spent 20 minutes chatting in the bathroom while he lay on the floor and fixed my leaky pipe. And he was right; the washer needed to be replaced, and there was a crack in the something or other. He had to run back out to his truck to get some type of tape until he could go and pick up a new joint for me, but he said it would hold.

"How do you know how to do all this and have all this stuff on hand? Are you a plumber or in construction?"

"Something like that," he smiled and winked at me as he sat next to me on the lip of the bathtub. I handed him a clean towel to dry off his hands as he bent over and gathered up his tools. *Damn, he's got a nice ass too.*

"What does that mean?"

"I'm a jack of all trades, master of none, as they say."

"So, just kind of a freelance handyman?"

"Amongst other things." Now he was outright snickering at me.

"Why so secretive, Mystery Man?"

It was his turn to laugh. "Mystery Man, I like the way you say that."

"Well, what else am I supposed to think?" I teased back. "You've been here for almost half an hour, and I know nothing about you. We've talked about me the whole time, and not by my choice, I may add. You're very good at turning questions around."

He joined me back on the edge of the bathtub, sitting fairly close for someone who has known me for less than an hour, and looked at me with an open and honest expression. "That's because I'd much rather get to know the beautiful blushing baker who lives above me than talk about my boring life."

"But what if I want to get to know the handsome Herculean handyman who lives below me instead of talking about *my* boring life?"

"Nice alliteration," he smiled.

"Thank you," I smirked back. "But in all honesty, Conner, tell me about yourself. Just one thing for now."

"Next time," he smiled and looked down at his watch. "I gotta be at work in an hour, and I still have to shower and eat first."

"So, he does have a job," I joked. "Do I get a hint at what you'll be doing tonight?"

"Sorry, Addy, no can do. I have to live up to my Mystery Man status now." He gathered up all the stuff he brought with him and headed for the door. "Besides," he said as he stepped onto the porch, "I'll just be *hanging* around."

As he walked down the porch steps and down the walkway to the side of the building, the way he said *hanging* clicked something in my head.

"*Ape Hangers,*" I called out. And if the way he turned back and smiled at me as he rounded the corner was any indication, I was right. He worked at the dive bar Kyle and I went to that one time.

The first piece of the Conner, last name unknown, puzzle slid into my brain. I loved a good challenge, and if that handsome man wanted to play, I'd be more than happy to play along.

"Hey, Kyle," I said as I opened the door. "What's up?"

Kyle stood on the front porch, a look of concern and admonishment on his face. "I just wanted to see if you ended up getting that tool you needed this morning or if maybe there was something I could do to help?"

My shoulders relaxed at the kindness in his eyes. Sometimes Kyle could be really pushy and overbearing, but then sometimes, when he smiled and acted like an adult and not a horny man-child, he could be really sweet. Yes, there were some things that I didn't like about him, but there were also some things that I missed. I missed our Thursday night pizza, beer and football nights before he won the bet and became cocky. I missed the helpful Kyle, who came to my rescue the day I moved in and taped up my cut hand. I missed the fun Kyle, who ran around my office with me, trying to grab the paint roller from my hands.

Part of me hated that I had written him off so quickly after only a few unfavourable encounters when I had some good memories, too. Maybe I just needed to give him a second chance and set some boundaries.

"That's really kind of you to check, Kyle. Thanks." I held the door open. "Did you want to come in?"

Kyle's face shone as if he couldn't believe that I was extending a friendly invitation to him. *Man, I was a bitch.* It crushed a bit of my soul to see how affected he was by my offer. Maybe our friendship had meant more to him than I thought.

"That would be awesome," he smiled as he made his way into my home. "I actually wanted to talk to you about something."

"What's that?" I asked as I grabbed a bottle of water from the fridge and handed it to him as we sat on the couch.

"I actually wanted to apologize for over-reacting about your ex being at your place at Christmas and if I've come across a little strong lately."

I was floored. Maybe he was more mature than I gave him credit for.

"The thing is," he continued, "I really like hanging out with you and think you're really sweet and kind and funny, and I wanted to get to know you better, but I think I came off a bit too arrogant when we went to *Ape* and I was bragging about my winnings. I didn't mean to be such an ass about it. I was just excited."

This was a different side to Kyle, back to the Kyle I first met. The Kyle who was caring, sarcastic, and fun to be around.

"And then when your ex came, and I acted like I was your boyfriend and was threatened by another guy coming to see you... I didn't think that way. I DON'T think that way. I got the message that you're not interested in me that way. I was just jealous since we kinda stopped hanging out after our date at *Rollies,* and I miss you."

"Honestly, I miss you, too, Kyle. This side of you. The old you. The Kyle I first met." I wanted to be honest with him. "But you changed after the bar. You didn't seem like yourself and were being way too forward. You started calling me Sweetness and hot stuff instead of my name, you let yourself into my place without knocking, and you just...changed."

"I know. I had some stuff going on with work, and I was under a lot of stress and not myself. And I know that sounds like an excuse, but it's the truth. I had a solid lead for a massive opportunity, and it slipped through my fingers." He grabbed both my hands in his. "I'm really sorry, Addy."

"As long as this version of Kyle is here to stay..."

"He is," he insisted, hand to his heart, "I promise."

"Okay." I smiled at him as we settled into our old, comfortable friendship. "I'd be happy to have my friend back."

"And I'd be more than happy to be your friend again." *Please don't let this bite me in the ass.*

Chapter 12

"So, does our renewed friendship start now? Did you have any plans for the rest of the day, or did you want to do something?" Kyle asked with excitement in his voice.

"What did you have in mind?"

"Well…" Kyle began, hope clear in his voice, "I was just on my way out to grab a quick lunch since I don't have anything in my fridge, and then I was going to drive into town to grab some equipment from work." Kyle crossed one leg onto the cushion so that he was facing me better, his arm resting against the back of the couch. "My boss just assigned me to a new project, so I just need to run in and grab more supplies from the warehouse. It'll just be a quick pop in and out, but how do lunch and a drive into town sound?"

He gave me such a charming smile. His blue eyes sparkled against his blond hair, fair skin and dark gray T-shirt. He just looked like a lost puppy, so innocent and hopeful, but something in my gut wasn't sitting right. Something was telling me not to go with him. As soon as he mentioned going into town to get supplies from his 'warehouse,' alarm bells rang, and chills skittered up my spine. The more I looked into the feeling, the stronger the internal alarms sounded. I had no idea why, but my body or soul or brain or whatever was telling me not to go with Kyle.

I went to ignore my internal warning system and tell him I could do lunch, but my heart started to race, and the chills up my spine turned into a shudder. "I have some stuff I need to do around the house this afternoon, so I can't really go into town with you today," I said, not really knowing where this was coming from since all I had to do was groceries and laundry, so I could do those anytime.

"Awe, come on, Addy, please?" He grabbed my hand and held it in both of his, the warmth of his skin nice against my chilled hands. "I'll be super quick, just in and out, I promise."

My stomach started to twist, and I didn't know why. What Kyle was asking me was completely innocent. Lunch and a car ride, but the warning bells wouldn't stop.

"Please, Addy?" he begged, "I just want to spend some time with you and try to get back to where we were. It'll just be like two and a half hours out of your afternoon. I'll speed and knock it down to two hours," he chuckled to himself, but it sounded forced. "Addy, please...see, I'm using your name and not calling you sexy or anything. I'm trying."

"How about this? I'll make us lunch here so we can at least hang out for a bit." The anxiety in my body calmed a little at the suggestion. I didn't know why I was having such a visceral response to Kyle all of a sudden, but it was clearly something I wouldn't and couldn't ignore.

The disappointment was clear on Kyle's face, but he accepted my lunch invitation anyway and followed me into the kitchen.

"So, what's the new project you're working on?" I asked as I pre-heated the oven and set about making some tuna melts and a garden salad.

"I actually can't really talk about it," Kyle said from the kitchen table as he set out plates and cutlery for me, "it's top secret." He wiggled his eyebrows at me and then gave me a playful smirk. I was relieved that Kyle was able to just fall back into his goofiness and not hold a grudge that I wasn't able to go with him this afternoon.

"Really?"

"Actually, yeah," he answered as he came to join me at the counter. "That solid lead I had at work last week that slipped through my fingers? Well, I've been working on a different angle, and it might still work out, but it's all hush-hush until it's a for-sure thing. Bossman is really excited about it and doesn't want anyone else noticing the potential we've seen."

"I actually don't even remember what it is you do," I smiled at him a little guiltily. "I know it was something to do with computers, right? Sorry, I'm not really knowledgeable when it comes to techy stuff."

"No worries, it's boring, really. I work in mergers and acquisitions."

"So, you buy out struggling companies to get ownership and fix them?"

"Something like that," he smiled as he took the salad to the table. "It's all about taking the unknown and making it public for everyone to enjoy." He gave me a wink at that just as the timer on the oven went off, and he took a seat at the table.

"And you're the one that finds the struggling companies?"

"Kind of." I pulled the tuna melts out of the oven and set the tray on a trivet in front of Kyle. He waited until I sat beside him before he continued. "They call me the 'Collector' at work. I find what we're looking for and present a plan to my boss about how we obtain what we want."

"Sounds like an important job."

"Oh, it is. Sometimes, it feels like life and death."

"Conner? What the hell are you doing here? It's not even 6 a.m.?"

I was half asleep, letting the doorframe prop me up as I stared at him on my front porch. I wore my red and black check pyjama pants, a black tank top, and a yellow zip-up hoodie overtop, and I knew my hair was all over the place, half falling out of the top knot I left it in last night. I let out a huge yawn, trying to protect him from the morning breath I knew I had.

"I know. I'm sorry, but I got the piece of pipe for your bathroom and wanted to get it installed before I went to work at 7."

"What?" That made no sense. I knew my brain was still foggy from sleep, but he left here for work yesterday around 3 p.m., and here it was 5:54 a.m., and he's talking about being at work at 7 a.m. again? A shiver racked my body as the cold morning air slid into the house. I held the door wider and motioned for him to come in.

"Leaky sink?" he smirked, closing the door behind him. "Ring a bell?"

"Yeah, I got the leaky sink part, but when the hell did you find the time to get the piece I needed?" I was squinting at him through just one eye. The other hadn't opened up yet and seemed to refuse to wake up for this conversation. "Didn't you say you worked at 4 p.m. last night? The hardware store closes at 6 p.m. on Saturdays, and it's closed today, especially this early in the morning."

"I know," he smirked, "I had the piece I needed at a job site, so I stopped by there on my way home after work last night."

"Job site?" God, this man was even more confusing. I thought he worked at *Ape Hangers*. Between Conner and all his secrets and the weird vibes I got from Kyle yesterday, these two were the strangest neighbours and were both messing with my head.

"God, you're adorable when you're tired."

I would have given him a snarky remark back if he wasn't herding me back to bed like I was a child, but I was too tired, and my brain was still foggy.

"Just go back to bed. I'll be as quiet as I can, and I'll let you know when I'm leaving so you can lock back up. Deal?"

"Whatever," I grumbled and flopped back on my mattress.

What seemed like only minutes later, as soon as I got back to sleep, there was a light tapping sound that filtered into my brain, stirring me from sleep AGAIN.

This time, I knew I let out an audible angry groan as someone laughed from behind me.

"All done," Conner chuckled as I rolled out of bed to glare at him.

"Thank you," I mumbled in return, now just grumpy because he was hot and helpful, and I felt like…well, like I hadn't gotten any sleep. And it was all his fault, too, not that he knew it. But I was up until 2 a.m. thinking about him, wondering what he was doing and trying to piece together the little things I knew about this man. He loved my cookies, worked out and often by the amount of equipment in the gym, had a beat-up truck with a buttload of tools, worked at *Ape Hangers*, was super handy, witty, kept up with my teasing, was very helpful and sweet, very mysterious, and so hot. The puzzle was starting to take shape, but really, they were only pieces.

"You're welcome, Addy. You can go back to bed now and get some beauty sleep. Looks like you might need it." He winked at me as he ducked the pillow I threw at him, chuckling lightly as he walked away.

"Jerk," I mumbled through a smile as he went through the front door.

"Remember to lock your door."

I waved him off and shut the door, locking it like he reminded me to and went back to bed. Unfortunately, freakin Conner, still no last name, was once again on the brain, and I couldn't get back to sleep. It was just before 6:30 a.m. anyway, so there was no point in putting off starting my day.

Sundays had officially become my "work day." It was my laundry and cleaning day, plus, so far, every Sunday, Cindy sent me the receipts of her sales for the week, and I balanced her account and updated her inventory list. Sunday was also the day I had set aside for writing. I had put on my list that I was going to allot one hour a week to work on my writing, and since I was already on the computer Sunday afternoons to do the stuff for Cindy, it made sense to just switch gears and work on the story I wanted to write.

It had been a project I'd wanted to start since I graduated from university but had never found the time. I had interned at a publishing house in my final year, and it built this desire in me to write. Amazingly, I stayed on at the publishing house for 10 years, moving around from Receptionist to Office Assistant and then to Office Manager. A posting came in for a Literary Assistant right before we moved, and it would have been a chance to work directly with the Literary Agent and assist in going through proposals and manuscripts, but it wasn't a job I could do remotely, and the move was already set in motion.

But throughout those 10 years working in publication and seeing all those amazing books being worked on and put out to print, it just made me want to see something I thought of being published. Something with my name printed on the cover.

I had a million ideas, but I had to think of a unique one that people would want to read. I had jumbled outlines that were out of order and random ideas jotted down, but nothing solid. But this was my chance, no 9-5 job to distract me, even though I looked online every day and still had my ad out there for freelance work. I just had to focus and write. I didn't think, didn't try and make a storyline; I just wrote what was in me, what was needing to get down on paper. My fingers typed, not really knowing where they were going, but I poured my heart and thoughts into the computer.

There are many different ways to love. You can love someone, and they don't love you back, or they could love you, but you don't love them. There's deep, needed passion where you can't get enough of each other, and then there's indifference. You love the person, but it's almost like the love is just routine and habit, like you almost don't feel it anymore — from them or yourself. You know it's there, but the lines are blurred between loving a person and being in love with them. You love them, but your world is no longer about them, taking care of them, making them happy. You love them because you always have. Your love has become lazy.

All my life, I have yearned for an all-consuming, passionate love. Unfortunately, life is unkind, and I've only ever experienced unrequited love or indifferent love. One where I care and love the person, but they don't feel it in return. My love is almost an inconvenience for them and for myself. It gets in the way and tries to make something out of nothing.

I don't know if anyone has ever truly been in love with me or loved me like I needed to be loved. And maybe that's the problem. Maybe I'm expecting too much. Maybe all the romance movies I watch and smutty books I read have created this desire to be loved in a way that just doesn't exist. Maybe I'm hoping for a type of love that is unachievable and has, inevitably, kept me feeling lonely and unwanted my entire life.

What I want is unattainable, but it's what my heart and soul are crying out for. It's what I need. I need to be wanted. I need to be needed. I need someone to look at me and know that they love me with everything that they are and that they would do anything to love me.

Is it selfish? 100%, but I don't know any other way. I don't know if I can help it. Can you stop your heart from hoping? Can you tell your soul to stop desiring and seeking its mate?

And all my heart, body and soul want is Tim, my married next-door neighbour who is currently being handcuffed and arrested for the murder of his wife.

I stopped typing and read what I just wrote over and over again. The Tim storyline could be interesting. I hadn't read any books where the main love interest was in jail before. That meant letters between each other, conjugal visits, dirty phone sex when he got phone time…there was possibility there.

But the reason that I kept reading the blurb over and over was because of what I wrote about love. I realized I was putting myself in the story, my thoughts, feelings and desires. I had never analyzed myself and my wants like that before, but it made perfect sense. Why I always felt alone and unloved in my marriage with Alex. Why I never felt like enough, or that our love was enough. Why it always felt like we both just settled. It was because it was *real life* and not some fantasized story in a fiction novel. I spent so much time longing for what I read about that I ignored the *real* love story I was living with Alex.

"Oh my God." *What if I made a mistake?*

Chapter 13

No. Divorcing Alex was the right thing to do. Clearly, he agreed that we shouldn't have been married anymore as he agreed to the divorce immediately. But it didn't stop my mind from going over all the unrealistic expectations I had put on him over the years. *God, I was a bitch.*

Addy: Hey.

A couple minutes passed before I got a response from Alex.

Alex: Hey

Addy: I just wanted to say sorry.

Alex: For the kiss? Don't be sorry, it was both of us. Plus, it was hot.

Addy: No, not the kiss, although yeah, for that, too. Sorry for being a bitch in our marriage.

My phone rang, showing Alex's name flashing on the screen.

"Alex..."

"You weren't a bitch, Addy. What's going on?"

"I started writing again –"

"That's awesome!" he exclaimed, genuine excitement in his voice.

"Yeah, it is, but then it got me thinking about our marriage and how I kept wanting this big romantic love story and wishing you would be completely devoted to me –"

"I WAS completely devoted to you, Addy," he interrupted. "100%!"

I huffed, "I'm not saying this right." I took a beat to figure out what I was trying to say.

"I never felt swept off my feet, never felt like I was the glue holding you together or that you couldn't breathe without me –"

"Addy…"

"And that's MY fault, not yours. Those weren't realistic expectations. You loved the real me, but I had these fantasy notions about what love should be, and that wasn't fair."

Alex was silent while I continued to gather my thoughts.

"Real love isn't someone being obsessed over you, throwing their whole life away just to pamper you, or walking around with boners all day, hardly able to control themselves around you because they need and want you so badly." Alex actually laughed at that last part. "What you gave me was real, and I'm sorry if I ever made you feel like it wasn't enough."

"You never once made me feel like that, so don't worry. You're thinking about it too much and making it into more than what it was. Our marriage just ended, Addy. It's not that we hated each other, or didn't get along or weren't happy together. We just knew our time as a couple had run its course, and we moved on. That's it. Turn off that brain of yours and stop overthinking everything."

That was something that Alex had told me often: that I was overthinking things. And, it was true. I always second-guessed things and over-analyzed what he said, and it drove him crazy. Truth be told, it drove me crazy too. I'd get so lost in my thoughts that I didn't know what was fact, my interpretation or if I was creating drama in my own life.

"We good?" he asked after a couple silent beats.

"Yeah, we're good. Just need to get out of my head."

He laughed at that. "I've been saying that for years."

BEEP BEEP

I pulled my phone away from my ear and saw an incoming call from a private number. I had left a message with the local paper to see if they needed any more work done, so I was hoping it was them calling me back.

"Listen, I gotta go. I've got a call on my other line, and I'm waiting to hear back from the paper."

"Okay, good luck. Love ya."

"Love ya, too."

I hung up, took a deep breath and answered the other line.

"Hello?"

"Heeeyyyyy, Sexy. How's my favourite neighbour?"

I pulled the phone away from my ear and saw the PRIVATE NUMBER showing, not the regular number he texted me from almost every day.

"Kyle?"

"That's me, Sweetness. What are you up to?"

"Ummm…not much. I was just doing some work. Where are you?" I asked as a loud horn blasted in the background.

"Toronto Harbour, why? You miss me?"

"No, it's just noisy in the background."

"You don't miss me?" he scoffed, "I'm hurt. We had an amazing lunch date yesterday before you ditched me, and now you don't miss me?"

Oh Lord, how was I going to cut ties with this kid? And yes, KID. The second chance I had given him yesterday was definitely biting me in the ass. He had called and sent me multiple texts yesterday when he went to Toronto to get his work supplies, and apparently, the super quick, in-and-out trip to the warehouse ended up being a party with some friends, which included a couple drunk photos being sent to my phone. Clearly, he had changed for just that day, and then things had gone back to normal after I fed him.

Thankfully, there was a knock on my door just as another horn blew through the phone line.

"Sorry, Kyle. Was there something you needed?" I opened the front door to an exhausted-looking Conner. I held up a finger to him, indicating I'd just be a second, but waved him in and watched as he flopped on the couch. I snickered softly as Kyle spouted on, most of which I missed.

"…and it was so hot, Sweets, it made me think of you right away. So, what do you think?"

"About…" I said, not wanting to admit I'd completely tuned him out. I made a drinking motion to Conner, and at his nod, I went to the kitchen to get him a bottle of water.

"About being my date for New Year's. I know you might not want to go because it's at the Rippers, but it's a really classy place, and the music is awesome, and it'll be so much fun, and the dancers-"

"Hold on," I interrupted, "are you asking me to be your date to a New Year's party at a strip club?"

Conner literally spat his drink all over the front of his shirt and gave me a *WHAT THE FUCK* look. I just shook my head and rolled my eyes. This had to stop. Kyle was talking, but I just cut him off.

"Look, Kyle. It's nice of you to ask, but no. I don't want to go to the strippers with you, and if you actually thought about it, you'd know that that's not me at all. And please stop calling me Sweetness and sexy and hot stuff and the other derogatory names you call me. I really don't appreciate it."

"Sweets, come on –"

"Goodbye, Kyle." I hung up the phone and threw it on my coffee table.

"Hi," I sighed to Conner, "are you okay? You look exhausted."

"Yeah, I'm completely beat, but I wanted to check on the leak before I crashed for the day."

"You didn't have to do that. You just installed it this morning. I could have just knocked on your door if it was leaking again."

"It's okay, I'm here now. Plus, I'm a really deep sleeper. I might not hear it if you knock." He finished the water bottle and patted the couch cushion beside him. "So, what did moron want?"

I chuckled at the accuracy of the 'moron' comment and sat down beside him. "He wanted me to be his New Year's date at a strip club party he was going to."

"Yup...moron." Conner dropped his head to the back of the couch but turned to look at me. "Is he giving you any trouble? He's calling you Sweetness and sexy and shit like that?"

"He's just a flirt that isn't getting the hint that I'm not interested in him. He calls, texts and comes around all the time, but he's just more annoying than anything."

"You sure? He's kind of a sketchy guy."

"What do you mean?"

Conner sat up, put his empty water bottle on the coffee table, and turned his body to face me.

"Two years ago, when Kyle moved in, the police were showing up all the time, questioning him about God knows what. I actually saw him being cuffed once and shoved in the cruiser. People were coming around day and night, banging on the door and making a ruckus. Pete, the landlord you bought the unit from, told me he was actually going to evict him, but I guess they came to an understanding, and things calmed down."

"Youthful indiscretion?" I put as much hope into the question as possible. If Kyle was really that much trouble, I would need to cut ties ASAP.

"Maybe? I tried to stay out of it."

Conner stood up and went to check on the pipe he replaced this morning.

"Alright, everything looks good, I'm off to bed."

"At 4:43 in the afternoon on a Sunday?"

"Yup," he drawled as he made his way to the front door.

"Any hint as to why you're so exhausted and going to bed so early?"

He cracked a smile as he stepped onto the porch. "Nope."

"Mystery Man," I teased as he walked down the walkway, throwing a wave over his shoulder in return.

It was strange; although I knew very little about Conner, I already felt like he was a friend. I didn't know his favourite colour, or where he grew up, or even his last name yet, but I knew that he was a caring man, someone who worked hard and looked out for others. The trivial things you asked when you got to know someone started to matter less and less. The more often I saw him, the more I saw little glimpses of the character and values of the person underneath. My Mystery Man was starting to show who he really was.

The one thing I loved about Hennington was how quiet it was. You didn't have the constant sound of sirens blaring, or the sounds of traffic, or transports driving down the highway or planes and helicopters overhead. But apparently, I *did* have a disgruntled neighbour overhead.

Stomping and yelling woke me up just after 2 a.m. Apparently, Kyle had come home after I hung up on him and was making a ruckus. That, or someone was not too quietly breaking into his place.

After a couple of minutes of trying to hear what was actually going on, there was a knock on my door.

"Adeline?" a voice said through my front door. "It's Conner, open up."

I ran to the door, not even knowing if I had bottoms on or just a T-shirt and underwear, and opened the door.

"What's going on?" I asked as I let him in and locked the door behind him.

"I don't know, but I could hear him downstairs. I just wanted to make sure you were okay."

A crash sounded above, like someone was throwing plates on the floor.

"Do you think someone broke in? Should we call the cops?"

"No, it's Kyle. I saw his car in the parking lot just now."

Well, at least that made me feel a bit better. Better to deal with the devil you know.

"Have you heard him like this before?" We made our way to the couch, and I threw a blanket over myself to help chase off the cold.

"Yeah, last summer when all the windows were open, but never through the floors like this."

The stomping and crashing continued, making me jolt at each sound.

"Hey," Conner said, putting a hand over my blanket-covered thigh, "it's okay. He's probably just drunk."

We were staring eye to eye, and even with all the chaos happening around us, I had butterflies in my stomach from just that one look. His eyes were so intense, a beautiful hazel mix of navy blue and brown. Guiltily, I got lost in his stare until another crash sounded from above and brought me back to reality.

"How was his parking job?" I asked.

"What do you mean?"

Another smash scared a flinch out of me. This time, Conner pulled me into his side and wrapped his arm around my shoulder.

"Well, if he's drunk, and you just saw his car on your way up, how was it parked?"

Understanding what I was getting at, he let out a sigh. "Perfect."

So, he wasn't drunk; something was going on.

A car door slamming made Conner bolt to the front window. The dark shadow of a body passed by as Conner peeked through the shades. And not three seconds later, there was pounding on my front door.

"Stay there," Conner ordered as he went to the door and threw it open. If I wasn't grateful for him checking on me before, I sure as hell was now.

"Who the fuck are you?" a voice growled from outside.

"Depends, who the fuck are you?" Conner's voice was strong and forceful, not taking any shit from whoever was at the door.

"I'm here for Kyle."

"Good, he's the other door. Get him the fuck out of here." Conner slammed the door and locked it. He made his way back over to me on the couch and pulled me back into his arms when he sat down. We didn't say anything as we listened to the pounding on Kyle's door, more yelling from upstairs and then Kyle stomping down the stairs.

"Let's go," the man outside grunted. The night was so quiet I could hear his loud voice in my quiet house. You'd think someone would whisper when they were outside at 2 a.m., but apparently not.

"I can't find my fucking cell," Kyle shouted back in a panic.

"Who the fuck cares," the guy barked at Kyle. "We're already late."

Kyle's door slammed shut, and their voices turned to quiet murmurs as they passed my window and eventually got in the car and left.

"You okay?" Conner's soft voice broke the silence that had surrounded us.

"Yeah," I breathed as I reluctantly pulled away from his warm side. "Thank you."

He gave a quick nod, his eyes locked on mine. He looked down before meeting my eyes again and reached over to rearrange the blanket that had somewhat shifted off my lap when I put distance between us.

"You're shaking," he whispered as he pulled my hands into his. I hadn't even realized my hands were doing that or that my leg was bouncing on the couch cushion.

"Adrenaline," I muttered, trying to take slow breaths to calm myself down. "I'll be okay."

"You sure? I can stay for a bit until you calm down and can get back to sleep."

Nah, I didn't need him to stay. Yes, it was scary for a bit there, but I was okay. I didn't need a man to take care of me. But before I could tell him that, my mouth opened, and the word "okay" came out instead.

"Okay," he smiled as he let go of my hands. "You okay if I grab a water bottle?"

"Sure, help yourself." I got up and held the blanket around me. "I'm just going to put some bottoms on."

I heard a chuckle come from the kitchen as I ran to the bedroom and shut the door. I was right. I was just in a T-shirt and my underwear. Thankfully the T-shirt came down over my butt but still, not appropriate for when the hot neighbour was holding you in his arms.

I threw on a pair of old joggers and a baggy university sweater and met Conner back on the couch.

"Here," Conner started as he passed me a water bottle.

"Thanks." I chugged half the bottle in one go, automatically feeling a bit better.

"Are you really okay?" The genuine concern was touching. But truthfully, I felt like an idiot.

"I'm fine. Nothing really happened besides some noise, so there's no reason for me to be freaking out."

"I don't want you having to deal with assholes coming to your door by mistake, Addy. That's not okay."

"Yeah, that part I was not okay with. That honestly really scared me, but the rest…well, it is what it is."

Conner continued to stare at me, giving me a disbelieving look.

"I swear. Can we just change the subject?" I pleaded.

"Fine." His voice still held concern, but he was obviously trying to placate me to make me feel better. "What do you want to talk about?"

I immediately seized my opportunity as soon as it popped into my mind.

"You."

Chapter 14

"Me?" Conner was already shaking his head with a smirk on his lips.

Beyond eager, I jumped right in, sitting up higher on the couch, my excitement overthrowing the fear and adrenaline from just seconds ago. "We can play Truth or Dare, and then I won't ask you any deep personal questions ever again."

"Ha," Conner barked. "What are you, 5?"

"Well, I don't know any other way to get any answers out of you."

"Nope, sorry," the smirk grew more mischievous on his lips. "I like the Mystery Man title too much."

"Please?"

"And what if I just keep picking 'dare'?"

"Then I'll 'dare' you to tell me something about yourself."

"So, this would really be a 'truth or truth' game?"

I smirked and just shrugged my shoulders at him.

He looked at me for a minute, warring with himself, before his shoulders dropped, and his smirk turned into a fake scowl. "Fine."

In all fairness, Conner was right. This was a child's game, and I was 35. I did know better and did have proper conversational skills, but it was 2:30 a.m., and I was tired but wired, and it was the first thing I thought of. Plus, I'd have to answer questions, too, so it wasn't just him putting himself out there.

I went first, starting with hopefully easy questions and not digging too much into his life right away. I asked his age, 38; his last name, Jensen; how long he lived here, five years in the tri-plex but 13 years in Hennington and if he was single. He laughed and said he better be, seeing how he had been sitting on my couch with me bottomless in the middle of the night.

Conner had a huge advantage since he already knew the basics about me from our chat when he was first looking at the bathroom leak. So, this time, he asked more detailed questions. He asked if I missed my ex, and I told him no, that I still talk to him all the time, and we're still close friends. *I thought he was my best friend? Why am I just saying 'close friend' to Conner?* He asked what my dream job was, and I told him a writer. He asked if I had written anything yet, and I told him I had started something but wasn't very far at all. He asked me about the premise of the book, and I told him about the woman who was in love with her neighbour who was arrested for his wife's murder. He seemed intrigued and said it sounded like a good book.

After going back and forth for a good while, no longer keeping track of questions but just having a good conversation, I asked what had been on my mind since I met him.

"What do you do for work, and why are you so secretive about it?"

Conner put down the cup of coffee he had gotten a while ago when we got comfy on the couch and gave a serious but shameful look.

"It's not my job that I'm secretive about. It's all the questions I get when I tell people what I do."

"What do you mean? I know you work at *Ape Hangers*. I just don't understand why it was such a big deal to tell me that. Are you a stripper or something?"

He laughed, and I could have sworn I saw his cheeks blush a bit. "No, I'm not a stripper. I work at *Ape Hangers*, but only when their regular bouncer can't make it in or they're short-staffed." He paused, and I refused to make a sound, not wanting to interrupt him when he was clearly struggling with what to say.

"When I was younger," he began, "I did things of…questionable legality. I was asked to drive packages places and drop them off at different addresses. Actually, 'asked' might be the wrong word. I was never really given the option. I was 'asked' with the understanding that there would be severe consequences if I said no.

"I never knew what was in the packages…never got any names, but I knew the guy I was delivering for was dealing with illegal shit. Drugs, weapons, forged documents…I had no idea what I was delivering. I just knew it wasn't legal.

"I grew up next to his parents' place. I saw the crowd of followers he built and kept my distance. He knew who I was and knew I didn't want to be involved in whatever he was running, but he still came to me when he was in a pinch. At the time, I was too afraid to say no and didn't know what would happen to me or my family if I did. There had been rumours about what would happen if you said no. People ending up in the hospital, houses catching on fire, pets found dead in the front yard…I didn't want to risk it."

He took a drink of his coffee, and I scooted closer to him on the couch, trying to provide some comfort while he expelled what happened to him in his childhood. "There would always be an envelope under the package with my name on it, full of cash. My cut of the transaction so that I would be just as implicated as anyone else. If he paid me, it meant I was working for him and was part of his crew.

"I always wore gloves, though, so my prints were never on anything. I knew it wasn't on the up-and-up and that I should have just walked away, but the money was good, and I was protecting my family." He took a breath before he broke eye contact and looked at his feet.

"When you're 16, poor and live in the rough part of town, knowing you'll never be able to afford to get out, and someone pays you a couple grand to drop off a package three cities over, you start to appreciate what that money could turn into. I'd take my family's old beat-up Camry and did runs for him every couple weeks for four years before I got the nerve to tell him I was done and couldn't help him anymore. The cops were sniffing around the neighbourhood more and more, and I told him that if I walked away, I could honestly tell the cops that I didn't know what was going on, didn't see anything or hear anything and that I could at least be an alibi for him telling the cops when I saw him at home. He wasn't happy about losing me as a runner but saw the value of having an alibi and went along with it. The Camry fire, a broken nose, three cracked ribs, and our dog's death were my payment for freedom."

"Oh, Conner," I whispered. All I wanted to do was give him a hug. His childhood sounded like a damn mafia movie. I had no idea this type of stuff happened in real life, and within a couple of hours of where I grew up myself.

He was silent for a while, just staring at the carpet before he continued. "I walked away with a lot of money, even though my conscience took a beating. I saved it all and finally invested it when I was 22. I tried to make an honest living working different jobs here and there so I wouldn't have to rely on dirty money, and only when work was slow would I dip into it, but barely enough to even touch the interest it was making. It's helped set me up for life," he turned his eyes back up to me, and I could see the battle he was fighting, "but at what cost?

"Over the years, I've thought about going to the cops, trying to clear my conscience, but I was honest when I said I didn't hear or see anything. A plain box would show up in the backseat with a sticky note on top that had an address. I never spoke to anyone, never saw anyone, nothing. It's a time in my life I regret beyond belief, but at the same time, I'm thankful for it since it allows me the freedom to do what I want now.

"I don't work or fit into the 9-5 world. I work when the work and needs are there, but I'm not living to work or working to live. I'm working to keep my hands busy and to help people out. I have friends who own construction companies and friends who own bars. If they need help, they know to call on me. It keeps me busy and helps out people I care about. I don't have a full-time job or a career. I don't even have a real employer, but I'm giving back when and where I can and the shit I did as a teenager has allowed me to do that. That and smart investing.

"I don't know what harm my part of running packages did, but I'm hoping that by helping out my friends whenever and wherever I can and giving back where I can, I'm balancing out the good and bad somewhere."

I sat in silence, taking in everything Conner said. It was so blatantly obvious that he struggled with his past and what he did. I couldn't imagine being forced into that situation in my teens and then finding the strength to get out of it.

Not wanting to sit in the heaviness of his confession, I swallowed the lump that had grown in my throat and asked my next question.

"What's your favourite food?"

He smiled at me, relief written all over his face that I didn't push or ask more questions. He reached out and squeezed my hand, entwining our fingers together.

"Popcorn."

I burst out laughing. "Really? Popcorn? Does it matter if it's microwave or movie theatre?"

"Nope," he smiled, "any popcorn will do."

It was like talking to my best friend I had known forever. There were no awkward moments, no tense, silent pauses. It was just...easy. Being with Conner, although I had really only met him the other day, was so peacefully easy. It was effortless. We continued talking until my eyes started to droop, and more than a few yawns had escaped. By then, we had already been talking for hours, and I had all but forgotten about the chaos from earlier on. Conner was so laid back and easy to open up to. I had never met anyone like him before, where I could just be myself and not have to worry if I was saying the right thing, if I looked okay or if I was acting properly. I could just be me and not have to stress. It was so freeing being around him.

When I had apparently let one too many yawns slip, Conner insisted it was time for him to let me sleep. We walked to the front door, our fingers still linked together and said our goodbyes. Our light banter stopped when we got to the door and was replaced by a lingering look in his eyes, and probably mine as well, and a deep desire for him to kiss me. As his eyes moved between mine and my lips, and he slowly leaned down, I thought that was exactly what he was going to do. But instead, he put a gentle kiss on my cheek.

"Sleep well, Adeline," he whispered, and with one final squeeze of my hand, he walked out the door, keeping his fingers twined with mine for as long as possible.

Chapter 15

KNOCK KNOCK KNOCK

I stood outside the doorway of Conner's unit bundled in my black leggings, a zip-up hoodie and my puffy vest. I was hoping to see Conner again today and thank him for the night before. Not only had he been concerned about my safety because of the ruckus upstairs, but he had opened up to me, had been vulnerable and told me some pretty personal stuff. Stuff that made me want to talk more and get to know him even better. Yes, he had a dark and mysterious past, but the fact that he had fought to get out and start his life over was really inspiring.

Conner's journey had put mine into perspective. His life had been in danger and at risk, yet he still persevered. I, on the other hand, had gone through a divorce, rejection from my family and the loss of a job – all things that I could and would eventually move on from - and had acted like my life had been falling apart. There was no denying that what I had gone through had sucked and was hard, but it was peanuts compared to being a transporter, or whatever Conner was, and getting beaten to within an inch of his life just to get out. Not to mention the car fire and the loss of his family dog.

I was about to knock again, as Conner had said he was a heavy sleeper, when I heard the sound of heavy bass music coming from the garage that Conner used as a gym. The sound of clanging metal was unmistakable the closer I got to the garage, and I knew there was no way Conner would hear me knocking on the garage door if I tried. So, instead, I just opened the side door I had used the first time I had visited the makeshift gym and let myself in.

As I made my way into the chaos of plates and bars and equipment, I found Conner at some sort of floor rack that held all the round plates. He was pulling them off the bar that was beside him on the ground and putting the colourful round plates back on the rack.

"Hey," I yelled as Conner rocked away to the music, headbanging as one more plate slid into place on the rack, clanging loudly against the one that was already there.

I could hear him softly singing along to whatever song was playing through the place as he grabbed another plate from the other side of the bar and put it on the rack. Deciding to enjoy the show, I sat on a bench that was about

10 feet behind him and admired the view of Conner in loose black shorts and a tight tank top.

"Holy shit!" he yelled as he turned around and noticed me watching him. I gave him a soft laugh and a finger-wiggle wave before I got up and joined him at the bar. He grabbed his phone and turned the music down.

"Hey, Addy," he smiled. "What are you doing here?" he asked as he grabbed another plate and put it away. Now that I was close to the bar, I could tell that he had four plates on each side, and each plate was stamped with a 55LBS marking on it. That was 440 pounds total on the bar, not to mention the smaller plates that he had already put away.

"Holy crap, were you just lifting this?"

Conner looked at me like I was crazy. "Well, I don't just put the plates on the bar to make it look pretty," he joked sarcastically.

"But that's like 440 pounds!"

"It was actually 515 pounds. The bar is 45 pounds itself, and I already put away the 5s and 10s."

"Conner…" I was flabbergasted. That just seemed like an insane amount of weight to be lifting.

"Yes?" he replied with a cheeky smirk. I remained silent as he continued to put away all the weights.

When he was done, he sat down on the bench I was previously occupying and chugged his water bottle. "So, what's up?" he asked when he finally finished his drink.

"I went to your place, but you didn't answer, so I thought I'd see if you were here." He pulled a box from one of the machines on the other side of him over and tapped it for me to have a seat. "I just wanted to say thanks for last night."

His face grew soft with concern as he listened to me start to ramble.

"It meant a lot that you came to check in on me when Kyle was throwing his tantrum upstairs, and then the creep came to my door."

"I'm glad I was there too. I don't want to think about what would have happened if you had opened that door alone. I want you to call me or come get me if shit like that ever happens again. I could kill Kyle for putting you in that situation."

"Me too." I looked down at my hands before I looked Conner in the eyes and continued. "But I also just wanted to say thank you for opening up to me and telling me about your past. I know it must have been hard digging all that up, but I really appreciate that you trusted me with that stuff. It helped put my situation into perspective."

"What do you mean?" He reached into the gym bag that was beside him and grabbed a towel, wiping the sweat that was scattered on his forehead.

"I just mean that you went through all that ordeal, got out and were able to start your life over again, whereas I got divorced and act like my life has fallen apart."

He just shrugged his shoulders before he got up and continued to clean up his gym. "People react differently to things, doesn't mean that they don't feel their feelings. Your life did fall apart. You're just handling it the way you need to in order to survive and move on. I'm not going to judge you for that."

That was probably the kindest thing anyone had said to me. It was surprising how important it was to have my feelings validated.

"Well, that was all. I just wanted to come over and say thanks." I got up to leave, but Conner had different plans.

"Where do you think you're going?" he asked with a smile. "You left my gym last time without touching a weight. That's a one-time exception. When you're in here, you're lifting weights."

I just laughed at him as I sat back down on my box. "Yeah, right, okay," I jabbed. "I don't do gym stuff, Conner. I don't even know what 99% of the stuff in here is."

"Then I'll teach you." I just shook my head at his comment, but he just kept going. "Take off your vest and come over here. Do you have anything on under your hoodie?"

I looked down at myself and saw the tight blue tank top I had underneath peek out of my hoodie. If I was being honest, I was starting to cook in his gym. He had to have heaters in here somewhere.

"I'm not letting you leave without at least just trying a deadlift. It's easy, I promise." Conner walked over to me and started to push the vest off my shoulders. The thought of him undressing me instantly shot my temperature up 10 degrees.

I lowered my face to hide my blush as he took the vest off me and put it on the bench seat. "And the sweater?" he asked.

I took a deep breath and unzipped my hoodie.

"Perfect," he whispered under his breath as he walked over to a wall that had about 10 different bars hanging on it and pulled one down. I followed him over and stood beside him as he grabbed two small plates from the plate rack thingy and put one on each side.

"Okay," he began. "The bar is 45 pounds, and I just have a 2 ½-pound weight on each side. It's only 50 pounds on here. Bend down and pick up the bar, but keep your back straight."

I just quirked an eyebrow at him. *Keep my back straight as I pick something up off the ground? Is he crazy? How the hell do I do that?*

He rolled his eyes as he stepped up to the bar and bent down to grab it. "Like this," he said as he pulled the bar off the ground, his back straight but leaning forward until he stood up straight and pulled the bar up to stop at his groin. He put the bar back down on the ground and then stepped to the side for me to take my place.

"So put your feet under the bar about shoulder width apart," he began. I did as he instructed, and he stepped up behind me. "Keep your hips straight," he continued as he put his hands on my hips and gently tapped the inside of my feet with his. "Just a bit wider."

I widened my stance a bit before he told me I was good. "Now, I want you to bend down with your knees, not just bend over at your hips, and grab the bar where the etching is."

I looked down at the black bar and noticed that there were three sections that looked to be about five inches long and etched like sandpaper. There was a rough section on both the right and left side, about halfway in from the end of the bar, and the third section was in the middle. I grabbed where the rough section was on each side of the bar, squatting down with my knees over the bar like Conner did, not just bending over at the hips like I was picking up my laundry off the floor.

"And lift!"

At Conner's words, I tightened my grip and started to lift the bar until pain poked me in my hands, and I dropped the bar, causing the plates to rattle at the ends.

"Owwww," I winced as I looked at my palms. "What the hell?" The sandpaper "etching," as Conner called it, completely dug into my hands as I began to lift the bar.

"Oh, toughen up, snowflake," Conner taunted. "It's just the bar. You're fine."

"Why the hell does the bar have pokey bits cut into it?"

"It's so that when you're lifting, your hands have something to grip onto instead of potentially having the smooth metal slip from your hands."

I looked at the bar and then at my hands again. There was nothing on my hands, no mark, no redness…nothing. I just wasn't expecting to feel anything digging into my palms as I was lifting weights. "Makes sense."

"Try again," he encouraged.

I bent down just like last time and grabbed the sandpaper parts again, now knowing what to expect, and lifted the bar. It was heavier than I expected, but I got it up to my thighs and then put it back down.

"Nice," Conner smiled as he went to the weight rack. "Want more weight on it?" I shrugged my shoulder and joined him at the rack. He handed me a plate that had a 5LBS marking stamped into it, and he took a matching one. We each took the 2 ½-pound plates off and replaced them with the 5-pound plates before I got back into position.

"Now this time," Conner instructed as he stood in front of me and bent down with me as I went to grab the bar, "try not to round your shoulders when you come up, but keep your back straight. Here," he said as he put his hands on top of mine. "Put your hands out a bit wider." He moved my hands just an inch wider on each side, still well within the sandpaper zone.

When he stopped repositioning my grip but continued to touch my hand, I looked up to see what was going on. We were face to face, only a couple inches apart. I gasped at the closeness and intensity in his gaze. He was looking at my lips and then up to meet my eyes. We were having a moment, an honest-to-goodness moment that felt like slow-motion.

But before I could even question what was going to happen, a car door slammed, and we heard yelling in the parking lot.

Conner pulled back as more yelling and banging sounded through the gym. The screaming voice sounded like Kyle's.

"What the hell?" Conner asked as he went to the door and peered outside. I followed him and saw Kyle crouched over in the trunk of his shiny black sports car, throwing everything from inside onto the ground around his feet. There were boxes, papers, clothes, water bottles, and a duffle bag that clanged as he dropped it on the cement. He had his phone wedged between his jaw and his shoulder as he threw everything from the trunk onto the parking lot.

"What the hell is going on?" I whispered to Conner as we watched Kyle kneel down and start to dig around the stuff on the ground.

"Who knows," Conner responded.

Kyle pulled his phone away, looked at it, and a look of panic took over his face. He pressed a button on the phone, stood up straight and then quickly threw everything back into his trunk before heading around the front of the building.

Conner turned around when Kyle disappeared around the building, and we were once again face to face, standing closer than what was appropriate. We were definitely in each other's space, but neither of us made a move to step away.

The tension between us was unmistakable.

But just like before, we were interrupted. Conner's phone rang through the speaker system in the gym.

"Shit," he said as he ran over to his phone as the loud ringing echoed through the speakers and the gym. "Hold on," he said into the phone before he pressed some buttons and the phone disconnected from the Bluetooth. "Sorry, hi."

I made my way over to the bench and put on my hoodie and vest as Conner spoke on the phone. "Give me thirty?" he asked as he walked over and mouthed the word "sorry" to me. "Kay, see you in a bit."

He threw his phone on the bench after he hung up and started to throw his water bottle and towels, as well as some long wraps that looked like fancy Tensor bandages, in his bag.

"Sorry," he said as he came up beside me, his gym bag slung over his shoulder. "That was a friend of mine, and he needs a hand moving something."

"No worries," I smiled at him as we both made our way to the door. "I needed to get going anyway."

We walked in silence to Conner's door before he gave me a flirty smile goodbye. I couldn't help the smile on my face either until I turned the corner to the front walkway and saw Kyle leaning up against his doorway on the phone. And by the sound of it, the phone call wasn't going too well.

"...this one's different, boss," he pled. "If we make this acquisition, I don't think I'll be able to sell it off in the end. It's too valuable."

I made my way to my door, trying to pretend to ignore Kyle to give him a small semblance of privacy, but he gave me a head nod and a sad smile. I could hear someone yelling on the other line until Kyle simply said, "Yes, boss," and hung up.

"Hey, Kyle," I said, "everything okay?" I couldn't help but take in his dishevelled appearance. I hadn't seen him all day and hadn't heard a peep from him since he stomped out of his place last night after all the ruckus.

"Yeah," he said, sounding exhausted and defeated. "Just crap at work. Plus, I had a rough night, so am dragging ass today."

"I heard." I gave Kyle a sympathetic but questioning look, hoping he'd explain what last night was all about.

"Shit, Sweets," he started as he leaned against his door and rubbed his hands over his face, "I'm sorry. I didn't mean to wake you up."

"It's okay," I offered, even though it wasn't. "I was just worried. I thought someone had broken in and was trashing the place."

"No, that was just me. I misplaced a really important piece of equipment for a job I'm working on and couldn't find it anywhere. My boss is going to tear me a new asshole when he finds out."

Kyle looked like he was about to fall asleep standing up and like he was facing a firing squad. Although we've had our differences, it was like I was looking at a wounded puppy.

"Anything I can do? Did you want to come in for some lunch or something?"

The smile that graced his face felt like the first genuine smile he had ever given me. If I didn't know better, I would have expected Kyle to break down in front of me from just the simplest form of kindness. *Man, his job must be killing him.*

He walked over to me and gave me a tight hug and a kiss on the side of the head. "Thanks, Addy, but I need to keep looking for that piece. If I don't have it by tomorrow, I'm toast." Without another word, he opened his front door and went inside.

Chapter 16

December 31st. The last day of the year. The last day to think about your resolutions and what changes you want to make. I didn't believe in New Year's resolutions, per se, but I did believe in looking at where you were versus where you wanted to be. This year, I had my list. The 10 goals I wanted to achieve by this time next year. I had already completed or was working on a couple of them, and I was proud of how seriously I was taking these tasks.

1 – make new friends who I can call upon, not just acquaintances

2 – try a new sport/outdoor activity

3 – Set aside an hour a week completely dedicated to my writing

4 – find a job I'm excited to go to each morning

5 – learn to make 5 new dishes from scratch (Lasagna – should be easy enough, an apple pie – crust and all, the rice paper pork rolls from my favourite Thai place – will save me money as well, my great aunts cabbage rolls, and the perfect thin crêpe)

6 – lose 20lbs so my clothes fit better, and I'm more confident in my tighter stuff

7 – buy a plant and keep it alive for the whole year

8 – start a self-reflection journal so I'm more aware of how I'm feeling and what is making me feel that way

9 – volunteer one day a week (ideally at an animal shelter if they're taking new volunteers)

10 – look into becoming a foster parent or adoption

I crossed off numbers 1, 3 and 8, although I had just purchased the journal and hadn't started writing in it yet. Conner had made crossing off number 1 on my list easy, especially after our gym escapade yesterday and the midnight chat the night before. He had definitely turned into a friend and not just a neighbour or acquaintance. Not to mention the tension-filled gym moment.

In all honesty, I had been bummed that we'd had two electric moments, which both got interrupted. I was definitely feeling the sexual frustration today.

Sundays, I did my work for Cindy and slowly worked on my writing, so number 3 could be crossed off, too. Number 2, I decided, was more of a spring/summer outdoor task, so I was okay with letting that one sit. And tonight, I was tackling part of number 5; I was going to try making a lasagna from scratch. I had gotten all the ingredients and found a recipe online that looked fairly simple.

My phone vibrated on the kitchen counter as I added the tomato sauce to the browned pork/beef mixture.

Conner: Orange

I laughed as I turned the heat down on the burner and picked up my phone.

Addy: For the master bedroom?

Conner: For the whole entryway, hallway and kitchen

Addy: Like a dark burnt orange that's almost brown?

Conner: Nope, like a bright orange highlighter.

Addy: Eeeee, well, that's a choice lol

Conner was helping a friend of his paint a new building on the other side of town, and we had a bet to see what colour they were going to be painting it: grey or beige. Clearly, we were both wrong.

Conner: What are you up to?

Addy: Just making lasagna before heading into the office. I still can't believe they called me back. I know it's just an advice column, but it's still an actual writing job.

The Hennington Hound was the local family-run paper, very small with just local distribution, and yesterday, they returned my call and asked if I'd be interested in writing a couple of advice columns that they could hold for when their paper was thin.

The paper only wrote about three things: local sports, community events and an advice column that Brian's wife Sharon wrote. It was a type of "Dear Abby" column that answered questions or gave advice to those who wrote into the paper, and that would be what I was taking over.

I had worked with Brian, the owner and one of two journalists the *Hound* had, on the Christmas Newsletter I edited last month and the article I wrote for the couple who was closing down their bakery after 55 years. After I submitted both articles to him, he asked me to send him some of the pieces I had done when I was on my university paper. I guess he liked what he saw and yesterday offered me the job. I only had to submit one piece a week, and apparently, there were hundreds of questions from readers I had to choose from.

Conner: Have you decided on what question you're going to tackle for your first piece?

Addy: No, I have to go into their office today and get set up with access to their network. Then, I can go through their folders and go over all the letters people have written in.

Conner: Good luck!

Addy: Thanks.

Once I had finished my lasagna, which was just as easy as I had hoped, I went over to the *Hound* and got all setup. I was given an ID badge, a key to the office, a laptop, and a desk in the corner. It was a pretty loose system where I could come and go as I pleased, work here or at home, and come in day or night, whenever and however I worked best. Being such a small family paper, there was a lot of trust that you would just get the job done. Plus, I was being paid per piece, not paid by the hour, so it didn't really matter to them how or when I got the work done as long as the pieces were submitted on time.

After I was granted access to everything and briefly walked through their network, I sat at my new desk and went through the folder of questions and comments that readers had written in. And Brian was right; there were hundreds of letters waiting to be answered. And they were quite varied as well.

There were the typical love, family and relationship questions:

- "I think my husband is cheating on me, but how do I make sure without ruining my marriage if it's not true?" ~ From Worried Wife
- "My son is 32 and still living at home. How do I kick him out?" ~ From Fed Up
- "My wife doesn't want to have sex with me anymore. How do I get her back in the mood?" ~ From Horny in Hennington

But then there were the unique ones that dealt with work, friendship and "who am I" questions. The ones where you could tell the people were really struggling. They were just regular people stuck in difficult situations and didn't know where else to turn for help and advice:

- "I love what I do, but hate my coworkers. I don't want to leave because I know I'll never find a job I love doing more. Do I just put up with my co-workers and keep quiet, or talk to my boss and rock the boat?" ~ From Job Lover/Co-worker Hater
- "All my life, I've been attracted to women, but a new guy started at my work last month, and I find him attractive, and I'm starting to question who I am. I know it doesn't matter if I'm straight or gay or bi, but as a 47-year-old man, isn't it a bit late for me to be discovering who I am and who I'm attracted to?" ~ From Questioning it All

- "My wife and I both work full time and try as hard as possible to live within our means, but we're running into serious financial problems. With a two-year-old with special needs, we can't really get additional jobs on the side since we're constantly having to take care of her and take her to appointments. We've both asked our bosses if there was any way we could get raises early or any additional work we could do, but no luck. We're worried we're going to have to start selling off our possessions soon just to get by. What do we do?" ~ From Desperate Dad

The last one really pulled at my heart, and I wanted to help them in any way I could. I knew I didn't have the answers. I wasn't a financial advisor or a loan officer who could just give them money, but I was willing to do as much research as possible to at least give them some hope.

I spent hours combing over websites looking for resources for *Desperate Dad* and his family. I found some grants through the Ontario ACSD (Assistance for Children with Severe Disabilities) Program and the Ontario Ministry of Children and Youth Services, which helped with the extra costs of caring for a child with a disability. I found an article about how to make extra money at home by doing things like renting out your car for the weekend, becoming a "shutterbug" and selling your pictures to websites, or participating in market research and taking surveys. I didn't know what *Desperate Dad* or his wife did for work, but those seemed like easy enough things that they could do when they had spare time. It wouldn't get them a lot of extra cash, but I figured if they were writing into an advice column, they were willing to take any help they could get.

By the time I had all my research gathered, it was dark outside, and my stomach was growling, a clear indicator that I had worked way past dinner. I packed up my laptop, excited to start on the actual article tomorrow. It wasn't until I looked around and realized I was the only one there that I noticed it was past 11 at night. I had been so submerged in going through the letters and then with my research that I had put in seven hours of work already and hadn't even realized it.

I walked the three blocks home, bundled in my winter jacket and boots. There were still people walking about, shouting "Happy New Year" to me as I passed. I had completely forgotten it was New Year's Eve, and a pang of loneliness sparked in me when I opened my front door to my dark, empty house.

Just like Christmas, this was the first New Year's Eve I'd be spending alone. It wasn't a big deal, really. Alex and I never really did anything and were usually in bed by 11 p.m. anyway, completely missing the ball drop, but it didn't make the fact that I was starting the new year by myself any easier.

I put my work laptop in my spare room where my desk was, grabbed a piece of lasagna from the fridge, and changed into some comfy PJs while I warmed my dinner up in the microwave. I turned on *Dick Clark's New Year's Rockin' Eve* and settled on the couch when my phone dinged beside me.

Kyle: Happy New Year, Sweetness. Wish you were here.

Attached was a picture of him with a stripper on his lap, giving him a lap dance. Ugh, I didn't want to see that. What happened to the sweet Kyle who was vulnerable with me on the front stoop just yesterday? I deleted the picture right away, not wanting that on my phone, and immediately exited out of Kyle's message. That was when I noticed a message from Alex that I had missed while I was working.

Alex: Happy New Year, Addy. I know it's been a tough year, but we made it through. Love you.

I smiled at his sweet text, a complete opposite of Kyle's and sent him a quick "Happy New Year. Love you, too" back. It was nice knowing that even though I was the only one in my house at the moment, I wasn't alone.

Just as they announced it was one minute to countdown, there was a knock on my front door. I looked out my front window, cautious in case it was one of Kyle's friends again, and saw Conner wave back at me.

"What are you doing here?" I asked as I opened the door. "I thought you were working at *Ape* tonight."

"I am," he said, coming in and shutting the door behind him, "but I told the boss I had to take a quick break."

"Is everything okay?" He was worrying me. I knew he probably only had 10 or 15 minutes for his break, and if he was here, something must be really important or really wrong.

"Yes," he said, his eyes focused on mine, and his breathing came quicker as he stepped closer to me, "I just needed to do this."

The ten-second countdown for the ball drop started in the background as Conner gently cupped my face in his hands.

"Happy New Year, Adeline." The words softly left his mouth before he pressed his lips to mine, capturing them in a soft but needy kiss. It was full of yearning and desire, where I could feel he had wanted to do it for a while and just couldn't wait any longer.

Our lips immediately opened to each other, both of us finally giving in to the desire and tension that had been building between the two of us all week. The longing looks and sly touches had been driving me insane, and I instantly melted against his lips. The smell, feel, and taste of him completely took over my body. This man devoured my entire being with a single kiss. There was no sound, no thought, no reality outside of Conner's big, soft lips on mine as one of his hands moved up into my hair and the other went around my waist and pulled my body tighter to his.

An involuntary moan left my mouth and travelled directly into his as our tongues swept across each other. My hands fisted in his tight black T-shirt, trying to hang on as my world shifted. This blew any kiss I'd ever had with Alex or the one Kyle and I shared out of the water. The want and need I felt in it, but the respect behind it, too. I never knew a simple kiss could shake me so much. It couldn't have been more than a fifteen-second kiss, just a teaser of what was to come, but already I could feel my body revving up. My nipples were hardening, my knees were weakening, and I could feel a heartbeat pulsing between my legs. I knew I was already wet just from our first kiss, and the power in that frightened me.

"I've wanted to do that since the first second I saw you standing in the gym," Conner breathed as he pulled away, resting his forehead against mine. I leaned in again, unable to get enough, and pressed my lips to his once more.

"Why didn't you?" We pulled back, forcing distance between us before we fell any deeper into our urges, but our hands still touched each other. I couldn't stop my hands from running up and down his chest, and his held me tight around the waist, occasionally rubbing my back and butt.

"I didn't want to scare you away." With a big sigh, he leaned in for another deep kiss before he went to open the door. "I have to get back to work."

"Conner?" I asked as he stepped outside.

"Yeah?"

"Happy New Year."

He leaned back in the door for one final kiss. "Best New Year's I've ever had."

Chapter 17

I stood in the doorway as Conner got back in his truck and drove back to *Ape Hangers* while my body pulsed with need. I silently cursed him for leaving me in this state.

Alex and I had been separated for three months before we signed the divorce paperwork and had our backslide into my bed. It had been 10 months total now that we'd been separated, and let me tell you, going seven months without sex was hard. I had wanted to get back out there, but I was still raw and self-conscious and in the process of finding who I was as a single woman. I had had nine years total with Alex, and now I had to try and date, and I had no clue what the proper thing to say was when you were so horny it physically hurt, and you just needed sex…lots and lots of sex.

True, I could have given Kyle a spin; he was definitely interested, but I was trying to be a stronger, better person who made smart choices, not add to the list of regrets I already had in life. Plus, on top of that, I was never the type of person who could have sex when my heart wasn't involved. I'd never been able to just pick up a guy at the bar, fuck him and then forget him. I didn't work that way. My heart and vagina were connected, which was why I was so shaken by Conner.

I knew I liked him. I knew from the second I saw him that I was attracted to him, but this *need* I now had for him made my heart clench.

I went to my bedroom and opened my bedside table, pulling out the purple vibrator I purchased for myself the day after the divorce was finalized. Not the typical celebratory gift, but knowing my head and my heart, I knew I would need it.

And it had been used more this week since I met Conner than ever before.

I turned off the lights, stripped out of my pyjamas and got under the covers. The quiet vibration made me feel like I was doing something naughty, but then I thought of the kiss. My fingers went to my mouth, and I could still feel the ghost of his lips against mine, sending shockwaves through my entire body from just that first touch.

A groan left my throat as I pressed the vibrating tip of the toy to my clit, and I jumped at the sensation. I was so wound up I almost came right away. *How am I this far gone by just a kiss?*

I moved the shaft of the toy through my wet lips, sliding it back and forth, pressing it over both my clit and my opening before I easily breached my opening and slid the silicone toy inside. I teased myself, pulling it out so just the vibrating tip was inside before I pushed it back in, tilting it just right so it rubbed against my walls. My back arched off the bed, just imagining it was Conner pushing into me, his lips on mine and his hands touching my body. My core was already shaking before I even put the clit stimulator into place, but once it was there, vibrations rocked my body, flowing outwards from my centre. I couldn't stop the moans and panting that left my lips as I clenched and pulsed around the toy in under a minute. My hand shook as I grabbed the pillow beside my head, as the other one still held the toy in place. My legs went stick straight, almost paralyzed and unable to move as the orgasm completely took over. My breath was stuck in my throat, my mouth opened in a silent scream, my head thrown back, and my eyes squeezed shut. My body jolted over and over, my clit and core pulsing and spasming harder than they ever had until I finally had to rip the toy out as it was becoming too much.

The entire ordeal took less than three minutes but left me panting and shaking between my sheets.

"Conner," I whispered into the darkness, "what are you doing to me?"

I had only known the man for a week, and yet I craved him as if we'd been separated lovers, missing each other for

10 years. The pull we had to each other was undeniable, and these past seven days have been the most aching, sexually frustrating, blue-bean-inducing time of my life. I was in big trouble.

Tears of frustration filled my eyes as I read the message for a third time and just put my phone down on the bed. I'd had enough. It was clearly time for me to cut ties with my only remaining friend from university. I had outgrown that friendship, and I didn't have time or patience for her ignorance or negativity.

I hadn't seen Nicole, my old university roommate, in years, and now all she did was complain about her kids and her husband and criticize everyone else. Every time we spoke, which was only ever when she texted, not when I initiated a conversation, it turned into nothing but a venting forum for her to bitch and complain about everything and everyone. I had tried to be supportive at the beginning when she first turned judgemental, but over the years, I had slowly started to ask if things were alright and why she was being so negative and nitpicky, even to me, about my own life. Eventually, whenever I added something to the conversation, it went overlooked, much like I had been when we were in school together. I had never met someone who was able to simply ignore a message or what was said and completely monopolize a conversation.

It felt like I had turned into her therapist or dumping ground.

I had questioned our friendship many times over the years, but beggars couldn't be choosers. She had been there for the good times but ignored me in the bad times when I needed support and guidance. It was a hard reality when I realized that she meant more to me than I meant to her, especially when I realized that I meant nothing to her at all.

She saw Alex and I together and thought we had an easy, perfect life. I could never complain about anything or stress over anything because she had two kids and was in a management position at work, whereas I was just a "childless assistant" – her words, not mine.

It didn't matter that I had suffered from depression at university and still struggled today. It didn't matter that I had a strained relationship with my family or that I was having a hard time finding a job. She had even told me to "suck it up and get over it" when I had shared with her a health scare that I had gone through a couple years ago. I was constantly beneath her, and she made that very well known.

But this morning was just too much. She was messaging me about this retreat she and husband number three were going on and mentioned that it was probably way too expensive of a vacation for me and that Alex and I would probably never be able to afford it with our jobs. It was at that point that I realized that she was completely oblivious to the divorce.

I couldn't believe it. I had told her when it happened almost a year ago. And I hadn't just texted, "I'm getting separated." I had actually called her when we separated, and Alex moved out. We had had an hour-long conversation about how we were getting divorced, how we were still best friends and close, that we were selling the house but both staying in Hennington, that it was no one's fault, and that she shouldn't hate him or choose sides.

Apparently, spilling my broken heart was irrelevant and something she ignored. I shouldn't have been surprised, though; it wasn't the first time. But it would definitely be the last. I didn't have space in my life anymore for someone who didn't care about me and only used me to validate themselves. Especially when I had already spoken to her about it multiple times over the years.

This time, I just texted, "We're divorced," and blocked her number. I wouldn't be reading or responding to any of her messages anymore.

I felt lighter, though, realizing that I would no longer have to put up with her ignorance and judgment. Just because we were friends at one point didn't mean we had to remain friends. Just like my marriage, we had some good times, but it was time to move on.

A thought made me rush to my computer. I pulled up my list of 10 goals for the year and deleted "6 - lose 20lbs so my clothes fit better, and I'm more confident in my tighter stuff."

In the spirit of removing judgement and negativity from my life, it didn't matter if I was 20 pounds lighter or 20 pounds heavier. I just wanted to be okay with myself and have that constant "not enough" feeling gone. My weight wasn't going to determine my worth or happiness, and neither was my group of friends or my relationship status. I just needed to filter out all the crap so that all I was left with was a happier me.

In the now-empty number 6 slot, I wrote, "do something brave just for you."

If blocking Nicole's number meant anything, it was that I shouldn't put up with being in uncomfortable situations or sit in discontent just because it was easier than facing possible negative outcomes or backlash. I had to start doing things for me, not for everyone else.

I looked down at my new list and smiled at the progress I'd made so far.

1 ~ make new friends who I can call upon, not just acquaintances

2 ~ try a new sport/outdoor activity

3 ~ Set aside an hour a week completely dedicated to my writing

4 ~ find a job I'm excited to go to each morning

5 ~ learn to make 5 new dishes from scratch (Lasagna ~ should be easy enough, an apple pie

– crust and all, the rice paper pork rolls from my favourite Thai place – will save me money as well, my great aunts cabbage rolls, and the perfect thin crêpe)

6 – do something brave just for you

7 – buy a plant and keep it alive for the whole year

8 – start a self-reflection journal so I'm more aware of how I'm feeling and what is making me feel that way

9 – volunteer one day a week (ideally at an animal shelter if they're taking new volunteers)

10 – look into becoming a foster parent or adoption

4.25 tasks were already crossed off (the lasagna making had to count for at least .25) in the two months at my new home. I was starting to feel like I had a purpose, a goal and some direction in my life. I could do this.

Chapter 18

"Kyle? What the hell?!"

I walked past my front door after saving the updates to my list when there was a single knock before Kyle let himself in.

"Happy New Year, Sweets!" He looked like he was still drunk or fighting a horrible hangover, at least. He stumbled over to me and threw his arms around my shoulders, then went completely weightless and crushed me under his body.

"Kyle!" I yelled, but soft snoring was my only response. Yup, the asshole had passed out. "KYLE!" I yelled even louder, trying to shake him awake without falling to the floor with him on top of me. Thankfully, I was pushed up against the wall for some support, but now I was just trapped between the hallway wall and my drunk-ass neighbour.

"This is unbelievable," I groaned as I tried to shove Kyle off me without him taking me down at the same time.

"What the fuck?!" Conner's voice boomed from the doorway, and he ran in and ripped Kyle off my body. Kyle, who was still completely passed out at this point, just fell to the floor and continued to snore.

"Are you okay?" Conner asked, running his hands over my body to make sure I wasn't injured. "I heard you yelling from outside."

"Yeah, I'm fine," I huffed, nudging Kyle's motionless body with my foot. "Idiot let himself in, threw himself at me to give me a hug and then passed out and went dead weight on me."

Conner was pissed. His hands were balled into fists, his jaw clenched tight, and his breathing was getting faster.

"Here," he stated as he picked up Kyle's body and dropped him onto the front porch, "not your problem anymore." He came back in, shut and locked the door and gave me a serious look. "That door stays locked from now on, okay?"

I nodded in agreement, "Okay." Between randoms showing up and Kyle letting himself into my place twice now, I wasn't taking any more chances.

"Come here." I walked into Conner's open arms and rested my head on his chest. "You sure you're okay?" His lips moved against the crown of my head before he put his fingers under my chin and tilted my head up to look at him.

"Yes, I'm fine. I promise."

The kiss that followed was almost automatic, the pull between us still there, maybe even stronger than last night. It was a quick welcome kiss, but the warmth and press of his lips still stirred excitement in me.

"Hi," he whispered, a boyish smile spread over his lips.

"Hi," I giggled back. Giggled like a damn schoolgirl with a crush. I was embarrassed for myself.

"I was just heading out to work but wanted to see what the yelling was about."

I backed away, reluctant to let him go. These quick meetings were getting annoying. I wanted to spend some real time with Conner, but it seemed like he was always doing something.

"Actually," he gave me a quizzical look, "you busy today?"

"Not really," I shrugged, "why?"

"Want to see what I'm working on?"

The surprise on my face must have been evident since Conner chuckled.

"Is that allowed?" I asked, really hoping it was since it would be another window into who Conner Jensen was.

"I'm allowing it," he smiled. "Go put on some old clothes you don't mind getting dirty. We'll be outside, and it's cold and muddy out."

He gave my ass a little swat as I walked by him, and if the look he gave me was any indication, he REALLY wanted to follow me and help me get changed.

Conner met me at his truck once I was all bundled up, and we made our way out of town. We hardly drove 10 minutes before he turned onto a dirt path that was bordered by thick, mature trees and took us behind the tree line that ran along the main highway in and out of Hennington. We drove down the tree-lined laneway until the highway was no longer visible in the side view mirrors, and the trees opened up around us into a large clearing.

Conner pulled up to a lot at the end of the dirt road and stopped in front of a partially built house. He wasn't lying; the entire area was dirt and mud and slushy, mucky snow, but the surrounding nature was beautiful.

"So? What do you think?" he asked as he passed me a hard hat from the back of his truck. There were three other guys that I could see working around, a couple work trucks parked at the front of the house where I assumed a front lawn and driveway would eventually be, two big industrial garbage bins, and some forklift-type piece of equipment. I had no idea what it was called or what it did, but I kinda wanted to drive it.

"It's going to be beautiful when it's done." I was in awe as I looked around. The house was nestled in amongst the trees, giving it privacy and a storybook feel.

The framing was all up on the house, wrapped in what I assumed was weatherproofing. The windows were in, and the metal roof was on. It looked like an old whimsical cabin with a covered wrap-around porch, double doors at the entryway, and large floor-to-ceiling windows all around the main level. The upper level had two window areas that were pushed out from the rest of the roof. They would be amazing reading bench seats. Those two windows had peaked roofs as well. The whole home wasn't too big, maybe 1500 square feet, two levels with a chimney poking out the left side. I noticed a cement foundation at the very back of the lot as well, which I assumed would be for a detached garage.

Conner and I walked up the front steps, him holding my hand as we stepped over tools and loose pieces of wood and into the main level, where everything was a disaster. You could see through the walls, but it looked like an electrician and plumber had already been in; wires, tubes and hoses running all over the place, and the floors were exposed sub-flooring.

"Just be careful where you step," he yelled over the buzzing noises of saws coming from the front yard. "This will be the living room," he directed as we walked to the left, "and over there," he pointed to the opposite side of the house from where we just came, "will be the kitchen and dining room."

Still holding my hand, he led me to the back, where he showed me the master bedroom and the ensuite bathroom, which took up the entire back of the house.

"Upstairs will be two guest bedrooms, a study/library/office and another bathroom." He pointed to the staircase as we passed it and made our way out the back glass doors to stand on a cement stoop. "Back here will be a large wrap-around deck that connects to the front porch." My breath caught as I looked over the trees and a small frozen creek that ran through the backyard.

"Conner, this place is amazing." We stood out back for a bit, the cold and wind making us shudder until he wrapped his arms around me from behind, and I leaned back into his warm embrace.

"I'm glad you like it," he pressed a kiss to the side of my neck before he whispered in my ear, "because it's mine."

"What?" I whipped around in his arms to look at him, a smug smile playing on his face.

"It's mine," he said proudly. "This is my property and my home." He looked out over his land with pride and spun me back around to enjoy the view with him.

"I got the land about three years ago and have been slowly working on clearing out the trees and building on it ever since. I'm trying to do as much as I can by myself and with the help of friends, so it's taking a while, but I don't mind."

As the wind picked up, Conner led me back into the house. "This is unbelievable." I couldn't believe he was building a house by himself. "So, this is what you do when you're not working? This is why you're never home?"

"Pretty much." He leaned up against some framing and pulled me back into his arms, his hands landing around my waist, just above my ass. He was looking around his home before his eyes came down to meet mine. "I'm out here as much as I can, but lately, I've been kinda distracted." He leaned down and pressed another tempting kiss on my lips. "You know," he taunted, his lips brushing against mine, "we're technically in my bedroom right now."

I pulled away and laughed at his boyish charm.

"Smooth, Casanova."

He laughed as we made our way back out front of the house, where Conner checked in with the guys who were there working. I warmed myself up in his truck, not wanting to get in the way.

"How would you feel about giving me a hand with something?" He jumped in the driver's seat and turned on the truck, the heat quickly filling the cab. I shoved my hands in front of the heater, trying to warm them up before he grabbed them in his warm hands and rubbed them together.

"What are you needing help with?"

"Well," he started as he turned the truck around and made his way back down the laneway, "it looks like we'll be ready to start doing the brickwork next week, so I wanted to go to look at samples and pick what colour bricks I wanted. Interested?"

"Sure," I smiled, my heart warming a bit. I'd only known Conner for just over a week, but he was inviting me into his life, and it felt right, unlike how it felt when Kyle invited me on a road trip.

Since Alex and I separated, I have learned to rely on my gut and listen to my sixth sense. The suggestion of going on the road trip with Kyle had set my nerves on end, but with Conner, there was no warning, only excitement. It felt like we fit.

I felt like now that I was older and dating again, things were so different from my first time dating in my teens and twenties. Now, I relied on my gut and did what felt right to me, not allowing myself to cave because I was worried about what the other person would think. I knew what I wanted and what I didn't and just went with it. There was no pretense, no fake personas. This was me; take it or leave it. And Conner seemed to be the same way. Conner and I had had some amazing conversations and interactions this past week, and we seemed to just slide comfortably into each other's lives and found our spot there, already ready and waiting for us.

We drove to a warehouse about an hour away, just outside of Toronto and talked about his plans for the house the whole way there. He wanted the cottage cabin feel, so was trying to stay away from siding as much as possible and wanted to keep the outside mostly wood, stone and brick. Inside, he said he was completely lost. He knew the layout but had no clue if he wanted carpet or hardwood in the bedrooms, what he wanted for a backsplash or countertop in the kitchen, and the showerhead options blew his mind.

"Seriously," he insisted, "have you ever gone to The Home Depot and looked at the amount of shower heads there are available? It's insane." I couldn't stop laughing at him as we pulled into a parking lot. This big, strong, goofy man, who was building his own home with his bare hands, was freaking out over the selection of a showerhead.

"Don't worry," I teased him, patting his thigh, "you can hire a decorator for all that stuff."

He put the car in park and grabbed my hand when I went to pull away. He linked our fingers together over the centre console and gave them a little squeeze.

"Or maybe I'll just ask my attractive neighbour for some help."

We got out of the truck at the building supply store that had bricks and stone out in their yard and started looking around.

"Well, you can," I picked up a bright yellow/orange brick, wondering who would ever use that for their home, before putting it back down, "but I don't know if Kyle's style will match yours."

"Hardy har har." Conner picked up a really pretty grey one with brown specks around it.

"Oh, that's nice." I took a picture of the brick on my phone so we could come back to it later.

We spent an hour looking at bricks and then stone work when I pointed out how nice some of the stone siding was before we eventually went back to the greyish-brown one that Conner originally picked.

"Now," he said as we got back in the truck to head home, "how about I take you on a long-overdue date?"

Chapter 19

The date so far was amazing. After going home to change out of our dirty clothes, we did the typical teenage dinner-and-a-movie night. Unfortunately, there wasn't much to do in Hennington in the winter besides the movie theatre. In the summer, there was a golf course and some trails to hike, but that was about it. Small-town living didn't offer clubs, or axe throwing, or escape rooms, or entertainment venues with concerts or comedians as options. We made our own entertainment or went outside.

The theatre in Hennington showed older movies during the day and then the new releases at night. Since we were seeing a matinee, the theatre was showing *Erin Brockovich*, which I had seen a dozen times over the years and really liked.

This time, however, I couldn't follow along. From the moment we took our seats in the old theatre and the lights all went down, my attention was solely on Conner. The way he relaxed in the seats with his long legs spread wide so he could fit in the squished rows. We were the only ones in there; the entire theatre was ours, but we still sat side by side.

The cinema was small, and the seats were packed tight, not that I minded being sardined next to Conner with his massive arms and shoulders brushing up against mine.

It was as if all my attention was zeroed in on wherever our bodies touched. His arm against mine, his legs brushed against my leg and eventually the feel of his warm hand on my knee, which slowly slid higher and higher but respectfully stopped mid-thigh.

I tried so hard to focus on the movie and not Conner's touch and focused in on one of my favourite scenes. I couldn't help but make a happy swoony sound when George knelt before Erin and simply said, *"You're someone to me."*

"Did you really just whimper at a line in a movie?" Conner asked as he tossed another handful of popcorn in his mouth. The teasing in his voice, however, was unmistakable.

"Hey," I began as I grabbed a kernel from my own bag. "It's every girl's dream for a guy to be open and vulnerable with a woman."

I could feel his shoulders shake in laughter as he looked at me with an "Are you serious?" look.

"It's true," I continued. "Half the time, guys are so closed off and tight-lipped with their emotions, women are left wondering what the guy's thinking and feeling, and hoping what they feel isn't just one-sided."

Conner put the popcorn down on the seat beside him and grabbed my hand. He lifted an eyebrow at me before he placed it right over his crotch.

"Conner!" I whisper-yelled. I could feel his dick twitching in his pants before he took that same hand and placed it over his heart. I could feel it racing under his shirt.

"I hope that helps clarify how I feel about you."

This was Conner's version of telling me that I had an effect on him, and I melted a bit inside.

"Now," Conner asked as he pulled the popcorn out of my hands and put it beside him. "Can I feel your heartbeat too?"

He placed his hand on my chest, just above my breast, but slowly started moving it down. I swatted his hand away with a laugh before he pulled me to lean into his arms, and he kissed the top of my head and whispered into my hair, "You're someone to me."

After the movie, Conner insisted on bringing me back to his place for dinner. He wanted me to just relax while we had a couple drinks, and he made the food.

"Seriously," I insisted as he shoved a beer in my hand, "the large popcorn you insisted on getting me since you refused to share was enough food for me."

"Hey, you know popcorn is my favourite food. No way in hell am I sharing."

"Fair enough," I laughed, taking a gulp of some apple cider beer he promised I'd like. "Huh, this is really good."

"When are you going to learn to listen and trust me?"

I was tempted to stick my tongue out at him, but I was too old for that. Instead, I just smirked at him as he shoved a pan of nachos into the oven.

"Besides," he grabbed his beer from the counter and joined me on his couch, "we can just nibble on the nachos. If you get hungry, they're there."

"So, what's the next step in the build? Are you ready to tackle the dreaded shower heads next?"

"Next is putting up the drywall and insulation, getting the bricks done, and hopefully starting on some of the inside stuff. Ideally, I want to get the wrap-around deck done too."

"That's so exciting."

"What's exciting is you down here with me on my couch."

I just sat there for a minute, taking in the man beside me, still not believing he was real. He was tall and muscular and just solid. And if the constant bulge in his pants was any indication, he was packing quite the weapon as well.

Conner wasn't the cocky, 6-pack, look-how-sexy-I-am type that you knew wasn't natural, but just pure power and strength. He had a slight tan from always being outside, even in the winter, and I could see some tattoos peeking out the bottom of both his T-shirt sleeves. But as dominating as his body was, his eyes and smile were completely honest and open. Yes, he had strong features, but when he smiled, his entire face transformed. He went from intimidating, bruting and sexy to sweet, heartwarming, and only a little bit intimidating. If I ran into him on the street, his presence, body and intense eyes would startle me, but seeing him here, smiling and relaxed beside me, I wanted to run to him and touch every inch of him.

So that's what I did. Setting the beer on the side table, I made my way across the couch and let him pull me down to straddle his lap.

"That makes you excited?"

He pushed both hands in my hair, holding my head gently in his grasp.

No one had ever looked at me with such lust in their eyes before. I had never had anyone stare at my eyes, down to my lips and have hunger written all over their face. I had never had anyone look at me with desire before. Even with Alex, it was never desire or passion. I never felt craved. I felt like a frozen pizza in the back of the freezer. No one *craved* frozen pizza. They wanted the freshly made, hot from the oven, ooey-gooey cheesy pizza with the fresh toppings. But it was easier to just throw a frozen pizza in the oven than to make your own or order from an over-priced take-out place. The frozen option was there in case you needed it; it worked and minimally satisfied your craving for more. And that was me, the frozen pizza that you really didn't want but that you settled for.

But with Conner, he looked at me as if he was drooling and couldn't wait to get a bite.

"You have no idea," he whispered before he crushed his lips to mine, pulling my face down to meet his. He went from zero to a hundred in a second. The desire seeped out of him and completely engulfed me. The bulge in his jeans pressed up to my centre, and I instinctively rocked against him. I wanted this man more than I understood. It made no sense; we barely knew each other, but he called to me. Everything about him just made me want him more. The way he joked with me, the way he checked in on me, the way we laughed together, and even the way he touched me. Everything about him just drove me wild.

Not to mention his delectable body that was rocking up into mine. He had one hand in my hair, holding me to him, as his other slid around my back and was creeping up under my shirt. The feel of his warm hand against my bare back sent shivers through my body. His touch felt like instant comfort and desire. His touch felt like home.

Just the simple brush of his fingers across my skin as he moved his hand from my back, around to my stomach and up to my breasts made my lady bits clench. His mouth devoured mine as his thumb brushed over my bra-covered nipple, and my hips rocked violently over his groin.

"God," I panted as I ripped my mouth from his to catch a breath. Conner's lips didn't leave my skin, though, and immediately attacked my neck and the tender spot behind my left ear. As soon as he kissed me there and applied a little suction, he pinched my nipple through my thin bra, causing my hips to grind hard into his lap again.

"Conner," I moaned as he growled into my skin and attacked my weak spot again, causing my body to grind against him once more.

His fingers slipped into the cup of my bra and took my full breast into his hand. He moaned as he returned his lips to mine and worked to bring my nipple to full, hard – to the point of painful - attention.

He pulled away, lifted me up off his lap and threw me onto the couch so my back was laying on the seat cushions. He spread out on top of me, holding up the majority of his weight but letting a delicious bit press me deeper into the cushions as his mouth once again captured mine. We were making out like teenagers, but the desire and want I had for him was pure carnal adult.

As my hips ground up to meet his again, he pulled away, pushing himself up on his arms, and just gazed down at my panting body. He pressed his forehead to mine, giving us both a moment to calm down. "I really like you, Adeline," he moaned as his lips travelled down my neck and over my shirt-covered breasts. He bit at my nipples through the fabric, and the small bite of pain radiated tingles throughout my body. He was slowing down, moving us from frantic desire to passionate need. I could hardly take it.

"I really like you, too," I panted as my hips lifted on their own accord, seeking friction my body knew his could provide, and he took it as an opportunity to start to take my pants down. If pull-on jeggings weren't the best things invented, I didn't know what was. My pants were ripped down my legs in two seconds flat.

He jumped up off the couch, went around the armrest and grabbed both my legs under the knees. Before I knew what he was doing, he pulled me down the length of the couch and rested my ass up on the armrest.

My underwear was the next thing to go, and Conner was kissing his way up my thigh, over my hip bones and planted a deep, open-mouthed kiss over my centre. He dove back in again, lips parted, tongue strong and wet, and licked from my centre to my clit, tasting every inch of me.

"Oh my God," I moaned, unable to hold back the needy sounds that were building in me.

I felt like I was a virgin again, being touched for the first time and not knowing what to do. Conner was doing things to me that Alex had never done. Alex hated going down on me and only did it three times in our entire marriage. And none of those three times were like this.

The feelings that were erupting through my body were unbelievable. My body wanted to stretch out but tighten up all at once. My hands wanted to grab Conner's hair, the couch, my breasts all at the same time.

The beautiful man between my legs was kissing and licking and sucking on me, moving from pushing his tongue deep into my centre to rolling it expertly over my clit. I could feel my wetness seeping out of me, and he just kept begging my body for more.

A large, thick finger danced over my lips and slowly around my opening before it pushed into me as Conner's tongue attacked my clit.

"Conner!" His name escaped my lips as I gasped for air. My body writhed under his touch, wanting to twist and turn, escape the onslaught of his mouth and finger, but somehow pull him closer.

Both my hands tried to grab hold of his short-cropped hair as I started to shake and twitch around his finger.

"That's it, Addy," he soothed as he pulled back to look at me while his finger thrust deeper and moved a bit quicker inside. "I got you," he whispered as he added another finger and then a third, moving them expertly inside me. He was gentle but determined. He clearly knew what he was doing, and all I could do was lay back and hold on.

My hand grabbed for his, which was still under my knee and held me up, and I held on tight as my insides shattered and quaked. His mouth was back on me, licking up the wetness that was seeping out past his fingers and gently kissing my clit and hip and thigh as I slowly started to come down.

A ringing in my ear was the first thing I noticed outside of my ragged breath, pounding heart and shaking limbs.

"Hang on," Conner ran to the kitchen and made the ringing stop, which I was slowly realizing was the oven timer for the nachos.

He scooped me up off the couch when he returned and carried me to the bedroom. "I'm not done with you yet." My arms went around his neck, and I pulled his mouth to mine, not caring at the moment that he had just swallowed my orgasm.

He laid me gently on his bed, then reached behind his neck and pulled his T-shirt off. He lazily unbuttoned his jeans and pulled the zipper down. His bulge immediately filled up the space the zipper created, straining against the confines of his underwear. He wasn't hurried or rushed, but there was no doubt he was eager as his eyes roamed over my body the whole time he undressed. I had seen his naked chest before, but Conner in just black boxer briefs made me quiver.

Strength and power just oozed off him. He was someone who looked like they would ravage you to the brink of consciousness, which I could attest to as he just did, and then ask for seconds, which he was currently doing. And yet, he had such a sweet heart, was kind and conscientious, and clearly a determined and motivated man. He was perfect inside and out.

I lay there, propped up on my elbows as he climbed on the bed, straddled my legs and started to lift my sweater over my head. As soon as it was off, however, leaving me in nothing but my bra, I started to shake. All of a sudden, I was worried, more nervous than I'd ever been before. This was the first man I would be with since the divorce, and I really liked him. I wanted Conner badly, but all of a sudden, I was overcome with the fear that I wouldn't be good enough...again. What if he just wanted sex and nothing else? I'd never been good at sex, and what if I ruined any chance of Conner and me being anything because I was bad in bed?

Conner sat back on his heels and gave me space, instinctively knowing something was wrong. The nerves took over, and my hands started to shake as I crossed my arms over my chest to cover myself.

"Hey...baby, what's wrong?" I couldn't help but melt just the tiniest bit when he called me that. It was said with care and emotion, not flung around like a derogatory name like it was when Kyle used his "terms of endearment." There was genuine concern in Conner's tone that showed that I mattered to him.

I sat up, putting us chest to chest. He wrapped his arms around me to hold me close.

"I just don't want to ruin this."

"What do you mean? Ruin what?"

"Us." The urge to look down and shy away was strong, but I forced myself to be open and honest with Conner and myself.

"Addy, having sex will not ruin us. Trust me."

"You might be disappointed."

"Okay," he said and put a bit of space between us so we could look at each other better. "Where is this coming from? Why would I be disappointed?"

"I'm not very good at this."

"At what? Sex?"

I nodded as treacherous tears slowly welled in my eyes. I was stronger than this. I would not cry over my fear of not being enough.

"Why on Earth would I be disappointed in having sex with you? And what do you mean you're not very good at it?"

"I'm not." My voice was barely a whisper.

"According to who?"

I took a large, steadying breath before I opened this can of worms. If Conner was able to be vulnerable with me about his past, I could do the same for him. "Alex." I wiped away the tears that filled my eyes before they ran down my cheek.

"Hold on, your ex-husband told you that you weren't good in bed?" He looked totally affronted and shocked, almost like he didn't believe me.

"Once or twice."

"Oh my God," he paused, scrutinizing my face, "you're serious?! He actually said you were bad at sex."

All I could do was nod.

"Well...I think it's time to prove him wrong and get some of your confidence back." He took my face in his hands again, gave me a deep kiss that I felt all the way to my toes, and slowly laid me back down on the bed.

Chapter 20

Conner's body covered mine, his lips and hands greedy as they travelled all over my skin. He pulled the cup of my bra down and sucked my nipple into his warm mouth.

The feel of his skin on mine, the brush of his lips, the soft roughness of his hands and the smell of him made me feel safe, eager and wanting. The fire he quickly built in me had my hands roaming over his strong back, finding comfort and desire in his warm skin. I was trying to be in the moment instead of trapped in my head, and as Conner licked, kissed and stroked my body, I drowned in his every touch.

He moved to the other nipple and gave it a quick nip before sucking it deep into his mouth. A yelp of pleasure and pain escaped my panting lips as my back arched off the bed. His touches, his caress and his desire extinguished my doubt, fanning the flames higher and higher. It had been seven months since I last had sex, and with how Conner was playing with my body, it felt like seven years. I was now desperate for his touch.

Conner rolled onto his side, bringing his lips back to mine as his hand drifted down my body to cover my sex. One large finger pressed into me again, teasing my entrance while rolling my clit with his thumb.

"God, you're so wet for me." He pushed another finger in, stretching me wider and driving me wilder. "You feel so good."

The teasing was not enough. My body craved more. I was still riding the high from him going down on me not five minutes ago, the remnants of my orgasm still thrumming and tingling through my body. The pure want that he built in me nearly brought me to tears. It was a physical ache for him. My body craved Conner. Yes, I had only known him a week, but the way he made me feel, the absolute need he built in me, was more potent than anything I had felt for Alex in the seven years we had been married. It was a need that was extinguishing all my worries and fears.

"More," I insisted, frantic to tell Conner what I wanted, what I needed. Quickly, it became very clear what I required. "I need you in me."

Conner climbed off the bed and pulled down his boxer briefs, freeing his thick cock. As if unable to control himself, he took his intimidating length in his hand and slowly stroked it as I quickly took my bra off and climbed under the sheets.

Without looking away from me, Conner went to his bedside table and dug around, coming up with a condom. I watched as he bit the corner, tearing it open with one hand, while he continued to stroke himself with the other, his movements getting stronger and faster. He rolled the condom on and crawled under the covers to join me. He captured my lips in a heated kiss, rolling on top of me and settling between my thighs. His cock slid over my lips until my folds were surrounding his length and slowly slid back and forth as he flexed his hips.

"You sure?" His lips barely left mine, just far enough so he could stare into my eyes and see the truth in my answer.

"Yes."

He sat back on his haunches, his erection held in his firm grasp. We both stared at his hand as he stroked himself one last time before he guided his cock to my opening. He slowly guided it in with his hand before an undistinguishable sound left him on a breath, and he lowered back onto his arms, pushing just a bit deeper.

The stretch was unbelievable as he slowly rocked back and forth, pushing himself in deeper and deeper with each measured thrust. The urgency to claim each other was palpable.

I widened my legs, giving Conner more room, and he slammed the rest of the way in.

"Fuck…" he bent down and captured my lips in a ravenous kiss before he started to pull back out and then slowly press back in. His hips moved in a slow rhythm, but the force behind it was intense.

Needy whimpers left my lips. My breasts were swaying with each flex of Conner's hips, and the bed started to rock underneath us as he picked up speed, the headboard hitting the wall with the force of his movements.

The feeling of him inside me was almost suffocating. I could hardly breathe; I was so full of him. Every inch of my inside was being rubbed by his thick dick. It completely took over every inch of my body. As corny as it sounded, I honestly didn't know where he ended, and I began. He was everywhere, and with each move he made, my body couldn't help but react.

Our lips hovered over each other, panting together, my breath exhaling as he inhaled as if we were sharing one breath.

He leaned back and pulled out before he flipped me over onto my stomach and lifted my hips up. In one quick move, he was back inside me and even deeper, if that was possible, the bed once again rocking beneath me. I buried my face in the pillow, and the smell of him filled my lungs. The smell, the feel, and the sounds we were making together, the slapping of skin, the tightness of his hold on my hips, the whimpers, groans and words of passion floating in the air lit a billion little sparks inside my body.

I reached back, desperate to touch Conner. One of his hands dropped to mine and held on while the other held my hip tight as he thrust in and out, harder and faster. He alternated between peppering my back with licks and kisses and grabbing my ass cheeks, giving them a light smack every now and then. And each move, each touch, was making my body pull tighter, my blood pump faster, and my nerves spark hotter. I felt like a balloon that kept expanding more and more, my body getting tighter and tighter, just on the verge of popping.

Sex had never been like this before. It had been a pleasurable act to scratch an itch, but it had never been so consuming. I had never felt it from the tips of my toes to the top of my head and every millimetre in between. And as Conner reached around me and found my clit, my toes actually did curl up as my entire body tensed before it exploded in every direction.

My eyes squeezed shut as light and sparks lit up my vision. My body quaked as he kept moving in and out, forcing his way through my clenching walls, taking my pleasure higher and higher, making everything so much more intense. My mouth was open in a silent scream, my breath trapped in my throat. I could hear Conner saying something as his thrusts became harder, quicker and jerkier, but I couldn't decipher what the words were. All I could do was feel.

I was finally able to release and catch a breath as his movements slowed, and I started to come back to reality. And unfortunately, that's when my brain kicked in as well.

"Adeline…" Conner's voice was almost reverent as his arms wrapped around me, and he pulled me down onto the mattress and into his chest. He pressed loving kisses into my damp skin until he reached and captured my lips. "…you are most definitely NOT bad in bed."

I laid in bed, staring at the ceiling while Conner was curled up against my side, snoring away, his head using my breasts as a pillow. We were naked and sated, and Conner was fast asleep, but I was completely awake, staring at the same spot on the ceiling for almost an hour now.

So many thoughts were running through my head, and I didn't have the room to process them all. Plus, I really had to pee.

Trying my hardest not to wake him, I slid out from under Conner's body and quietly got out of bed. I took a second to admire the beautiful man who had definitely captured my heart and body, unable to believe that someone like him would want someone like me. I grabbed his T-shirt from the floor and quickly threw it over my naked body as I tiptoed to the bathroom and shut the door behind me.

I needed to think about what just happened, needed to analyze it, and I couldn't do that with him right beside me, holding me while he slept peacefully.

As I left the bathroom and made my way in the dark to Conner's kitchen, I tried not to think about the fact that he had just given me two orgasms within an hour. I tried not to dwell on the fact that Alex had only gone down on me three times in our entire relationship, and yet Conner had seemed to love it and didn't want to stop. I definitely didn't think about how there was more passion in my first time with Conner than in the entire time I was with Alex. I couldn't think about those things, not while I was still at Conner's place and he was sleeping just down the hall.

I grabbed a glass of water, scolding myself for comparing Alex and Conner. It wasn't fair to either of them, and they were both good men.

I slid down to the floor in front of the kitchen sink, hugging my knees to my chest and tucked them under the shirt to keep warm. I couldn't stop the arguments from seeping into my brain.

I just couldn't believe how different sex with Conner was. How…overwhelming. And I could tell that Conner was with me for every second of it. He was completely into it. Completely into *me*. Maybe it wasn't me who was bad at sex. Maybe Alex and I just weren't compatible, but like everything in our marriage, whenever something went wrong or didn't seem to work as hoped or expected, I was to blame, once again letting the little knives cut me and let the water erode away the rock that I was.

We didn't do oral sex all that often, so I became incredibly self-conscious, thinking it was because I tasted bad or he didn't like how I gave head. And every time we had sex, it always seemed rushed. When I asked Alex why, he said it was because I would just lay there and make him do all the work, so he tired quickly. And instead of participating more, I took that as I was bad at sex, and he didn't like it.

Somehow, I thought it was always my fault that we were never in sync. But if what Conner and I just had was any indication, Alex was the problem and not me. Alex and I just didn't fit, but Conner and I most definitely did.

In the middle of this massive and life-changing revelation, one that, after all these years, finally gave me a bit of self-worth and confidence back, I heard light footsteps in the hall.

"There you are." Conner walked into the dark kitchen in all his naked glory and sat down on the floor beside me. He pushed my hair behind my ear and kissed me with a gentle softness that just melted my entire body. "The bed got cold, and you were gone when I woke up. How long have you been out here?"

I lifted up my now half-full glass of water and indicated to the top of the glass. "Since about here."

Conner let out a breathy chuckle as he grabbed my glass of water and chugged the rest. "Well, now that it's empty, are you coming back to bed?"

With a new lightness and a boost of confidence back in my life, I got up off the floor and held out my hand to Conner. "Lead the way."

We walked back to bed hand in hand and settled into a soft and passionate round three.

Chapter 21

Dear Desperate Dad,

First off, please know you are not alone. With the rising cost of living, from groceries and gas to our utility bills and house and car insurance, many people are struggling just to get by.

Last year, the national inflation rate went up over 6%, with grocery store prices going up almost 11%. I don't know anyone who received a 6% wage increase this year or even the past few years combined. Our employment wage increases are no longer proportionate to Canada's annual inflation rate. And when we struggle to handle a life that we had previously been managing fine, we tend to think we're doing something wrong.

This is not your fault! Living paycheck to paycheck is now the norm, and for a lot of people, even that is not enough.

Add the additional struggles that people may face, like a one-income household, only being able to find part-time or contract work, or, as in your situation, taking care of a child with special needs and getting by, let alone getting ahead feels hopeless.

I pulled up my research from the other day and added those hopefully helpful tips and links to the article. I didn't know if *Desperate Dad* would use the information I gave him, but at least I tried.

I saved the article, wanting to go over it and tweak it a bit before I submitted it to Brian and maybe do one more look online to see if there was a resource I had missed that could help this family. I knew I was going overboard, that this was just an advice column, but I figured if people were taking the time to write in with their genuine concerns, I should take it seriously and help them in any way I could.

The sound of Kyle running down his steps pulled my attention from the computer. Lately, it had seemed like he was stomping around more, almost like he was purposefully making extra noise to remind me he was there. Conner and I had talked a bit about Kyle's interest in me after he had let himself into my apartment yesterday, and it was clear that Conner was suspicious and weary of Kyle, and I didn't think it was in a jealous or protective kind of way.

What he had told me about the police coming to Kyle's place a couple years ago and Kyle being taken away in handcuffs hadn't left my mind either. I definitely needed to put distance between us, but stupid me didn't know how to do it without hurting his feelings, and for some strange reason, I was concerned about that.

The sound of Kyle's front door slamming was quickly followed by a knock on my door and a quick jiggle of my door handle. Thankfully, I had listened to Conner and kept the front door locked at all times now after Kyle had let himself in. Luckily, Conner was asleep on the couch after a long day working two different jobs outside in the cold and didn't seem to hear what was going on.

"Hey, Kyle," I greeted as I pulled a wrap out of my closet, herded Kyle outside onto the front stoop and shut the door behind me, not wanting to wake up Conner and get him involved.

"Hey, Sweets," he greeted with a confused look. "Why are we outside?" His face changed into an excited smirk. "Are you taking me somewhere?" Of course, he had to add a wink to the end of his question.

"No," I huffed, quickly losing my patience with him and his constant need to make everything suggestive. "I have someone over and didn't want them to overhear."

"Who is it?" he asked as he tried to lean over and see in my front window. "Is it another girl? Maybe the three of us can have some fun together, Sexy." He moved back over to me and ran his hand down my arm.

I stepped back to break the contact. "Enough, Kyle." I shook my head as I put even more space between us. "I've asked you multiple times to stop calling me Sexy and Sweetness and stuff like that. I'm not interested in you like that, and it makes me really uncomfortable when you keep throwing sex into every conversation we have."

"Addy, come on, you know there's something between us —"

"Stop," I ordered as he tried to move closer again. "Just stop, Kyle."

He was silent as he just stared into my eyes. A chill came over my body, and it had nothing to do with the cold January weather. His blue eyes turned from flirty and friendly into something sinister in the four seconds of silence.

"Okay," he said in a low tone before he quickly pulled on his friendly façade again and smiled at me. "No worries. Sorry if I was making you uncomfortable. It was just flirty fun, and I thought you were into it, but no biggie." He gave me a small wave and made his way down the walkway to the parking lot out back.

It was like a Jekyll and Hyde act right before my eyes. He went from flirty Kyle to darkness in his eyes and back to flirty seamlessly. If I hadn't been paying such close attention, I completely would have missed it. The same warning bells I had when he had asked me to join him for a ride to his warehouse were ringing in my head again.

I stood there until he was out of sight to make sure he didn't double back on me or anything. I honestly didn't know what to do anymore. This was a new side to Kyle and one that I was honestly very uncomfortable with.

I went back inside and relocked the door. The ominous feeling I had when Kyle changed right in front of me didn't leave, though. It was still there, sticking to me like cobwebs you could feel but couldn't see.

I peeked around the corner and saw Conner sprawled out on the couch, sleeping while *Seinfeld* played on the TV. At least I had managed to keep this interaction with Kyle away from him. Who knew what would have happened if Conner had answered the door.

I crept over to him and placed a kiss on his forehead, gently waking him up.

"Ready to eat?" I asked as he opened his tired eyes and smiled when he saw me. We had gotten up at 5 a.m. so that he could go and help one friend deliver some lumber to a job site before he worked all day doing clean-up and dump runs for another friend who had just bought a hoarder house to flip. The man was pooped.

"Yup," he yawned, "I'm coming, Cricket."

"Cricket?" I asked as I watched him stand up and stretch his arms over his head. His white T-shirt rode up and showed the smooth skin of his abdomen. Poor guy had been out in the cold and rain all day and was just drained. I had sent him a text to just come over after work and relax and that I'd take care of him.

"Yeah, Cricket," he smirked as he started to follow me out of the living room. "Did you know you rub your legs and feet together in your sleep? It's frickin' adorable."

I blushed as I went to the kitchen to grab the bowls for the chilli I had cooking in the slow cooker all afternoon, but when I turned to put them on the counter, Conner was just standing in the doorway, his arms above his head, gripping the door frame, watching me. His frame took up the entire doorway.

"What," I asked. My heartbeat instantly rose, arousal building in my chest and…down below.

"Nothing. Can't I just look at my girl?"

His girl? I quirked an eyebrow at his audacity but swooned a bit at the same time.

And the cheeky bugger knew exactly what he was doing to me. He sent a wink my way, which was VERY different from the winks Kyle gave, before he grabbed one of the bowls I was still holding, planted a kiss on my cheek and gave my butt a quick swat on his way over to the food.

"Hey!" My ass stung from the tap, the pleasant sting radiating across my cheek.

His chuckle followed him back out into the living room, a steaming bowl of chilli and a side plate with dinner rolls and a pickle in his hands. Conner definitely brought fun and lightness into my life, but I still couldn't shake off the darkness from Kyle's visit.

It seemed like my talk with Kyle had worked to some degree. Over the next two weeks, he didn't come over or send any more inappropriate texts. We had seen each other in passing, and he'd just given me a polite "Hi, Addy," a smile and a wave, and that was it. Although there were very few interactions, it did seem that I was seeing him more and more, almost like he was looking out for me coming or going before he'd appear. Either that, or I was letting my mind get carried away.

And although I wasn't too thrilled about seeing more of Kyle, the complete opposite could be said for my basement neighbour and potential new man-friend. I saw Conner every day after our first night together. Sometimes, it was as simple as Conner knocking on my door to give me a kiss and tell me he was going to work or just coming home and going to bed to crash. Other times, it was going for a walk or Conner coming over to help me renovate the house. Most times, it was just us hanging out at my place, watching TV and having a meal. It was nothing big, no expensive dates, just two people relaxing together and getting to know each other better.

It was easy, with no pretense or expectations. We just simply enjoyed spending time together, even if we did nothing. But the more time I spent with Conner, the more time I wanted to spend with him, both in and out of the bedroom.

With Conner, the pressure was gone. It was just enjoyment and maturity and tender kisses for no reason other than he wanted to taste and feel my skin under his lips. Conner knew what he wanted, and so did I. We weren't testing things out, trying to figure out what we liked and what we didn't. We knew what we wanted, and clearly, we wanted each other.

We had fun together, wanted to share our days with each other and just hang out. Conner was someone I wanted to be around. He was good for my self-esteem and mental health. He was bringing joy back into my life. He was easy to be with and made me realize that life didn't always have to be so hard and so serious.

What we had was a different kind of friendship. We weren't in a relationship that was based on sex but on who we were and the enjoyment we had together. It was as if I had found my best friend. My best friend, who I got to touch and kiss and lick and fuck.

And after two weeks of seeing Conner every day, I wanted to have "the talk" to see if he was in the same place emotionally as I was. I was already falling for him…hard. But I didn't. I didn't want to spook him and send him running for the hills. He was making an effort to see me every day, so that had to mean something. I liked being around Conner. I liked who I was when I was with him. He made me smile more than I ever had before. But I was trying hard to just go with the flow. I didn't want to think too much about it or analyze the fun we were having together. I just wanted to be with him.

"It's just poker, Cricket," Conner said, his nickname for me sending a rush of warmth through my body, as it did every time he said it. "You'll be fine, I promise."

Conner was hosting a poker night for some of his construction buddies. There were four guys who did this every month, rotating houses each time, and tonight was Conner's turn to host at his place.

"Plus," he continued as he put salt on the pretzels and shoved them in the oven, "the girls always come, too."

I walked over to Conner and leaned against the counter beside him as he proceeded to pour beer into the homemade cheese sauce for the pretzels.

"But won't it be kind of awkward since I don't know any of them?"

"This is how you get to know them." He smiled at me as he tasted the cheese sauce, removed it from the heat and set it aside.

"Look," he said, turning to face me, "there's no pressure. If you don't want to come, you don't have to, but the guys know I've been seeing you and the girls want to meet you. They're a great bunch of guys; loud and unfiltered and rowdy, yes, but they're still great guys. Plus, you love reading, and the girls always talk about all these smutty books they read. I thought you might have fun."

That did actually sound like fun. Meeting people was always awkward for me since I wasn't very outgoing, but making new friends, especially ones who already knew Conner and shared my love for smut books, sounded like an entertaining evening.

Conner's friends started arriving just before 7 p.m., and he was right. The guys were loud and sarcastic and didn't hold back any punches with each other, but the laughter that flowed through Conner's home was genuine. These guys were obviously close friends.

The guys were already smack-talking each other over the poker table while the girls were all sitting in the living room drinking wine and laughing at the hilarity coming from the guys in the kitchen.

"So, how did you meet Conner?" I turned to see four sets of eyes looking at me. All the girls had been so incredibly sweet and welcoming, and once they found out I was a reader too, they latched on to me like they wanted me to join their raunchy reading cult.

"I actually live upstairs," I smiled at the group, who were genuine in their interest in me. "I had a leaky pipe in the bathroom and asked Conner if I could borrow one of his tools." Honest to God, all four of them silently "awed" at the same time.

Kate and Max were in their mid-twenties, met at a party and got married three years later. Brie and Thane met at college, pretty much got married right away and had two kids. Jess and Austin were in their late thirties, like Conner and I, had met at a bar years ago but didn't really have a need to get married. Jess had a son from a previous marriage, and they were happy with their mixed family dynamic. Tasha and Josh were the babies of the group, in their early twenties, and they pretty much grew up together. Their parents were best friends.

They were all really welcoming ladies who seemed to just be open and honest people. They all introduced themselves right away and pointed out their partners when I met them. The interesting part was they hung off every word I said as if getting a glimpse into Conner's life was like finding a hidden pirate treasure.

"And how long have you been dating?" Brie asked. She was very sweet and genuine, very motherly and seemed to just love love. She was the one who seemed to be asking the most questions.

"Really, only a couple weeks," I said as I lifted my drink to my lips. "I moved in just after Halloween, but with Conner's work schedule, I didn't actually meet him until just after Christmas."

"That sounds like Conner," Kate laughed. She was an outspoken and forward woman, and I envied her confidence. "That man never takes a break. Idiot never knows when to say no. I've talked to Max about it before and said that the boys kinda need to look out for Conner to make sure that people don't take advantage of him."

"Does that happen a lot?" I asked Kate, but my eyes flit between all the ladies.

"Kinda," Jess said, her shoulder lifting to one side before she got up to refill her wine glass. "He's always been the type of guy who was always helping, always doing something. At the beginning, it was just that he was new and eager to help, so people just put more and more on him." She sat back on the chair after putting a new bottle of red wine in the centre of the coffee table. "But it never really ended. Not until recently. Even when he was engaged to Sasha, he worked like a machine and picked up anything and everything that was up for grabs. It's nice to see him happy and taking time for himself for a change."

The girls kept chatting in the background as my mind picked up on one shocking point.

Engaged to Sasha. Who the hell was Sasha?

Chapter 22

"Okay, so Tuesday, you're coming to my place, right?" The poker night had been a blast, and the girls were a hoot. And through it all, Tasha was persistent that I join their Tuesday Night Smut Night. Out of all of them, Tasha was the quietest, so I was shocked when they told me that she was the one who started it all and hosted it every week.

"Yes," I told her, nervous but glad to be included in their little group. "I'll be there. Just text me the name of the book again so I can download it on my Kindle."

"And don't let the cover or the title fool you," Brie jumped in with her sweet, caring tone. "So far, it's been a really good book. I thought it would be just raunchy crap when Kate picked it, but," she fanned her face with one hand before resting it over her heart, "It's been charming, actually."

"Fair enough," I smiled as I hugged them all as they made their way out with their partners. Conner came up behind me and threw his arm over my shoulder, bringing me into his side and kissing the top of my head. "So, good night?" He asked as he led me back down the stairs to his apartment.

"Yeah," I smiled, "it was fun. The guys are completely insane, and the girls are a bit wild and crazy themselves, but they're a good group."

"Did I hear you say you were going to join them for the book night thingy?"

"If that's okay with you…"

Conner pulled me down to sit with him on the couch and put his head in my lap. My hands instantly went to his hair and started to scratch his head.

"Of course, it's okay. You don't have to run your nights past me. If you want to hang out with the girls, I'm all for it. I think you'd really like them."

"I already do."

We sat in silence for a bit before we got up, cleaned up the kitchen and headed to bed. Conner was out instantly, the beers and head scratches having put him in a tired state. I, on the other hand, downloaded the book as soon as I got the text from Tasha and started reading.

"No way," Jess laughed. It was Tuesday, and I was at Tasha's for the Tuesday Night Smut Night, and we were deep into the food, drinks and book discussion. "There's no way that could happen," she continued. "And if it could, there's no way I would get myself into a 'two hotdogs, one bun' situation. I'm not a masochist."

"You've pushed out a child," Tasha giggled, "that's a whole hell of a lot bigger than a DP situation."

"Double penetration is totally different!!! My baby was coming out, not going in!" We all burst out laughing. "Plus, I had drugs, lots and lots of drugs. I was praising the epidural Gods the whole time."

"It can happen," I added, "if you can push a child out of you, two dicks can go in one hole. I can't imagine it would be pleasurable, though. All I would focus on would be the stretch and the pain. But the book made it seem like it would be really hot…"

"Yeah, but her poor vagina," Brie said sympathetically. Everyone laughed again except for Kate, who seemed to be suspiciously quiet and just smirked through the conversation.

"Kate?" I asked. I didn't know her well at all, but I found it funny that the loud, outgoing, and blunt woman I met at poker night was just sitting there quietly observing.

"You seem awfully quiet about the topic. What do you think?"

Brie, Jess, Tasha and I all dropped our mouths open in shock when all Kate did was shrug her shoulders, take a drink and say, "Max and I have a very healthy and adventurous sex life and some VERY good, close friends."

"Are you shitting me?!" I was shocked again to find that coming from Brie, the quiet mother of the group. "You and Max have threesomes?"

Again, Kate just shrugged a shoulder and took a drink.

"No, no, no, no," Tasha threw back, "you can't just say that you and Max are all porn star, wild sex, adventurous threesome people and then not expand on that."

Brie, Jess and I were completely enraptured while Tasha kept asking Kate questions, and Kate just kept shrugging and sipping her beer.

"Do you do two hotdogs, one bun?"

Shoulder shrug.

"Have you done front and back door at the same time?"

Shoulder shrug.

"Is it always the same guy?"

Shoulder shrug.

"Have you done MORE than two guys at once?"

This time, it was a wink and a shoulder shrug.

"DAMN IT, WOMAN!!!" Tasha burst out. "I NEED ANSWERS!"

The rest of us lost it in hysterical laughter, and the book was forgotten, and Kate's sex life became the topic for the night.

I couldn't even imagine taking Conner and another man at the same time, let alone two Conner's in one hole. My insides involuntarily quivered and clenched at the thought, and I could feel my face flush.

A throat clearing brought my attention back to the group to find Kate pointing at me. "What's that blush for, little miss Adeline?"

I knew 1000% that my blush grew as everyone turned their attention to me, and smiles grew on their faces.

"Nothing," I said with a small shake of my head, "I was just thinking that I could never take two of Conner at once. It would rip me apart."

Brie, Jess and Tasha all nodded in agreement, but again, Kate just shrugged, and I caught her sending a wink my way. "So," Kate asked, "how are things with you and Conner?"

"Things are…" I thought about Conner, the place he now fit in my life, not just as a partner but as a true friend. Someone I could talk to, rely on and be open and honest with. I was…happy. "Easy," I answered. "Things with Conner are easy. I don't have to worry about what I look like, what I say, how I act. I'm just me, and I honestly think that's a first."

When I got home, I was hot and bothered. There was no avoiding it. Talking about a book that was MMF, had male/male partnering, male/female partnering, and all three at once, plus the inquisition into Kate and Max's relationship…a woman couldn't help but be affected by it.

I pulled into the driveway to find my living room lights on and saw Conner through the front window as I passed by. I had left Conner alone at my place at his insistence when I mentioned that I was planning on hiring someone to replace the bathroom vanity I had ordered online and had delivered yesterday. He had called me an idiot for wasting my money when I could have simply asked him. He said to leave it to him, and he'd get Josh to help him install it while I was with the girls. I couldn't wait to see how it looked, but honestly, I was more excited to see Conner.

"Hey you," I smiled as I entered the foyer and hung my jacket up.

"Hey," he answered back with a breathtaking smile.

I just stood there, staring at the amazing man relaxing on my couch. He was in dark blue jeans and a cream long-sleeved T-shirt, and I instantly felt tingles. Everywhere.

I walked over to him on the couch, straddled his lap and planted a needy kiss on his lips. My arms wrapped around his neck as I pressed my hot centre right over his crotch. He was still soft, but his bulge was always there. What could I say? He was a show-er AND a grower.

"I'm guessing it was a good book," he chuckled as he gently pushed me back.

"Why are you laughing and pushing me away?" Embarrassment flooded my system, instantly extinguishing all the little fires that were burning inside.

"Because this isn't like you. I'm always the one to instigate things."

"So?"

"I'm just surprised, that's all. You've never jumped on me like that before."

"And you're complaining?" I swivelled my hips that were still pressed against his bulge and felt the jerk of his dick as it started to harden.

The teasing smirk left his face, and desire filled his eyes. "Fuck no," Conner breathed before he yanked my head back to his and plunged his tongue between my lips, meeting my tongue in a frenzy.

He stood up, effortlessly picking me up along with him, and carried me to the bedroom. My legs wrapped around his waist as his hands kneaded my ass cheeks. We weren't two steps into the bedroom before he wrapped his hands around my waist and literally threw me on the bed. I giggled in exhilaration as I bounced on the mattress a couple times before Conner pounced on me.

With no words between us, Conner and I ripped each other's clothes off in desperation. Within seconds, we were naked together, lying on the bed, the condom beside Conner's head on the opposite pillow while I was between his legs, my tongue licking up his warm, hard shaft.

A soul-deep moan left his throat as I engulfed the tip of his head and took him all the way to the back of my throat, taking only half his length into my mouth. His hips involuntarily lifted off the bed as his fingers wound in my hair. "Do that again," he groaned as I pulled back so just the tip was in my mouth and then sucked him down deep again.

I did this over and over, taking him to the back of my throat to the point of gagging, before swirling my tongue around the crown of his head when I pulled up.

My need for him was growing. I could feel myself getting wetter and wetter with the sounds and words that were coming out of this amazing man's mouth.

The next time I took him deep, I got the need for more. I needed more of him. I pushed deeper, to the point that I was gagging, and tears filled my eyes before I forced myself to focus on my throat and relax. I was able to take him just a bit deeper, maybe three-quarters of his entire length, before I had to pop off to get some air.

"Holy fuck," Conner moaned before he pulled me back onto his cock. "Deep, baby, take me deep again."

I pulled off, pushing against Conner's control so I could take a deep breath and then slowly sucked in his length, going past my gag reflex, although I did gag again, and took him into my throat.

The groans, whimpers, and pleas for more had me deep-throating him over and over again until he made a slight whining sound, almost like he was about to lose control, and he ripped me off his dick to lift me to the bed beside him. He grabbed my legs and threw them over his shoulders, had the condom on and was inside me in five seconds total.

"That's my girl," he praised as he easily slipped his shaft all the way in, "so wet and ready for me."

I couldn't say anything as I was biting my forearm to stop myself from screaming. His thrusts were so powerful and desperate that he was moving the bed, shaking the entire frame and ramming it against the wall. There was no doubt that Kyle was hearing what was going on down here.

He moved my legs so that both of them were over one shoulder and held them tight as he leaned forward and braced himself on his other arm. His body had mine folded in half. His lips brushed over my skin, everywhere they could reach, as his hip thrusts slowed but were deeper and more powerful, sending sparks and tingles to my centre. I could feel myself tightening, almost pushing him out as I began to shake.

"Jesus…fuck…Addy…I'm not going to make it…" he whimpered before his hips gave one more powerful thrust, and the bed cracked. Neither of us stopped, though. Conner kept coming inside me as my pre-orgasm state levelled out at the peak. All it took was for Conner to reach between my legs and tweak my clit, and I was coming around his cock.

"I think we broke the bed," he panted when we finally came down, and he pulled out of me. He went to the bathroom to dispose of his condom while I grabbed his discarded shirt and threw it on. I was still panting when Conner came back in, turned on the light on his cell and got down on his hands and knees to look under the bed.

"Yup," he said, his naked ass sticking up in the air. I reached over the side of the bed and gave it a swat. It was a fine ass. "We broke one of the support posts on the bed slat in the centre." He stood up and looked at me, a proud look on his face. "Totally worth it."

Chapter 23

Conner and I broke one support post and two actual bed slats by the time we were done in the morning. We had tried to be gentle, him going down on me and then tenderly making love to me, but our need for each other had taken over both times. Clearly, Tuesday Night Smut Night was going to be something we would both enjoy.

I was in the kitchen toasting a bagel while Conner was in the shower freshening up when there was a knock on my door.

"Good morning, Sweetness," Kyle sang as he pushed his way into my foyer. "Don't you look ravishing this morning in your cute PJs and your hair all rumpled?"

I looked down at myself and confirmed that I was in baggy flannel pants that had pictures of golden retrievers on them and a gray hoodie. Definitely nothing sexy or revealing, but the way Kyle was staring at me, I might as well have opened the door in just a housecoat with the front open, revealing my body to the world.

"Ummmm…thanks?"

"So, what are you doing today? I've been missing you and wanted to do something. I haven't seen you since New Year's when I came over to give you a New Year's kiss." *So, I guess he's just pretending the talk we had on the front porch two weeks ago didn't happen?*

"I was thinking," he continued as he pushed a piece of stray hair behind my ear, causing an involuntary shiver of NOT lust to shake my body, "maybe you could get all dressed up for me, maybe something hot and sexy, show me those beautiful tits again, and I'd take you out for the night." He ran his hand down my bicep and took my hand in his. "I'll show you a good time. I promise. Maybe a couple of good times." The wink he sent me made my thoughts go from "Yeah, I don't think so" to "Ugh, you're disgusting."

"Kyle," I huffed as I grabbed my hand back and crossed my arms over my chest, hiding my nipples from the laser-eyed glare he was shooting at them. "That's not appropriate, and I've told you to stop with the names and the flirty shit. It's not wanted, and it's *really* not appropriate since I'm with Conner."

"Oh," he feigned surprise, "you're with Conner? I didn't know you were seeing anyone."

"Yes," a deep voice came from behind me. I turned around to see Conner coming out of the bathroom in just a towel. Steam from the shower billowed out behind him, and I swore he started to walk in slow motion. It was as if I was watching a commercial for body wash or, you know, the beginning of a porno. My mouth instantly went dry as I took in the water droplets that slid down his skin. "Addy and I are together. What's it to you?"

Conner came up beside me, kissed the top of my head, and wrapped an arm over my shoulder, leaving no doubt that we were together and that he had been in the shower because he had been dirty, very, very dirty. And I had the broken bedframe to prove it.

"And as you can see," Conner continued as he readjusted the towel that was low on his hips, "we're kinda busy. So, what do you want?"

The look Kyle gave Conner was one that actually shocked me. It wasn't loathing or hatred or jealousy like I would have assumed, but one of violence, almost as if seeing Conner with me clicked the "irrationality" switch in his head.

"I wasn't talking to you, buddy. This is between me and my girl here."

I closed my eyes in despair as I KNEW that Conner immediately saw red at Kyle's statement. "She's MY girl," he growled, "and she's not going anywhere with you." He put a hand on Kyle's shoulder and turned him towards the door. "And if you ever speak to her like that again, you and I will have a problem that won't be fixed with words." Conner, not too kindly, pushed him out of the house, slamming and locking the door behind him.

"Was that completely necessary?" I asked as Conner turned around to walk back down the hallway.

"Yup."

"Seriously? You're now making decisions for me and deciding who is allowed to spend time with me or allowed in my home?"

"Yup."

"So, what, I have no say in my own life now? He was just talking like an idiot like he always does, and you came barging in, swinging your big dick and completely took over a conversation that had nothing to do with you."

Conner let out a deep breath as he walked into the bedroom and started to get dressed. His temper was getting the better of him, but I wasn't letting this go.

"You basically just peed all over me, Conner, stating 'she's mine.'"

"Well, you are mine," he threw back as he pulled a sweater over his head, "just like I'm yours."

"Yes, but that doesn't mean you have to act like a possessive caveman and mark your territory."

"Seriously, Adeline? With all the shit he's pulled with you? Letting himself into your house, the incident with the banging upstairs and the dick at your door, plus how he talks to you? Asking to see your tits again? Again? When did he see your tits?"

"It was an accident. One fell out when I was lying on the couch. I didn't whip it out for him or anything."

"You better not have…"

Now I was fuming. "And what is THAT supposed to mean? I can't have a past or have shown my tits to someone else? Since when are you this possessive?"

"Damn right, I'm being possessive and letting him know that I'm with you and that he better watch his back. I won't have him messing with you, Addy. I don't trust him, not for a second. And if I have to protect you by showing him that you're mine and I'm here, then I'm damn well going to do it."

"He was just coming over to see if I wanted to do something with him."

"Yeah, something that involved you getting dressed up all hot and sexy for him. I heard what he said, Addy, and it was not okay."

"Yes, well…we can agree on that."

"So, what's the issue?"

"The issue is that, although I love that you want to stand up and protect me, you have to let me fight my own battles. The more you defend me, the more I feel like the damsel in distress who is losing her voice."

"That's not what I was doing…"

"Yes, it was. When you just jump in like that, what am I supposed to think? It was pretty much a 'shut up and let me handle this' move. I was left just standing there, quiet, while you men-folk duked it out over the pretty, helpless girl who was going to be the prize."

"Oh, come on, now you're just making shit up."

"No, Conner, I'm not. You can't dismiss how I'm feeling, and what you just did made me feel like what I had to say didn't matter. I was yours, your possession and yours to protect. I wasn't even a person in that situation, just your plaything."

"Addy…" Conner huffed as he sat on the edge of the bed and grabbed both of my hands, pulling me to stand between his legs. "I'm not trying to dismiss how you feel. You have every right to feel the million and one emotions that go through that beautiful head and heart of yours every day. But as your PARTNER, not your owner, but your partner, I have the right to say something when my partner is being treated like a sex toy by the creepy, stalker neighbour upstairs."

I took a calming breath and tried to listen to what Conner was saying. I didn't agree with how he handled it, but I understood where he was coming from. He wasn't going to just stand by and let Kyle say shit to me, and in his mind, speaking up and stepping up was him showing a united front. He was showing he cared, just not in the same way I would have.

"Okay," I breathed as I wrapped my arms around his shoulders, "I get what you're saying. I want a partnership, too. It just didn't feel like it back there."

"I'm sorry," he whispered as he kissed my belly through the hoodie.

"Me too," I whispered back as I kissed the top of his head. Conner looked up at me with tender eyes, and I bent to kiss his soft, plump lips.

"How about we get out of here," he suggested, "get the stuff to fix the bed, and we can have makeup sex?"

I shook my head but couldn't stop the smile that spread across my face at the wink he sent me as I went to the bathroom to get ready. As much as Conner and I might disagree and argue about things, the big goof always had a way of making me smile and making sure we were okay.

Being with Conner had become effortless. We laughed and joked, relaxed and did mundane things together. We didn't care what we did as long as the other person was there. And it was more than just being in the same room or doing things together. We genuinely cared about each other.

Conner checked in on me every day. Lately, he was checking to see if I had had any more encounters with Kyle since he had tried to let himself into my place again a couple days ago. Conner had greeted him at the door and had given him an earful.

He also knew that the one-year anniversary of my divorce was coming up and checked on my emotional and mental well-being. I felt like I was doing okay, but just like Christmas, I didn't know how the day would hit me until it came.

And I was worried about Conner and how much he was working. The man was constantly tired. He was either go-go-go, or he was dead on his feet, on the brink of falling down. The man needed a vacation. I understood where he was coming from, that he wanted to help wherever he could and didn't want to say no when someone called to see if he could help, but he wasn't taking care of himself, and one of these days, he was going to crash.

But in the end, it was like hanging out with my best friend every day. Best friends who couldn't get enough of touching each other's bodies and had amazing sex.

And as the weeks of dating turned into months, Conner and I had sort of formed a routine. Tuesday nights, I would do the Tuesday Night Smut Night with the girls while Conner went to *Ape Hangers* with the guys, all of them making sure they were home by 10 p.m. to eagerly await our return. It quickly turned into my favourite day of the week.

The girls were a blast, and we often texted in our group chat, but I always looked forward to Tuesdays the most. The night was full of laughter, wine, and so much fun with the girls, but when I got home, it was full of passion, and possession, and deep intimacy. Whether it was hard and rough or soft and deep, Conner always made me feel amazing.

During the week, if Conner was working, I would either work on a new article for the *Hound* or spend some time trying a new recipe. Conner was a great guinea pig. When he went to work at his house, I usually went along with him and tried to help wherever I could, which mostly consisted of being the fetcher of tools and supplies from his truck.

He was patient with me, teaching me about what he was doing, what tools he was using and what the next steps were. He even surprised me one day with some black pull-on work boots that were bright purple on the inside and a matching hard hat. He wanted me there with him, and he wanted me safe. It was his way of showing he cared.

He constantly did little things like that. He would rub my feet when we sat on the couch to watch TV, he brought me Skittles and my favourite iced tea when my cramps were especially bad one day, and he got me "just because" gifts because he saw something he thought I might like. He learned fast that giving me flowers was a bad idea because I couldn't keep them alive for more than three days. But plants, I was doing okay with plants. The first one he gave me was almost a month old now and still looked green and lively. The second plant we didn't talk about. I was convinced it was half dead when I got it.

"What?" Conner asked, noticing the instant change in my demeanour and my eyes locked on my car. "What's wrong?" He turned to follow my gaze, and I knew the instant he saw what I did as his body went rigid, and he stepped slightly ahead of me.

There, in my parking spot, was my car with all four tires flat and the word "SLUT" written in black marker across my windshield. But the disturbing part wasn't the damage. It was the fact that Kyle was standing right beside my car, looking at it as if he was proud of a job well done.

Chapter 24

"What the fuck?" Conner barked as he rushed up to Kyle, cornering him against the car but making sure not to touch him.

"I was just coming to get you," Kyle said as he peered around Conner to look at me and completely ignored Conner's threatening presence. "I just got home and saw it like this."

He was lying. Both Conner and I knew he was lying. We had both been at my place all night and hadn't left the house yet today. We had heard him walking around and talking on the phone to people all morning. Conner and I had even grimaced when we saw two girls walk past my front window, heard them go upstairs and then heard the bed slamming against a wall while Kyle was saying filthy, degrading things to both of them. It was like we were forced to listen to degradation porn through the ceiling.

He was lying, but I didn't know why. Well, I knew why; he was guilty, but I didn't know why he would do this.

"Why, Kyle?" I asked as I moved around Conner to face him. "Why would you do this and lie about it? We both know you were home all day. We heard you. The flooring isn't that soundproof."

"Oh, trust me, I know, and I like it," Kyle smirked and sent a taunting look to Conner before he looked back at me and winked.

Conner went instantly ballistic. "You son of a –"

I grabbed Conner's arm and pulled him away from Kyle before he did something that could get him arrested. Kyle would deserve it with what he was alluding to – that he listened to us having sex through the floor – but I didn't have bail money to get Conner out of jail if he was charged with assault for kicking Kyle's ass.

"Why?" I asked again. "Why would you do this?"

"I don't know what you're talking about, Sweets," Kyle shrugged as he brushed imaginary dust off his jacket. "Like I said, I just found your car this way."

Conner pushed forward again, trying to get at him, but respected my warning when I put my hand out to block him. "DON'T call her Sweets!"

With a roll of his eyes, Kyle stepped away from my SUV. "He seems very possessive of you, Addy. I hardly get to see or talk to you anymore, and now he's telling me what I can and can't call you? Seems very controlling." He cupped his hand around his mouth in a fake whisper. "Wink if you need me to rescue you from this guy."

"Just go," I told him as I put my hand on Conner's arm and led him to his truck. "What happened to you?"

"I don't know, Sweetness," Kyle said as he started to make his way down the driveway, a cocky swagger in his step, "maybe I just miss my girl. Want to get together and hang out like old times?"

I just shook my head as Conner and I made our way to his truck. Kyle's laughter followed us until we were inside and the doors were shut. It took Conner a good two minutes to calm down enough that his jaw unclenched and his breathing evened out.

"You okay?" I asked as I put my hand on his thigh.

"I hate that guy," he grunted. "I don't trust him. There's something sketchy about him and something going on. He's never been this in-your-face before."

"I know," I huffed, "he's an ass. He wasn't this bad when I moved in, but lately, it's just non-stop. Did I tell you that he started texting me again?"

"WHAT?" Conner barked in surprise, twisting in his seat to stare at me. "What is he saying?"

I pulled out my cell and handed it over to Conner so he could read the string of texts himself.

Kyle: Hey, Sweetness

Kyle: Miss you, hot stuff

Kyle: When can we hang out again?

Kyle: Why aren't you writing back? Don't you miss me?

Kyle: Want to come with me to Toronto this weekend? Huge party all weekend long. We could have some fun 😌

Kyle: Why don't you answer me? Is Conner not letting you talk to me?

Kyle: What does that behemoth have that I don't?

Kyle: You know I could satisfy you more than he could 🥒

Kyle: Let's get together like we used to. Pizza, beer and football on the couch. I guarantee we'll have fun, maybe a touchdown or two ourselves 😉

Kyle: I saw you watching me pull into the parking lot today. Were you waiting for me?

Kyle: Listen, bitch, if you don't want to talk to me, fine, but then stop smirking at me and flirting and shaking your ass at me when we see each other. No one likes a tease.

"They started the day you had that pissing contest with Kyle at my place," I told him as I took the phone back and put it in my purse. "Looks like you poked the bear, and now he's trying to start shit."

"He can start shit all he wants," Conner mumbled as he started the truck, "but I'll finish it."

"Where are we going? I need to call the cops and report this."

"We'll call when we get back. I need to get away from that asshole before I do something I won't regret but will put me behind bars."

I just rolled my eyes at his alpha-male bullshit and put my seatbelt on. I hated when Conner got like this, all protective and overbearing. It was cute at the beginning when he was dealing with Kyle's friend who came pounding on my front door at 2 a.m., but now, it was just annoying. Didn't he know that Kyle didn't stand a chance with me? He could send as many texts and say as much stupid shit as he wanted in front of Conner, but it wasn't going to make me run into his arms. If anything, it just put me more solidly in Conner's. If only Conner didn't instigate him back.

"Here," Conner said once we were on the road. He held out the sleep mask for me. "Let's not let him ruin our day anymore."

I knew he was right. The more I dwelled on Kyle, the more power I was giving him. With a resolute breath, I took the sleep mask and put it over my eyes.

Chapter 25

We drove for a long time without any stops, and my anxiety was getting the best of me, especially since I was blindfolded and couldn't see where we were going. I thought we were maybe going to the new house, and he was going to surprise me with what he'd done next, but he just kept driving and driving...and driving.

Luckily for him, Conner kept me entertained with stories of Max, Thane, Austin, and Josh and the shenanigans they got to on job sites. I swear, all of them were children when they got together. I'd been to two poker nights now, and between what I'd seen at those and the stories that Conner told me so far on the drive, including trapping each other in the outhouses after one of them was just in there and made a stink, nail gunning their tools to the floor, and grabbing the back pocket on someone's work pants and ripping it down, more times than not ripping part of their pant leg off too, I was convinced that there wasn't an adult amongst them. But as shocked as I was at the pranks they pulled on each other, I was jealous of their friendship. I was starting to talk to the girls more and more and had now gone to a couple Tuesday Night Smut Nights, but these guys had years of being together, and they were his family. It was nice to see.

"So, when do I get a clue where we're going?" I asked when the radio announcer said the time, hinting that we'd already been on the road for forty-five minutes.

"Never," Conner said, the smile evident in his voice.

"Really? No hint at all?"

"All I'll say is that we're almost there."

It was about five more minutes before the truck slowed down. I could hear more traffic, and we had stopped a couple times at stop lights before the truck stopped one final time, and Conner turned it off.

"So, are you ready?"

If I wasn't blindfolded, I would have given Conner the stink eye. He refused to tell me what he had planned for today, insisting it was a special surprise date. And if the hour-long drive was any indication, the date was taking place in Toronto.

"Depends," I tensed, "do I get to take this blindfold off?"

We had parked in a noisy lot, and Conner had helped me out of the truck but had yet to let me see where we were.

"Yes, Cricket," he chided, "you can take the blindfold off now."

I quickly ripped the thing from my face and deflated a bit when I saw that we were at The Brick.

"Seriously?" I turned to see Conner laughing as he took the blindfold from my hand and threw it back in the truck before he guided me to the store. "This is my surprise date? Going to a furniture store?"

"Yes," he said as he kissed the side of my head, "but you don't know what we're doing at the furniture store." The laughter in his voice was making it hard to stay disappointed with his "special date."

"Alright then, Smarty Pants, what are we doing at The Brick that makes it such a special surprise date?"

Conner opened the door for me and then took my hand and led me to the bed showrooms. "We're picking out furniture and appliances for the new house."

"Isn't it a bit early to pick out appliances and furniture? You don't even have proper flooring down yet."

"I know, but I can select them now and then order them online when I'm ready. I just need the product code."

"Okay…"

"Plus, I want your help to pick out the mattress." He wiggled his eyebrows at me, acting like a horny teenager. I just shook my head and chuckled under my breath as he led me through the bedroom displays.

"So," he started, "what are you thinking?"

"Well, it's not up to me, babe. It's your house, so your furniture and style."

"I know," he said as he stopped beside a light wood set that had lamps built into the headboard, "but I want you to like it too." He pulled me past the bedroom sets and took me to the dozens of mattresses on display.

"Plus," he added as he laid down on one mattress, rolled around, made a face, and got up to try the next, "I want you to be comfortable on the mattress." He patted the mattress he was currently lying on for me to join him and scooted to his typical side of the bed. "You toss and turn all night on mine, Love, so I know it's not comfortable for you." *Did he just call me Love?*

"It's fine," I told him as I lay on my side and looked at him, trying to calm my heart down. "It's your mattress, so you need to be comfortable."

"I know," he said before he sat on the next mattress and moaned as he flopped back. "You have to try this one." I shook my head in amusement as I joined him on the huge king-size mattress. As soon as I sat down on it, Conner grabbed my hand and pulled me down to lay beside him. I sighed in comfort as my body sank into the soft pillow top.

"Addy," he said as we turned to face each other, still lying on the most comfortable bed I'd ever been on. "I want you to be part of this. I want you to be part of my life. And I want you in my bed, and not just for sexy fun time." I took a deep breath and looked into his eyes as he pushed a piece of hair behind my ear.

"I know, Conner, but…this is hard for me." He began to interrupt me, but I pushed forward. "You know that I don't have a lot of people in my life, no one really close to me, no friends or family. People always tend to push me out and push me away…and I have a hard time seeing my own worth because of that. And I don't want to get my hopes up here. If you want me to have that big of a part in your life where we're picking out furniture together, we need to have a conversation about that and be honest with each other about it."

Conner sat up on the bed and pulled me back so that I was sitting against the headboard with him. "What conversation do you want to have?"

I looked around the department store, not believing that this was where we were having our heart-to-heart, but it seemed somehow perfect for us. We found little moments to connect in everything we did, from grocery shopping to working on the house. This was just another random moment where we were opening up and connecting.

"You said that you want me to be part of your life and to help you make decisions. And I'm not fishing for anything here, but aren't those kinda big decisions and declarations?

It's kind of a big deal if you want me to have input on how you finish your house or what mattress you choose."

"Yes, and…"

I chuckled, "What do you mean 'and'? You're talking like this is it, like we're building this house and life together, but this," I said as I waved my hand back and forth between us, "is still fairly new, generally speaking. And if we're talking about building this life together, I have to know that you're serious about us, and you're going to be with me when I have moments when I hate myself. When I push you away over and over again because I don't think I deserve you. You need to know that I'm a bitch and an emotional wreck sometimes, and I need to know that I can count on you to be there when things get hard between us…and I don't mean in the bedroom kind of way. I don't want to read too much into this and think that us picking out furniture together means more than it does. I don't want to be picking out furniture for your house if you're not serious about this. I don't know if I could take that type of teasing."

"Addy, I know what I'm getting with you. I know you're a stubborn ass and that you always think you're right. I know that you think shit of yourself no matter how often I tell you you're beautiful, or sweet, or amazing. I know you go from laughing to crying while reading a book. I know you have your moments, but so do I, and I KNOW it's all worth it. I want you to be comfortable in my bed and in my home and in my life."

He looked at me with such tenderness in his eyes, "Because I'm not going anywhere. You're stuck with me. I love you, Addy. I love you just the way you are. You should have figured that out by now."

My heart pushed against my chest, my emotions jumping and spiralling inside, begging to burst free. Here, sitting on a demo mattress in a big box store, surrounded by customers and employees, the man whom I had only known for 11 weeks spoke the words my heart had been saying all along.

I held his face in my hands and kissed him with all the love I had inside.

"I love you, too."

We could barely keep our hands off each other as we continued to walk through *The Brick* and pick out the furniture and appliances for Conner's home. Every few minutes, Conner's hands would either go to my ass or would "accidentally" brush against my breasts. At one point, when we were looking at fridges, he actually came up behind me and thrust up against me as I was bent over looking in the freezer.

When we had picked out a new washer and dryer, stove, dishwasher, fridge, and bedroom set, Conner returned to the mattress demo area and flagged down a staff member. He had told the sales associate that he wanted the mattress where we had first said "I love you" to each other. And he emphasized he wanted that exact mattress, the actual floor model itself.

And if I thought Conner had been handsy while we were walking through the store, the drive home was a hundred times worse. His hand was constantly rubbing up and down my thigh, sneaking up to my mound and at one point, he undid the button and zipper of my jeans and snuck his hand inside.

He had pulled me into the centre of the bench seat when I had first gotten into the truck, and it was clear as he was rubbing my clit that this had been the reason why.

I had one mini orgasm on the ride home, and when I tried to give him road head, he stopped me, saying he wouldn't be able to concentrate on the road if I put my mouth on him at the moment.

But when we got home, all the horniness and need withered away like a deflated balloon once we saw my SUV.

"I guess I should call the police and insurance," I stated when we got out of the truck and walked over to my vehicle. "I still can't believe Kyle did this."

"He wants you, Addy, and he's not taking you saying no very well."

"Yeah, but to destroy my car? Clearly, he doesn't think this is going to make me run into his arms."

"I don't know what to tell ya, Love. The guy is messed."

Our love bubble had popped as we went down to Conner's place, and I placed the call to the police.

It was disappointing to find out there was nothing we could do. We didn't have a video of Kyle doing the damage and hadn't seen him doing it ourselves. All I was told to do was call my insurance and get the car repaired, but if I thought it was Kyle, to try and stay away from him as much as possible.

Conner didn't like that answer and told the officer that Kyle had let himself into my unit multiple times already, was saying inappropriate things to me all the time, and generally wouldn't leave me alone. The only direction we received was not to engage with Kyle in the future.

But that didn't stop Kyle from trying to engage with me. In the days following the vandalism to my SUV, Kyle's texts had gotten more frequent and more…forward. On top of that, he was coming down more often to "check on me." He claimed to be worried about how possessive Conner seemed and wanted to make sure I knew I had a friend I could turn to if needed.

The creepiest part was that as the nicer weather started, a random folding chair had appeared on our front stoop that Kyle seemed to used to watch the neighbourhood to "make sure nothing else in the tri-plex got damaged," as he put it. And although he pretended it was to watch over the property, it seemed like he was only interested in watching me. Whenever I left for work, he was out on the front stoop.

When I came home, he was there. When we went to the new build, to get groceries, to get the mail...Kyle seemed to be at his post, keeping an eye out. But when I asked Conner about it, he said he only noticed Kyle when he was with me, not when he was out and about by himself.

It seemed like I had a new shadow.

Every day, he showed me he cared and that I was important to him, and every day, I fell a little more in love with him, and that scared me beyond words. We had only known each other for such a relatively short time, and already, he was so incredibly important to me and felt like a missing piece of my life.

When I divorced Alex, I resigned myself to the reality that I might be alone for the rest of my life. But here I was, two months into dating Conner, and we'd been inseparable since day one, having spent time together literally every single day. It was something that I loved and counted on, something that just felt right.

"So, where are you taking me?" I asked as Conner and I walked out my front door and around to the parking lot. He had told me he wanted to take me on a special date today but had refused to give me any details.

"Can't tell ya," Conner smiled as he lifted our entwined hands and kissed my fingers, "it's a surprise." He let go of my hand and pulled a sleep mask out of his pocket.

I burst out laughing. "Oh, hell no, I am not going to be blindfolded and allow you to do God knows what to me, Mr. Jensen. I don't think so."

"What? Don't you trust me?" The sarcastic and wicked look in his eyes told me I should say no, but when I looked past him to the parking lot, my instincts were to hold onto him tighter and trust him 100%.

Chapter 26

Conner and I tried to keep to ourselves as much as possible and ignored Kyle when we saw him. We refused to let Kyle keep us housebound. We continued to live our lives as normal and tried as hard as we could to pretend that Kyle wasn't there, but admittedly, we did start to spend more days and nights at Conner's place than mine.

Fridays had become our domesticated days. We tried to reserve the day just for us, neither of us working if we could help it. We'd have a lunch date and then help clean each other's places before going grocery shopping together.

We now spent every night together as well. It didn't matter if I was at his place or he was at mine. If he had to get up at 3 a.m. for a job or didn't get home from work until 3 a.m., we spent the night in each other's arms. Conner had become my safe space.

It wasn't as hard as it used to be to stay out of my head and just enjoy what Conner and I had built together over the past couple of months. Ever since he told me he loved me, I felt more secure in our relationship, no longer worrying that it was just one-sided. I got excited when he started leaving clothes at my place or when he gave me a key to his. And although we had been moving fast and were secure in the love we had, part of me was waiting for the other shoe to drop. There was no way that my first relationship after my divorce could be this smooth and perfect. There had to be a hidden past or an angry side that I didn't know about. And as predicted, one Friday afternoon, the other shoe dropped.

"God, Conner! What do you want from me?" We were sitting in his truck in the Walmart parking lot, yelling at each other.

"Everything," he reared back, "I want all of you."

"You have all of me," my hands flew out wide in exasperation. "We spend every day together and sleep in the same bed every single night. What more do you want?"

"I want us to move in together."

"I know, that's what started this conversation." The deep breath I took to try and calm my freakout did absolutely nothing. My heart was still racing. "I just don't understand why. We pretty much live together now, and we've only been dating for three months."

"Addy, I want to be with you. We're not teenagers dating around, trying to figure out what we want. I know what I want. I want you. My lease is up for renewal, and I don't want to renew it. I want to move into your place, and then when the house is done, I want us to move in there together."

"What, and get married and have 2.5 kids?" I was completely freaking out. This was too soon, too fast. It felt like the ink was still drying on my divorce.

"Would that be so bad?"

My heart literally stopped a beat, my breath caught in my throat. Was he serious? Dread seeped through my core, my hands shook, and sweat beaded on my forehead. I hadn't told Conner about mine and Alex's infertility issues. If he was serious about us moving in and starting a life together, which apparently included marriage and 2.5 kids in his books, he needed to know that it couldn't happen with me. Once again, I wasn't going to be enough for someone, and I would end up broken and bleeding as he walked away.

"No," I started, having to take a pause to swallow the lump in my throat, "it wouldn't be so bad." I looked up to him, my throat tight from holding back the tears I knew were just waiting to come out. "But if that's what you want, then it can't be with me."

"What does THAT mean?" The hurt in his voice was like a knife to my heart.

"Let's just go. I don't want to have this conversation in a Walmart parking lot." I turned to face the windshield and put on my seatbelt, effectively pausing our talk for now.

The ride home was silent and full of tension but thankfully short. When we got home, Conner walked ahead of me into my place, using the key we just got made for him to let himself in and went straight to the spare room to put the pack of toilet paper and Kleenex boxes in the closet.

We still hadn't said a word to each other, and I was mentally preparing myself for the end. My heart was already breaking. When Conner found out I couldn't have kids and wouldn't be able to make him a father, would he still want to be with me? He was 38 years old. He probably didn't want to wait much longer if he was hoping to start a family.

I solemnly went to the kitchen but hadn't even put the bags down before my head snapped to the sound of Conner's voice yelling from down the hall. I followed the sound and ran into my bedroom to see Kyle standing between my bed and the window, looking cocky and confident and almost a bit annoyed at being interrupted. *What the hell is he doing in my house?!*

"What the fuck are you doing here?" Conner grabbed him by the shirt collar and shoved him hard against the wall, making it impossible for him to move away.

"Her bedroom window was left open, and a squirrel ran in. I came in to try and get the damn thing out before it destroyed the place. I'm trying to be neighbourly."

"Bullshit!" Conner growled, knocking Kyle's back once again against the wall. "The window was locked. I checked it this morning."

"Well, I don't know what to tell ya, friend," Kyle sneered, "but it was open when I walked by."

"Addy," Conner still kept his eyes locked on Kyle, "call the police."

"Conner," I said, "do you really think I need to call –"

"Call them!" He had never spoken to me with such anger before. Rage was pouring off of him, and I honestly didn't know what he was going to do. All I knew was that I didn't want to poke the bear.

I ran to the living room, looking for where I had left my phone when we went to Walmart. As soon as I found it, I called 911 and hurried back to the bedroom where Conner had released Kyle but had him cornered between the wall and closets.

"911. Police, fire or ambulance?"

"Police, please."

The line clicked and started ringing again before a gruff voice picked up and spoke on the other end. "911 police, what's your emergency?" My mouth opened and closed like a fish while I watched the stare-down take place in front of me. What did I say? I came home, and my friend (or former friend, really) was in my house? That didn't sound like an emergency to me.

"Hello, this is 911 police. What's your emergency?"

Conner grabbed the phone out of my hand. "My girlfriend and I just got home and found someone in her house. I have him cornered in her bedroom."

I couldn't hear what the officer said, and Conner was not so discretely trying to herd me back out of the bedroom.

"No, no weapons that I can see."

The officer spoke again before Conner chuckled, "Yeah, we know who he is. He's the guy who lives in the unit above her who has been pretty much stalking her for the past four months."

"Conner," I went to object, but the quick look he shot me shut me up right away. Kyle hadn't been stalking me. He'd just pushed the line of being too friendly and too forward, grabbing my ass, letting himself in, hanging around my door all the time…and acting a bit sketchy as of late. And yes, this was definitely over the line. I just nodded to Conner as he returned his eyes to Kyle, gave the officer our address and listened to what the officer was saying.

"Go to the front door, Addy. There's an officer just a couple of blocks away."

I ran to the front door, opened it wide and watched for the red and blue lights as Conner stayed with Kyle in my room on the phone with dispatch.

The police pulled up almost right away, and I led them into the house. One look in the bedroom, and the officer sighed and shook his head.

"Mr. Martin," the officer bit out, "we meet again."

"Officer Brink, my favourite pig."

I was shocked at the attitude that came off Kyle. It was once again the Jekyll and Hyde act he had pulled on me. He still had the sneer on his face from when Conner caught him in my room, but now his arms were crossed, and he was leaning back against the wall, completely relaxed, not having a care in the world. And calling the officer a pig? Where did that come from? This was not the same Kyle I met a few months ago.

"Come on, Kyle, turn around. You know the routine."

The routine?! What the fuck?

Conner moved out of the way while Kyle got cuffed and was led out of my room. He winked at me and blew me a kiss as Officer Brink dragged him out of the house and put him in the back of the cruiser.

"Get your purse," Conner barked as he grabbed his keys. "We're following them down to the station and getting a restraining order."

It was hours later by the time we got home. After learning that I, in fact, couldn't get a restraining order because Kyle and I never lived together and didn't have children together, and we couldn't get a peace bond because I didn't have proof that Kyle was in my house to hurt me instead of just robbing me, Conner and I were stuck. There was nothing we could do. Plus, there was no damage to the house, no broken locks or windows, so they couldn't disprove Kyle's "window was open and saw a squirrel go in" story. It was completely his story against ours, and neither of us had proof to back our story up. All that we managed to get was a "We'll see what we can do," when we told the officer we wanted to press charges for breaking and entering.

"Thanks, Pete." Conner hung up with his landlord and came into the bedroom. "Pete said he'll be over in 20 minutes with an eviction notice and will change the locks so Kyle can't get back in."

"Thanks," I said, not really paying attention at all. I was focused on my room. Kyle was in here. What did he do? What did he touch? Was there anything missing? Did he go through my drawers, sniff my underwear? Did he lay on my bed and do God knows what to himself and my pillow?

I felt nauseous. It felt like my world had been contaminated with an unknown disease, and I didn't want to touch anything. Nothing *looked* out of place, but it was the unknown that made it so much worse.

"I can't stay here," I leaned back into Conner's embrace as he walked up behind me and held me to his chest. "He's tainted everything."

"I know, Love," he pressed a kiss to the top of my head and hugged me tight. "We'll stay at my place until we can figure some things out."

I just nodded absentmindedly, my eyes still scanning my room.

"Do you want to grab some clothes, or are you okay with what you have downstairs?"

"I'm good. I just want to get out of here."

In the morning, I'd throw everything in the wash, the bedding, the pillows, all my underwear, just to be safe. I had no idea what Kyle had done in there, and I didn't want to take any chances. The mattress I couldn't do much about besides steam cleaning it, so that went straight to the top of my to-do list.

"There has to be something, right? We can't just hope he doesn't come back. You saw how he was completely indifferent to the police. And they knew him by name, Conner. The officer knew who he was."

"I know." I could still feel the rage pouring off Conner as we worked together to put away his groceries that had been sitting in the truck the whole time we were dealing with the Kyle situation. We were now down in Conner's unit, but the tension and anger remained. "We'll figure something out. I'll keep you safe. I promise."

"Keep ME safe? What about you? Who's going to keep you safe when he decides he wants to get you back for throwing him against the wall? You could have been charged with assault."

"I can take care of myself." He wouldn't even look at me, not once since we came down to his place. He walked right by me to put his pre-workout in the cupboard and acted like I wasn't even there. No brush of the hand across my back or smack on the ass as usual. He was keeping his distance from me.

"Hey," I grabbed his arm as he passed me for the third time, "what's with you?"

He slammed the loaf of bread on the counter, effectively squashing the whole thing as his hand continued to press down on it.

"Are you breaking up with me?"

So, that's what this was about, the truck conversation at Walmart that was still on pause.

"No." My hand slid down from his arm to grab his hand and gave it a squeeze. "No, I'm not breaking up with you, but you might be breaking up with me."

"Addy, what the fuck is going on?" He pulled his hand from mine and took a step away, putting even more distance between us. He crossed his large arms over his chest and glared at me. The man I was in love with was actually glaring at me, and my heart broke just a little bit more. "What happened between this morning when you were giving me a blowjob that literally made me see stars to sitting in the truck and telling me I don't have a future with you?"

"I can't have kids, Conner." The words came out flat and lifeless. I just ripped the Band-Aid off and let the wound show. The truth just fell out, my mouth not giving my brain time to overthink how I was going to break this to him. We were both in our thirties and knew what we wanted in life, and it was better to let him know now that I couldn't give him what he wanted before we got any deeper into this relationship. In all honesty, I knew I should have told him a long time ago.

"Okay?" He looked at me with confusion and accusation.

"You said you wanted to get married and have 2.5 kids. I can't –"

"No," he interrupted, "YOU brought up the marriage and 2.5 kids. I just asked if that would be such a bad thing for us."

We stared at each other on opposite sides of the kitchen as the conversation in the truck replayed in my head. He was right. I was the one who brought it up.

"Look," Conner made his way over to me, his arms wrapping around my waist and erasing the space between us, "do I want to be a father? Yeah, sure, I'd love that, but if it doesn't happen, it doesn't happen."

"You need to be sure about this, Conner." My hands slid up his chest, pleading for him to take this seriously. "I don't want us to be two years down the road, and you change your mind, and then kids become the deal breaker that breaks us up."

"I want you." His eyes were intense and peering right into me. "I love you. If being a father becomes something I can't live without, then we can look at adoption or fostering, but only if you want. Or we get a dog." He smirked at the last part, clearly trying to lighten up the conversation. And I appreciated it, but there was still more we needed to sort out.

"Sasha," I said.

"What about Sasha?"

Bringing up Conner's ex was probably a dick move. No, it was DEFINITELY a dick move. But from what he had told me about his relationship with Sasha when I asked him after that first poker night, I had to be sure, and then I'd never bring it up again.

"You were with her for four years; you were even engaged, but you broke up with her because she couldn't give you what you wanted. I don't want that to be me."

"I broke up with Sasha because I didn't want to be with her. I only proposed because I was getting pressure from both our families to do it. She was older and was getting pressured to get married and have kids before it was too late. I proposed, and she said yes to appease our families, and then when we realized we didn't want to get married, we called it off."

We were silent for a moment before he continued.

"Addy, I'm old enough to know what I want. We might only be dating for a few months, but I don't want this to end, especially not over something you have no control over. Please just trust and believe me when I say that I want to be with you, and the rest doesn't matter. We'll figure it out."

He pulled me to him and kissed me with sweetness and adoration.

"I love you," I whispered against his lips.

"Does this mean we can stop using condoms?" he whispered the words back against my lips before he dove back in to deepen the kiss, but I pulled back and let my laughter run free. It was nice to laugh after the day we had.

"Yes, I guess it does."

Chapter 27

In the four days since the break-in, Conner wouldn't leave my side, even turning down work so I wouldn't be alone. He came with me to the *Hound* when I went in to print out my article for final revision. He came with me when I went to get a new mattress after I decided just to replace the 10-year-old one that I had originally gotten when Alex and I first got together. Conner even came with me to the pharmacy when I went to grab more tampons. It was almost like he was watching for something or knew something bad was going to happen.

Even when we were back in my place after washing and cleaning everything we could, Conner was there, almost following me from room to room, not wanting me to leave his sight.

"Okay, that's enough," I finally said when he got up from the couch and followed me into the kitchen.

"Addy –"

"You followed me into the bathroom this morning, Conner. I know you're worried, but I'm okay."

"Addy," he started again, "shut up for a minute."

"Excuse me?!"

"Shhhh!" He held a finger to his lip to silence me. That was when I noticed that he wasn't looking at me but was looking around the room.

We stayed quiet for a minute, my eyes looking around, trying to figure out what the hell was going on with Conner before he grabbed my hand and pulled me from the kitchen. He actually pulled me right out the front door. The man was lucky I was wearing slippers at the time, and he had grabbed a jacket on his way out.

"Conner! What the hell?" I pulled him to a stop on the front porch, refusing to go out any further.

"Something's not right."

"What do you mean?" I put on his jacket and bundled myself against the windy April afternoon.

"I noticed it the other day when we came in to clean. No matter what room we're in, there's a buzzing and clicking sound when we get quiet, and it seems to follow us from room to room."

The seriousness in his tone made me freeze. He grabbed my hand and pulled me farther away from the front door and around the back of the house to his gym. If what Conner was saying was true, it would explain why he was so quiet yesterday and today. But what was he suggesting? That someone was listening to what we were saying? That the house was bugged? This wasn't a true crime thriller movie. Why would anyone give two shits about us that they would wiretap my house?

"I've been thinking," he started again as we stepped into his garage, "I think someone is watching us."

"Conner," I placated, "why would people be watching us? We're nobodies."

"Just listen!" He was serious, and I didn't know if I should be worried about the situation or about him. "For the past three days, you've been getting phone calls from unknown numbers where it's just dead air, right?"

"Yeah…" I didn't know where he was going with this.

"And you left your phone at home the day we went to Walmart and came back and found Kyle in your place, right?"

I hadn't even thought of that. The phone calls had started right after Kyle had been arrested. I just nodded.

"That's the same time I started to hear the noises. I first heard it when I had Kyle cornered in the bedroom, and you had run to get your phone. Kyle and I didn't say a word to each other, and I could have sworn I heard a light buzzing and clicking sound. I thought I was just hearing things, but I've heard it now every time we've been at your place."

I had nothing to say. I hadn't heard a sound, or at least not one that I didn't think of as just regular house noises. But Conner was serious about this.

"Keep going," I encouraged.

"And I've had this feeling for a couple days now like we're being followed."

"Babe," I tried to take any pity, confusion or appeasement out of my voice and just speak smoothly but sincerely. Conner turning into a paranoid boyfriend was not going to help me get over Kyle's break-in. "I hear what you're saying," he immediately pulled back, his shoulders dropping, and he shook his head.

"I'm not crazy, Addy."

"No, baby, you're not, but you're starting to sound paranoid."

"Or cautious."

"Okay, cautious. But what do you want to do? I haven't heard any noises in the house, and people get scam calls all the time where there's no one on the other end."

"I don't know." Conner started pacing back and forth in front of me. "I just can't shake this feeling."

"Okay. So, let's figure out what to do about it. Is it really freaking you out this much?"

"Yes, it is." The worry in his eyes convinced me. Conner had never seemed like a paranoid person before, so if he was this worked up over something, there was a reason.

"Okay, so what do you want to do?"

We spent the next 10 minutes in the garage, coming up with a plan. I would start tracking the time of day when I got the unknown calls, noting the number and where I was at the time.

When I suggested we go back to how life was before, with him going to work and us spending our days apart, he wasn't happy. But after I explained it was the only way to determine if the noises in the house were there when I was in the room with him or when it was just him, and if he got the feeling of being followed when he was alone, he reluctantly accepted.

I still wasn't sure any of this was necessary, but having a plan made Conner feel better.

We did our experiment for a week, our routine going back to normal with Conner accepting any calls for work, me working from home, and us going to work on the new build together. In the time I was home, I never heard any of the buzzing or clicking Conner was talking about. I never felt like I was being followed, but the phone calls kept coming with no pattern I could discern.

They'd come in all day, never at night, maybe two to three calls a day, and either flashed "Suspected Scam" on my phone or listed a Province or State underneath the number.

Whenever I picked up, there was no sound, just a hang-up after a couple seconds. Eventually, I just stopped picking up.

One week turned into two, which turned into a month, and everything went back to normal. Conner continued to hear random buzzing throughout the house but started to believe me when I said it was just normal house noises.

We only saw Kyle once after he broke in when he came to move his stuff out. Conner and I had stayed in the living room of my place and watched the whole thing through the front window. I had felt like a creeper, but Conner had said he wasn't going to give Kyle a chance to try and say goodbye to me and wanted to make sure he didn't try and get into the house again if we were out. I had to appreciate where he was coming from and curled up with him on the couch as we pretended to watch *Shameless* on the TV.

Kyle had two guys help him move, and the amount of computer towers, monitors and just tech stuff that was brought down was astonishing. It was like his house was a Best Buy. I would have said that with the amount of equipment, Kyle was a big-time gamer, but I had never once heard computer game sounds through the floor, and he didn't really seem like the gamer type to me.

On his last trip down, my doorknob rattled as Kyle tried to get into my place. Conner immediately went to stand up, but I put my hand on his thigh and just shook my head at him. He huffed but listened to me as Kyle came to our front window, knocked on the glass and yelled a "See you later,

Sweetness" through the window. I knew for sure I wasn't planning on ever seeing Kyle again, but deep down inside, I had a feeling he wasn't going to walk out of my life so easily.

Chapter 28

"You piece of shit!" I yelled at the ripped rice paper in my hand and threw it on the growing pile of ruined food. I was finally attempting to make the rice paper pork rolls from my favourite Thai place, really wanting to cross another thing off my goal list, seeing how it was already mid-April and I hadn't made any progress on it since New Year's.

The rice paper was the hardest part of the whole thing. The pork was cooked perfectly, the vermicelli was all set, the lettuce and mint were cut up and waiting, and the peanut sauce I was ready to just eat by itself since it was so good. But the damn rice paper was either not wet enough and would crack, or too wet and would tear or was sitting out too long and stuck to itself when I tried to roll it. With a huff, I vowed to try one last time before I just threw everything in a bowl and ate it that way.

Just as I was filling the last piece of paper I had with the food and started to roll, the doorbell rang, scaring the crap out of me since I was concentrating so hard on my food. And, of course, when I jolted from the doorbell, my finger poked right through the rice paper.

I swore softly under my breath as I went to let Robin in. She was the girl who had moved in upstairs a couple weeks ago and who I had kind of taken under my wing. She was only 19, living on her own for the first time and was always coming down to see if I could help with something or if she could borrow something.

I didn't mind. She was a sweet girl, and kind of reminded me of myself when I was her age: shy, closed off, polite and never wanted to ask for help. But I had insisted she come over this afternoon so I could help with a paper she was struggling with for a class she was taking online.

Except when I opened the door, Robin wasn't the one who greeted me. It was a man in his late 40s to early 50s who was dressed impeccably in a navy blue suit, his hair slicked back, not a single strand out of place. He stood there, all the confidence in the world as he pulled on the shirt cuffs under his suit jacket sleeve. This had to be a door-to-door salesman or a politician vying for votes.

"Can I help you?" I asked, my annoyance evident in my voice.

"Hello, Ms. Peters," the gentleman almost purred my name. "I'm looking for Mr. Jensen." He had a sinister smirk that lifted the left side of his mouth as he stared at me, looking as if he knew all my deepest secrets and was holding them against me. That was when I really took in his appearance. He had cold dark brown eyes that stared straight to my soul and made me shiver, short black and gray scruff that dusted over his jaw, and his full head of black hair was gelled and combed back without a receding hairline in sight. There was also the tip of a tattoo that peaked out of his shirt collar, but it was too covered to see exactly what it was.

But besides his older, powerful look, his face was littered with tiny scars. There was one on the corner of his lip, one that I could barely see under his covered jawline and a large one that ran across the entire length of his right eyebrow. I closed the door a bit, hiding part of my body behind it. *Who is this man, and how does he know my name?*

"Um…Conner doesn't live here. He lives downstairs. His doorway is out the side of the house."

The dark-haired stranger leaned against the doorframe, crossing his arms over his chest while he slowly took in the amount of my body that wasn't hidden behind the door. "And I bet you love having Mr. Jensen below you, don't you, Ms. Peters." His smirk returned and crinkled his assessing brown eyes.

"I'm sorry, but who are you?"

"Oh, how rude of me," he straightened up and took a step closer to me, trying to walk through the doorway. Immediately, I pushed my hip against the door and shoved my leg behind it so that he couldn't get in anymore. Unfortunately, a hand flew out from around the other side of the doorframe, preventing me from closing the door even more on him.

Two men appeared and flanked his sides, pushing their way into the house and protecting the suited man's back. They must have been hiding on either side of the door as they appeared out of nowhere. The one goon pushed the door wider, allowing the suited man to enter into my home. I shoved my leg farther behind the door, trying to prevent them from coming in, but goon number one threw his shoulder into the door, easily throwing it all the way open with unbelievable force. The door slammed into my knee and ankle and bounced back. I stumbled back with a cry. All three of them entered my home as goon number two softly closed and locked the door behind them, trapping me and these three strangers in my entryway.

"My name is Mitchell Erbing, Ms. Peters. I'm an old friend of Mr. Jensen's. I'm wondering if you would pass a message on to him for me."

All of a sudden, as if on some silent command, his two bodyguards rushed me, each grabbing an arm and shoving me against the wall, using their legs to pin my body down, making it impossible to move. Goon number one started sniffing my hair while goon number two trailed a hand down the side of my body.

I bucked away from them, using all my might to try and pull away, but moving away from one only pushed me closer to the other. I saw Mitchell raise his hand just before he backhanded me into goon number two's face. I cried out as my face was whipped to the side.

"Please, Ms. Peters. Be still and pay attention." Mitchell's voice was calm as he readjusted a huge gold ring on the hand that just struck me. I inched away from goon number two's face as he leaned in and licked up from my chin to the corner of my mouth. I tried to get away but was still being held in place by the two men.

"Please tell Mr. Jensen that I'm looking for him. All these years, I've been watching him live off the money that I provided him with. It's time I called in a favour, don't you think? I want him to meet me in one hour at the corner of Reeler and King. And Ms. Peters, if he doesn't get the message, next time…" Mitchell stepped into me and shoved his face into mine, crushing his lips to mine. I tried to pull away, but he bit down hard on my bottom lip, cutting it instantly with his teeth. I could taste the blood as it trickled into my mouth. "…I'll send it to him in pieces…" his finger slowly ran down my cheek, over the bruise I was sure was forming over my left cheekbone from the hit. "Understand?"

All I could do was nod as the two goons released their hold on me. I quickly stepped back further into my home, trying to put as much distance between us as possible, but my ankle was swelling from being smashed when they opened the door, and I stumbled to the ground. My hand had reflexively gone to my burning cheek, and I felt wetness there. From tears, sweat or possible blood from his ring cutting my face, I wasn't sure. I just knew I couldn't take my eyes off Mitchell as he started to leave.

"Oh, and Adeline, dear, it's a pleasure finally meeting you face to face. You really are quite lovely." He pulled out a piece of paper and threw it at me as he stepped out the door, but I didn't move from my spot until I heard the car doors close. Only then did I scurry on my hands and knees to the piece of paper he threw down for me. Unfolding it, I gasped in horror. It was a picture of my bedroom, and in the middle of the picture was an arial view of Conner and I having sex. It was from last night from the date stamp. There we were in black and white, me on top, riding him with my head thrown back and my mouth open.

And I bet you love having Mr. Jensen below you, don't you, Ms. Peters. Mitchell's words came back to me. He'd been watching. Conner was right; we were being watched. But by who? Who was this man?

I quickly stumbled to my feet and hobbled to the living room window to make sure they were gone. As soon as the black SUV pulled out of our driveway and was around the corner, I grabbed my keys and my phone and limped to the car. I didn't even bother with my purse or a jacket.

I took a quick glance in the rear-view mirror as I backed out of my parking spot and caught my reflection in the mirror. I had a small gash on my cheek, some dried blood and a pretty impressive bruise starting, not to mention the swollen and bloody bottom lip. I threw on my sunglasses that I kept in my visor to cover my bruise and drove as quickly as I could out of town. I tried calling Conner's cell over and over, but no answer.

Desperately trying to remember where Conner said he was working today, I went to the new build first, hoping Conner would be there. As I pulled into the laneway, I spotted Conner's truck parked at the side of the yard, but I couldn't see him outside. There were a couple guys moving in and out of the house, but no Conner. I parked my car behind his truck and limped up to the laneway and onto the porch. I spotted Conner in one of the front rooms, measuring and cutting drywall as I walked in. The music was blaring, and he didn't realize I was there until I tapped him on the shoulder. When he turned around, his face went from annoyance at being interrupted to joy at seeing me.

"Hey, Cricket. What are you doing here?" He pulled me into his arms, causing me to stumble into him as my ankle rolled. I stifled a whimper and tried to regain my balance, but Conner immediately pulled back, noticed my busted lip, and held me at arm's length.

"What's wrong?"

I lifted my sunglasses and perched them on top of my head.

"Holy fuck, Addy. What happened?"

"Someone named Mitchell stopped by my place." Tears started to fall as the fear and panic of the situation finally caught up with me. "He said he wanted you to meet him in one hour downtown, or he'd send the message again…in pieces." I handed him the picture that I still held crumpled in my hand. "He also gave me this."

Conner took the piece of paper from my hand and quickly opened it. His eyes bulged out before his jaw clenched, and his hands crushed up the picture.

"I'll kill him," he growled before he gently pulled me tight into his arms. I hobbled as close to him as possible and squeezed him tight.

"Who is he?"

Conner ignored my question as he checked out my ankle, knee and cheek before helping me back out to our vehicles. He said that the swelling was already pretty bad and that I needed to get my leg elevated and put some ice on it. The cut on my cheek and lip wasn't too serious. Just needed to be cleaned and bandaged up.

He lifted me into his truck, saying he'd get someone to drive my SUV home. He still hadn't answered me about who Mitchell Erbing was, and once we were on the road, I asked again. I wasn't going to let this go. I couldn't.

"Conner, who is he?"

Conner took a big breath, looked over at me and squeezed the steering wheel so tight I was afraid he was going to break it.

"Remember how I told you about my old neighbour and how I used to deliver packages for him?" All I could do was nod. "Well, that neighbour was Mitchell Erbing. He was in charge of everything. Apparently, from what I've heard, he now runs a not-so-small gang and is into drugs and prostitution. I've been trying to keep an ear to the ground to make sure he didn't come back. It's been over 15 years since I last spoke to him. I thought I was in the clear." He paused for a second before he continued. "Apparently not."

"Why is he back? What does he want from you? And why did he come for me?"

"I don't know, Love, but I'm going to find out."

We were silent for the rest of the drive home until we pulled onto our street. When Conner pulled into the parking lot, he put the truck in park but kept it running. He didn't turn to me, didn't move, nothing. The air became thick with tension as I unbuckled and opened the door to get out. The new house was only about a 10-minute drive from where we currently lived, and between me waiting for Mitchell and his goons to leave, driving out to the new build, our conversation in the house, and us coming back, we'd already wasted a good 45 minutes of Conner's 60-minute time limit. He had less than 15 minutes now to get to the meet-up spot, and I didn't want to stall him. I didn't know what the consequences would be if I did.

"Adeline," he said, waiting for me to turn towards him. I turned back around in the truck seat, one leg hanging out the truck door and faced him, although he wasn't looking at me. He was still looking straight out the front window. "If I'm not home by 10:00 tonight, you need to run." He finally turned his face toward me, and I didn't like what I saw. "Not 10:10," he continued, "not 10:01. 10:00 on the dot."

He reached into the glove box of the truck and pulled out a key ring. There was a non-descript copper key on it, as well as a key with a "GMC" rubber cover over the top of the key. Nothing else.

"If I'm not back," he handed me the keys and took my face in his hands, "take out the bottom right drawer of my dresser. There'll be an envelope under the drawer with an address, a name and a phone number. Get yourself to the address, leave Hennington, and call the number."

I was taken aback and shook my head. Conner's hands only held my face tighter. Leave Hennington? What was he talking about?

"Conner, what's going on? Why won't you be back?" I started to hyperventilate, and my chest was squeezing tight. I grabbed his wrists, his hands still holding my face, and stared into his eyes as mine started to tear up.

"I love you, Adeline. More than you'll ever understand. This is the only way I can make sure you're safe."

I pulled back from his hold and pushed my back against the open door, as far away from him as the truck cab would allow without me actually getting out of the truck. My panic was full-blown at this point. He had contingency plans to keep me safe? How much danger was he in? How much danger had he put *me* in? Who was this man?

"Conner, what the fuck is going on? Why won't you be back? Why do I have to leave Hennington?" I paused as the real question finally slipped past my trembling lips. "Who *are* you?"

"I've never lied to you, Adeline. I'm exactly who I said I was. The man you fell in love with." I sagged against the door as the love he spoke about filled my eyes. "Nothing is different. I was always prepared in case this day came. I just hoped it never would. I never thought I would find someone who I loved so much who would be caught in the middle of it. Promise me," he pulled me into his arms and held me tight, his face pressed into my neck. "Promise me that if I'm not back by 10:00, you'll do as I say."

Chapter 29

At 9:58, I was sitting on Conner's bed, his dresser drawer pulled out and on the bedroom floor with the key ring he gave me and the envelope from under the drawer in my hand. My purse was beside me, as well as a small bag with a hoodie, my phone charger, a water bottle, some granola bars, deodorant, and a change of underwear. I didn't know how long I'd be gone; I was just told to run.

9:59, and still nothing. No call, no text, no sound outside the building of cars driving by. Of course, like a bloody horror, angst-driven movie, it had started to rain when the sun went down. I peered up out his bedroom window, which looked over the driveway, hoping to see headlights turn in. I stared and hoped and prayed that Conner would come home. He had to come home. He just...

BZZZZZZ

The sound of the alarm I had set on my phone interrupted my panic attack. It was 10:00 on the dot. I grabbed the phone, turned off the alarm and ran up the basement stairs and out to my SUV. I locked myself in and tore open the envelope. Just as Conner said, there was an address, a name and a phone number. I put the address in the GPS and sped out of the parking lot.

I pulled into an old storage unit lot in the middle of nowhere about half an hour later, triple-checking that the address was correct, and drove up to the unit number that was on the piece of paper. I looked at the door for maybe a minute, hyping myself up to do this and not just go to the police, until I reminded myself that Conner had a plan, and if he didn't want me to just go to the cops, there must have been a reason. I had to trust that. I had to trust *him*.

I took the key ring Conner gave me out of my purse and made my way to the old, rusted bay door. As predicted, the old copper key on the ring fit into the lock on the door. I didn't hesitate to throw the storage unit door open as the rain continued to pelt down on me. Inside, unsurprisingly, since the other key on the ring was a key to a GMC, was a vehicle covered by a dusty tarp. I ripped the tarp off and revealed a truck that looked older than me. *Why do I have to use his truck when I have my car?*

But after remembering the fear in his eyes after he kissed me, told me he loved me and that he was sorry he dragged me into this and drove off, I stopped questioning him. I grabbed my purse and my bag from my car, threw them into the truck and switched out the vehicles, pulling mine into the storage unit after pulling the old clunker of a truck out and locking the unit back up.

The truck shook and bumped as I drove it to the exit of the storage complex. I didn't know where to go from there. I didn't want to push the truck too hard; I had no idea how long it had been sitting or how long it would last. I could either go East towards Toronto or West towards farming country. On the one hand, I could find accommodations in Toronto, where I would disappear in the millions of people that lived there, but on the other hand, Conner had said to get out of town, so did that mean to stay hidden or just to leave Hennington? But if I went West and the truck broke down, I'd be a sitting duck for hours before someone could get to me.

With the truck rumbling as I idled at the entrance, I dialled the number on the sheet and made a snap decision, heading East with the hope that being lost in the sea of millions would be better than being alone on an empty road and completely out in the open.

I checked the piece of paper one last time, confirming the number and memorizing the name "Anders" before I hit the CALL button.

"Yeah?" a voice huffed after four rings.

"Um...I'm looking to talk to Anders, please."

"SARG, line 2 for you!" I was immediately put on hold. *Sarg?* Was this the police? There was no greeting, no automated message, just a grump on the other line. And if this was the police, why hadn't Conner just told me to go there in the first place?

"You can stay here tonight. We'll put you in one of our holding cells. At least it has a bed and a guard 24/7."

I was two seconds away from running out of the station and just driving until I ran out of fuel. I called the number Conner had given me, and now I was going to be locked up in a cell. I tried to keep calm and figure out what was going on, but I was completely lost and panicking.

Once I got a hold of Detective Sergeant Anders and told him what was going on, he asked me to come into the Toronto Police Headquarters right away. I hadn't even been here 30 minutes, and I'd already given him a statement, passed over the piece of paper from Mitchell and the card that Conner had given me, and was now being taken into a cell.

"It's the safest place for you right now." I nodded as Det. Sgt. Anders and I walked through the station and to the line of four cells at the back.

Det. Sgt. Anders was an older, gruff man, probably in his mid to late 50s, with a short buzz cut on his graying hair.

He was completely bald on top and had wrinkles at the corner of his bright blue eyes. You could tell he'd been doing this a while; his body was still strong and always on alert, and his eyes roamed, taking in everything at once.

"I gave my card to Conner when he was still a teenager working for Erbing. I could have brought him in and held him for 48 hours for suspicion of drug trafficking, but I could tell he was a good kid. He must have held onto the card. Damn glad he did." Anders shook his head as he led me into one of the cells and sat beside me on the cot. He was silent for a beat before he spoke, almost as if he was talking to himself. "We're going to catch that bastard."

"Am I really in danger?"

He looked at me with sympathy in his eyes, but the determination and fury in his posture alone answered my question. He looked back to the ground as if he was bowing his head in prayer, talking to God, asking for help while confessing a sin.

"I'm not going to lie to you, Ms. Peters, the shit that Mitchell Erbing is involved in isn't pretty. A lot of women have gone missing, and a lot have turned up dead – somehow, they all have a connection to him. We know he's involved in drug trafficking, using women as drug mules, and we know he's part of a human trafficking ring, both for child slavery and sex trafficking.

"The thing is, we can't make anything stick." He shook his head, clearly far beyond frustrated. "We've already arrested him dozens of times, but he's a slippery fucker with enough money and power for the best lawyers in the Country. He always gets out after our 48-hour hold since we don't have enough solid evidence to hold him longer and make the charges stick."

He looked over at me, assessing me once again. "You're quite pretty, Ms. Peters, so I would have no doubt that if you hadn't listened to Mr. Jensen, you would have ended up in Mitchell's hands, and we never would have seen or heard from you again."

I looked at my phone, and only three minutes had passed. I'd give it two more minutes, and I'd try calling him again.

I had been here for hours, and I still hadn't heard from Conner. I had texted and called him a dozen times since Det. Sgt. Anders left me in here by myself an hour ago, but I haven't been able to reach him and haven't heard a peep back. I was so exhausted I just wanted to curl up on the cot and sleep, but I was too worried, and my nerves were shot.

I sat back down after doing 92 laps of the cell – yes, I counted. I was so deep in my Sand Trap, questions flying at me from every direction, that I was sure I was having an anxiety attack. Was I really in that much trouble? Was I still? And what about Conner? Where was he? It was past 1 a.m. at this point, and still, no call, no text, nothing. Was Mitchell holding him and torturing him? Was he dead? Tears fell down my face as a throat cleared at the door.

"Ms. Peters." My head jerked up at the man standing at the doorway to my open cell. He wore a black suit, white shirt and black tie and had an air of superiority to him. Very *Men in Black*. "I'm Superintendent Harper with the RCMP ERT - Emergency Response Team. I'm head of an elite unit that has been looking into the workings of Mr. Erbing for quite a while now –"

"Do you know if Conner's okay?" I interrupted him, not caring if it was rude or not. My focus was on Conner and whether he was okay. Anything else was insignificant.

"Sorry, ma'am. I don't have an update on Mr. Jensen at the moment." He pointed to the end of the cot I was sitting on, and when I nodded, he sat down. "I spoke to Det. Sgt. Anders and he filled me in on what happened tonight, but I was wondering if you could tell me what happened in your own words."

"Okay."

It was the third time I was re-telling the story tonight. First was when I called Det. Sgt. Anders from the truck, and the second time was when I got to the station, and he took my official statement. You'd think by now it would have been easier to tell, but it wasn't. Every time I thought of the evil in that man's face or the fear in Conner's, it terrified me.

However, I went over the events again. I told the Superintendent about Mitchell and the two guys coming to the house, what Mitchell said and how he hit and bit me. I reluctantly told him about the picture of Conner and I having sex that Mitchell had given to me, and he looked appropriately apologetic when he said that Det. Sgt. Anders had shown it to him as part of evidence. I cringed at the thought of a picture of such an intimate moment for Conner and me being part of the evidence. Finally, I told him about Conner's reaction and how he instructed me to wait until 10 p.m. and, if he hadn't returned, to run.

"And Mr. Jensen knew Mr. Erbing from before?"

"Yes, Conner said when he was a teenager, he did runs for Mitchell for a couple years but got out and left the city and hasn't heard from him for like 15 years."

Superintendent Harper nodded along, taking notes in a little black book he had, but almost the whole time, my eyes stayed glued on the cell door, wishing for a miracle that Conner would come running in.

"Ms. Peters," Superintendent Harper continued, "before yesterday, when Mr. Erbing showed up, did you or Mr. Jensen notice anything out of the ordinary? Mail going missing that you should have received, cars following you, phone calls where there was no one there or a hang-up, things like that?"

I could feel the blood drain from my face. The picture Mitchell had, the phone calls I was getting, the feeling Conner had of being followed…Conner was right. Someone had been watching us, and not just in the bedroom. It was all connected.

"Ms. Peters? Are you okay?"

I swallowed the rising bile, and I numbly nodded. "Yes, we had strange things happen. My neighbour broke into my unit, and after that, Conner swore he heard buzzing and clicking in different rooms at my place. He said he always felt like someone was watching us, and I've been getting two to three calls a day from either suspected scam numbers or just different area codes from different Provinces and States. There's never anyone on the other line."

"Do you mind if I see your phone?"

I handed it over right away. I knew he didn't have a warrant to search it or anything, but he was trying to help. Giving him any information I had could only be a good thing.

"I kept a log of calls, days, times, numbers and what I was doing at the time in my notes."

"Can you show me?"

He handed the phone back to me, and I pulled up my notes. There were pages of information that I had tracked for him to look over.

"Can I take this for a little while? I want to pull these numbers and see if I can trace them. A couple of these numbers look familiar."

"Of course, but if Conner calls or texts back, can you please bring me my phone back? I'm really worried about him."

"Will do. One more question. What's the name of the neighbour who broke in?"

"Kyle Martin."

His nostrils did a slight flare, his perfect façade breaking just the slightest bit.

"Thank you, ma'am." And with that, I was left alone in my cell without even my phone to distract me.

I could barely stand it. I wanted to get out and walk around the station, demand answers and that someone go out and find Conner, but I knew that going out there and making demands wouldn't help anything move any faster. I just had to be patient.

"I'm really sorry, Ms. Peters," Superintendent Harper stated as he returned almost an hour later, "but we're going to need to keep your phone and log it in evidence."

"Why? What did you find?"

"Unfortunately, I can't share many of the details with you as this is an open investigation, but since you already know Mr. Martin, and it looks like at one point you had regular text and phone conversations with him, I can tell you that he is known to our ERT and is someone we have been monitoring for the past year. Four of the numbers you have logged in your phone are registered to him."

I almost threw up. Kyle was connected to Mitchell. He had been trying to get close to me since the day I moved in. Was he the one who planted the camera in my bedroom? Was that what he was doing when Conner walked in on him? Had he been watching me the whole time?

"We believe that you were Mr. Erbing's next mark."

And this time, I did throw up, barely making it to the sink in the corner in time.

Somewhere around what I guessed was 3 a.m., I was finally able to close my eyes a bit. I was nowhere near sleep, but my body had finally given up and needed to rest. My eyes were shut, but my brain kept running over everything that had happened, only now, it went all the way back to when I moved in and met Kyle on that first day. Every look, every touch, all the jokes and cheek kisses. The fact that in all that time, I had never been up to his place. The invite to New Year's at a strip club, which I probably wouldn't have returned from if Superintendent Harper's admission of me being the next mark was correct.

How did I let this happen? How hadn't I been more aware? I knew I wasn't comfortable around Kyle, but I was too afraid of hurting his feelings to put distance between us, and it was almost too late. It almost cost me my life.

"Ms. Peters?" I opened my eyes to see Det. Sgt. Anders at the cell doors. "Sorry, we're going to have to move you. We need the cell."

I got up and followed Det. Sgt. Anders through the station and into his office.

"I shouldn't be doing this, so appreciate that I'm trusting you here. You can stay on the couch, but please, *stay* on the couch. Don't go walking around, looking at stuff and keep the door open. I have case information in there, and if my Chief of Police sees this, both our asses are on the line, but it's either this, or you're out in the hallway on a plastic chair. I'm being nice, so don't abuse it."

"Thank you, Detective Sergeant."

With a nod and an obvious non-verbal command for one of the officers to keep an eye on me, he left the office and went out the back door of the station. Not two minutes later, he came back, and this time he wasn't alone. There, being escorted in by Det. Sgt. Anders and Superintendent Harper, his hands handcuffed behind his back and his body bent over, was Kyle.

Chapter 30

"Adeline!"

Before I was fully awake, I was ripped off the couch and crushed in a pair of massive arms. But as soon as he touched me, as soon as I smelled him and registered his voice, I knew it was Conner. I wrapped my arms and legs around him and bawled into his neck.

"Where have you been?" I cried as I pulled away and kissed him with more passion than I knew was in me.

He sat down on the couch, pulling me on top of him to straddle his lap and held me tight to him as tears of relief fell down my cheek. Knowing he was safe and here was overwhelming, and all the fear and anxiety I'd been feeling for the past almost 12 hours, since we parted in the driveway, was pouring out of me.

"Shhhh, Love, I'm here." Conner rubbed soothing hands up and down my back, peppering kisses on my head, cheek, neck, shoulder, anywhere he could touch without letting me go. I hugged him to me, my tears quickly subsiding. I needed answers, but I spared one more second to kiss the man I loved.

There was an obvious throat clear before Det. Sgt. Anders joined us in his office. "Sorry to interrupt. Mr. Jensen, glad to see you're okay." Conner just nodded at the Sergeant and watched as he moved to his desk. "We have some questions for you."

"Of course."

"Ms. Peters, one of the officers will take you to our lunch room to grab a coffee while I speak with Mr. Jensen."

"If it's okay, I'd like her to stay." I had moved off Conner's lap when Det. Sgt. Anders went to his desk, but Conner's hand was gripping mine and refused to let go. I didn't mind one bit.

"That's up to you," Det. Sgt. Anders responded. Superintendent Harper knocked on the door, waiting for a head tilt from Det. Sgt. Anders before stepping into the office and closing the door behind him.

Conner looked at Superintendent Harper but didn't falter in his conviction. "I'd like her to stay." He squeezed my hand, and I squeezed his in return. There was no way anyone was separating us right now, not when I just got him back.

"Okay," Det. Sgt. Anders allowed. "This is Superintendent Harper. He's the lead of an Emergency Response Team run by the RCMP that has been following Mr. Erbing's activities for a couple of years. He's already spoken to Ms. Peters and me about what happened yesterday, but we'd like to hear your side."

Conner looked to Superintendent Harper and asked, "I'm assuming you know about my history with Mitch?"

"Yes, I do. Det. Sgt. Anders updated me on his initial interactions with you back in the day, and we actually have a record of your involvement as Mr. Erbing's runner in our file. Why don't you start with what happened yesterday."

Although Conner didn't seem surprised to hear he was part of Mitchell's file, I was shocked. If they knew about Conner's involvement from 15 years ago, they must have a pretty in-depth case against Mitchell. But then why couldn't they make anything stick?

"Adeline came to my job site at around 5:00 limping, with a cut on her cheek and a busted lip. She told me that Mitchell had shown up with two guys looking for me and threatened her. He…" Conner paused to swallow, taking a deep breath and looked at me, sorrow in his eye. "I always had a backup plan in case he came looking for me again. I knew when he let me walk that I was never really gone from his world, but I didn't think he'd go after Addy. I should have known better." He kissed the top of my head, my hair muffling his voice. "I'm so sorry, Love."

"So, after you dropped Ms. Peters back off at her place, where did you go?" Det. Sgt. Anders was watching us like we had no hope, like we were facing the firing squad and he couldn't do anything to stop it.

"I met up with Mitchell —"

"And where was this?" Superintendent Harper interrupted.

"Reeler and King in Hennington." At Superintendent Harper's nod, Conner continued.

"Mitchell spouted off about how it was good to see me again and how it was nice to see what I had done with his money, the life I had made for myself with the fancy truck, the garage full of gym equipment and not having to work. He said he wanted his money back and wanted me to join his crew as an investor so that I could keep making him money. When I told him I would never work for him again, but I'd happily give him the money if he left Adeline and me alone, he started to make a couple comments about Adeline."

"I'm assuming the comments had to do with the picture he gave Ms. Peters of you two?" Det. Sgt. Anders eyes flashed quickly to mine but then returned to Conner.

"Yes, and about other things too. He knew about the work she was doing, the food she cooked, her fucking underwear collection… he said he'd been watching us for a while, and she was more beautiful in person."

"Did he say how he knew all this?" Again, Det. Sgt. Anders asked for clarification.

"Not exactly, but he said he'd been *watching* us, so I'm assuming he has cameras planted at her place."

"And what happened after that?" Superintendent Harper asked, obviously wanting to move the conversation along.

"His two guys threw a huge box in the back of my truck, and Mitchell gave me an address. He said I had to make the drop by 10 p.m. or he'd pay a visit to our old neighbourhood."

"Why does that matter?" I asked, not following the threat.

"My parents still live in the same house they did when I was growing up. Mitch's parents were my parents' neighbours."

Both Superintendent Harper and Det. Sgt. Anders wrote something down, nodding at Conner to continue.

"So, I put the address in the GPS, thinking it might be helpful for you guys to track later, drove halfway to Hamilton where the drop off was, just to make sure I wasn't being followed, then turned and headed for my parents' house. I had to make sure they were okay, so I drove there, woke them up and shoved them in my truck. I took them to the closest Police Station and told the cops there what had happened. I gave them your name, Anders, hoping they'd connect and keep my parents safe."

"Yes, their Inspector called a couple hours ago and said they'd put your parents in a safe house for the night with a patrol outside."

"Thank you," Conner gave him a small smile as his shoulders dropped in relief. "And then I just booked it here to make sure Adeline was okay."

"How did you know I'd be here?" I asked.

Conner looked down at me with tender love but guilt and sorrow. He wasn't going to let what happened to me go anytime soon, at least not until the bruise on my cheek and my busted lip healed. "I figured as soon as you called Anders's number, he'd have you come in."

"What did you do with the package?" Our eyes moved to Superintendent Harper as he stood from his chair and pulled his cell out of his pocket.

"It's still in the back of my truck."

Superintendent Harper dialled a number and barked into the phone that he needed someone to meet him here immediately and left the room.

Conner, Det. Sgt. Anders and I shared a look before Det. Sgt. Anders stood to go after Superintendent Harper. "You two better sit tight. I have a feeling this is just getting started."

Chapter 31

"Is it safe for us to go home?"

It was morning, and we were still at the station. Det. Sgt. Anders was right; our part in this wasn't even close to being over. Once they recovered the box from Conner's truck, the shit-storm only grew. I guess we couldn't really blame them since inside the box was a 7-year-old girl who was tied up like a pretzel and out cold. Thank God she was alive, but her discovery only turned Superintendent Harper into more of a pit bull.

When Conner asked if there was any way we could go to a hotel and get some sleep, Superintendent Harper threatened to lock Conner up for human trafficking if we didn't stay at the station and comply with everything he asked.

"Honestly, no," Harper sneered. I had removed the "Superintendent" title when he turned into a power-hungry dictator, throwing his weight around, although Conner and I had been completely compliant and helping in any way we could. He was a completely different person from when he first came in and was talking to me in the holding cell. It seemed like Conner and the girl was the break he needed in his case against Mitchell, and he wasn't letting us out of his sight.

"At this point," he continued, "I don't think anywhere is safe for you to go. Erbing's clearly been watching you both for a while, so he knows everything about you. He knows all your safe spots, everywhere you go, the vehicles you drive, the places you hang out…your entire life is a roadmap for him to find you at any time."

Harper barked a command to one of his men before he continued. "When we let you go, we'll put two undercover officers on you at all times." *LET us go? Were we being detained without our knowledge?* "Under no circumstances are you to acknowledge these officers. Do I make myself clear? You do not look at them, you do not approach them, you pretend that they are strangers. You will have them following you everywhere you go. Every time you go to the grocery store, they will be there. Every time you go to church, the mall, work, to visit your family, to the bathroom…they will know where you are and what you are doing."

Harper paused, and he looked between Conner and me. "Conner is our one shot at catching this fucker and making it stick. Erbing knows the drop wasn't made, and he'll come back for revenge. If we put you in hiding, we would be losing our one shot at catching him. We have to use you as bait, Conner. It's the only way to get him."

"No," I protested vehemently, "no way in hell am I going to let you use Conner as bait and put our lives in danger. Put us in witness protection or something. Get us away from that maniac. There's no way you're putting Conner at risk."

"Sorry, Ms. Peters, but it's not up to you. You have no choice. This is so much bigger than you and Conner. You're going to have to come to grips with this and fast."

"This is my life!" I had never been so angry or desperate before. "I get a say."

I could tell that Harper was losing patients fast. Conner was brooding silently, letting me speak for myself and stand up for both of us, just squeezing my hand in support. We were showing a solid united front, and he was allowing me to take the lead. Finally, Harper huffed out a big breath and shook his head.

"Sorry, sweetheart," he mocked, "but if it's between you and Conner and stopping a drug and human trafficking ringmaster, you and Conner better learn how to be some convincing bait."

I hated Harper. I didn't hate much in life, but that man, I absolutely hated. By the time we were finally "let go" and got back to Conner's place, we had been away from home for four days.

Legally, Conner and I hadn't been held for 48 hours for questioning, but that was just semantics. Realistically, once Conner arrived at the station the day after I had, we were told we couldn't leave until they were done with their questions and their preliminary search of the truck so that they could "clear Mr. Jensen of any connection to child trafficking or child endangerment." It was a complete dick power-move by Harper, but Conner and I agreed not to push it, just help where we could and completely comply with what they demanded to try and get this over with as quickly as possible.

Obviously, Conner's truck was in evidence since that's where the girl was found, and it had the drop address saved in the GPS. The ERT was also hoping that the two guys who were with Mitchell when he attacked me and who had put the box in Conner's truck might have accidentally left a fingerprint or DNA somewhere. This, we completely understood. We just didn't understand why we had to stay at the station for them to do it.

We could tell that Det. Sgt. Anders didn't agree with how this was all going down, but Harper's "Superintendent" status outranked Anders's "Detective Sergeant" ranking by miles, so he couldn't do a thing about it. He tried to make us as comfortable as possible, brought us food when he could, blankets and some old police sweats they had in their uniform closet, but he was limited in what he could do, especially since there were other cases and arrests going on. At least we were given a cell with a bed in it; once Kyle was taken out of the station, that is. They were adamant that it was vital that Kyle not know we were there.

Then, yesterday, just as we were told we could go, I was presented with a search warrant for my home. Harper's team wanted to look for and retrieve the hidden cameras and recording devices that they believed Mitchell had Kyle install when Kyle had broken in. Their hope was that they'd be able to trace them back to a server somewhere and add "voyeurism" to the massive list of Mitchell's criminal charges. My home was now part of the investigation, and I couldn't return until I was given the "all clear."

Everything was a complete nightmare. The only silver lining was that Conner would be driving us home in the old GMC clunker that had been in the storage unit for years, so odds were no one would recognize it as one of our vehicles.

But all the relief of being out of the police station and home was squashed the minute we pulled up to our tri-plex and saw the police tape over my door. Thankfully, there weren't any vehicles or any detectives there at the moment, except for the unmarked car that had followed us all the way from town and was now parking on the other side of the road, a couple houses down. How were we supposed to live like this?

Since my phone was logged as evidence, Conner received a call early in the morning from Harper – I still refused to call the jerk Superintendent – saying I was permitted to return to my residence to grab anything I needed, that there would be two agents who would be there watching me so that I didn't contaminate their crime scene, but that I couldn't yet return home.

"It'll be okay," Conner assured me as he grabbed my laptop and my work computer from my office while I tossed some clothes in a suitcase. "We'll figure it out."

"I know we will," I replied, huffing as I folded another pair of jeans and placed them in my suitcase. "But honestly, I'm not even comfortable staying at *your* place."

"I know. I'm not either."

The RCMP had given me a warrant for my home but hadn't mentioned Conner's at all. I guess there wasn't enough evidence to warrant a search warrant for his house as well, as there was nothing leading them to believe his home had been tampered with, but I still didn't feel safe.

goodness it was a mild spring, as we had already gone on three walks today just to talk. "But unless we stay at a hotel for God knows how long, I don't see another option. We know the house is safe; no one has been there but me and my crew, and we know every wire in that place. If something was tampered with, we would have found it. We just put the walls up this week."

I let out a huff before he continued.

"I have my camping stuff we can use: an air mattress, sleeping bags, a camping stove, and we can use the outhouse we have set up for the work crew. I know it's not ideal, but would you rather stay here?"

"No," I agreed, "I don't want to stay here. Kyle was too close for us to just hope he left your place alone."

"Just think of it as fancy camping. We'll be roughing it but with the luxury of being indoors."

We debated letting Harper know what we were doing but decided just to pack up and go. The undercover officers who were watching the house would follow us, and no doubt keep Harper updated on what was going on.

We grabbed all of Conner's camping equipment, packed up his suitcase and grabbed some food to take with us before we loaded the old GMC and headed out of town. We stopped at Walmart on the way, grabbed ice to fill his cooler, some fresh produce, and a new phone for me before we arrived at the dark house.

"Well, this feels ominous," I half-joked as we parked the truck and grabbed our stuff. The house was dark, and being out in the middle of nowhere, there weren't even street lights to guide our way. We were just surrounded by trees and the night sky.

"It'll be fine," Conner encouraged. "We'll make this work."

I followed Conner up to the house, where he unlocked the front door and then double-checked all the window locks once we were inside. At least we knew the house was secure. It took a couple trips from the truck before everything was unloaded, and we began setting up our new living arrangement in what was the master bedroom at the back of the house.

As he had indicated, Conner's camping bin was loaded with everything we'd need, or I should say bins, as he had three. There was an air mattress and pump, sleeping bags, a camp stove with multiple propane containers, bags of batteries of every size, flashlights and lanterns, cooking pots and pans as well as plates and bowls, a small radio, and even a small portable power station. He said that it wasn't much and really would only help us keep the phones charged, but it was more than I expected. Clearly, Conner was more of an outdoorsy man than I'd known.

"Here," Conner reached out and handed me a camping knife.

"What the hell do I need this for?" The thing was massive, at least the size of my forearm.

"We're inside, but the outhouse is outside, and so is the creek, which will have to be our main source of water for now until I can get something finagled here." The look of confusion and bewilderment must have been very evident as he continued. "We're out in the country, Cricket. There will be animals out, especially since we have a fresh water supply. There are coyotes, raccoons, foxes, deer, and that's just what I've seen on the property. I'd rather have you safe than sorry."

He seriously wanted me to defend myself against a coyote with a camping knife?

"How about when we venture outside, we do it together?" I handed the knife back to him. I'd much rather he kept it than me trip and fall on it or something. The house was still a construction zone, after all.

Chapter 32

I lasted a week in our isolation before I started going stir-crazy. Conner had been able to keep busy working on the house, but I needed to do something to keep my mind off why we were in this situation to begin with. I decided to use my cell as a data hotspot and signed into the network at *The Hennington Hound* to go through some of the new letters that had been submitted.

Since the publication of my *Desperate Dad* advice column, I have been getting 20-25 emails and physical letters written in a week asking for help and advice. It had become so popular that Brian had decided to make it a weekly piece, not just a piece that was added in when the paper was light as he had originally offered. I was loving it, and with every new piece published, more and more letters came in. I went through the new written-in submissions and saved about ten of them to my computer, unable to decide which one I wanted to tackle first. I wanted to jump right in and work on a couple different pieces since I knew it would occupy my time and mind, but my laptop only had so much battery life, and I didn't want to waste the limited power the little portable power station had by charging it.

Conner had done what he could with the water and electric people, but we were being held up with red tape since the house hadn't been inspected yet or something. He was going out of his mind trying to do what he could at the house but still stay safe and not venture out too much or bring people to us.

By the middle of week two, we were starting to snap at each other. I loved Conner, but being stuck with the same person 24 hours a day for 10 days straight, with nothing to do since we STILL had no power, was taxing. The hardest thing was that it was the situation, not each other, that was driving the wedge between us. It wasn't Conner's fault that the electrical inspector got turned away by the cops guarding the driveway, preventing us from getting the power turned on. It wasn't my fault that we were running out of food, and all I had left to cook was soup and stew.

But the smallest things were setting us off.

"I WAS ON MY PERIOD!"

"Oh, trust me, I know."

"What the hell is that supposed to mean?" Conner and I were circling the kitchen area, yelling over where the kitchen island should go. Or at least that's where the conversation started. It went from kitchen island location to sex on the kitchen island, to us not having sex in the past 18 days, to "I WAS ON MY PERIOD!"

"It means that just because we can't have sex on your period doesn't mean we couldn't have at least done something."

"Conner, we were at the station for four days before all this. I wasn't going to fuck you in a cell!"

"But what about after, huh? What about when we got here, and I tried every day, and you kept pushing me away."

"I WAS SCARED!" Tears sprang to my eyes. I had been trying so hard to hold it together during this whole situation, but I was done. It had been a horrible 10 days. The air mattress we slept on was killing my back, the food we ate was all canned and boxed stuff that we normally didn't eat, so it didn't agree with my stomach, and we were in the middle of nowhere. If something happened to us, if Mitchell found us, we'd be dead. I was constantly on alert for anything, a strange sound or a branch to move unnaturally that I was strung so tightly, any little thing would set me off.

Conner came to my side and pulled me into his arms. "I know, Love. I'm scared, too."

"I can't stop," I cried into his chest. "Whenever I relax for two minutes, I think that's when he's going to get us." I pulled back and cradled his face in my hands, just needing to touch him and confirm he was still there. I had been doing that a lot since we were at the station. "Those 12 hours that you were gone were the scariest moments of my life. I thought I had lost you, and he's still out there, hunting us. I can't stop being on alert. I can't give myself to you, relax into you, be with you without worrying. I can't lose you...I...I..."

Conner took my lips in a fierce kiss, crushing me to his chest. I held on tight as he pushed me against the kitchen wall, lifting me up to pin me between his hard body and the drywall. My legs wrapped around his waist as I lost myself in the desperation of having Conner in my arms. I honestly thought I had lost him that first day at the station and hadn't truly recovered since.

"I love you," he growled against my lips. "I won't let anything happen to you."

"I love you more."

He pulled back to look me in the eyes, passion and love shining so evidently, emotions got caught in my throat. "That's not possible."

Conner carried me to the bedroom, our lips feeding on each other the entire way. We fell onto the air mattress, and I rolled on top of Conner's body. Our hands worked frantically to pull away clothes. Luckily, we were both wearing sweatpants, so there were no buttons and zippers in the way. With quick tugs and a couple kicks, we were both pantless and ready. I needed him so bad, but there was also this pull not to let my guard down.

"Addy," Conner whispered, his hands rubbing up and down my thighs as he gently rocked his hips. "I promise I won't let anything happen to you."

"But what about you?" His hard length was sliding in between my folds, coating himself in my wetness.

He sat up, bringing us chest to chest and wrapped his arms around me. "As long as we're together, watching out for each other, we'll be fine."

He kissed me languidly, with soft, unhurried movements but deep caresses of his lips. He lifted me up and slowly lowered me onto his straining erection. The feel of him inside me was like a piece of me returning. 18 days was a long time for us not to be intimate. Although we didn't have a relationship based on sex, touching, kissing, holding, and caressing each other was a daily thing. And when we did get together, it felt like home.

Moans and whispered words left both our mouths as I rocked on top of him. Conner's arms held me tight, the need and urgency in both of us building into a type of desperation.

Conner laid on his back, pulled me down on top of him and caged me to his body. His hands grabbed each butt cheek as he started to ram up into me, jolting my body with every thrust. He was so deep that a sting of pain erupted every time he pressed deeper into me. But I couldn't stop. The feel of him moving in and out, faster and harder, was building an inferno inside me, and the need to come overtook everything.

"Why don't we go to the house," Conner suggested.

I looked up from zipping up my suitcase – I didn't know how long I was going to be locked out of my house, so I was taking as much as I could with me – and saw Conner leaning in the bedroom doorway, a laptop bag over each shoulder. In his hands were my Kindle, a bag with my bathroom supplies and my purse. Of course, there was an officer behind him, just like mine was in the corner of the bedroom watching me.

"But the house isn't even close to ready."

"It's not perfect," he led the way back to the front door, the two agents keeping a close eye on what we were touching and taking, "but it's got walls, insulation, windows. The water and electricity are all hooked up. We just don't have them connected yet. It could work for now until we think of a better plan."

"Conner, the place doesn't even have floors or a toilet yet."

"You guys all done?" the officers who had been following Conner interrupted, eager for us to leave the property.

"Yeah, I think that's all that I need for now."

We took everything I packed down to Conner's place.

"Look, I know it's not ideal." Conner stopped me at his doorway before we went downstairs. We had agreed that until we were 100% sure that his house wasn't bugged as well, all private conversations would be had outdoors. Thank

I pushed off his chest, needing to move my hips. I rocked on top of him as he held my hips firm and continued to push up into me in turn. My head fell back, and a cry ripped from my lips when he angled my hips differently, hitting a spot inside me he'd never hit before.

My body shuttered and exploded around him as he continued to jut inside me, my body squeezing so tight it was hard for him to keep thrusting.

"Don't push me out," he grunted, flipping me onto my back and then tossing me onto my belly. He grabbed my hips, jerked them up and then was back inside me a moment later, pushing through my still-quivering walls with a hard thrust.

"Fuck, I missed this." Conner ploughed into me, going harder and deeper. He wrapped an arm around my body and brought my back up to his chest so I was sitting on his thighs, and he was still fucking me from behind. One of his hands grabbed a breast, and the other slid down to my clit. His thrusts slowed but were just as deep and strong, prolonging the fire that burned inside me. His lips met my shoulder, giving it a bite before his mouth trailed up my neck, peppering my skin with nips and licks. My hands grabbed onto his to stabilize myself as I felt my second orgasm teeter on the edge. My one hand squeezed his harder over my breast while the other met his at my clit, then slid past to find where we were joined, and he was sliding in and out of me.

The feel of his wet shaft sliding past my fingers and into me sent me over the edge, my body falling back into his as my orgasm took over. But Conner pushed me forward, back onto the air mattress, and powered into me a couple more times before he went over the edge himself, spilling into me with grunts and curses.

"See," he panted, falling onto the air mattress beside me and pulling me into his arms, "I promised I wouldn't let anything happen to you."

And as if fate had a horrible sense of humour, there was a knock on our door as soon as the words left Conner's mouth.

Chapter 33

My heart thudded in my chest, racing with the panic of someone knocking on our door when no one should know this place existed, let alone that we were here.

"Get in the closet," Conner commanded as he put his pants on, grabbed his camping knife and went to the front window to see who it was.

"Fuck that," I whispered as I grabbed the small campfire hatchet that was by the back door and followed behind him, quickly pulling my sweats on as I went.

The pissed-off look Conner gave me didn't matter. He wasn't going to deal with this alone if it was Mitchell. We were in this together.

I stood behind the front door as Conner looked out the window and gave a sigh when he apparently recognized who it was.

"What are you doing here?" he barked as he opened the door, but he kept me hidden behind it.

"It's nice to see you too, Mr. Jensen." Harper's voice was cutting. He clearly didn't want to be here. "Can I come in?"

Conner opened the door, letting the man in and closed and locked it behind him.

"Ms. Peters," Harper nodded at me as I came to stand beside Conner. Always a united front. Conner and I remained quiet as Harper looked around the house, taking in all the construction that we were living in the middle of. When his eyes came back to us, they quickly landed on Conner's knife and my hatchet and his hand immediately went to the sidearm under his jacket. "Do I need to be concerned that you're holding weapons while talking to law enforcement?"

We both put our weapons down and put our hands up, slowly backing away.

"We're just being careful. We're still bait for Mitchell, right, and no one's supposed to know we're here." Conner had venom in his voice, still salty over being classified as "bait" and being refused protective custody. I was right there with him. If they wanted us out there, we had the right to protect ourselves.

"Well," Harper gloated, "that's actually why I'm here. Mr. Erbing has been brought into custody, and we're removing the protective watch we had on you, effective immediately."

"What? You got him?" The words were out of my mouth before I could register what Superintendent Harper said. Yes, he was now back to Superintendent if, in fact, he did have Mitchell in custody.

"We were able to use the drop location you had in the GPS of your truck and locate one of his associates. The guy had a rap sheet almost as long as Mr. Erbing's. He agreed to cooperate with our investigation in exchange for a reduced sentence and sang like a bird. We were able to pick up Mr. Erbing last night."

"That seems a little too easy," Conner looked at me, a confused and concerned look in his eye. I had to agree. They'd been after this guy for how many years, built case after case and brought him in on charges, but they'd never gotten anything to stick. All of a sudden, someone was willing to talk, and they got Mitchell right away? Something wasn't adding up.

"Five years of my life dedicated to bringing this guy in is not 'easy,' Mr. Jensen." Harper, yes, back to Harper, stepped closer to us, kicking the knife and hatchet that were on the floor out of the way. "Time, dedication, evidence, planning, gut instinct, and excellent detective work got us this break. It wasn't just luck."

Convenient how he left out that this was all thanks to Conner's insight, planning and forethought in putting an emergency plan together in case Mitchell ever showed up again. If it hadn't been for Conner putting the address in the GPS and keeping Anders's contact all these years, Mitchell would still be out there. *No, you're right, Harper. This win is all because of you.* I really had to fight to not roll my eyes.

"What are the chances of him lawyering up again and getting everything dropped?"

"Ms. Peters, the associate that we have spilling all the dirt was the one who didn't get his package delivered by Mr. Jensen here. He wasn't too happy with Mr. Erbing and made that very clearly known to him. Once Erbing's healed enough to move from the infirmary, he's going straight to prison."

Conner and I just looked at each other again, both of us obviously thinking the same thing. Something wasn't right. Erbing, one of, if not THE top child, drug and sex trafficking ring leaders in Canada, got taken down by a business partner, completely unaware, without the other guy getting injured and none of his guards there to protect him, and then was just left to get picked up by the cops? This didn't seem suspicious? Either I watched too much crime drama, Harper was a blind idiot who was getting fooled, or Mitchell had just given up. My money was on the second option. This wasn't over.

"So, are we free to go home?" Conner asked, hesitation in his voice. This felt like a trap.

"Yes, you're free to go back home, but I should tell you. Mr. Kyle Martin made bail. He left the city, and we don't know his current whereabouts."

Conner and I packed up our camping gear as we prepared to go back home…at least for now.

"This doesn't feel right."

I looked across the bedroom as Conner came back in from loading one of the full totes back in the truck.

"I know." I sat on the floor and continued to put the leftover food at the bottom of another tote. "That was too easy. Five years of trying to catch Mitchell, and then all of a sudden, they find him beaten up on the side of the road, just waiting for the cops? Plus, Kyle's out?" I folded my hands in my lap, trying to stop them from shaking. "This is a trap."

Conner made his way over to me and joined me on the floor. "It feels that way."

"So, what do we do? Going home feels like we're walking into the lion's den, but staying here without the cops guarding us feels like we're sitting ducks."

"I don't know."

We just stared at each other for a minute as Conner held my hands in his, calming the shaking in them just a bit.

We were fucked, and we both knew it.

If Mitchell was truly behind bars, we had no idea who his second in command was and what orders they had been instructed to carry out. Clearly, Conner was a priority since his lack of a drop was the reason Harper's Emergency Response Team was able to find and turn one of Mitchell's associates, leading to his apparent beat-down and arrest.

And then there was Kyle. I didn't know if his obsession with me was his own or because he was looking for new women for Mitchell. I knew he had wanted me. The makeout session we had had when he helped paint my office and then the constant little kisses and the erection I had felt in his pants had been a dead giveaway, but had that all been a ruse for Mitchell? Had he wanted me for himself or to hand me over to the ringmaster?

I prayed that with being in my mid-30s, I was too old to be taken into a trafficking ring, but I wasn't an expert. I had done some research, and trafficking could encompass anything from sex trafficking to forced labour/involuntary servitude and even trafficking for the removal of organs. If Kyle had caught me for Mitchell when I had first moved in, I could have ended up being a drug mule, put into a forced marriage, given as a sex slave, and the list went on. At the time, being an unemployed divorcé who didn't speak with her family and didn't have many friends, I would have had no one to care or come looking for me. I would have been the perfect candidate to be taken without anyone noticing. No employer would have wondered where I was, no spouse would have come looking, and family members wouldn't have wondered why it had been so long since I called. I would have been exactly the type of woman who could have disappeared.

Until Conner. Conner would notice if I was gone. Conner would come looking. Hell, Conner would tear the entire world apart until he found me. But Kyle's obsession with me started before Conner was in my life. He had always come over, had always watched out for me, always flirted with me to gain my trust. He had always bad-mouthed Conner as well as if to ensure I hadn't made friends with anyone else but him.

So even if the Mitchell situation was taken care of, which I highly doubted it was, the Kyle threat was still very much real.

Chapter 34

I stood in my entryway and looked around. My house was a mess. The "Do Not Enter" tape had been removed from the front door, the door had been locked, and none of the windows had been broken, but it looked like someone had broken in and completely trashed the place. It seemed that when an elite team run by the RCMP was told evidence was somewhere, they didn't care about cleaning up after the mess. They just wanted to find the evidence.

There were muddy boot prints all over my beautiful hardwood floors, my lamps were all tipped over and pictures removed from the walls. Closets were emptied, and their content was strewn all over the floor, and down the hallway, I could see bedding and books falling out of the doorways.

But it wasn't just the mess that made me stop at the entryway. I didn't *want* to be here. I didn't want to move back in and have life return to normal. My house had been permanently tainted. I couldn't look at the hallway and not see Mitchell there towering over me with his goons. I couldn't look in my bedroom without seeing Kyle creeping around. I couldn't stand in this structure and not feel like I had been violated. This was no longer my home. This was no longer my fresh start after the divorce. This was the birthplace of my nightmares.

"I have to sell this place," I said into the open air.

"And you'll move in with me." Conner pulled me into his chest as we continued to look around my former home. I just nodded into his chest, acknowledging this next step.

"Into your house?" I didn't know if Conner was thinking the same thing, but living downstairs wouldn't be much better than living here.

"Into *our* house." He kissed the top of my head before he took the suitcases back outside to the truck. I grabbed the garbage bag that held all our dirty clothes and towels and followed him back out. "I'll call Pete and tell him I'm cancelling my lease," he continued, "and tell him I'll be out in what, two weeks? That should be enough time to get the inspectors back out for the electrical and water, at least get the flooring in the master bedroom done and our stuff moved in."

I nodded and followed him back into the house. He went straight into my bedroom and threw everything off the bed before grabbing the corner of the mattress.

"What are you doing?" I rushed to his side and helped him lift.

"If we're going back to the house, we're taking a real mattress with us this time."

We loaded the mattress into the back of the truck and strapped it down. We grabbed whatever else would fit into the cab of the truck with us - bedding, towels, laundry detergent, pretty much anything small that we could squish in garbage bags - and made our way back to the house.

We did a couple trips back and forth to grab stuff from both our places before the sun started to set and the house became dark. We lit the candles, turned on the camping lights around the house, and sat in our bed to eat a very late dinner.

"Do you feel better staying here, or do you still feel like we're sitting ducks?"

I munched on my cold Thai food as I gave his question some serious thought.

"I still feel like we're sitting ducks since the house and land are in your name, so it could easily be found, but it's better than in town."

"It's actually not," Conner replied, putting his now empty beer bottle on the floor.

"What's not?"

"The land," he continued as he bit into his spicey pork, "it's not under my name."

I paused my eating and looked at him in complete shock. "Go on..."

"It's under Matthew Lichti."

"And who is Matthew Lichti?"

"Matt's the guy who owns the 70 acres around us. I helped him build a couple of his barns, and in return, he said I could build on this plot of land."

"So, this isn't actually your house. It technically belongs to Matt?"

"Technically, yes. He holds the property in trust for me since I didn't want it in my name in case something like this happened, but it will move to my name once he dies. These five acres of land are willed to me."

"Isn't it kind of a big deal for someone to leave you property?"

"He has no real family left; his wife was the aunt of one of my roommates from when I first moved to Hennington and lived in a 2-bedroom house with four other guys. When I told them I was looking for work, one of the guys connected me with Matt. He was looking for someone to help out around the barns while his sons dealt with the business side of things. A year later, he lost all three of his sons in a barn fire. I helped him take down and rebuild his barn. He lost so much. Not only his boys but half the chickens on his poultry farm. It took us years to rebuild everything and for him to get back on his feet."

"Poor man."

"I know. He's the nicest guy, too. I was in my early twenties, had just gotten away from Mitchell and Toronto and didn't know shit. Matthew taught me how to work, how to lay a level foundation, how to put up walls, shingle a roof, frig, how to properly use a drill." He chuckled and grabbed another beer from the drink cooler. "I didn't know the difference between a Phillips and a Robertson screwdriver when I met him, and he completely took me under his wing. I felt bad taking money from him when he was trying to rebuild his life and was teaching me so much, so he promised me some land in return. I didn't know it would be five acres in the woods with a fresh spring running through it."

"Lucky you."

"Yeah," Conner turned to me and kissed me tenderly. "Lucky me."

Life went back to normal, as much as possible, within the next couple of weeks.

The inspectors came out and gave the okay for us to connect the water and power within the first week. In that time, Conner managed to lay the hardwood in the bedroom and closet, the tile in the ensuite bathroom, hook up the toilet and install the shower and tub. I'd never been so happy in my life to see a toilet flush. No more outhouse for me.

By week two, all the flooring was done throughout the entire house, the light fixtures were up, the kitchen cupboards were installed – the countertop was coming in three days – and the appliances were ordered. Most important, however, was all our stuff was moved in. We knew it was out of order to have the house furnished before the walls were even painted, but we wanted out of the triplex. I met with a realtor the day after I decided to sell and had it listed two days later. We were holding offers until tomorrow, and then I'd be done with that place.

I looked around our half-done home and smiled. There was a mix of Conner and me in every room. The master bedroom had the new bed set we picked out together but his area rug and my recliner in the corner. The kitchen had his kitchen table, but my hutch. The living room had his entertainment centre with the new sectional and tables we purchased with the sale of my living room set. We had sold a lot of our furniture, not needing double of things like kitchen tables or sets of dishes, pots and pans.

I grabbed a drink from the bar fridge that was originally from Conner's gym - we had it hooked up in the kitchen until the appliances came next week – and made my way upstairs to one of the spare rooms that we had set up as my office. I had been trying really hard to crack down on my work for Cindy and *The Hennington Hound*, trying to make up for the time Conner and I had spent here in hiding.

I managed to write three articles for the paper last week and emailed them to Brian this morning, along with an apology for being distant the past couple of weeks and a promise to be in the office tomorrow. He had emailed back almost instantly, telling me not to worry, that he was impressed with what I had written so far and had no problem with me working from home. I was so appreciative of the freedom that Brian had given me and told him a thank-you batch of cookies was on their way.

I logged into the inbox that people used to submit their pieces for the advice column and found another letter from *The Neighbourhood Watcher*.

I first received a letter from *The Neighbourhood Watcher* after my advice column to *Desperate Dad,* and I have received a new one every week since. I first thought that it was just someone who wanted to vent, but I was drawn to the letters they wrote. Every letter was about things they noticed around Hennington that didn't sit right with them, and almost every week, I added one of their letters to my "prospective article" folder.

I had responded to one of their letters, the first one they wrote, but I tried to be as fair as I could and wrote an advice column for a new person each time. As much as I would have loved to answer more of the letters from *The Neighbourhood Watcher*, it wasn't fair to the other people who wrote in asking for help or guidance. Everyone deserved to have their letters responded to.

And as I scanned the emails in the inbox, I clicked on *The Neighbourhood Watcher*'s letter first.

Dear The Hennington Hound,

I don't know what to do.

I'm really worried about the woman who lives in the apartment below me. She's amazing, a great friend, and I adore her, but out of the blue, she's pulled away. I have done nothing but be kind to her. I helped her when she first moved in, spent nights with her so she didn't feel alone, and even brought her a drink every time we hung out together. She treated me like a best friend, always with a kind smile, a hug, and constantly having me over to her place.

I've tried to be a nice neighbour and a good friend, but then she started dating this guy who was controlling, aggressive and incredibly arrogant. I tried to be there for her, but now I hear she's selling her place, and she didn't even tell me she was moving.

I can't help but feel like it's the guy she's dating. He's not good for her. She's such a lovely woman, and he's a beast who is squashing who she is. He has taken over her life. He is always around her, won't leave her alone for a second and has told her to stay away from me.

How do I get her away from this guy? I'm worried about her and the G.I. JOE she's dating. He's going to get her in trouble if he hasn't already. I'll do whatever I can to have her back in my life and make sure she's safe from him.

~ The Neighbourhood Watcher

I read the letter over and over again; something in this one was just not sitting right. Besides the fact that a lot of people had problematic neighbours, something felt personal about this one. Friends pulled away, neighbours helped each other, and people didn't always like who their friends were dating. This was all normal. Something kept pulling me to the last paragraph. I must have read it ten times before I looked up and saw Conner coming out of the garage in the back of the property that was his gym.

"Nah, sorry, Sweets. I don't really have any tools, but you should check with G.I. JOE."

"Who's G.I. JOE?"

"He's the guy who lives downstairs. You still haven't met him?" At the shake of my head, he continued. "He's probably out in the garage working out or something, but he has tools."

G.I. JOE.

That was how Kyle first described Conner to me, and here it was again, in a letter about a neighbour who was worried about the girl in the apartment below them. Kyle helped me move in. Kyle spent nights at my place and always brought me a beer. Kyle hated Conner. My house was for sale, and I was moving. It all lined up.

I clicked on my deleted items and my "prospective article" folder and pulled up everything that *The Neighbourhood Watcher* had written in. I went through them all with a "Kyle" lens. I made it three letters before my hands were shaking, and I was on the verge of a panic attack.

The first letter was about how people were becoming too judgemental of each other and forgetting that it was okay to let loose and have fun, that life didn't have to be so serious all the time. People were becoming too sensitive and turning into prudes. They didn't know how to just hang out and have a couple drinks anymore without judging people for being "inappropriate": our night at *Rollies*.

The second was about how stupid cellphone companies were and how they were giving out people's phone numbers to telemarketers who would just call and say nothing: my hang-up calls.

The one I just read that pushed me over the edge was about how safe Hennington was, how you didn't feel like people were staring at you or watching you, that you were free to do whatever you wanted, be with whoever you wanted, and you didn't have to worry that your neighbours were watching or listening in; the cameras in the house and the picture Mitchell had of Conner and me having sex.

They were all innocent letters. There was nothing scary or troubling about them until I looked at them as if Kyle had written them. Suddenly, all the letters pointed to me.

"CONNER!" I screamed at the top of my lungs, quickly hitting PRINT on all the articles, my printer kicking to life.

Conner sprinted up the stairs, having never heard me bellow for him like that before, and found me clicking away on the computer.

"What is it? What's wrong?" He looked around, the same panic in his eyes as mine.

"Read these." I threw pages at him as soon as they were done printing. There were 16 letters in total, one submitted each week for the past four months, starting the day after my first advice column was published.

Conner was quiet as I watched him flip through the sheets. "What are these?"

"It's Kyle."

His eyes snapped up and looked at me, then flew down to the pages again.

"Are these letters to you?"

"They're pieces that were written into the paper for my advice columns."

Conner went back to the beginning of the stack and read them all over again. "We need to call Anders."

Chapter 35

"I know it all just sounds like random coincidences, but when you look at it all together…"

"You're right, it's definitely more," Det. Sgt. Anders nodded while he typed something on the computer. "Okay, start from the beginning. How does this person contact you? What's their name and email address? And let's start a list of everything you have in common with these letters."

Conner and I were back at the police station, having decided it was best to talk to Anders in person and show him the physical letters. We sat in his office, the letters strewn over his desk like someone was playing a game of 52 Pick-up.

"All the letters were emailed to the *Advice@HenningtonHound* email address," I began, "not my personal work email."

Anders wrote everything down. "Who all has access to that account?"

"I don't know, I guess just Brian and I."

Anders's eye snapped up. "Who's Brian?"

"He's the owner and publisher of the paper."

His head went back down, and he continued to type. "Have you mentioned anything to Brian about these pieces?"

"No. Once I saw the G.I. JOE reference and went back through all the letters, I told Conner, and we came right here."

"Okay, don't say anything and don't change your pattern. Mr. Martin clearly knows you're the one who monitors the inbox and reads all the letters. Is it only you who responds and writes the advice columns?"

"Yes, it's just me. I just took the role over on New Year's from Brian's wife."

"And have you responded to any of the letters that this *The Neighbourhood Watcher* has written?"

"Yes, that's what made me start watching out for who was writing in. I had written a piece in response to their letter, and two days after the article was published, I noticed they wrote back in."

Det. Sgt. Anders looked at the letters that were laid out on his desk. "Which one was the letter that you responded to?"

As if Kyle had given me a glimpse into the future, his first letter had predicted what happened to me just last month.

"It was the one about not feeling safe in her complex anymore since their friend caught someone in their house when they got home."

Det. Sgt. Anders picked up the letter and re-read it, empathy in his eyes as he looked back at us. "Just like Mr. Martin did to you." The memory sent a shiver down my spine.

Det. Sgt. Anders had no doubt that all the emails had come from Kyle. There were too many similarities between the letters and my life since I had moved into the tri-plex. He took all the letters and my work laptop and spoke to someone in their cyber division to see if they could trace where the emails came from. They didn't get very far, though. All they discovered was that the emails were sent from an anonymous email address and sent from a secure network through an incognito browser. It hid who set up the email address, the IP address, and anything else that could have given us even a hint of proof that it was Kyle. We had nothing.

"Come on, Love. Harder!"

I let out a deep groan. Sweat had dampened my skin as I lay on my back. Conner was on top of me, his weight pressing my body into the floor.

"I can't," I puffed, barely able to catch my breath.

"You can, Addy. Push harder."

"Conner, we've been at this for almost an hour. I'm exhausted."

"I don't care."

I looked deep into his eyes, both loving him and hating him at this moment. "I don't want to hurt you."

"I swear to God, Adeline. No more excuses."

"Conner..."

"Adeline! You can do this!"

"FINE!"

I took a deep breath and got myself ready. Conner gave a firm nod in encouragement when he saw the resolve on my face.

"Watch your thumbs."

I readjusted my hands, which Conner held pinned above my head, and looked into his eyes. "I love you."

"I know."

Without any more delay, I thrust my hips up as hard as I could, trying to throw his 230-pound frame of solid muscle off my body and bit into his arm that was right beside my face.

"Son of a..." he yelled as he shifted away. I took his moment of distraction as my opportunity and punched him as hard as I could in the face. I was aiming for his nose but slammed my fist into his jaw instead. Blinding pain immediately radiated through my fist.

"FUCK!" I rolled onto my side and cradled my hand to my chest. Tears immediately sprung to my eyes. I barely registered the fact that I was able to move, and that meant that I knocked Conner off my body.

"Damn, that hurt," Conner gritted through his teeth, rubbing his jaw. "Good job, Cricket." He sat beside me on the floor and helped me up into a sitting position. "That's how you get away." There was pride in his eyes, even though I could clearly see blood forming in the bite mark I left on his arm. "Let me see your hand." He carefully examined my knuckles. They were red and swollen from the hour of training Conner had just put me through.

After we left the police station, we both agreed that I should learn how to defend myself in case Kyle popped up again. As soon as we got home, Conner took me out to his gym at the back of the property. For the last hour, he had taught me how to throw a punch, how to react if someone grabbed me from behind, and how to defend myself with jabs, eye pokes and kicks to the junk. It was all practice up until he said I should try for real it in a controlled setting. No matter how much I protested, he insisted that there was no better way to learn to fight than to actually fight. Kyle wasn't going to go gentle on me if he came to get me, so Conner didn't want me to hold back.

"How's your face?" My left hand hovered over the red mark that was growing on his jaw while he continued to examine my right.

"Better than your hand." He looked worried as he went to the cooler in the corner of the gym and grabbed some ice. "You didn't hold your wrist straight, did you? It looks like you hit more with your knuckles than your fist."

"Got you to move, though," I said through a wince as Conner tried to straighten out my fingers.

The sly smirk he sent me made me feel strong, but I knew if I ever had a run-in with Kyle, the whole situation would be very different.

"Come on," Conner said as he helped lift me up off the floor. "Let's get washed up and stretch out your muscles."

Conner and I walked back to the house and directly into the master bath. He turned on the hot water while I stripped out of my gym clothes, wincing with every move and trying not to use my right hand.

"Stop," Conner whispered. He gently lifted my shirt over my head before wiggling my bike shorts down.

"Go get in the hot water. It'll make you feel better. I promise."

He helped me climb over the side of the huge clawfoot tub, and I settled into the warm bath. My body instantly relaxed, my aches melting away in the heat. It wasn't even dinner time yet, and I was ready for bed.

Conner climbed in behind me, careful not to press on any of the bruises I'd collected in the past hour. He pulled my body back against his and held the ice pack over my, thankfully, not broken hand.

I could have stayed like that for hours. Submerged in the steaming heat of the huge tub, Conner's strong and warm body behind me. It was heaven. His wondering hands rubbed my tired arms and legs, eventually gliding over my stomach and up to my breasts.

"These two must be exhausted," he whispered against my neck as his lips found my skin in a warm kiss. "They were confined in your sports bra for a long time."

I rolled my eyes at his corniness but couldn't help the moan that slipped past my lips as he squeezed my breasts tighter and kissed the side of my neck, right under my ear; my weak spot. Every time his lips touched me there, it was as if he turned a switch on inside me, and my body came alive.

One hand continued to knead my now aching breast while the other slid down below the water and between my legs. His lips continued to move all over my upper body, kissing and licking and nipping everywhere he could reach. His lips didn't leave my skin as his fingers spread my lower lips and started to play in the folds.

"Do you have any idea how sexy it was seeing you out in my gym today?" My back arched as his finger slowly rolled over my clit. "How hard it made me seeing you all sweaty after pushing yourself and fighting back?"

His hand slid lower, and two fingers entered me. I couldn't keep the panting and noises from escaping as Conner's hands removed all my aches and pains and replaced them with pleasure and desire.

"Seeing how powerful you were," he pushed his fingers slowly in and out, teasing me, "how fierce." His hand sped up, and his other moved up to my chin to turn my head. "How determined." He captured my lips in an intense kiss that completely took my breath away. I was only able to whimper out his name before all words and thoughts left my head, and the desperation for Conner took over.

I turned in his arms, the water lapping over the edge of the tub and straddled his lap. He immediately thrust his fingers back inside me while the other hand wrapped around my neck and brought my mouth back to his.

Although Conner and I were out of the "honeymoon" phase of the relationship, there was still a need that took over us from time to time, a yearning to climb all over each other and pull the other closer, to get him deeper in me. I held onto his shoulders as I rocked on his fingers, but it wasn't enough. Impatiently, I swatted his hand away and grabbed his dick, positioning it for me to slide down. Within seconds, he was deep inside me, and although the stretch and fullness were unbelievable, it still wasn't enough. I could feel my blood pumping, my heart racing and my climax building, the need in me only getting bigger and wilder.

Our foreheads were together as I writhed on top of Conner, my movements fast and hard. We were both panting, our lips randomly crashing together before they were ripped apart by our need to breathe. And in between each kiss, Conner moaned and whispered words against my lips. "…fuck, Love…you feel so good…harder…I love you so damn much…that's it…fuuuuuck…God, you're so tight…Addy…God, Addy…"

His words were like little love letters that went straight to my centre and pushed my climax higher and higher. Even when he just moaned "Fuuuuuck," it made me want to push even harder, make him feel even more and push him right over the edge to bring him his release. I wanted to be the reason he felt amazing, the reason he came, the reason his body shook as he spilled into me.

I grabbed as much of his now somewhat grown-out hair as I could and yanked hard as I pushed my body to its limit, trying to get us both to the end. Although this felt amazing, and I didn't want to stop, I knew this was only round one. We were in one of our desperate moods where one orgasm was not going to be enough to take the edge off.

Conner's hands wrapped around my hips; one went to my clit, and the other went to my back door. At the same time, he put pressure on both parts and shot me right over the edge. I jolted on top of him as my entire body shook. I could feel my walls squeezing him over and over as he moved my hips with his hands and thrust up into me. I was panting for air as the blood pressure rushed to my head, all my muscles locked tight in my climax. It was so intense I was dizzy when Conner suddenly stopped, stood up in the tub, our bodies still connected, and left the bathroom, his wet footprints trailing behind him as he carried me to bed. Only it wasn't to sleep. He wasn't done with me yet.

He threw me on the edge of the bed, lifted my legs to his shoulders and pushed right back into me. He stood at the end of the bed and thrust hard and fast. His thumb zeroed in on my clit and went back to work, instantly pouring gasoline on the fire that was still burning inside me. Within minutes, my walls were pulsing around Conner again, squeezing him tight. My climax was so powerful it felt like I had been electrocuted, but in the best way. The shockwaves of heat, fire, and pleasure flowed through my body, freezing it in a state of utter bliss, even stopping my lungs from working.

"Fuck, Love," Conner grunted as his thrusts became desperate and ragged, "I can't get enough of you."

I managed to squeeze out an "I don't want you to" before he came inside me, and my body started to slowly release its hold on my limbs. I floated back to earth, panting as the squeezing and twitching of my body finally ceased.

"Never leave me," Conner begged as his body folded in half on top of me, his shaky arms barely holding up his weakening knees. I wrapped my arms around him and pulled his body on top of mine.

"Never."

Chapter 36

The sound of a phone ringing woke me from a nap I didn't remember taking. Conner and I were both naked, cuddled together on top of the comforter. We couldn't have been out for more than half an hour since the tips of my hair were still wet from the bath.

"Babe," I pushed Conner on his chest, "your phone."

All he did was grunt and pull me closer to his chest. "Don't push me away. You're keeping me warm. Why are you stealing my blanket?"

I giggled at his sleepy ramblings. I had learned that barely-awake Conner said some ridiculous things sometimes.

"You're cold because we fell asleep naked."

"Mmmmm, naked Cricket," he pressed a kiss to the top of my head, and his hand slid down to grab my ass. "My favourite."

The phone continued to ring as Conner fondled my ass and leaned down to press a very not sleepy kiss to my lips. The passion in it astounded me, as did the erection growing against my belly.

"Ready for round three?" He rolled on top of me and slowly rolled his hips against mine.

"How about you answer your cell first." As much as I wanted a round three…and four, my lady bits needed a bit of a break. Conner was a big man all over, and my hoo-ha was still sensitive from rounds one and two.

Conner made a teasing sound of frustration and rolled over to get his phone. I curled up on his thigh as he sat up to answer, his half-woodie just inches from my face. I couldn't resist the man.

"Down, girl," he snickered as I licked him from balls to tip and deep-throated him in one go. With him only half erect, it was much easier to take him in. When he was fully hard, forget about it.

I chuckled and gave his tip one more lick before I sat up with him, pulling a throw blanket up over us to help hide temptation.

Conner shook his head as he answered the phone. "Hey, Phil."

I had met Phil a couple times. He was the owner of *Ape Hangers* and had been giving Conner a hand with moving all our stuff in and getting the house finished. He was a huge, scary, tattooed man with a shaved head and a graying beard, but he was the biggest goof. He reminded me of Terry Crews, but with tattoos everywhere.

I couldn't hear what Phil was saying, but I took the look of shock and happiness on Conner's face to be a good sign.

"Hold on, let me check." He turned his cell away from his face and smiled at me. "Ian's wife just had the baby."

Ian was one of the bouncers at *The Ape Hanger*. His wife was getting close to her due date, and Conner had offered to cover a couple of his shifts so he could be with her and their new baby. We had been waiting for this call.

"That's amazing. Does Phil need you tonight or tomorrow?"

"Ian was mid-shift when he got the call from Janet that her water broke, so it'll only be like four hours tonight and then tomorrow. He had the rest of the week booked off anyway."

I waved my hand at him, shooing him out of bed. "Go, go," I encouraged, getting out of bed with him and following him into the walk-in closet.

"Sure, Phil, I'll be there in 30."

Conner was driving down the laneway not 15 minutes later, leaving me hot and needy after the passionate kiss he gave me at the door. That man was going to be the death of me and my vagina.

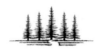

Kate: I don't accept that. Get your ass over here.

Brie: We miss you, Addy. We haven't seen you in weeks.

Addy: I know. I miss you, ladies, too, but things are crazy here. With the house, trying to catch up on my writing for the paper after the trip and just getting back from helping my family on the farm, I haven't had time to breathe.

It was a complete lie. All of it was, and I felt like the worst person alive for lying to the girls. Conner and I had decided when the Mitchell Erbing fiasco started, and we went to the Toronto PD Headquarters that first night to try and keep as many people out of the know as possible. If Mitchell was willing to threaten me to get to Conner, we had no doubt that he would go after people we knew if he didn't get what he wanted. Hell, he had already threatened Conner with harming his parents. The man clearly knew no bounds.

Conner had told the guys, and I had told the girls that we were going on a vacation, then that we were at my parent's farm helping out because my dad was injured and then that we were spending all our time at the new house because we wanted to finish it together. The lies kept building, but we didn't know what else to do.

Tasha: That sounds like a great reason to come over for some wine and smut. I don't care if you haven't even read the book. We just want to see you.

Jess: Exactly. Plus, the book Brie picked this week was crap anyway. We'll probably just be harassing Kate for more details about the Kate/Max/lover #2/lover #3 bombshell she dropped last week while you were away. I KNOW you don't want to miss out on that. Apparently, piercings are involved.

Brie: HEY! The book wasn't crap. It was just different from what we were used to reading. I thought I'd introduce you ladies to a different perspective.

Jess: Like whips and chains and submitting to a man??? No way. I'm not bowing before any man and giving him all the power.

Kate: Don't knock it until you try it 😏

Tasha: Fuck no! You let Max tie you up?

Kate: 😏

Tasha: KATE!!!!!

Brie: How's the book coming along, Addy?

Leave it to Brie to change the subject in an attempt to keep the peace.

Addy: I actually haven't written anything in a long time. I've just been too busy.

Jess: But it sounded so cool when you told us about it.

Kate: Prison sex, married man, the scandal of it all...mmmmm, sounds delicious.

Tasha: Seriously, Kate, what is wrong with you?!?!

The texts between the girls went on, and tears filled my eyes. I missed them. They were so much fun and lived life how they wanted. They were the breath of fresh air that I needed in my life, and it was torture having to lie to them. But we needed to keep them and the guys safe. At least until Kyle was found. I couldn't have their lives on my conscience if anything ever happened to them.

And somewhere in the bottom of my gut, I had a feeling that the more people I had in my life, the worse *their* lives were going to end up. My gut was telling me that this wasn't even close to being over and that the worst was yet to come. That danger was out there, watching us, just waiting for the perfect moment to strike. I was not going to hold our friends' lives in my hands and decide whose life I could put at risk of getting hit in the crossfire. This was between Kyle, Mitchell, Conner, and myself, and we were going to try and keep it that way for as long as possible...we hoped.

Chapter 37

Tim…Tim, Tim, Tim, Tim.

After texting with the girls, I decided to take another crack at the story I had started writing months ago. Sadly, it hadn't been touched since Kyle broke into my house and our lives went into a tailspin of chaos. Being in hiding and being scared for your life didn't really lend to a productive and creative environment. But the story of Mary/Kathy/June - I hadn't decided on the main character's name yet - and her love for her neighbour Tim, who was arrested for the murder of his wife, had been dancing around my head lately. Maybe it had been all the time I had spent at the Toronto Police Headquarters.

I knew a couple things about the story, but I didn't know how to get from point A to point B. I knew it was going to be a happy ending, I knew I wanted super smutty but with action in it, and I knew I wanted to call Tim's innocence into question, making the reader guess until the very end, but I didn't know how to get from where I was to where I wanted to be. How did I make my main character fall in love with a married man, still be in love with him while he was in jail and not make her seem like the villain or desperate or a prison groupie?

Instead of stressing over a linear timeline and what to write next, I just thought of what scenes I wanted in the story and started making notes.

- Conjugal visit
- Flirting behind wife's back
- Wife has a stroke and is on bed rest
- Main character goes over to help Tim as much as possible
- She goes over one day, she catches him jerking off in the shower, and he whispers her name
- They never kiss, never cross the line
- He admits that he wants her but can't divorce his wife. He still loves her, but he has feelings for 'main character' too
- Flirty touches at backyard BBQ
- They write letters to each other while he's in jail, and they become dirty letters about all the things he's dreamed of doing to her over the years. How he always looked out the window to see if he could see

her, how he would see her gardening and want to just throw her on the ground, how he worried about her in the house all by herself

- Hug too long and too tight to just be a friendly hello
- Main character is actually friends with the wife and is jealous when neighbour tells her stories about Tim
- Tim is arrested, and all he does is yell over to main character that it wasn't him
- Pills/drugs???? How does she die?
- Police investigate and find more and more evidence to prove he killed her

Evidence, something they lacked when it came to Kyle. There was no way to prove that he was the one to send the emails as *The Neighbourhood Watcher,* but Anders, Conner, and I knew it was him. But how did we prove it?

I sat, staring out my office window into the forest behind us and the small lazy creek. The property was beautiful, and I could see myself growing old here with Conner if we lasted that long. With Kyle in the wind and who knew what was going on with Mitchell, it wasn't a guarantee that I would get a happy ending or get to grow old with Conner. People were after us, and neither of us was really equipped to deal with it. Neither of us was a violent person who would be able to defend ourselves if we needed to. We didn't know how to shoot a gun or even have a gun. And we weren't investigators. We didn't have resources at our disposal. All we had was the knowledge of what had taken place and Anders, who trusted us.

One thing Anders said at the station the other day popped back into my head.

"Okay, start from the beginning. How does this person contact you? What's their name and email address? And let's start a list of everything you have in common with these letters."

Start from the beginning…start a list.

I closed my story down, saved the notes I made, and opened up a new Word document. I needed to start from the beginning and make a list of anything that could prove useful. I knew things were probably going to be out of order, but I needed to get everything down regardless.

- Met Kyle when I moved in. He was at my side the moment I tripped and fell. He ran up and grabbed a first aid kit from his place and bandaged my hand up. Said he used to get a lot of injuries from soccer, or hockey, or football or something

- I invited him over first, and he was flirty right away. Football, pizza and beer Thursday became a thing

- Always at my place, had never stepped foot in his home

- Make out after painting room, then next day, he barged in and threw me against the wall, kissing and groping. Very intense and dominant

- Walked to *Ape Hangers* for our "date night" after he won thousands on a football game

- Gambling. High-stakes gambling. Started to become cocky and arrogant. Kept going up to the waitress to get more drinks and kept eying the dancer
- Let himself into my home twice
- Blew up at me for Alex coming over at Christmas – was he watching the driveway or watching my front door?
- Came over to apologize for acting off and coming off as abrasive – gave him a second chance
- Went out to *Rollies* for our date – got drunk and handsy
- Invited me to New Year's in Toronto
- Showed up drunk the next morning
- Guy banging on my door
- Kyle stomping and yelling upstairs
- Kyle freaking out in the parking lot and then was sombre and defeated when I talked to him on the porch – said it was work
- Incident with my car
- The break-in and cop knew who he was

The cop knew who he was. How did the cop know? What other and how many other charges had been laid on Kyle that a cop would know him by name? Conner had said that Kyle almost got evicted because of the noise, rowdiness and cops showing up, but Conner said he only saw him get taken away in cuffs once. One time in a cop car wouldn't make the cops know you by name. There was way more to Kyle's history that I didn't know, especially how he was connected to Mitchell. We just knew from Harper that they were "associates" and that Harper assumed I was Mitchell's next mark.

But everything was an assumption at this point. We didn't know anything definite, and millions of questions were running through my mind. How were Kyle and Mitchell connected? Were Kyle and Mitchell actually two separate issues that were connected but not? Was Kyle breaking into my place not actually connected to Mitchell and the video cameras? Did Mitchell have another way of getting the pictures of Conner and me? Were Kyle and Mitchell really just associates and didn't actually work together?

I was thinking of so many different questions; it was like a snowball rolling down a hill, collecting more and more snow as it went, getting bigger and bigger. I'd think of one question, and that would spur another one to pop into my mind to the point that my brain wouldn't stop turning. My brain was in complete chaos and didn't know up from down. I wasn't even sure what was true anymore. There was so much information floating around my head I was starting to second-guess everything.

Conner and I had assumed that Kyle was connected to and working for Mitchell because Harper had said a number of the scam calls I got were from numbers registered to Kyle and that Kyle was known to the RCMP and the ERT, but were we right to assume that him breaking into my place was how the video cameras were set up and how Mitchell was able to watch us? What if it wasn't? What if Kyle was there for a different reason, and Mitchell had someone else break in and install the cameras, and we never knew it?

But they had to be connected. They just had to be. I wasn't unlucky enough to have two different criminals after me. What was their connection? What was I not seeing?

All of a sudden, the phone conversation I overheard Kyle having on the front porch with his boss after he freaked out in the parking lot came to mind. *"...this one's different, boss...if we make this acquisition, I don't think I'll be able to sell it off in the end. It's too valuable."*

Had he been on the phone with Mitchell? Had he been talking about me? Was I the acquisition that was too valuable?

I felt like I was going to throw up. All I knew for sure from Harper was that Kyle and Mitchell knew each other; a couple of the numbers that had called me with no one on the other end of the line were registered to Kyle, and Harper believed Mitchell had his eye on me. That didn't mean Kyle was involved, though...did it?

"Hey, Cricket," Conner smiled as he came over and placed a kiss on my head. "What are you doing?"

"I'm trying to look for something I missed."

"What do you mean?"

I pushed away from the computer desk to face Conner and stretched my aching back. "With Kyle. Something that I missed that could tie him to the emails. Something that's hard evidence that he's behind all this."

"He's not, Addy. Mitchell is."

"I know that, but Kyle's the one that's out and free and…"

"Addy, you have to stop."

"Stop what?"

"You have to stop this. Stop obsessing over Kyle."

"I'm not obsessing."

"Yes, you are."

"Conner – "

"Have you had dinner tonight?"

I turned back to my desk and held up my spoon that was stuck in the jar of peanut butter that sat beside my empty bottle of water.

"That's my point," he chided. "You're not eating. You're not sleeping."

"Yes, I am." I was starting to sound like a teenager contradicting their parents.

"No, Addy, you're not." Conner grabbed my hand and led me to the couch we had against the opposite wall from my desk. "Not since Mitchell attacked you. And it's understandable, but you're hurting yourself."

"No, I'm not. I'm just making sure I haven't left anything out. Our lives are at risk here, Conner, and I'm going to do whatever I can to keep us safe."

"You talk in your sleep." I was so taken aback that I wasn't able to formulate words. I just shook my head in denial.

"You do, Addy, and you have ever since the break-in. It's not every night, but at least once a week you start whimpering, tossing and turning, and crying out 'no' and for Kyle to leave you alone. You're obsessing."

"I...I..." I had no idea what to say to that. Clearly, I didn't know that I talked in my sleep. Conner had never mentioned it before. But he was getting irritated...and with me. All I wanted to do was make sure I hadn't forgotten anything important, and he was getting annoyed at me because of it.

"Conner, I'm not obsessing," I pressed, trying really hard not to get mad at him for caring about my well-being, "I'm trying to be thorough."

Conner got up and went to my desk. "Love, there's being thorough, and then there's trying to write a transcript of every conversation and interaction you've had with someone over the past six months." He scrolled through the pages of information I had on my computer and shook his head. "You have to give this a rest. I'm worried about you."

"And I appreciate that, but I'm not going to sit around helplessly and do nothing." I got up and tried to calmly walk out of the room. "I'll give it a rest when Kyle is in jail with Mitchell, and we're safe."

That was the first night that Conner and I slept in separate beds since we'd gotten together.

Chapter 38

I had only lasted one day in the guest room before I crawled back into our bed, but the distance between Conner and I could have been an ocean. He was right. I couldn't turn my brain off. For the next three days, all I could do was think and overthink and, yes, obsess over every little detail. I hadn't gotten any sleep at all. It was to the point where I was more concerned about Kyle than I was about Mitchell.

Kyle had a personal connection to me; we had been friends. He had been in my home, and I had opened up to him about Alex and my family and my life. I had been vulnerable with him, open with him. He was my first friend after the divorce. To find out that he had been connected to Mitchell and was now out with his whereabouts unknown, I couldn't handle it.

Mitchell was on Harper's radar, and the Emergency Response Team had eyes on his crew and their goings-on, but Kyle was in the wind, and our relationship had been too close for comfort.

When Conner came into the kitchen on day three of our 'fight' and saw me with bags under my eyes and my eyelids drooping at the kitchen island, the worry in his eyes almost killed me. He was still angry at me for refusing to let this go, but his concern for me was at the forefront.

"Love, you need to sleep. Go take a nap." Little did he know that it didn't matter if I was awake or asleep. My brain just kept working.

"I can't," I whispered, emotions clogging up my throat. "I can't turn my brain off. I can't just do nothing and just wait for the next attack to come. How can you just sit there and not worry?"

"I'm not just sitting here, Addy. I'm moving on. I'm taking my life back and showing Mitchell that he doesn't control me. I'm not giving him or Kyle any more power over our lives." He made his way over to my side of the island and wrapped his arms around me from behind, lightly kissing my shoulder. "I refuse to live my life being afraid. That's not a life, Addy."

I leaned back against his chest, his strong arms comforting me. A tear leaked out of my eye, the build-up of exhaustion and fear finally getting the better of me.

"Come on," he pleaded as he picked me up and carried me to our bed. "Just lay with me for a bit and try to sleep."

Conner held me tight to his body, his arms wrapped around me, giving me comfort and support. Silent tears fell from my eyes onto his chest as I prayed for my mind and body to just let me sleep. And for the first time in three days, my brain allowed me to rest. All the details didn't matter anymore. We knew that Kyle and Mitchell worked together. In all honesty, the how and why didn't matter. All that mattered was that Conner and I stayed safe.

Addy: Happy Birthday, Alex. Hope you have a fantastic day. Miss you. Love you.

I looked at the string of texts that I had sent Alex over the past couple of weeks, and my heart sank. Not a single reply. I knew things were different between us; he had started seeing someone, and I had Conner, but we still kept in touch. We were still friends; at least, I thought so. I knew that the texts and phone calls would dwindle off eventually, and we would no longer talk every couple of days, but to go a month without hearing from him, especially when I had reached out a bunch of times, was odd.

I hit the call button on my phone, and it immediately went to voicemail.

"You've reached Alexander Adams. Sorry, I can't come to the phone right now. Please leave a message, and I'll call you back as soon as I can. Thank you." BEEP.

"Hey Alex, it's me. Happy Birthday. I'm just checking in. I haven't heard from you in a while. I hope everything's okay. Call or text me back, please...I miss you."

After I hung up, I looked through my phone. Three calls out, none returned, and seven texts unanswered. I was starting to feel like a stage five clinger refusing to let go of the guy she was interested in. But I knew Alex. I had nine years of history with him, and although people did change, he was someone who was religious about checking messages and getting back to people. He considered it rude otherwise. Something wasn't right.

"Conner," I called as I made my way into the kitchen to grab the keys to the truck. I had sold my SUV after the Mitchell attack since both he and Kyle knew our vehicles. The police still held Conner's truck as evidence, and even if it was released, we'd sell it right away. We were getting by using the old GMC that had been in storage.

"What's up?"

I turned around to see him coming in from the front door, where he was working on the railing for our wrap-around deck.

"I'm heading into town to check on Alex. Something's wrong."

"What do you mean?"

"I've sent him a bunch of texts and phone calls, and he hasn't answered any of them. I'm starting to worry. I just want to go and check that he's okay."

"Have you tried calling his girlfriend or his work number?"

"I don't have Jenny's number." I scrolled through my contacts and found his work number. I called, but again, he didn't pick up. A painful thought came to my mind. What if he didn't want anything to do with me anymore? I knew being divorced would separate us, but I, maybe naively, always thought he'd still be in my life. Was he ignoring me on purpose?

Wanting to test my theory, I held out my hand and asked Conner to pass me his phone. He looked at me with confusion but handed it over anyway.

I called Alex at work again, but with Conner's phone, just to see if my suspicions were correct.

"Alexander Adams," he greeted with a cheerful welcome.

"Alex, it's me," I sighed, glad he was alive and okay but pissed he was now clearly dodging my calls and texts. "Are you okay?"

There was a pause before he responded with a clipped "Yes." I looked at Conner, and when he mouthed, "What's going on?" I immediately hit the speakerphone button, so Conner could hear the conversation.

"What's going on?" I pressed, cautious of the distance he created, as soon as he knew it was me. "I've been texting you for weeks with no answer, and I just called twice, and you sent me to your voicemail both times."

His only response was a soft "Uh-huh." I was completely thrown by the disinterest and clipped tone of his voice. I could tell Conner was confused, too, as this wasn't the Alex that he had heard me talk about.

"Alex…"

"Look, Addy, you either want to talk to me or you don't. You can't send your boyfriend over to rough me up, telling him that I won't let you go and won't leave you alone, and then continue to text and call me."

My eyes flew to Conner, the question burning clear in my gaze.

"Wasn't me," he defended, hands risen and shaking his head.

"Alex," I pressed, "what are you talking about?"

"Your boyfriend showed up at my office one night and caught me when I was getting in my car. He beat the shit out of me, telling me to leave you alone, that you were his, and if I didn't stop talking to you, he'd put me in the hospital next time."

"I swear to God, Addy," Conner pled, looking paranoid and confused, "it wasn't me."

"What did the guy look like?" I waited for Alex to answer, afraid I already knew what he was going to say.

"It was the blond guy that lives above you. I recognized him from when I came over to help you set up your new place."

Kyle. I fucking knew it.

"Alex," Conner jumped in, "it's Conner, Addy's actual boyfriend. Listen," he pulled out his wallet and grabbed a card, "Kyle's dangerous and has been stalking Adeline since she moved in. He vandalized her car, broke into her place, put cameras throughout her house to spy on her and is connected to some really dangerous criminal rings in Toronto."

He showed me the card he pulled out, the one with Det. Sgt. Anders's name and number on it. I nodded, agreeing that we needed to keep Alex safe.

"Kyle got arrested for being part of Addy's attack and just made bail a couple weeks ago," he continued.

"What attack?!" Alex bellowed.

"The guy Kyle works for deals in human trafficking," I explained. "He came to my house with a couple of his goons and roughed me up a bit. I'm fine, and I went to the police, and Kyle got arrested."

"Addy, why didn't you tell me?"

"Because you haven't been returning my calls or texts!" I was exasperated with this whole situation, but it looked like Alex was now involved. I understood why he pulled back, Kyle threatening him and all, but he needed to be careful. He was now one of Kyle's targets.

"When did he approach you?" Conner asked.

"About five weeks ago."

I turn to Conner. "That was right before the attack."

"Do you have a pen?" At Alex's confirmation, Conner continued. "You need to call this number and ask for a Det. Sgt. Anders. He's the Police Sergeant who's been helping Addy and me with Kyle and Mitchell."

"Who's Mitchell? Is there more going on?"

I looked into Conner's concerned eyes as he nodded his head. He'd been getting really good at reading my looks lately, and it was clear he knew exactly what I was thinking.

"Maybe you should come over tonight," I offered. "There's been a lot going on, and if Kyle knows who you are and where you work, there's some stuff you need to know."

Chapter 39

"So, this is all your fault."

As much as I had hoped that Alex and Conner were going to become friends down the road, the death glare Alex was shooting Conner's way was a clear indication that that wasn't going to happen anytime soon.

"Alex, that's not fair," I protested, at the same time as Conner gave a solemn "Yes." My head snapped to Conner, and I could have punched him.

"This is not your fault! Mitchell is a freakin criminal mastermind who threatened you as a child and attacked me to try and get you to do work for him. If it wasn't for you and your plan, we'd probably both be dead by now, so quit this 'my fault' bullshit!"

I was exhausted. Alex had come over about two hours ago, and we had been sitting in the living room going over the whole Kyle/Mitchell/Conner story since he arrived. Conner wasn't happy about revealing his connection to Canada's most wanted human trafficker, but we both understood that Alex was now part of this and needed to be made aware of what was going on.

"It's true, Addy," Conner rebutted. "If it weren't for my past, Mitchell would have no connection to you or Alex."

"True," Alex unhelpfully chimed in. I shot him a "shut up" look in return.

"Regardless," I said to both of them, "he's in our lives now, and we all need to be careful. I don't think Mitchell is after me specifically. If he wanted me, he would have taken me when he attacked me at the house, so Kyle's threat to you," I looked pointedly back at Alex, "seems to be Kyle acting on his own."

"So, what do we do?" Alex asked.

"We don't know." It was the truth, as depressing as it was.

"Have you called Det. Sgt. Anders yet?" Conner asked.

"No," Alex answered, taking a swig of his beer, "I came right over as soon as we hung up."

"I think maybe it's time to give him a call."

Alex called Det. Sgt. Anders and told him the situation. Almost immediately, Alex put the call on speakerphone.

"Okay, they're on." Alex put the phone on the coffee table between us, and we all leaned in.

"Ms. Peters, Mr. Jensen, I have some not-so-good news to share and thought it might be prudent to let all three of you know at once since it seems like Mr. Martin's behaviour has become more reckless. Mr. Erbing is free."

"WHAT?!" Conner roared as he bolted from the couch.

"Superintendent Harper called me this morning to advise that the person they had detained and who was being held in the infirmary was not Mitchell Erbing but one of his associates."

"You've got to be fucking kidding me. Why didn't Harper call us? And how the FUCK did he mistake Mitchell for one of his flunkies?" Conner was pacing back and forth, and I sat there in shock. My hand shook as I reached out for Conner. Mitchell was free and had been out this whole time. He could have been watching us for weeks, watched them pull the protective detail off us.

Conner turned around when he felt my hand on his leg and rejoined me on the couch, pulling me close to his side.

"Turns out that the associate they arrested had gone through facial reconstruction to look like Mr. Erbing as retaliation for a bad deal and then was left for us to pick up. The arresting officers thought the swelling and cuts were a result of Mr. Erbing's fallout with their informant. As for Superintendent Harper, I'm not at liberty to divulge any information about his ERT, the work of the RCMP, his decisions, his agenda, or the case. All I know is that Mr. Erbing is on the loose, and they've lost his trail again."

The frustration in Det. Sgt. Anders's voice was as clear as day. We knew his hands were tied in regard to Mitchell. All he could do was help us on the Kyle front. But the two were connected, and I was honestly grateful that he was keeping us in the loop at all.

"So, what do we do?" I asked, my voice as shaky as my limbs.

"For right now, just keep watching out for each other and call in whenever something new pops up. It's up to Superintendent Harper if he wants to put a protective detail on you again, but seeing as he didn't even let you know about Mr. Erbing, I wouldn't count on it. You can always hire personal security, but it might draw attention to yourselves, but that's up to you and how safe you feel."

"Knowing our luck, if we hired security, they'd probably end up working for Mitchell anyway," I mumbled.

"That is a possibility, yes." Det. Sgt. Anders replied. The helplessness in his voice showed how much his hands were tied. Kyle was in the wind, and there was no evidence besides hearsay to prove that he was stalking me through the paper or had attacked Alex. And Mitchell was free, assigned to a useless specialized team who arrested the wrong man a month ago and just found out that the real villain had been out this whole time.

After a few more words and a sincere "good luck" from Det. Sgt. Anders, Alex disconnected the call and looked at us with worried eyes.

"I'm sorry you've been going through this, Addy."

"Me, too," Conner whispered against the top of my head.

"I gotta go," Alex said, worry in his voice. "I need to go check on Jenny."

That night, Conner and I went to bed, the camping knife in his nightstand and a baseball bat beside mine. It was time we became prepared for the worst.

"Here."

Conner came into the gym, where I was trying my hardest not to get beat by the punching bag. Every day, Conner and I trained together, going over self-defence, fighting, escaping, and just general stamina and muscle building. He didn't need it, but I for sure did. I had never been athletic or coordinated, and if someone had decided to chase me, all I would have been able to do was throw my shoe at them and hope I didn't trip when I ran away. But now, I was starting to feel like I had some skills. Not enough to fight back and save my life, but maybe enough to get away and hide until help came.

"What's this?" I ripped off the navy blue and pink boxing gloves Conner had gotten me with my teeth and shook them off my hands.

Conner was holding a small gift bag out for me to take but didn't say anything. I sat down on the weight bench, guzzled half a water bottle and opened the bag. Inside were three small packages: one in a clear baggie and two in small boxes.

I put the gift bag between my legs and picked up the baggie to open it. It was a silver ring with a flower on top.

"Pretty," I smiled up at Conner as I fit it to the middle finger on my right hand.

"Turn the rose."

I looked up at Conner in confusion before I tried to turn the top of the ring. It was tight, but after a good twist, it started to turn and came right off. Under the flower was a tiny blade that stood straight up, no bigger than the post on an earring.

"What the —"

"It's a self-defence ring," he explained. "It's time we take your safety seriously."

The joyfulness of receiving gifts and a beautiful flower ring disappeared with the seriousness of the gift. I screwed the flower top back on so I didn't stab myself and quickly grabbed the remaining items out of the bag.

The second thing was a safety keychain where if you removed the top, a high-frequency alarm would sound. I learned that the hard way before Conner took the thing from me and replaced the pin to silence the alarm.

"Damn, that's loud." I rubbed my ear, trying to get the ringing to stop.

"That's the point," Conner chuckled as he tossed the keychain back in the gift bag.

The last box I pulled out was a pair of connection bracelets. I had seen them all over Amazon. If one person touched the face of the bracelet, the other person's bracelet would light up and vibrate. They looked just like a small Fitbit.

"These are nice, but are you planning on going somewhere?" The bracelets were meant to connect you with your loved one when they were far away, and by him giving them to me, along with self-defence items, I was worried that Conner was planning on hunting down Mitchell on his own or something.

"No, I'm not going anywhere. I just thought that if one of us were ever in trouble, it would be a way to signal to the other they needed help."

"You're starting to worry about Kyle and Mitchell, huh?"

"Not worry, but I want you to be protected as much as possible. Kyle and Mitchell are sneaky bastards. They've gotten away from the police and Harper. Who knows what they have going on, or even if we're still on their radar, but I'd rather be safe than sorry."

I stood up and wrapped my arms around Conner's neck, bringing him in for a gentle kiss. "Me too. Thank you for all this."

He took the bracelets from the box, secured one to my left wrist, and then put the other on his wrist. "Never take these off." He squeezed my right hand to indicate the ring as well as the bracelet.

"I promise."

Conner had another short shift at *Ape Hangers* and left just before dinner. I still wasn't comfortable being in the house by myself, especially knowing that both Kyle and Mitchell were out there, but Conner was right. We couldn't keep living our lives in fear. It only gave them more power. So, as hard as it was, my goal for the evening was to try and forget that our lives were in danger and start to finish up some projects I was working on in the house.

The house was almost completely finished. In the time we had been living here, Conner had made finishing the inside his full-time job and was teaching me along the way. I no longer just handed him tools but actually helped him put the house together.

Almost everything was done, and so far, it was beautiful, with an amazing combination of rustic and modern. Both the kitchen and living room had an amazing mixture of clean white and natural wood and stone. The flooring throughout the entire house was hardwood laminate and just made the house feel like a hidden cottage in the woods, which technically it was.

The kitchen, bathrooms and laundry room had all their appliances in them, and all cabinets, countertops and vanities were installed. The walls were painted, floor trim installed, and the furniture Conner had ordered had started to arrive. All the main construction work was done. All that was left was simple things like hanging the lighting fixtures, putting the hardware on the kitchen cupboards, putting all the covers on the electrical and lighting outlets, assembling some of the furniture, hanging up the curtains and blinds, and hanging the doors to the bedrooms, closets and bathrooms. And those were some of my tasks for the night.

I started in the front of the house, hanging up the curtain rods, sheers, and the rich brown curtains we had purchased in the living room windows, then the wide wood slat blinds we had custom ordered for the kitchen. It was once I got into the master bedroom I ran into some issues. And by some issues, I meant the feeling that I was being watched.

Chapter 40

I knew I had been over-cautious and paranoid since the whole Kyle/Mitchell disaster started, but this felt different. This felt similar to when someone was standing behind you, and you felt a presence in the room. Goosebumps littered my skin, and the hair on my arms stood on end. This wasn't me overreacting; this was my body registering a warning.

The sun had set, and the backyard was dark, but the solar patio lights illuminated the property enough that I could see the first row of trees. And that was where I saw the slightest movement. I bolted for the bedroom lights and slammed them off before I went back to the French doors that led out onto the back deck. I tried to look out to see if I could see anything and prayed the dark bedroom kept me hidden.

"You live in the middle of nowhere," I told myself, trying to rationalize what was going on. "There are animals out there that could be moving the trees." But the feeling of being watched wouldn't go away. I kept my eyes locked on the spot where the middle of the tree line shook again.

The strange and scary part was that, although the trees were so packed tightly together that if one moved, the surrounding trees usually did as well, the movement I just saw was only from one tree. Something was moving the branches about six feet up, and it wasn't the wind.

I reached into my back pocket to grab my cell, but it wasn't there. I had left it in the living room, streaming music throughout the house.

"Fuck," I whispered, debating if I should go grab it or keep watch out back. The decision was made for me when the tree shook again, and a figure slowly stepped out of the tree line.

Panic flooded my body as I pressed my back to the wall and moved away from the French doors. "Holy shit," I panted, terror taking over. I knew I had seen something moving in the trees, and it was DEFINITELY not a fox or a squirrel. I slowly turned and looked back out the door but kept my body hidden. If I had seen them, they could have seen me.

"Please be a bear, please be a bear…" I chanted over and over as I looked out. There, at the edge of the tree line, stood a person staring at the house, just standing still. They were still covered in shadows, just barely in the scope of the patio lights, but I was able to see that it for sure wasn't an animal. It was a person.

I whipped my head away from the door, pressing my body back against the wall, unsure what I should do. If I ran for my phone, whoever was out there would see me through the glass doors. Plus, all the lights were on in the living room, pretty much putting a spotlight on me.

I looked around the bedroom in hopes of finding something that could help. We didn't have a landline in the house; my laptop was up in my office, and Conner had his phone with him. The only thing I saw that could potentially help was the bat that sat beside my bed. It wouldn't help me call for help, but I grabbed it anyway, arming myself just in case. I had to make a run for my phone and hope the person outside didn't see me and come charging into the house. I didn't even know if all the doors were locked.

I did one more scan of the room as I slowly shimmied across the wall, farther away from the doors, and across the bed towards the bedroom door, when I saw the gift bag Conner had given me sitting on the chair in the corner. *The connection bracelet!* I looked down at my wrist, having forgotten I was even wearing it, and pressed the top button over and over, hoping it would signal Conner. But nothing happened. I tried again and again, cursing the damn thing, but it wouldn't turn on. It couldn't connect.

"Fucking piece of shit." I refused to cry as pure fear and frustration took over. I had to get my phone.

I took one more peek out the door, the figure still standing exactly where they were before, and bolted to the living room. Once I was about 10 feet away from my phone, my wrist vibrated, and not five seconds later, my phone started ringing. I grabbed it as I ran past the coffee table, not bothering to slow down as I ran to the front door to double-check it was locked.

"Help!" I yelled as I answered the phone. I didn't see or care who was calling; I just needed help.

"I'm two minutes down the road. What happened?" Conner's voice hurried through the phone, concern taking over his normal calm tone.

"There's someone in the backyard." I ran back into the bedroom and back over to the French doors, double-checking they were locked, too. The person still stood there, right at the tree line and just looked at the house. I couldn't tell if they were looking in at me or if they were scoping out the house, but I didn't care anymore. I had the bat in one hand, Conner on the phone in the other, and he was just pulling up the laneway if the sound of rocks hitting metal in the background of the call was any indication.

"I'm almost there, Love, just hold on."

"I'm not going anywhere." I stared down the person and refused to cower in the corner. If I saw them lift an arm as if to point or saw a red scope light, I'd have ducked for cover, but until then, I was keeping my eye on them.

Seconds later, the person simply backed up into the trees, not bothering to turn around and run. The truck lights lit up the backyard as Conner's body came running around the house. I hung up the phone and shoved it in my back pocket before I threw the doors open.

"They just ran back into the trees," I called as I joined Conner outside.

"Get back in the house!"

"I don't think so! If you're out here risking your life, so am I!" Plus, if the person had a gun and was going to shoot me, they would have done it already.

I ran down the back deck and joined Conner on the back lawn.

"They were over there." I pointed to the bank of trees right beside the creek.

We ran over, Conner, of course, beating me there and insisting I stay behind him, and stopped at the tree line. He bent down, looking at something on the ground before turning on the flashlight on the cell in his hand. But instead of looking into the trees like I thought he would, he had the phone aimed at the ground, right over a set of footprints.

"Call Anders." Conner flipped off the flashlight and started taking pictures of the footprints. He followed them just to inside the tree line and then came back out.

"There's no answer." I ended the call as Det. Sgt. Anders's voicemail kicked in. It was already 9 p.m., so it didn't surprise me when I got the voicemail, but it made me wonder if I should call 911 or the Toronto Police Headquarters and have them get in contact with Anders themselves.

"Hi, this is Conner Jensen. I need to speak to Det. Sgt. Anders immediately." I looked up to see Conner with the phone to his ear. "Headquarters," he whispered, reading my mind once again. I nodded as I looked down at the footprints and followed the trail just like Conner had. "We've had an incident at the house and need to speak to him right away. It's an investigation he's working on…thank you."

Conner turned his flashlight on and joined me at the edge of the tree line. "They're going to call him at home and have him call us back." I just nodded as I looked around, shining my light everywhere I could, praying I didn't find a pair of eyes looking back at me.

"Did you see who it was?"

"No, it was just a figure with a hood over their head. At least that's what it looked like. They were barely in the light from the porch, so they were pretty much just a shadowy figure, but I felt like someone was staring at me as soon as I got into the bedroom."

"Come on." Conner grabbed my hand and pulled me back towards the house. "Let's go get some things from inside so that we can keep watch while we wait for Anders to call. I don't want you out here alone. We have footprints, and I don't want anyone coming back trying to erase them."

Thank God we lived in the middle of nowhere, or else the flashing lights would have pissed off all our neighbours. Det. Sgt. Anders had called us back within five minutes and said he would contact Hennington OPP to get someone to come out and secure the scene until he got here.

Conner and I had waited outside in the backyard to make sure no one would come back to erase the footprints that were there. We stood back-to-back; Conner watched the tree line while I watched the house and laneway, both of us with flashlights in our hands. My bat and Conner's camping axe sat at our feet. I was going to protect this evidence if I had to lay my body on top of it and shield it myself.

It took twenty minutes before the first police car showed up. When I told them what happened and they saw the footprint going into the trees, they immediately called another car for backup. I guess Hennington OPP knew who Kyle Martin and Mitchell Erbing were and didn't want to take chances either.

Our backyard was lit up like a stadium, with police lights flashing, headlights beaming around the property, and the police car's spotlights pointed into the trees. Two officers circled the property while two sat inside with us to take an official statement.

"So, you have no proof it was Mr. Martin or Mr. Erbing." The young female cop was curt but wasn't rude or arrogant. She was cut and dry, the give-me-the-details type, and I appreciated that. Facts I could stick to without getting emotional, but facts required evidence, which we didn't have.

"No, I didn't see who it was, just a tall person, medium build."

"But you're assuming it was Mr. Martin or Mr. Erbing?"

Conner returned to the kitchen table and brought the two officers cups of coffee and me a glass of water. "Kyle has been stalking Adeline for over six months," Conner started as he sat down beside me. "We've been working closely with Det. Sgt. Anders from Toronto PD for about a month and a half now as more and more stuff has popped up."

"What stuff?" The second officer was an older gentleman with kind but assessing eyes. He had been quietly watching so far but piped in every now and then when something piqued his curiosity.

"Why don't you grab your laptop and show them the list?" I looked at Conner and felt like a complete moron. The list. Of course. The damn list that I had made about my history with Kyle.

I was out of my chair in a flash and ran up the stairs to my office. I could hear Officer Two asking, "What list?" in the distance.

"Adeline was getting frustrated that whenever something new happened, we'd take it to Det. Sgt. Anders but there was never any concrete evidence that would legally allow him to go after Kyle. Everything was always hearsay."

I rejoined them at the table and turned my computer to them. "I've been working on a list of my history with Kyle, hoping that something would click or act as proof that he's been behind everything."

"He was your neighbour," the female cop started, perusing the document out loud, "hit on you... broke into your home... vandalized your car... beat up your ex... stalked you through your paper? What does that last one mean?"

"I write the advice column for *The Hennington Hound* and recently discovered that Kyle had been writing in pieces to me that were all related to things that were going on in my life." There was a knock on the door before the handle turned, and Det. Sgt. Anders poked his head in. I had never been so happy to see that man in my life.

"Mr. Jensen," he nodded, and he shook Conner's hand when Conner got up to greet him. "Ms. Peters. You both okay?"

"Shaken up a bit," Conner answered as he welcomed Anders into the house, "but we're okay."

"Good to hear." He turned to the two officers and introduced himself. "Inspector Anders, Toronto PD." He shook both officers' hands.

"Inspector?" I asked, happy for the man who had been trying to help us. "You got a promotion?"

"I did." A smile barely touched his lips, but it was there. "It's been in the works for a while, but I refused to give up this case. The Chief of Police finally agreed to my condition that I remain the point person on the Martin/Erbing file."

"Congratulations…and thank you," I said with complete sincerity. He believed us and wasn't giving up on us. We had someone going to bat for us in our corner. Anders was a good cop, and it was a relief that someone else wouldn't be taking over our situation. Anders just nodded and took a seat at the end of the table.

"So, catch me up." The officers told Anders what they'd seen outside on their preliminary search, and I explained what had happened and showed him the list of my interactions with Kyle. Anders took over explaining my history with Kyle and Kyle's connection to Mitchell. It was frustrating how many times he said the word "allegedly" when he was talking about what Kyle had done, but I got it. We couldn't make allegations without proof.

"Did you see anything when you came home?" Anders looked at Conner, who had been sitting quietly so far.

"Nothing but some branches moving."

"And you couldn't make out who was in the backyard?" I could tell he regretted asking me the question because he clearly knew the answer. I just shook my head no. "And you don't have any surveillance or cameras on the property?" Conner and I both shook our heads. "So once again, we have no evidence that it was Mr. Martin behind this. All we have are a couple boot prints, which we can't use to identify him."

"Pretty much." I was as dejected as he was.

"Okay," he huffed, "walk me through it. Where were you when you saw him?"

All five of us walked through the house to the master bedroom and to the French doors. I took them outside and showed him where our visitor emerged from the trees and then sulked back in. Inspector Anders looked around, crouched down to look closer and took a flashlight from one of the officers circling the property before venturing into the trees.

"We'll have to tape off the area and explore the trees deeper in the morning when it's lighter out." Anders handed the flashlight back and addressed the Hennington OPP crew that had gathered around us. "Do you think your Chief would sanction an overnight watch here?"

"It doesn't hurt to ask," one of the officers who had been circling the property said. "I'm good to stay if she gives the okay."

The older cop who had been in the house with us nodded and volunteered as well before he walked away to call their Chief of Police.

The Chief insisted on talking to Anders. It looked like since all of the incidents with Kyle (and at least one with Mitchell) had happened in Hennington OPP jurisdiction, but Toronto PD had an active investigation on Kyle, and the RCMP's Emergency Response Team was dealing with Mitch, this was going to turn into a jurisdictional nightmare. But that was going to have to wait until Hennington Chief of Police got in contact with the Toronto PD Chief and Harper. For right now, it was going to turn into a joint investigation. To me, the more people who kept an eye out for Kyle, the better, but at the same time, I didn't want Inspector Anders to get pushed out. He knew the history and had the connection to Mitchell, too. He was vital to this whole thing.

"What are you thinking?" Conner was standing behind me in the living room, his arms wrapped around my waist as we watched one of the cruisers leave for the night while the other one repositioned itself in our laneway so that it wasn't so out in the open. The Chief had allowed the two officers who volunteered to stay, but only for one night. She was going to come out herself in the morning, look at the footprints and see what part the OPP would be playing in the investigation. From what Anders told us, she was under the "no evidence, no case" mentality. We had nothing concrete on Kyle, so the OPP had better things to do than waste their time on a fishing expedition. Anders, however, told us that he was fully committed and wouldn't leave us alone in this.

I shrugged before answering Conner, both of us still looking out the front window. "Just wondering if this is pointless."

"What do you mean?"

"Kyle and Mitchell are bad people who think and act like bad people. We're good people who are trying to fight them within the boundaries of the law. We're trying to stay safe, look for logic and evidence, and follow the due process of the legal system, whereas Kyle and Mitchell couldn't care less what they do and who they hurt. We aren't on an even playing field as them. How are we ever going to get them when they're not afraid to get their hands dirty? We're 100% playing defence while they're on the offence, not giving a shit what they do and who they hurt."

"So, how do you fight bad people without turning bad yourself?" His arms pulled me tighter into his chest, and he placed a soft kiss on my shoulder. He understood what I was getting at.

"Exactly. I don't want to be pessimistic and give up, but I'm at a loss for what else we can do."

"I'm heading out," Inspector Anders announced as he came back into the living room. I had printed off my Kyle history for him to take as he was heading over to Hennington OPP headquarters to brief the Chief on the investigation before she came to look at the footprints and deeper into the tree line tomorrow morning. "I'll be back in the morning."

He shook mine and Conner's hands before heading out the door. "Please try and get some sleep," he urged. "You've got officers on site to keep you safe."

And I did feel safe until about 4 a.m. when I heard yelling coming from the back of the house and a single gunshot.

Chapter 41

I bolted upright in bed, but Conner had already opened the French doors and was halfway out.

"Conner!" That man was *not* running *towards* the sound of gunfire. If he didn't get shot, I was going to kill him myself.

"Stay there," he yelled as he jumped down the steps and took off towards the gym, where the garage lights were on.

I jumped out of bed, not caring that I was only wearing a long T-shirt and sleep shorts, and ran after him in bare feet. It didn't matter how much it hurt or how cut up my feet were going to be; something was going on, and Conner was heading straight for it.

I caught up to him just as he threw the garage door open and ran inside, only to be shoved back out.

"Stay back," the officer barked. Conner and I both crowded the doorway, trying to see in. The older cop was in the middle of the gym, his gun drawn at someone lying face down with their hands clasped behind their head. The younger cop was cuffing the person and hoisted him to his feet.

"Pete?!" Conner shrieked and pushed back into the garage, ignoring the cops. "What the fuck?" I followed Conner in as he stopped just in front of a man in his early thirties and the two cops.

"You know this guy?" the younger cop asked, carrying most of Pete's weight. It seemed like the gunshot we heard had resulted in a gunshot wound in Pete's thigh.

"Yeah, he's my old landlord," Conner sneered.

"And Kyle's old landlord, too," I added, realizing who this man was.

"Conner," Pete begged, "I'm so sorry, man. I had no choice."

"What do you mean?" The younger cop sat Pete down on the weight bench while the older cop grabbed a towel from a shelf at the end of the gym, pressed it against the gunshot wound in Pete's leg and radioed for an ambulance.

"Kyle," Pete gritted through his teeth. "He threatened my girlfriend if I didn't come here, scope out your place and take pictures."

"Do you have any proof of this?" the younger cop asked as the older officer continued to apply pressure to the gunshot wound. Clearly, they weren't worried about Pete going anywhere or thought that he was a threat.

"Not really. He approached me in the parking lot after work two days ago and said if I didn't get him pictures of your house, he was going to…" he swallowed hard, tears filling his eyes, "he was going to kidnap her and rape her before he killed her."

"And you believed him?" the young cop asked.

"He had pictures of her on his phone. He'd been following her all over town and even had pictures of her from in our bedroom."

Holy shit. Another camera in a bedroom. Then, my thoughts immediately went to Alex. Kyle approached him in the parking lot at work, too. It was a pattern! If only we could prove it.

"Pete, where do you work?" All eyes turned to me. I had an idea; I just prayed it worked out.

"At the accounting firm on Main St."

"Do you have cameras in the parking lot?"

"No, but there would be one at the car dealership across the street. Don't know if it would hit our lot or not, though."

I turned to Conner, hope in my eyes for the first time. "Kyle approached Alex in his parking lot, too. And we had cameras put in my bedroom." I turned to the cops. "It's a pattern. If we can get the camera feed from Alex's job and from the dealership across the street from Pete's work, would that be enough evidence to go after Kyle?"

The two cops looked at each other. They both seemed a bit lost, not knowing everything that we had gone through with Kyle, but they were at least taking my theory seriously. "Possibly. It would give us enough to consider him a person of interest but not enough to arrest him."

"And the pictures from your bedroom," I turned back to Pete. "We think it was Kyle who put the cameras in my bedroom, too, and the cops took them as evidence. Can we compare the cameras? If they're the same, that has to be something, right? That's something solid connecting Kyle to all of this, and it would be a solid connection between Kyle and Mitchell since Mitchell had the printout. It would be the evidence that we've been looking for."

"We should call the Chief," the younger cop said.

"And Anders." Conner came forward and brought Pete a bottle of water from his gym fridge. He put a hand on Pete's shoulder and helped him take a sip. "Can we take the handcuffs off?"

"I'm sorry, we can't." The older cop who was looking at the bullet wound sounded torn. "He was still trespassing and tried to run when we told him to stop."

"We're not pressing charges," I jumped in, "and his girlfriend's life is on the line. He had no choice but to run. Plus, you shot an unarmed man. It's the least you could do." I moved to Pete's other side and nodded down at Pete as he looked up at me in thanks. Pete was another victim of Kyle's. We all had to stick together.

Both officers looked at each other and shrugged their shoulders. It seemed like we were in a very unique situation, and neither one knew if they needed to follow official protocol here.

"Fine," the older officer said, the young one on the phone with their Chief of Police, "but don't move from the bench and don't think for one second that we won't take you down again if we need to."

The officer uncuffed Pete, who sighed in relief and laid down on the weight bench. He was clearly in pain and eagerly finished off the water bottle Conner had given him. Luckily, an ambulance pulled up not five minutes later and got to work on his injury right away.

By the time the paramedics were done, the Chief of Police and Anders had arrived.

"And what were you supposed to do with the pictures?" The Chief of Police was a striking woman who was incredibly intimidating. She had beautiful black skin, natural black curly hair and eyes that didn't stop moving around, taking everything in, and just radiated power and authority. I was instantly envious of her confidence.

"I'm supposed to put the cell on top of my rear tire when I go back to work at 8 a.m."

"And has Mr. Martin contacted you on your phone?"

"No," Pete said, "it's actually not my phone. Kyle gave it to me and said to take pictures with it and then leave it for him."

The Chief of Police had confiscated the phone and was clicking through it as Pete spoke. She evidently hadn't found anything as she clicked it off, dumped it back in an evidence bag and took off her gloves.

"There's nothing on it besides a couple pictures of the back of the house," she said to Inspector Anders.

Anders just nodded. He had barely said anything since he arrived. He had just been taking everything in. But something was bugging him. That much was clear. "Parking lot and bedroom cameras."

"That's what I was thinking, too," I said to him. "Can we pull camera footage of Alex and Pete in the parking lots and compare the bedroom cameras to the ones Superintendent Harper took?"

"We could, but that's not what's bothering me," he looked at Conner and me, ignoring the others in the garage. "I've been following Mr. Erbing for over fifteen years, and Mr. Martin for about seven, and this is the first time I've seen any indication of a pattern or repeated behaviour. It's sloppy. Mitchell Erbing doesn't do sloppy. It's almost as if Mr. Martin is getting desperate."

"Let's hope he's getting desperate. When people get desperate, they make mistakes." The Chief of Police made her way over to our little group and joined in the conversation. "I'll call my team and get them to collect the camera and check on Pete's girlfriend."

"And what do you want to do about the drop?" Anders questioned. He was deferring to the Chief of Police as the hierarchy of police ranking dictated, but you could tell it was hard for him. He'd been working so long and hard on the Kyle/Mitchell case, even putting off a promotion until his superiors agreed he could keep the case, only now having to give up control to someone who was just brought up to speed less than 12 hours ago.

"The drop goes as planned. We will have one of our officers pose as Pete, drive to his work and plant the phone. Pete and his girlfriend will be brought into protective custody until after we've caught Mr. Martin doing the pickup."

"And if Kyle figures out it's not actually Pete?" Conner was on the same wavelength as me. This didn't sound like a solid plan.

"It's our only shot," the Chief said. "The drop is supposed to take place in three hours. We don't have a location for Mr. Martin, but we know he'll be there somewhere. Even if he's watching and sees it's not Pete, he'll be in the area watching. I'll have a dozen officers in plain clothes watching out for him."

My anxiety was crippling. Conner and I waited at the house with one of the cops while everyone else was in town getting ready for the stakeout. I had a bad feeling deep in my gut, and it clawed at the back of my head. This was the moment we'd been hoping for, and so much could go wrong. Kyle could already have Pete's girlfriend and do unspeakable things to her. He could discover that it was a setup and become even more unhinged.

And then there was the whole Mitchell element of it. Was Kyle doing all this for Mitchell? If Kyle failed at his task, was Mitchell going to get involved in our lives again? Inspector Anders hadn't given us an update on Mitchell since he told us he was never actually arrested, which meant he hadn't received one from Harper either. In this case, no news was *not* good news.

Conner and I weren't able to get back to sleep after everyone left, so we scrubbed the gym floor, all the mats and the bench with bleach to get Pete's blood off of everything. Once that was all done, we drove to the 24-hour Walmart in Hennington, the cop who stayed to guard us followed a safe distance behind, and grabbed a surveillance home security system. Cameras were going everywhere: front yard, back yard, by the garage, in the garage, on the porch at the front door and back French doors, and even one down the laneway. We weren't taking any chances.

Conner was outside setting up the cameras in the gym while I was in the house setting up the recording hub and installing the software on the laptop and my cell. We were trying to keep busy and keep our minds off the drop that was happening any minute.

"How's the setup going?" Conner asked as he came in and flopped on the couch. He was sweating and exhausted. We'd only gotten five hours of sleep over the past two days, and he had just installed seven out of the eight cameras. He was completely worn out; we both were. Constant anxiety and stress, plus no sleep, wreaked havoc on a person's mental and physical capacity.

"It's almost done," I replied as I connected the hub to our router. "The system is up and running, and I have the app on my phone. We just need to sync everything up."

"Perfect." Conner let out a big huff before he pushed himself off the couch. "I just have the camera at the end of the driveway left, and then we're done."

"Do you need help with that one?"

"Yes," he replied as he came over to give me a quick kiss, "I'll need you in here to tell me how far down the laneway I can go before we're out of range with the hub."

"Sounds good."

Once all the cameras were synched, Conner took the last one and started down the laneway. I watched him from the front window as he walked and kept an eye on the hub, which indicated each camera signal. Once the connection went dead on his camera, I gave him a call on his cell and told him to back up about 10 feet. Once his camera was reconnected, I gave him the go-ahead to install it.

I stood up from where I was crouched by the hub, and a sharp sting pricked the side of my neck. For a brief second, I thought it was a muscle spasm since I'd been bent over for so long, but when my legs collapsed under me, and I couldn't move or talk, I knew something was really, REALLY wrong.

"Hey, Sweetness. Ya miss me?"

Chapter 42

Kyle.

I couldn't move my head to see him, but I knew that voice. He silently walked into my line of sight as everything tilted and went blurry. I saw a syringe in his hand as he crouched down beside me and gently pushed a piece of hair behind my ear. He had drugged me.

"Damn, I forgot how sexy you were." He grabbed the front of my shirt and pulled my torso up off the ground to his chest, planting a firm, wet kiss on my lips. I couldn't move away or even turn my head. I just lay there frozen as he pulled away from the kiss and licked up the side of my face. "This is going to be fun," he whispered in my ear before he threw me back to the ground. The last thing I saw was his fist coming towards my face.

I woke up sometime later in what had to be a trunk. No matter how dopey and groggy I was, the dark, confined space, carpet underneath me and the smell of exhaust and gasoline equalled being trapped in a trunk. I took a quick inventory of my body. My face killed from where the asshole punched me, but I could see, and the fogginess in my brain was very slowly dissipating. My body was cramping, but I figured that was from being crammed in a tight space for a long time. My arms and legs were tied, and I had something shoved in my mouth. When I tried to spit it out, I discovered I had something tied over my lips as well.

I tried to feel around to see if there was anything in the trunk with me when my connection bracelet hit the ground and pressed into my wrist, reminding me that it was there. I pressed the button, hoping for a vibration to indicate that my message connected. Conner needed to know that I was still alive somewhere and conscious enough to use the bracelet. To my utter relief, my wrist vibrated, and not two seconds later, a vibration came back in return. That meant two things. 1 – my message got through to Conner, and he responded, letting me know he got it and 2 – my phone was nearby and still on. I swept my hands back and forth, trying to reach the back pocket of my jeans to see if I could feel it, but with my hands tied behind my back and being cramped in a trunk, my arms couldn't reach it. I tried to roll onto my back to see if I could still feel my phone in my back pocket where I had last had it, but when I got to my back, I didn't feel anything pressing into my butt. Kyle must have taken it.

Think, Addy. Use your brain! As terrified as I was, panicking now wasn't going to solve anything. I had to be smart. I had to pay attention and remember every little detail I could.

- Lots of car noises
- Lots of horns and construction sounds
- Felt like stop and go. It was fast and then breaking
- There was no talking coming from the car, so fingers crossed it was only Kyle
- Not very many turns – were we on a highway?

It felt like hours before the car slowed. We took a bunch of turns and then came to a stop. The car idled for a couple minutes before it shut off. I listened carefully to every sound I could hear; a car door opened and then shut, and I heard footsteps along with what sounded like birds squawking. The sound of traffic had diminished but was still there in the background, and I could hear a loud horn in the distance. I'd put money on it we were in Toronto and by water.

"Wakey wakey, Sexy Lady," Kyle sang from the other side of the trunk. He flipped the lid open, and sunlight blinded my eyes. "Damn," he groaned, "you look so good tied up like that."

My stomach turned at his words and the desire in his eyes. He reached in, and as much as I struggled away from him, there was no point. There was nowhere for me to go while I was tied up in a trunk and still a bit foggy from the drugs.

"You know," Kyle started as he picked me up and carried me over his shoulder to a non-descript door, "this is all Conner's fault." He kicked the door hard, and the door immediately opened. I was upside down and getting dizzy, but I looked around and tried to get any type of clue as to where we were. But even from upside down, as soon as we stepped into the main part of the building, it was obvious that this was a strip club. There was no doubt in my mind that it was the one he invited me to on New Year's. The one that, if Harper was correct and I had been Mitchell's next mark, I probably wouldn't have returned from.

"Mitchell just wants his money back and for Conner to keep working his accounts." Kyle marched us across the main floor; the music was blaring, and the lights were muted. There were tables on one side of me and a couple stages on the other. The space looked empty except for a person sitting in one of the booths in the corner of the room. I wiggled and tried to scream to get help from the man in the booth, but he just stared at me.

"Hey!" Kyle yelled and smacked my ass hard. "Behave and stop wiggling around." I ignored him and tried to wiggle myself off his shoulder. He smacked my ass harder, but this time, he left his hand there, his fingers playing with the seam of my jeans. "You keep wiggling like that, and I'm going to give you something to wiggle on." He smacked my mound hard through my jeans, and the fear of him touching me there made me freeze. "That's better."

I tried to lift my head up as much as I could since I could feel all the blood rushing to my brain. With the drugs still lingering in my system and now being carried upside down, I was going to pass out soon. Kyle took his time as he walked me through a bunch of different doors and hallways, talking the whole time. He was feeding me valuable information, which meant he wasn't worried about me escaping and telling anyone. Kyle was talking because he never planned on me getting away. I was never getting out.

"Did you know that Conner has over $12 million because of investments and interest and stock market trades?" He walked down some stairs and into a dark room. "And although Mitchell is calling the shots, NOT from behind bars, mind you," he sneered as his hand slid up my thigh and over my ass, "I'm really looking forward to getting reacquainted, Sweetness."

Unwelcome tears came to my eyes. This was all Mitchell and not just Kyle with a stalker crush. And if Kyle's roaming hands were any indication, he was going to use our time together any way he wanted.

He bounced down some old, dark stairs, knocking my stomach into his shoulder with each step, causing the wind to be knocked out of me. There were only two more turns before he opened a heavy metal door, and we walked inside.

He flicked on a light switch, and some old, flickering, fluorescent lights buzzed on. We walked into what looked like an old changeroom with benches, lockers and an adjoining bathroom, and he flipped me over his shoulder and onto a metal chair. The force of it jolted up my hip and spine, making the headache I was fighting from being hung upside down since we got here even worse.

"Conner is one of Mitchell's long-term investments," Kyle continued as he pulled zip ties from his back pocket and secured my arms, which were still tied behind my back, and my legs to the chair. "Mitchell has decided it's time to cash out." Kyle pulled my cell phone out of his back pocket and waved it at me before he went to my back and pressed my thumb to the sensor to unlock it. "If Conner proves himself to no longer be useful," he whispered in my ear from behind me before he took my earlobe into his mouth to give it a suck and a nibble, "he will be disposed of, and you, my dear, will be gifted to me for a job well done."

Fear and nausea took over. No matter how much I told myself to breathe, stay calm and be smart, this situation was just getting worse and worse. I didn't doubt Conner had turned Mitchell's money into a fortune. He had told me himself that he had done some smart investing, but $12 million? That was an unbelievable amount. What was Mitchell prepared to do to me in order to get Conner to give him that money and to have Conner work for him again? If what Conner had said at the police station was true, Mitchell wanted Conner to be his investor and work Mitchell's money like Conner had done his own. If Conner had turned his money from Mitchell into $12 million, the amount of money he could potentially make Mitchell was mind-boggling. Mitchell was not going to let that potential go.

Breathe, Adeline. Be smart. I took a couple deep breaths to try and calm the panic that rose in my chest. Kyle kept talking, but I was more focused on my surroundings. I needed to see if there was a window or a door or anything I could use as a weapon if, by some miracle, I got my hands free. I took in the room I was in and realized it was an old multi-stall shower. The walls and floors were covered with tiny, once-white, square tiles; there were no dividers between the stalls, but there were three shower heads on the wall. There was only one small window up high, as we were clearly in the basement, and only one open doorway in and out.

"There," Kyle announced, bringing my attention back to him as he put my phone on a tripod that was set up in the corner of the shower. "Now your tracking is off, and he won't be able to trace this."

Kyle pressed a button on my phone, and the record sound beeped loud in our echoey shower.

"My dear Ms. Peters." My head whipped to the sound of a voice coming from the doorway. Slowly, Mitchell Erbing entered the shower stall in a black pinstripe suit. "I can see why Kyle has been so taken with you all these months. You look positively lovely tied up like this."

Fear shook my body as if I was having a seizure. I was in the same room with the devil, and I was his sole focus.

With slow, confident steps, Mitchell made his way over to the side of my chair and looked down at me with pure pleasure. "So pretty," he purred into my ear as he crouched down beside me and started petting my hair. "I could get a lot of money for you." He gently ran a finger down my cheek before he refocused his attention.

"Kyle," he called as he stood up straight, "mind joining us?"

My eyes flashed back to Kyle, having momentarily forgotten he was there behind my phone, recording the whole encounter. The smirk on his face sent shivers down my spine as Mitchell continued to pet my cheek. Surprisingly gentle, Mitchell reached behind my head and untied the material that was over my mouth. "Let's see those pretty lips, shall we?" As soon as the material was gone, I spat out whatever was in my mouth. It looked like one of my kitchen washcloths. But before I could say anything, Kyle's lips were on mine.

"Bite him," Mitchell whispered in my ear, his hand, which he fisted in the back of my hair, held my head immobile, "and I'll cut your throat."

Kyle continued to kiss me. His tongue slid over my lips and sought entry into my mouth, but I kept my jaw clenched shut. Kyle's one hand went under my shirt to grab my breast, squeezing it painfully hard, while the other held tight around my neck. Tears streamed down my face as he squeezed my breast harder and harder, eventually forcing a cry from my mouth and my jaw to unclench. His tongue drove into my mouth as Mitchell yanked on my hair, reminding me of his warning.

Kyle moaned into my mouth as I struggled to get away. "I wonder if she's wet for me," he panted as he pulled back and readjusted his now-hard dick in his pants. "Let's check, shall we?" He looked to Mitchell, who gave a chuckle and a nod for Kyle to proceed.

Kyle stepped to the side so that everything he did was seen by my phone. He knelt down beside me and slipped the button through the hole in my jeans.

"No," I cried as I tried to shift my hips away. With a flick of the wrist, Mitchell pulled out something that was gleaming gold from his suit jacket pocket and pressed it into my throat within two seconds. I moved my eyes down, not moving my head a millimetre, and saw Mitchell's hand wrapped around a gold handle with black marbling peaking out. By the feel of the sharp edge against my neck, I'd put money on it he was holding a switchblade.

"Move…" he sneered as he pressed the sharp tip deeper into my neck. "I dare you."

Kyle unzipped my pants and shoved his hand inside as I sat, tied to the chair, a switchblade pressed to my throat, trying to hold my emotions together. They were recording this for a reason. They were going to show this to Conner, and I couldn't let him see how I was dying inside. I had to be strong, or he was going to do something stupid and reckless and get himself killed trying to rescue me. But as soon as I felt Kyle touch me, my whole body recoiled at the feel of pure evil. It was as if that one single touch killed anything good that had ever happened in my life and painted over everything with an oozing blackness.

My hips involuntarily jolted as Kyle's fingers slid under my underwear and brushed over my folds. And as Mitchell had hoped, my jolt had caused my neck to slide over his blade and cut it before I forced my body still. I could feel a small drip of blood slide down my neck.

"She's smooth," Kyle moaned, his fingers pushing through my lips but thankfully nowhere near my entrance. "But she's dry." He removed his hand and brought it to his nose for a long, deep sniff. My stomach churned at the sight. "I'll just have to try harder next time." He stuck his fingers into his mouth as he walked back behind the camera.

"Hello, Conner," Mitchell started, "I hope you've been enjoying the show so far. But let's cut to the chase." He grabbed the cloth that had been over my mouth and wrapped it over my lips again.

"You've been my longest and most profitable asset so far, working my money for me all these years, playing the market like a pro. I think it's time I get my payout and you rejoin my employ as my investor. I want my money back, all of it, plus everything you've made off of it, and once I have every cent, you'll work your magic on my money for me. I've let you be free long enough, don't you think? It's time you come back and work for me. And for every hour you make me wait for an answer, I'll be collecting a bit of interest of my own."

The knife that had been sitting against my throat moved up to the tip of my chin and dug in, dragging from my chin all the way under my jaw to my throat. A scream left my mouth but was muffled by the material covering my lips.

"For every hour you make me wait, another four inches will be cut into beautiful Adeline's skin here. One inch for every year you worked for me and profited off my money and generosity." He removed the switchblade from my skin and wiped it off on my shoulder. I could see the red stain on my gray T-shirt from my blood. "You have one day. That's 24 hours, or 96 inches, if you'd prefer to look at it that way. And if I don't have my money by then, sweet Adeline here will belong to me, and I'll get my money from her instead."

He stepped closer to the camera, blocking it from my sight. "I'll be waiting at our old hang-out, but don't worry, I'll leave your lover in the capable hands of her former neighbour."

As soon as Mitchell left the shower stall after he did the inaugural first cut, Kyle stopped the recording, sent it to Conner and stomped on my phone, destroying it completely. He walked over to me, grabbed my chin and placed a hard kiss on my lips right over the material that covered my mouth. "I'll see you in an hour," he breathed into my ear before he grabbed my nipple through my shirt and bra and tweaked it hard.

Once I was alone, I started to take inventory of my surroundings. I had to be smart and remember the training Conner had given me. I pushed back the pain and the sight of the blood dripping from my chin and neck and soaking my shirt and focused on the situation. My hands were zip-tied, not tied with rope, same with my legs. The chair was metal, not possible to break like a wooden chair would be. I was in a shower stall, with only a tiny window up by the ceiling and only one way in and out. Music was pounding through the club upstairs, so screaming for help wouldn't do anything, even if I got the gag off.

The shower heads looked dry and corroded, so this was probably the old change rooms that weren't used anymore. I couldn't count on anyone stumbling in here to change or shower to help me. The only things I saw were an open walkthrough from the change room into the shower, the tiled floor and ceiling, and a small drain that the chair was positioned on top of.

There was nothing in here to help me get out. Except for me.

Mitchell had said to the camera that he would leave me in the hands of my neighbour, so I at least knew it would always be Kyle who would be coming back every hour to cut me and not some random who might do more than just cut me. Plus, Mitchell didn't seem like the type of guy who liked getting his hands dirty, except if it was to make a point. So, I had Kyle to contend with. Maybe if I finally gave in to Kyle, I could convince him to let me go? And then I'd only have Kyle to deal with and not Mitchell? Maybe? But was that option any better? I knew what Kyle wanted, and the thought of giving myself over to him almost made me gag.

I couldn't hear anyone out in the changing room, didn't hear a radio, shoes tapping on the floor or breathing. I was going to venture a guess that I was completely alone.

I took inventory of everything I had on me to see what could help. I was wearing a plain T-shirt, jeans, slip-on shoes, my connection bracelet (which wouldn't work since Kyle smashed my phone and they needed your cell's Bluetooth to connect) and my rose ring. The ring could help if I could get my hands out from behind my back and somehow cut through zip ties with the tiny blade without breaking it. That was all I had on me.

I had to figure something out and find a way to get out of here. I couldn't just sit and wait for Conner to come to rescue me, although he probably knew where I was since my phone had still been working when we arrived before Kyle turned off the location settings.

One thing I knew for sure, this was going to be a long and painful process. If there was ever a time to practice patience and keeping a level head, it was now. The cuts were going to hurt badly, and who knew what else Kyle was planning on doing to me, but I couldn't let myself break. Kyle and Mitchell were not going to win. No matter what Kyle put me through and how long it took, I was getting out of here.

Chapter 43

By the number of cuts in my skin, it had been four hours that I had been tied to the chair, including when Mitchell and Kyle had made the video for Conner and given me the first cut. And as Mitchell had promised, for each hour that I had sat in the chair, Kyle had cut another four inches into my skin, joining one cut to the next, a jagged, bloody line that ran down the centre of my body.

But honestly, they weren't four-inch cuts. Kyle hadn't come in with a tape measure or a ruler. He had just cut into me for as long as he had wanted – sometimes three inches and sometimes six. The pain was unbearable. One wound would just be healing in time for him to come in and start another.

Each time Kyle came back, it was the same routine. He brought a shot glass of water, a small dish of pretzels and

Mitchell's switchblade. It had almost been like a dance to Kyle: enter, taunt, cut, water, feed, touch, leave. He would grab a part of my body when he sliced another supposed four inches into it, moaning as he did. After the cut, he forced the water on me. He held me by the throat and poured the shot glass of water into my mouth. Then came the pretzels, and as soon as the food was gone, it was a kiss or lick, a lingering touch somewhere on my body, and he would leave me alone for the hour.

I sat in the chair, shaking as I thought about the hours that had gone by and the torture I had been put through.

Soft footsteps echoed in the changeroom, alerting me to someone's presence. My heart raced, and my body shook as I waited and feared who would come around the corner.

I was torn. Part of me hoped it was Kyle, as he was the devil I knew and not another one of Mitchell's goons who would probably do more than just cut some inches into my skin. But another part of me was hoping it was just a random who could help me escape. Maybe it was one of the dancers who was using the basement changeroom or showers for more privacy, and she would see a helpless woman tied to a chair and help get me out?

But as the soft footsteps turned into heavy, purposeful steps, I knew instantly that it was a man.

The first thing that passed through the shower doorway was a man's hand holding something shiny and gold. As the rest of the body entered, my eyes lifted, and I stared right into Kyle's eyes. He gave me a flirty smirk and a wink as he flicked Mitchell's switchblade open and closed, and open and closed as he walked slowly into the room.

"Hello, Sweetness," he purred as he swaggered up to my chair and squatted down in front of me between my legs.

The click of the switchblade opening and closing over and over again was the only sound as Kyle looked me over, lust shining in his eyes. The black marbled handle had been a stark contrast to the bright gold of the blade, which was just slightly tarnished at the tip with what I assumed was my blood.

With one final click of the switchblade, Kyle rocketed to his feet and joined his first four-inch cut to the end of the one Mitchell had left, right at the base of my throat. I screamed into the cloth that was still covering my mouth as my body thrashed and tried to move away. Mercifully, the cut went by quick as Kyle seemed to be overeager, and the moan that left his throat was unmistakable.

As soon as the cut was done, he took a step back and just stared at me, his chest heaving with desire. He bent down and picked up a small bowl and a shot glass that I hadn't noticed he brought in with him. He gently took the material off my lips and held up the shot glass for me.

"Here, Sweets," he whispered as he tipped the shot glass to my lips. I gladly took the small drink of water, unhappy that it was only a shot glass worth and not more. My mouth was so dry ever since he had shoved the washcloth in my mouth when he first took me from the house. Achingly, that small shot of water looked like a little show of mercy, but I couldn't think that way. Kyle was the enemy. He was only giving me the water to keep me alive.

Only, it wasn't water. Or at least it wasn't 100% water if taste was anything to go by. Taste, and the fact that as soon as he pulled the shot glass away from my lips, my stomach instantly turned, and I threw up over the side of the chair.

I panted as I sat back up, Kyle silently watching me the whole time. Maybe it was the nerves of being kidnapped and tied up, the pain from the cuts, or having a severely empty stomach, but I couldn't be sure. Thankfully, Kyle left right after that, leaving the gag off my mouth so I didn't choke on the vomit that I could feel rising in my esophagus again.

For the next hour, I panicked and foolishly wasted my time on anything except creating an escape plan. I couldn't help it. I threw up two more times and was now not only worried that I had been kidnapped and was going to be tortured but also that Kyle had poisoned me.

And as much as I tried to fight against it, I started to cry. I was going to die. There was no way Kyle would be letting me loose, and I wasn't some superhero who could take on Kyle and Mitchell myself with my hands literally tied behind my back.

I was screwed. Truly and royally fucked. This was how I was going to die. My big risk of jumping into the unknown of getting divorced and starting my life over again was going to end with me bleeding out in the grungy, dirty strip joint shower.

I cried, screamed and begged for someone to help me, but all that I got back was the echoes of my pleas. Until I once again heard the sound of footsteps in the changeroom.

"What's with all the noise, Sweetness?" Kyle asked as he sauntered back into the shower, the switchblade twirling in his hand. "Did you miss me that much? I was hardly gone 50 minutes."

"Stay away from me!" I yelled as Kyle came closer.

The smell of beer, pot and sex surrounded me and overtook the smell of vomit as Kyle came up next to me and ran his finger down the first eight inches that had been cut into my skin. But no matter how much I thrashed and tried to move, I couldn't get away.

Kyle's hand shot out like a snake, grabbed my throat right over the cut and squeezed. I gasped as I could feel the cut that had just closed tear back open, and small trickles of blood started to roll down my neck.

"You know," Kyle whispered, as if he was whispering declarations of love to his soulmate, "the more you fight, the harder I get. And the sight of your blood…" he moaned the words in my ear before he smashed his lips to mine and held my head in both his hands, trapping my mouth to his. His tongue came out and licked over my lips as one of his hands dropped right to the crotch of my pants and started to rub me hard through the denim.

He quickly straddled my left leg and started to move his hips over me, his hard erection moving up and down my thigh. The hand that was holding my head moved to my throat, and I could feel his thumb gliding over the cut in my skin, smearing the blood all over my neck.

Don't fight, *I told myself, as my heart and spirit were breaking.* The more you struggle, the more he enjoys it. *This was the moment, I knew it 100%. This was the moment that would change the rest of my life. It would change how I felt in my own skin, how Conner's touch would feel if I ever saw him again. I was dying inside as this monster- who I had actually kissed and made out with in my home office — took what he wanted from my body while he assaulted and violated me.*

Kyle's lips moved to the side of my neck, licking it and biting it as I cried for him to get away. But his hips continued to rock on my leg, his hand continued to press hard into the crotch of my jeans, and more and more moans left his mouth before he pulled his head back, opened his mouth in a soft groan, and his body gave a couple hard twitches. "It makes me come," he panted into the space between us. Kyle stood back up, removed his hand from my crotch and gave my face one long lick from chin to cheek, right over my lips.

My tear-filled eyes immediately shot down to the front of his jeans, where his erection was still straining against the zipper. The sight made me throw up all over the floor again, and this time, it was from the obvious quick-draw orgasm he just had at the sight of my blood, not from whatever he had forced me to drink.

"Now look what you've done," he tsked as the hand that was holding the switchblade rearranged the front of his pants.

"Kyle, please," I whimpered as I stared into the eyes of the man who used to be my friend. The fear I felt was suffocating, making it hard to breathe and making me want to give Kyle whatever he wanted in order for him to stop. But he completely ignored my begging.

"You know," he continued as he moved in front of me and ran his finger down my chest to the deep V of my T-shirt. "It could have been different for us. If you had just listened to me and stayed away from Conner, we could have been together. You could have worked for Mitchell, helped be a mother to the younger girls we brought in and then

come home to me every night where I would have ravished you. Worshiped you. Loved you. But now..." with a quick flick of his wrist, the blade was at my collarbone, stabbing into my chest, "now I have to teach you a lesson. I have to share you with Mitchell and the crew and watch as other men get to touch and fuck what's mine."

The pain from the cut forced a scream from my throat as the edge of the blade ripped through my skin, creating another 4-inch cut down my body. He pulled the knife away from my chest where the newest cut ended and licked the blood off the blade. "On the plus side," he continued as I tried to hold back the vomit I could feel moving up my throat, "I get to do whatever I want to you and make this pretty skin bleed. And when we're done here, you'll be mine anyway."

Kyle put the knife in his back pocket and then rubbed the thumb of one hand over my bottom lip while he held the shot glass to my mouth with his other, but I refused to open my mouth. "Swallow the shot, Sweetness," he said teasingly, "or I'll give you a shot of something else to swallow." At that remark, he moved the hand that was brushing my lip to his zipper and slowly started to pull it down.

I quickly opened my mouth wide and swallowed the water.

Once the shot was swallowed, he shoved a couple pretzels in my mouth and put his hand over my lips so I couldn't spit them out. While I chewed, he kissed and licked the side of my neck while the hand that had just unzipped his pants roamed up my body to fondle my breasts. I quickly learned that the sooner I drank and ate, the less time Kyle had to explore my body.

But once he left, I broke. The ghost of his hands on me, his tongue, and his words made me feel like I was covered in cobwebs. I couldn't see the violation he had caused, but I could definitely feel it. It took a couple of minutes to try and stop the tears that ran down my face and the tremors from racking my body, but within that time, I once again vomited, this time all over my pants.

I needed to get out of here and fast. I had a feeling that the next time Kyle came back, his violation wouldn't be so "innocent" and with clothing in the way. I had to be stronger than this. Smarter.

I looked around the room again, hoping that I had missed something in my original inventory of the space, but nothing was different. I could hobble with my chair over to the window, but I was still tied to it and wouldn't be able to get out. I could bang the legs of the chair on the grate below me to try and get someone's attention, but I knew that if I made noise, Kyle would once again come back early.

I rubbed my wrists together, trying to rip the zip ties apart, but all that did was kink my shoulder since my arms were still tied behind my back. I tried seeing if I could stand up enough to slide my arms under my butt and bring them to the front, but my arms were secured through the slats in the chair. Lastly, I tried to sit up to see if I could at least get my feet free, but all the moving around I had done had opened up the wounds, made my stomach roll, and I vomited again.

I could feel myself getting weaker and more and more tired. It seemed as if any exertion I put out caused me to vomit, and once I was done, my body was drained.

When Kyle came back, far quicker than I thought the hour had been, and saw the vomit all over my pants and top, he undid the button and zipper and slid my jeans down my legs.

"*Can't have such a beautiful woman sitting in her own vomit now, can I?*" He cut one of the zip-ties and pulled my pants off one leg. I immediately flailed and tried to kick Kyle with my free leg, but he caught it with one hand and waved the switchblade at me in warning.

"*Ah, ah, ah,*" he chided, "*let's not make this any harder than it needs to be.*" He shoved my leg back down and tied it back to the chair leg with a new zip tie he pulled from his back pocket. He cut the other zip-tie free to remove the other pant leg, repeating the process. He skimmed his hands up my bare legs until he reached my shirt and pulled my top up over my head, leaving it behind my back, giving him a clear view of me in my bra and underwear.

"*Much better,*" he sneered as he flicked his wrist and cut open my bra, baring my breasts to him before he put the next cut right down the centre between my breasts. I tried to hold in the scream as the pain seared my chest, taking my breath away. But just like the two times prior, once the cut was done, he produced the shot glass of non-water and the small bowl of pretzels.

This time, however, instead of kissing or licking me, he bent down, sucked one of my nipples into his mouth and bit down hard.

"*FUUUCCCKKKKK,*" I screamed as the pain from the cut was momentarily eclipsed by the feeling of Kyle's teeth digging into my sensitive nipple. He popped off my abused breast, gave the other one a soft kiss and left to go, chuckling on his way out the door.

I tried to take a deep breath to steady myself. I was feeling more and more woozy as time went on. I didn't know if it was from the poison I was sure Kyle was forcing on me or from all the blood loss from the cuts. Either way, I didn't know how much more of this I could take. I *could already feel all the energy draining out of my body; my heart rate was beating faster, and my head was starting to spin.*

I focused on what I could control. I controlled my breathing...until I vomited again. I wiggled my hands and fingers, trying to keep blood flow going to them as they were far past tingling and losing feeling. I tried to see if I could remove the top of my flower ring to expose the blade and possibly cut through the zip-ties that held my hands together, but the chair slats that the zip-ties were fed through kept me from moving my hands in the right position. And the more I moved around, the worse I felt.

The cuts stung and weren't healing as quickly as I'd hoped, in part due to my constant struggle to get away from Kyle and my attempts to escape. Not to mention constantly bending over to throw up. Recently, the vomiting was accompanied by cold chills and dizziness. I was feeling shaky and sick. I couldn't stop throwing up and had already heaved six times since Kyle left. I would put money on it that he was trying to dehydrate me by giving me a vomiting agent in the water and then forcing me to eat dry, salted pretzels. If I was dehydrated and vomiting, I was weak, and if I was weak, I couldn't fight back or escape.

Kyle had me just where he wanted me.

Chapter 44

The pain from being cut open woke me from passing out. I hadn't even realized that I had been lightheaded to the point of blacking out, but it made sense. I barely mustered enough energy to cry out in pain; the most pitiful whimper was all that left my lips.

"Welcome back, Sweetness," Kyle whispered as he finished the cut that ended right under my belly button.

My head lolled as I tried to hold onto my consciousness and focus on my surroundings. Kyle cradled my head against his chest as he poured the shot glass of water into my mouth. It was strange. This time, it felt like Kyle was taking care of a sick loved one. He was gentle with me, soft with me. He brushed the hair out of my face, wiped away the vomit that I could feel crusted on the edge of my lip, and kissed the side of my head when I moaned and tried to turn away from the shot glass. *Mind games. He's now wanting me to trust him.*

I slowly pulled myself out of his grasp and swayed as I tried to sit up on my own.

"Slow, Sweets," Kyle pled, his hands hovering over my shoulders to catch me if I passed out again. "You scared me when I came in and you were unconscious. You can't do that to me. I was so worried." *If he really cared, he wouldn't have sliced into my abdomen while I was passed out.*

I ignored Kyle's sweetness and tried to piece together what had happened since I lost consciousness. First was the fact that I did, in fact, pass out. I had been awake for quite a while after Kyle's last visit, so I couldn't have been out for more than 15 minutes.

Second, was the lack of pain in my shoulders and the burning feeling radiating in my hands. I flexed my hands and noticed right away something was different. I looked down in shock. It seemed that while I was passed out, Kyle had released my hands from behind my back and retied my wrists to the arms of the chair. The blood that now rushed back into my fingers and palms tingled to the point that it felt like my hands were burning. It was incredibly painful, but it was a good thing.

The third thing I noticed was the brain fog and how weak I felt. The dehydration and blood loss had definitely kicked in. Although it had only been four hours and four small shot glasses of vomiting agent-tainted water, it also meant that with Mitchell's inaugural cut, I now had five cuts into my body and over twenty new inches where blood trickled out. I was dizzy, my heartbeat was racing, and I had a hard time catching my breath. I was almost panting as I shook in the cold metal chair.

"It's almost over, Sweets," Kyle cooed as he squatted between my legs and rubbed his thumb over the freshest cut, once again smearing the blood over my skin. "Just a little while longer. You can do that for me, right? Hold out just a little bit longer for me? Just until Conner gets in contact with Mitchell? Then it'll all be over, and I'll take care of you and get you better, and we'll start our lives over, this time with you knowing the truth about it all."

Kyle kept blathering on about his delusions, but I got stuck on one word: Conner. Conner was still out there worried about me. I had to let him know I was okay before he did something stupid like trade his life for mine. I shook my head to try and remove the fog that was settling over my brain, but it just made things worse. The dizziness was instant, and I leaned forward, throwing up minimal bile right in front of Kyle.

He quickly jumped out of the way and came to rub my back as my body kept dry-heaving over and over.

"It's okay, Sweets. It's almost over."

Kyle gave me one more kiss on the head before he left, and for the first time since Mitchell first came into my life, I had hope. Kyle was right: this would be over soon.

With my hands no longer behind my back, I was finally able to put my plan into place, as long as I could keep focus between vomiting and trying not to pass out. With my hands now tied beside me, I had the dexterity I needed to try and cut through the zip-ties. It took me longer than it should have to turn the rose ring around on my finger and start to unscrew the top. I had to wait until the next round of vomiting came before I let the rose top drop onto the floor, hiding the sound of the piece of jewelry hitting the metal grate under my chair with my retching and choking. I knew cutting through the zip-ties with a tiny blade the size of an earring post would take forever, but I had to focus, which was extremely hard with the dizzy spells coming quicker and quicker. If I rushed, I'd break the blade or end up cutting myself.

With my wrists still tied to the chair, I bent my upper body down and put the back end of the ring into my mouth, careful to keep the blade away from my lips. With what little saliva I could manage, I, ever so slowly, grabbed the ring with my teeth and pulled it up over the knuckle of my finger.

"Thank God," I whispered to myself as I slumped back on the back of the chair and moved the ring down to my first knuckle. I wasn't able to reach the zip-ties with the ring in its normal place. I had to move it up my finger and pray to every God and Goddess out there that I didn't drop it.

Carefully, I spun the ring around my first knuckle and pinched it between my thumb and the chair, gently pressing the blade over the zip tie. I made tiny motions back and forth, not wanting to press too hard and break the blade.

I kept my eyes focused on the doorway, and my ears locked in for any sound of someone coming. Sadly, that small amount of progress I made tired me out and made me vomit again. And apparently, having bent over opened up some of the cuts on my abdomen.

On top of that, I was feeling lightheaded and dizzy again, and my vision started to fade around the edges. I was going to pass out. With the minimal strength I still had, I bent back over, put the ring back in my mouth and slid it back into place at the bottom of my finger. I couldn't risk the ring falling off when I passed out again.

I looked down as the world tilted to see if I had made any progress on the zip-tie. For the first time today, I smiled…only a little. Right before my world turned black, I saw it. A tiny nick in the zip-tie. The ring had worked. My plan was going to work. I just needed…

The sound of footsteps woke me from the nothingness. It was harder this time to come back to reality, but the noise was so loud that I couldn't ignore it.

"Honey, it's dinner time," Kyle called as the sound of his footsteps entered the changeroom. I struggled to sit up from my prone position, leaning over the side. My head was deadweight that I didn't seem to have control over. It flopped to one shoulder and then back, so I was looking at the ceiling once I was finally able to somewhat sit back up in the chair.

"There's my beautiful girl," he purred as he made his way over to me. "Look at you dripping with blood. You're making my cock hard again." All the sweetness that was in his voice last hour was completely gone.

I flopped my head forward to look down at my practically naked body and saw that the wound under my belly button was still bleeding. It was slow, just a tiny drop…drop…drop, but it hadn't scabbed over yet. Unfortunately, I figured that meant one of two things: 1 - Kyle had come back before the hour was up, or 2 – my blood was no longer clotting because something was wrong with me…really, really wrong. I had noticed that everything was sluggish, my body almost feeling like a rag doll, either motionless or being flopped around. It made me wonder what was in the last shot glass Kyle had given me an hour ago.

"You know," Kyle said, the switchblade playing over my skin as he squatted between my legs, "you've never looked sexier." He grabbed my face and pulled me to sit properly in the chair. I felt so weak my body easily followed his lead, but thankfully, my brain was working. Slow, but it was working.

Still squatted between my legs, Kyle moved his hand down to his zipper and slowly pulled it down. There was nothing I could do as he freed his erection from his boxers and started fisting himself. His eyes raked over me, starting at the top of my head, to take in every line and crease on my face and weariness in my eyes. He bit his lip and moaned as his eyes followed the jagged line of cuts down my bloody throat, between my breasts and down my body until it was as if he couldn't stand it anymore and jerked up to lick up the spilt blood from the most recent cut up to the first.

"Fuck," he moaned as he grabbed his cock again and started pumping it harder. He squatted back down between my legs and focused right in front of him. My legs were open, each ankle tied to the foot of the chair, and my pants had been taken off hours ago, leaving me spread before him in just my underwear.

With one hand pumping away on his dick, he raised the other, which was holding the switchblade and quickly flicked it under the seam of my underwear, cutting them away from my body.

"Kyle, please..." I begged as tears filled my eyes. Was this where Kyle was going to rape me? Was this when he was going to take what he ultimately wanted?

Kyle groaned as I started to cry harder, begging him over and over again to stop. The panic and fear had me vomiting over the side of the chair as he came all over his hands and the floor.

"Sweetness, what you do to me." He licked the inside of my thigh before he tucked himself back in his pants. He ran the blade over my lower stomach before puncturing the skin and dragging the knife down.

"Ooops," Kyle smirked as he flicked the end of the blade and cut an extra two inches into my skin. The end of that cut was right through the very tip of my outer lips. If he had gone half a centimetre more, he would have cut my clit. When he was done with the water and pretzels, instead of kissing my cheek, he bent down and kissed the cut he just finished.

I shook in fear as his lips pressed right above my vagina, afraid that he would move lower or his tongue would come out to play. I had to get out of here before the next hour came, or Kyle would end up cutting through my lips, clit and centre.

I now had six long cuts down the centre of my body. You didn't realize how long twenty-four inches, or two feet, was until it was cut into your flesh.

As soon as Kyle was out of the room and his footsteps faded out the changeroom door, I looked down and examined the small cut I had managed in the zip-tie. It was barely a millimetre, but it was there, which meant it would have weakened the strength of the zip-tie.

I tried to pull my wrist and snap the rest of the tie, but I wasn't strong enough. I was getting weaker as time went on, and if I didn't get out of here now, I knew I wouldn't be leaving here conscious or alive.

Without wasting more time, I bent over, put the ring back in my mouth and slid it back down to my first knuckle. And, instead of making small, shallow cuts, I pushed the blade of the ring as hard as I could into the centre of the tie and punctured the cut wider. It wasn't much, but it was enough that with one more surge of energy and power, I was able to flex and twist my wrist, loosening the tie enough that I could squeeze my hand out.

I quickly took the ring off and used it like a knife to free my other hand before I vomited again and had to rest. With all the moving around, the latest cut wasn't scabbing over, and the blood flow wasn't slowing. I was queasy and getting disoriented, my vision starting to blur as the blood ran down my legs. *Five minutes. I can give myself five minutes to rest.*

I grabbed the underwear that Kyle had cut off me and pressed the material into the newest cut to try and slow the bleeding. Hygienic? Not at all. Necessary? Absolutely.

I looked around, attempting to catch my breath and settle my head, and tried to figure out how I was going to get out of the strip club once I cut my legs free. I couldn't leave out the front door, obviously, and to get to the back door where we came in, I'd have to go through the club. The only option for me was the window. I wasn't going to try searching for another exit upstairs and risk getting seen.

So, I had a plan. A shitty one, but the only viable one I could see with the clock running down.

I bent over to cut my legs free, and the vomiting and dizziness came back. I didn't stop cutting, though. I cut while my stomach retched and my head swam. I nicked my ankle with the blade, but I didn't care. One more cut to add to the collection. With my one ankle free, I was able to stand up on wobbly legs, slide the zip tie off the bottom of the chair leg and free my other foot.

I was free. Dizzy and had to use the chair as a support, but was free.

I grabbed my T-shirt, threw it on, and did a quick sweep of the room to see what I could use to break the window. All there was in the room was the chair, my vomit-covered jeans, my cut bra and underwear, and my shoes, which I grabbed and slid on, and in the corner was the tripod and my smashed phone.

I waddled over to the corner of the room, checking that no one was in the changeroom as I passed the open doorway, and grabbed the tripod and my phone. Although it was smashed, I tried to turn it on, praying it was just the casing and the screen that was smashed, but when the screen remained black, I knew it was dead.

I carried the tripod and chair over to the far wall and prayed my plan worked. I stood up on the chair and used the tripod to try and smash out the window. I was still so weak that it took three tries for me to lift the tripod over my head and hold it steady enough to swing at the window, but my aim was good, and the sound of breaking glass was barely heard over the pounding beat of the music in the club, but still brought a small smile to my lips.

I swung the tripod around the broken window frame and cleared out any jagged pieces of glass. I had to flop back down in the chair to catch my breath and steady my vision again. *Hurry up, Addy. If Kyle catches you now, you're dead.*

I left the tripod on the floor but grabbed my vomit-covered jeans and wrapped a leg around each hand. I stepped back up on the chair and grabbed the window frame with my denim-covered hands so that I wouldn't lose any more blood cutting them on the sharp glass. I leaned against the wall, my hands gripping the window ledge, and tried to pull myself up. I was barely able to pull myself to my tippytoes before my arms gave out from my exhaustion, and I slumped back down into the chair. I didn't have the strength or energy to pull myself up. I could barely stand.

Tears sprung to my eyes as I realized I wasn't getting out that window. I only had one option left, and it would either get me free or get me caught. I had to risk it, though.

I picked up the tripod from the floor and tied my jeans around the end of it. I stood back up on the chair, my legs shaking and my abdomen still bleeding, and shoved the jeans and tripod out the window, waving it like a flag.

"HELP!" I yelled as I moved the tripod, hoping the movement would catch someone's attention. "HELP ME!"

The typical Toronto city noise was loud on the other side of the window, and my weak screams were probably whispers in the background. I was running out of strength and knew I was running out of time. I had been moving so slowly that my hour had to be almost up.

With all the strength I had left, I waved my denim flag and screamed "HELP!" as loudly as I could, praying it wasn't Mitchell or Kyle or one of their goons who found me. But no one came. I had to be facing a back alley or a loading dock or something. There were no cars or people passing the window. Just ambient city noises.

I slumped against the wall, the tripod slipping through the window and through my fingers to clatter on the floor, and let out one last whimpering, "Someone, please help me," before I slid down the wall and curled up on the chair.

My plan had failed.

Kyle had won.

He had managed to drain me to the point where I could barely stand. Six hours of being drugged, six hours of constant vomiting, even when there was nothing left in me to expel, six hours of bleeding, and twenty-four inches of fresh, open cuts had weakened me to the point of hopelessness. I didn't want to concede. I didn't want to give up. I was a fighter. If this past year had taught me anything, it was that no matter what shit life threw at me, I could survive it, but this…I didn't see a way out of this. My entire body gave out, and I tumbled to the floor as the realization hit me. This was over. I was done. I was either going to end up dead or be taken and tortured, die inside and *wish* I were dead. My future held only death or misery under the hands of Kyle and Mitchell and their trafficking rings.

My body shook as I wept on the floor. I hardly had enough energy or moisture left in me to produce tears, but my eyes stung, and my throat tightened up. I couldn't believe I was in this situation and that losing my husband, losing my dream home, losing my job, and losing my family had led me to this.

And then Conner. I found the most amazing man who had a troubled past but persevered and pushed through it to be a kind, giving and loving person who, by some miracle, chose to love me, a broken woman who was still trying to find out who she was and what she was made of. Conner was the love of my life. He was my future, and it seemed that future may no longer be possible.

But I wanted it. I wanted it so badly. I wanted that life for myself and that future. I wanted the home in the forest, the Friday lunch dates, the excruciating gym workouts, and the fun shopping expeditions. I wanted the conversations, the arguments, the sarcasm, the jokes, the love, the touches, and the intimacy.

I thought about how much my life had changed. The friends I now had, the job I loved, the confidence I had found in myself to speak my mind and not be worried about what people thought. I thought of the woman I was now compared to a year ago, and I was proud of her. She had a life; she had joy, love, adventure, and a future waiting for her.

I wanted that future.

That want and need took over everything else inside me. Took over my fear and hopelessness. I looked at the open window and saw a way out. That window HAD to be my way out. I couldn't give up.

I pushed myself off the floor, brushed the dirt and broken pieces of glass off my naked rear end, and stood back on the chair. I grabbed the window ledge and prepared to try to pull myself out again. If I wanted that life, I had to put on my big girl pants and go get it.

The music blasting in the strip club upstairs almost made me miss the shuffle of footsteps and hurried whispers that came through the window. I quickly ducked back down to the floor and grabbed the tripod, shoving it out the window and waving it like a maniac. Even if it was Kyle, Mitchell or one of his goons, they'd either pull me out and someone would possibly see me, or they'd catch me inside, and that would be that. This window was my only hope for a future.

"HELP!" I screamed as loud as I could. "SOMEONE HELP ME, PLEASE!" I swooshed the tripod and jeans back and forth as hard as I could and kept screaming.

Hurried footsteps slapped across the pavement, coming closer and closer. This was it. It was either someone who would rescue me or Mitchell and his crew coming to end me.

"Adeline?"

"HERE!" I yelled as I waved the tripod once more.

I could barely see out the window, only glimpses of cloud and sky, so I had no idea how close someone was. But when the tripod was ripped from my hands, and a head poked through the window to peer down at me, it was the most beautiful sight I had ever seen.

"Inspector Anders," I sighed as tears of joy sprung to my eyes. "Quick," I reached out for him, "Kyle will be back any minute."

"Hold tight," he instructed as he clasped his hands with mine and started to pull me out.

"WHAT THE FUCK!?" The shout was heard just a second before the sound of a gunshot reverberated through the shower stall, and blinding pain shot through my thigh.

I screamed in agony as Inspector Anders let go of my hands, dropping me back onto the chair below. He immediately stuck his head back through the window and aimed his gun behind me.

"Drop it, Kyle," he ordered. "That's your only warning."

Kyle lifted the gun to me again, and two shots went off at once. One landed in the tile wall not an inch from my head, while the other was a perfect kill shot. Right in the centre of Kyle's forehead.

Chapter 45

Inspector Anders lowered himself down through the window and swept the shower and changeroom before coming back to check on me.

He stood before me in full black tactical gear.

"All units, move in. Package has been secured." He took in the blood that had soaked through my shirt, the blood that was pouring out of the gunshot wound in my thigh and the vomit all over the floor. "We need medical here now!"

I could feel my consciousness slipping away, the adrenaline quickly seeping out of my body, and the loss of blood taking over.

"Conner?" I whispered as my head fell back against the wall, and my body slid out of the chair to the floor.

"Stay with me, Adeline," Inspector Anders said as he rushed to me and pressed his hands into my bleeding thigh. "He's in protective custody. He's fine."

I barely managed to get out the "thank you" before everything went dark.

Waking up in the hospital sucked. My diagnosis was pretty grim. I was right that Kyle had given me a vomiting agent to try and dehydrate me. My body was filled with a toxic amount of Ipecac that the doctors were trying to counteract. Although I had only had it in my system for six hours, the amount that had been forced on me could have been fatal. As it stood, I wasn't going to die from it, but they were worried about the lasting effects it could have on my heart.

On top of that, I had severe dehydration, needed a blood transfusion and had over 120 stitches down the centre of my body. The scars, I was told, would never go away. The jagged red line that ran from chin to pelvis would always be there.

But the worst of all was when Inspector Anders told me that Mitchell wasn't at the club when the raid happened. He was still out there.

Conner had been by my side every second since I woke up. Inspector Anders had pulled as many strings as he could and had arranged for Conner to have a full-time protective watch when he wasn't in the safe house. Now that I had been found, he straight out refused to go back to the safe house and pretty much lived with me in the hospital. The nurses had to send in security a couple times as he refused to leave me even for a second, regardless of exams, medical tests, confidential discussions about my medical diagnosis or visiting hours. I believe the words Conner had said to security were, "You can shove your visiting hours and go fuck yourself. I'm not leaving her." We had to call in Inspector Anders to smooth things out. But when the nurses and security heard the story of what Conner and I had been through, they understood and left Conner alone. Inspector Anders putting a cop outside my room helped, too.

"Thank God Kyle was an idiot." I shook my head while Conner filled me in on what had happened during my six hours in hell.

Conner hadn't known I had been taken until about twenty minutes later when he had the security camera in the laneway hooked up and came back into the house and found me missing. He and the cop who had stayed to guard us while everyone else was at the cell phone drop Kyle was supposed to be at looked everywhere and found nothing. No sign of struggle, no forced entry, nothing. It was as if I had just up and vanished.

At the same time, Anders and the OPP Chief of Police realized that the drop Pete was supposed to do was a setup and were scrambling to figure out their next steps. I was gone, and no one knew where I had gone or where to look next. It wasn't until they looked at the security cameras we had just installed that they confirmed that Kyle had taken me and disappeared into the trees behind the property. They found ATV tracks deep in the trees, but they disappeared once they hit the highway.

But it was the fact that Kyle had left my cell phone on during the drive that they were able to trace my location. That and the fact that I had connected with Conner over the connection bracelet which confirmed that I was with my phone. Unfortunately, bureaucratic bullshit between Hennington OPP (because I was kidnapped within their jurisdiction), Toronto PD (because they had an open case on Kyle) and Harper's Emergency Response Team (because Kyle was working for Mitchell) slowed down the entire process.

It had been almost two hours that I had been gone before the text message popped up on Conner's cell phone with the video of me and Mitchell's ultimatum. Once Conner showed it to Anders, they put him in protective custody right away as he was losing his mind and tried to drive to the strip club himself. Anders went straight to Toronto PD to log the video in evidence. Once the Chief of Police saw the video, he pretty much ignored all hierarchical systems and sent in a tactical unit to get me back and take down as many of Mitchell's men who were there as possible, completely ignoring protocol.

"Harper is pissed," Conner said as he tucked me in and then curled up on the cot the nurses had brought in for him. This was our third and final night in the hospital. If my test results were okay tomorrow morning, I was getting discharged. "He's blaming Anders and the tactical unit for not 'leaving it to the professionals' and letting Mitchell get away. I could hear them yelling out in the hall when Harper came in to question you when you were first brought in and still passed out."

"What a dick." I shook my head as I turned to face Conner, who was now spread out on his cot beside my bed. "Harper's only concern is getting Mitchell. If it were up to him, he probably would have let Mitchell kill me if it meant that he got his arrest."

"Probably," Conner agreed. We just stared at each other for a moment, absorbing the fact that I was back with Conner and I was alive. "I was so scared," Conner whispered, reiterating his fear for at least the fourth time since I'd woken up. "If Anders hadn't shoved me in protective custody right away and put four guards on me, I would have hunted Kyle down and killed him myself."

I reached my hand out of the bed and held on tight to his.

"I know, babe, but I'm here. I'm banged up and will need a lot of therapy, but I'm here."

"You have no idea how crazy I was going while I was trapped in that house." By the bruises and cuts that were taped on his knuckles, I could only imagine what the state of the walls was in the house they kept him in. Conner wouldn't have just sat quietly and waited. He would have been a caged animal, clawing and punching to get free.

"I'm here," I reassured him.

"I know. I love you so much," he whimpered as the reflection of moisture in his eyes drew my attention.

"I love you, too."

I got the all-clear. The doctors checked my stitches and blood work first thing in the morning and packed me a goodie bag of ointment, dressings and painkillers to go, plus a new snazzy cane to help me walk out. The bullet wound in my thigh was still healing and gave me a wicked limp, and the stitches down my torso were tight and pulled whenever I moved. I felt like a 90-year-old man with the quad base cane, but it helped.

Conner had my overnight bag all packed and was just throwing his PJ pants in his bag when the room phone rang beside my bed. Inspector Anders had been calling every day to check in, and I told him I was probably getting out today, but I would let him know.

I picked up the phone with a smile. "Good morning, Inspector Anders."

"Ms. Peters…" I froze on the bed as the voice on the other end of the phone sent ice down my spine.

Mitchell.

Chapter 46

"I'm glad to hear you're doing well and getting discharged today." My body shook as Mitchell's smooth voice crooned over the phone line, sending fear and dread racing through my body.

"Mitchell," I breathed into the phone. Conner dropped his bag on the floor as soon as he heard the word slip past my lips. He stared at me for a beat before he ran to the door and grabbed the cop stationed there.

"It's Mr. Erbing to you, my dear," Mitchell sneered. "We haven't become…familiar enough with each other yet for you to address me so informally." Both Conner and the guard rushed back into the room and crowded around me. "Let me cut to the chase, as I'm sure you've already flagged the officer guarding your room." He took a purposeful pause, letting me absorb the fact that he knew what was going on in my hospital room. "You have taken away one of my best collectors, so now you owe me a replacement. Shall it be you or Mr. Jensen?"

He was baiting me. His voice was snide and taunting. He knew that I knew he held all the power, and he was letting that knowledge sink over me. He knew that Conner and I were, in a way, responsible for Kyle's death and, ultimately, his loss of "product," and he was coming to get his revenge. Seeing how he already had his eyes locked on Conner for the money, it was clear he was hoping to get a two-for-one deal and take both of us down.

Conner grabbed the handset from me, hit a speaker button on the phone cradle attached to the wall, and softly put the handset back in the cradle. He then pulled out his cell and opened a voice recording app, pressing the record button to record the conversation as the cop pulled out his cell phone and started texting someone. Fingers crossed, it was Anders.

"Well…" Mitchell prompted when I didn't answer, his tinny voice filling the room from the small phone speaker, "what's it going to be?"

"I," I had to swallow a couple times before I could form a sentence. Mitchell knew where I was. He knew I was getting discharged today. He had eyes and ears everywhere. He could have doctors and nurses in his pocket. Frig, for all I knew, he could have had the doctor put a tracker in me when they were stitching up my cuts. "I'm not going to pick either of us. We've done nothing wrong."

"Tsk, tsk, tsk," Mitchell mocked, "I'm very disappointed in you, Ms. Peters. I would think you would want to save Mr. Jensen. After all, he is the love of your life, isn't he?"

The hospital room door burst open, and Harper barged in, ready to kill anyone in his way. I whipped around and held my finger to my lips, praying the arrogant asshole would listen and be quiet and not just push his own agenda for once. For being a "Superintendent," the guy had the tact and finesse of a bull in a china shop.

"He's a much better match for you," Mitchell continued, hopefully not hearing the new arrival. "Your dear ex-husband Alex just seems too safe, too…boring." My heart leapt at the mention of Alex as Harper joined our circle around the phone and gave a nod when he noticed Conner recording the conversation. "But not Mr. Jensen. He's feisty and exciting, isn't he, Ms. Peters? It's because of his dark past, you know. One that I'm well acquainted with. All those jobs he did for me, knowing it was wrong and against the law… make him a bad boy. You love the bad boy, don't you? That edge of danger in the reformed man. Plus, all the money he accepted for the jobs…you'd be set for life.

"And that beautiful house he has built for the two of you? Even I have to admit that it's a nice piece of private, secluded property. The things you two could get up to out there on that big piece of land." My eyes shot to Conner's. He knew about the house. Fuck, of course he did. There was probably a tracker on the phone that Kyle gave Pete. "I'd hate for something to happen to it because you couldn't make a decision and weren't following my directions." I heard Harper's teeth smash shut as he tried not to interrupt Mitchell, spouting threats and ultimatums.

"I won't pick either of us." A little power filled my voice, surprisingly, because of an encouraging nod from Harper. "Kyle got himself killed. We didn't kill him, so we shouldn't have to pay that price."

"Hmmmm," Mitchell hummed and hawed, "I guess you do have a point there, Ms. Peters. However, it was because of his obsession with you that he was killed nonetheless. So, this is what I'm going to do. I'll give you a choice." The taunting and arrogant sound slid through the phone. "You can either choose yourself or Mr. Jensen or, if you don't have the lady bits to make the decision yourself, you can defer that option to me."

"No," I quickly said, "I don't want you to choose. No one is being chosen." I was glad I had finally found my voice.

"Okay, then," we could all hear his smile through the phone. He had me right where he wanted me. "Who is it going to be? Are you going to give Mr. Jensen back to me to replace Kyle as my new collector, or are you going to come, stand by my side and be the obedient merchandise my clientele gets to sample?"

"Keep talking, Mr. Erbing," Harper answered. My heart sank knowing this was where he would step in and take over. Part of me was glad, though, as it gave me time to figure out how to answer Mitchell's ultimatum. There was no way he was letting that go. "You've already admitted to stalking, espionage, uttering threats, kidnapping, sexual slavery, entrapment, and racketeering just in the short time I've been privy to this conversation."

"Superintendent Harper," Mitchell happily exclaimed. "It is such a joy to hear your voice. I had assumed it would be Mr. Jensen or Inspector Anders who would have jumped in. What a delightful surprise to speak to you again."

"Cut the shit, Erbing," Harper barked. "I got you this time. Your high-priced lawyers won't be able to talk their way out of this."

"Well, that depends," Mitchell taunted. "Is your proof of this 'confession' based on an illegal wiretap by chance? Or did you get Mr. Jensen to record the call so you wouldn't have to get a warrant?" Inspector Anders walked in as Harper looked at the phone, seething. "Either way, you yourself admitted to only hearing part of the conversation. Who knows what Ms. Peters, Mr. Jensen and I were talking about before you barged in and interrupted a private conversation… that would all be hearsay."

Harper cracked. "You manipulative son-of-a-"

"Mr. Erbing," Inspector Anders interrupted, "Inspector Anders here. What are your terms?"

Harper shot Inspector Anders a murderous glare, clearly pissed that an Inspector interrupted him and pulled his focus. I shot Inspector Anders a serious look and a quick nod. The less Harper said, the better.

"Inspector Anders. Glad you could join us, and congratulations on the promotion. I hear it was well deserved."

Mitchell's tone changed from goading to professional when he went from Harper to Inspector Anders. Even Mitchell could tell Harper was a kid with a short fuse and way too much audacity.

"As you know," Mitchell continued, "Mr. Martin was shot. By you, as I understand."

"Yes, he shot Ms. Peters and refused to stand down when ordered. He shot again, and I was forced to take him out."

"Understandable, but very unfortunate. You see, Mr. Martin was a colleague of mine and was a wonderful asset to my company. As he was taken from us because of Mr. Jensen and Ms. Peters, I'm requesting one of them join my employ as a replacement. I have left that choice up to Ms. Peters."

"Not happening." Inspector Anders left no room for negotiation in his tone.

There was a silent pause before Mitchell spoke. "Well, it looks like we're at an impasse." It almost sounded like sadness in his voice. That he had seriously thought this cat-

and-mouse game was going to end with me picking either Conner or myself to join his evil empire.

"Conner…Adeline…" Conner and I shared a shocked stare before we both looked back to the phone. Mitchell hadn't referred to us by our first names this entire conversation so far. "I'm sorry we couldn't come to an agreement. And I'm sorry you didn't pick the easy way out of this situation. It's just going to get harder from here." The room went silent, and then the tone sound of the phone buzzed through. Mitchell had hung up on us.

The hospital was just a couple blocks away from the Toronto Police Headquarters, so Inspector Anders had us follow him over so that he could get caught up on what he had missed. He had sent the guard who had been stationed at my hospital room to head out to our home to check it over before we drove back. Thankfully, Inspector Anders didn't want to take any chances.

Of course, this was all after Harper reamed Inspector Anders out for overstepping and potentially "fucking up years of work." Harper's words, very unprofessionally yelled across the hospital room with Conner and I present, had had no effect on Inspector Anders. Inspector Anders had looked at Conner and me, asked if we had everything, and then led us out to the nurses' station to finalize my discharge.

"So," Inspector Anders started as he closed his office door behind us, "fill me in on what happened before I arrived."

Conner told him about the phone call, how he went out to grab the guard and that he started recording the conversation. Mitchell had clearly known where I was, what my prognosis was, when I was being released, and where we lived. He had clearly been keeping a closer eye on us than anyone had thought. Apparently, killing Kyle had just pushed him over the edge, and it seemed like his interest in us was no longer just about getting Conner's money and having Conner as his investor. On top of that, he now wanted either Conner to be Kyle's replacement or for me to do God knows what for him.

"I hate to ask…" Inspector Anders said, nodding to Conner's cell phone on the desk.

"I know," Conner answered, unlocking the phone and passing it over. "You'll need to hear the full recording and log it into the growing pile of evidence."

"Yup." Inspector Anders, for all his dedication and allegiance to us, looked resigned. "The growing pile of evidence that seems to be doing none of us any good."

"So, what do we do?"

Both men's eyes turned to me at my question, both holding looks of resignation. There wasn't anything we *could* do. We knew if we found Mitchell, he'd be out within 24-48 hours, even with the huge pile of evidence there was against him. Plus, it wasn't our call. Harper had stated very plainly that any movement on Mitchell was going to be *his* call and with *his* men. Harper had viewed the green light Inspector Anders's Captain had given when I was rescued as "an act of treason," and today's confrontation between Inspector Anders and Harper was strike two.

"Nothing." A deep voice spoke from the doorway and had all of us whipping around to see where the sound came from. A tall, built man with lush black hair stood just inside Inspector Anders' office, fully decked out in a navy blue suit decorated with badges and medals all over his chest and arms. "We do nothing."

"Chief Oliveri," Inspector Anders stood and waved the Chief in, "please, come in. This is Adeline Peters and Conner Jensen." We all stood and shook hands before returning to our seats, Chief Oliveri taking a seat on the couch I had spent the night on when Mitchell first came into my life.

"It's nice to finally meet you both," Chief Oliveri said with a small smile before he turned to address Inspector Anders. "Unfortunately, I don't come with good news. I just got out of a meeting with the Ministers of Public Safety. They've demanded I pull you from the case."

"Fuck." Inspector Anders breathed out the curse, but he might as well have yelled it through a megaphone.

"I'm sorry," I interrupted, "but what do the Ministers of Public Safety have to do with this?"

"The Ministers of Public Safety are the top of the top," Chief Oliveri answered, a look of resignation set on his face. "They're Superintendent Harper's boss's boss. They are who the very head of the RCMP reports to, and they're appointed by the Governor in Council on the advice of the Prime Minister himself. They are the final say of law enforcement. If they've given me the order to have Inspector Anders stand down, we have no choice. We were able to remain part of the investigation because we were investigating Mr. Martin, but now that he's gone, we've lost our only connection to the case." He turned to Inspector Anders. "I'm sorry, Patrick. I know how much this case has meant to you and how long you've been working on it, but it's out of my hands."

"So that's it?" I squeezed Conner's hand as my focus bounced between Inspector Anders and Chief Oliveri. "Conner and I are on our own now? We have to put our trust in Harper, who would rather use us as bait than actually protect us?"

"Not exactly," Chief Oliveri said, "I might have an idea or two."

"What if it doesn't work?" We had been home for two days now, and the peace and silence we were experiencing were unnerving. Both Conner and I were on high alert, waiting for something to happen, some type of retaliation from Mitchell.

"It's our only option, Love," Conner said as he gently cleaned around the cut that ran the length of my torso and covered it lightly with a non-stick bandage. We were back at home, and I was sitting on the bathroom vanity in our ensuite in sleep shorts and a zip-up hoodie. "Plus, I trust Oliveri. If he's willing to put his neck on the line and work the system so that Anders can continue to work with us in whatever capacity he can, then he has my vote."

"But faking termination papers so Inspector Anders can work as our personal security? He has a wife and kids. What if Mitchell goes after them like he did with Alex and Pete?"

"Inspector Anders, or I guess Patrick, or just Anders now since he's no longer Inspector, knew the risks when he took the job. He knew the risks when he started going after Mitchell over fifteen years ago. He knew the risks when he agreed to Oliveri's plan. We have to trust that he's okay with the amount of risk he's taking."

"But…"

Conner put the medical supplies down on the counter and took my face in his hands, forcing me to meet his eyes. "Do you trust him?"

"Of course I do."

"Then trust him fully."

I let my forehead rest against Conner's before my lips met his in a soft, hesitant kiss. I had to be careful with how much I moved my jaw and neck. Those cuts were taking the longest to heal as they were the ones that got moved and stretched the most.

I yearned for the time when I could have pushed the kiss deeper, wrapped my legs around Conner and ground myself on him, but that time was gone. And it wasn't just because of the physical limitation of my injuries. Conner barely wanted to touch me anymore, afraid that he would touch me wrong and hurt me.

And I...I had a hard time being touched. Every so often, I would get a flash of Kyle's hands on me or his tongue licking up the fresh cuts and tasting my blood. I felt constantly dirty, no matter how many showers I had had in the past two days we'd been home. I felt grotesque. Conner didn't deserve to have to look at my scarred body and pretend it turned him on.

I didn't feel like this was my body anymore. I didn't want to be in this skin. All I could do was absorb the moments when Conner held me in his arms, like now, and pray that he wouldn't look at me like I was tainted.

The knock on the door pulled us apart.

"Rain check?" Conner asked as he kissed the side of my neck on the sweet spot just below my ear.

"Yeah," I huffed as he helped me off the counter, grabbed my cane for me, and walked to the front door.

Anders stood on the front porch, his arms straight as he leaned over the railing, his back to us and his head dropped down.

"Anders," Conner greeted when Anders didn't turn around when the door opened. "Everything okay?"

Anders turned around, and my heart immediately dropped. There was sympathy in his eyes, and his jaw was clenched tight. "We need to talk," he said as he came to the front door. "You might want to sit down."

Chapter 47

I stood at the back of the church as the pastor talked about how my mother was now returning to her place with God and living amongst the angels. It had been five days since the barn fire that had killed my mother and left my dad in a coma in the hospital.

My aunt Bethany - who was my parents' neighbour, had seen the fire, called 911 and made all the funeral arrangements - hadn't even called me to let me know. I would have just been notified by police as next of kin if Oliveri hadn't stopped the process and spoken to Anders, and I was eternally grateful that he did. Clearly, when the Peters family disowned you, they disowned you fully, regardless of the circumstances.

Anders had told us that the fire was under investigation. There had been no lightning strike, no electrical problems, not on an overly hot day that grass, hay or straw would have overheated and started smoking. One minute, everything was fine, and then the next, it was completely engulfed in flames, faster than the sprinkler system could handle. There was no smoke or anything beforehand, but there was a clear ignition point.

The police had deemed it arson, and we all knew who it was. It was Mitchell. The fire took place the day after I was released from the hospital. This was clearly Mitchell's retaliation for not picking me or Conner to join him to replace Kyle. I took one of his, so now he took one of mine. This was what he had meant when he said I should have taken the easy way out and not made things harder. Unfortunately, there wasn't any evidence tying it to him, so Toronto PD couldn't open an investigation on him, and Anders couldn't resume his position as Inspector.

I was flanked at the back of the church between Conner and Anders, pillars of strength holding me up. I was leaning heavily on my cane, as none of my former family left a spot for me to sit during my own mother's funeral, and my gunshot wound and my abdominal sutures were screaming at the effort it took to stand there through the whole service. Conner at least had his arm around me, taking some of the pressure off my recovering body.

No one looked at me when we arrived at the church, and no one told us where the funeral reception was being held. Not a single member of my family spoke or even looked at me the entire time I was there. I would have thought for sure the gnarly scar and line of sutures that ran from my chin and disappeared under my neckline would have gotten a look or two, but nothing. The only interaction I received was when my Uncle Jacob pushed my hand away when I reached out to touch my mother's casket as it was being taken out of the church.

We stayed until the church was empty, every member of my family and community gone, and everything was silent.

"This is my fault," I whispered as I hobbled up to the picture of my mother that stood on the raised altar at the front of the church. "I'm the reason she's dead."

"Adeline…"

"No, Conner, it's true." I turned around to face him as he stood on the step below me, pain and sorrow in his eyes. "If I had fought harder when I got divorced, we might have been able to repair the damage, but I just threw them away like they threw me away. I could have been the bigger person. I could have tried harder. I didn't fight for them." I turned around to face the picture of my mother again. "And if I had just given in to Mitchell…none of this would have happened."

"Except it would have killed you, Addy. It would have killed both of us. Do you really think Mitchell would have had you sitting behind a desk doing an inventory of the women he controlled and traded? He would have tortured you, raped you, sold you to someone else to do God knows what to." He came up behind me and gently put his arms around my centre, being careful of my injuries. "And it would have killed me too. I wouldn't have survived if he got a hold of you."

I understood what Conner was saying. If Mitchell had gotten a hold of him, it would have destroyed me, too. But was my life more important than my mother's? Wasn't I playing God now, deciding that my survival was worth more than the other people in my life who were now targets? How was I supposed to deal with this?

"Come on," Conner whispered as he walked me back down the aisle. "Let's go home."

Anders stayed behind us in his own car the entire two-hour ride home. It was almost as if he was worried we would be ambushed on the drive. And the whole way, Conner and I were silent, stuck in our own thoughts. Every so often, I would see Conner's hands squeeze the wheel before he would put his hand on my thigh as if to make sure I was still there. He would look at me, give me a sad smile and then grab my hand and hold it over the centre console.

I didn't know what to do. I was so caught up in my thoughts that I was starting to think that there was no way out of this situation that didn't involve either Conner or me paying a larger price than we were willing to consider. If I went to Mitchell, Conner would lose his mind and probably end up being shot trying to get me back. If he went to Mitchell, I would probably be captured trying to get him out, and we would both end up under Mitchell's thumb.

The police couldn't do anything, the courts couldn't do anything...frig, a specialized Emergency Response Team run by the RCMP couldn't do anything. What hope did Conner and I have?

And why me? Why us? Why were we so special that Mitchell was now after us?

Conner. It all started with Conner and Mitchell wanting his money back and wanting Conner to be his new investor. He wanted Conner to do one more drop for him as a runner to prove that Conner had never really gotten away. Conner had always been under Mitchell's thumb, even though he never knew it.

I shook my head, immediately removing Conner from blame. Even if Conner had never been part of my life, Kyle had been interested in me from day one. He had his sights set on me from the day I moved in. I would have been pulled into Mitchell's world regardless.

If Mitchell just wanted the money back, Conner would have happily given it to him just to keep him away, but at this point, I didn't think anything would keep Mitchell away. I had a feeling my parents' farm burning down and my mom dying wasn't even going to be seen as retribution for Kyle. My mom's life wasn't even going to be enough. He wanted us in his world, and he seemed eager to force our hands to submit to him. No matter the cost.

"Stay in the car!" I refocused my thoughts out of my Sand Trap, only to realize that we were home and both Conner and Anders were running towards the front porch, both their eyes locked on something. I started to get out, only to have Conner yell at me again to stay in the car. I lasted all of one minute before I saw Anders pull out his cell phone and make a call. That was all the reason I needed to get my ass up there and see what was going on.

I hobbled over to join the men on the front porch and noticed a knife stabbed into the banister railing, pinning a photograph below it.

"What the…" I broke off when I got a good look at the picture. It was of my dad. In the hospital. Tubes and wires running all over him.

"Don't touch it!" Anders barked as my fingers involuntarily went to touch the picture. "I already called Captain Oliveri, and he's on his way."

"But my dad…"

"He's putting an officer outside his hospital room."

I looked from Anders to Conner and back to the picture at least a half dozen times before I flopped down on the patio chair in defeat. This was my second warning. I hadn't even walked into the house yet after my mother's funeral, and there was already another life on the line. If I didn't choose between myself or Conner, my dad would be the next to pay the price. Mitchell was letting me know he was one step ahead and not afraid to follow through on his threats.

"Come on, Addy. Let's go inside."

Conner gently helped me up from the seat, my sutures screaming in protest. I immediately pressed my hand that wasn't holding the cane to my abdomen, where they stretched and moved the most. The gunshot wound in my leg still ached a lot but was healing, and the sutures were starting to dissolve, but the cut down my centre still felt raw and sore. Just the simple task of talking moved my chin and pulled on the cut from my chin to my neck. It was going to take a long time before it didn't hurt to do the simplest movement. I was just finally able to wear a sports bra yesterday without the pain of the band digging in.

It had been 10 days since I was tortured and pretty much cut in half, and it looked like I would be feeling the pain of it for quite a while yet. The physical scars were starting to mend, but the mental ones would remain with me forever. I was still unable to look at myself in the mirror without cringing and getting emotional, and I had yet to look at myself fully naked. Whenever I saw the scars, even the ones on my chin and neck, I felt like I was going to throw up. I couldn't look at myself that way, looking like a monster with a jagged pink scar down my body, covered in black sutures.

Mitchell hadn't realized it yet, but he had already won. He had permanently scarred my body to the point that I was broken inside and couldn't even face myself. I felt like Adeline Peters was already dead.

Chapter 48

If I could have punched Conner in the face hard enough for him to be knocked unconscious until we sorted out a better option, I would have. I was furious.

"NO!" I yelled. "Are you fucking crazy?!"

"Ms. Peters…" Captain Oliveri began, but I shot him a murderous glare from across the kitchen table.

"No," I stated emphatically. "He's not giving himself over to Mitchell. Are you all nuts? Mitchell will kill him!"

"Love –"

I turned my glare to Conner and cut him right off. "Don't you dare 'Love' me. What's your plan? Go back to the strip club in Toronto, knock on the door and say what? 'Hi, I'm here to work for Mitchell. Where can I start?'"

"Ms. Peters…" Anders started, but I just sent him the same look I sent Captain Oliveri. None of these men were going to convince me that Conner turning himself over to Mitchell was a good idea. "We're just throwing out ideas, seeing if something makes sense."

"Well, this one sure as hell doesn't," I pushed back.

"Addy –"

"No, Conner. This doesn't make any sense."

"But –"

"No buts. You do this, you die. We both know it. And then what? What would you have accomplished…"

"Will you just –"

"No, if you're going to keep talking shit, you can just leave and leave this to the rest of us to figure out."

"DAMN IT, WOMAN! WILL YOU JUST SHUT UP?" Conner bellowed. "I have a plan."

"And that would be…" I shot back. I was not in the mood for him to play the martyr and was not going to sit here and waste what little time we had listening to him explain a plan that would end up with the love of my life dead and the man responsible still on the loose.

Mitchell had made it very clear by the note written on the back of the picture of my father that we had until the end of the day to make a decision. It was either going to be Conner's, mine, or my dad's life. One of us was going to have our life taken away within the next six hours. And the elementary school checkboxes didn't make the threat any less terrifying.

You have until midnight. Who's it going to be?

☐ Ms. Peters

☐ Mr. Jensen

☐ Dear old dad

"If you would shut up for a minute and listen for once. I know you're scared, but fuck, you need to listen and think with your head, not with your heart."

The room went quiet as I waited for Conner to proceed, all eyes on the two of us.

"I contact Mitchell and tell him I want to meet." Conner held his hand up to me to stay quiet when I went to interrupt. "I meet with him, explaining how since I got us into this mess, I'll work for him if he leaves you alone."

"No," I cried, tears forming in my eyes.

Conner grabbed my hand as a tear fell down my cheek, already picturing the next funeral I would be attending...alone.

"I'll give him all the money back and take over for Kyle if he leaves you and your family and friends alone. This is all because of me."

"This is not your fault," I whimpered as I tried to scoot my chair closer, but the movement tweaked my stitches, and I flinched. Conner instinctively knew what I needed, pulled my chair closer to his, and wrapped his arms around me.

"It is, Love," he whispered into the side of my head. "If you'd never met me, you wouldn't be in this mess, and your mom would be alive."

"That's not true," I pleaded, looking into his deep hazel eyes that I loved so much. "Even if I'd never met you, Kyle already had me in his sights the day I moved in. Guaranteed, I would have ended up in Mitchell's world regardless."

"We'll never know for sure, but all I know is that it has to be me who ends this."

"We've had something in the works since you were attacked," Captain Oliveri piped in, allowing Conner and me a moment to hold each other and absorb as many minutes as we had left. "We knew as soon as Anders killed Kyle that our stake in this game was done. But I have connections to some pretty powerful people who were willing to help…off the books."

"What does that mean?" I asked. I took a calming breath, wiped my tears away and pulled myself together. I tried to move back to sit properly in my chair, but Conner's arms just held me tighter, rearranged me so that I was leaning back against his side, and he pressed a kiss to the top of my shoulder.

"Have you ever heard of tracking chips?" Captain Oliveri asked.

"You mean like the tracking chips in people's cell phones or like AirTags?"

"Something like that. It's like a cross between an AirTag and the microchips people put in their dogs, but this allows GPS tracking, not just identification." At the nod of my head, he continued. "There's a company in Mexico that has created GPS tracking-enabled chips that can be implanted under the skin. It's been used for years to help with kidnapping cases and has a very high success rate. The problem with implementing them in stakeout or undercover missions is that they're metal, so when the person gets swept, the chip is detected. This is where my contact comes in."

Captain Oliveri pulled out his cell phone and handed it over to me. The screen was an extreme close-up picture of a piece of technology that looked like a grain of rice.

"One of my contacts works in a government lab and has been working on making that tracking chip undetectable to any type of scanner. It's made of plastic, silicone and stainless steel. It's not fully developed yet, but he's moved onto his human trial phase." If I hadn't been looking at Captain Oliveri, I would have missed the quick flick of his eyes over to Conner. It took me a minute before it all clicked together.

I pushed myself out of Conner's arms and sat fully back in my chair, staring at him in disbelief. "No!"

At Conner's nod, I knew I was already too late.

"When?" I asked, my mind trying to figure out when Conner would have had the time to be briefed on such a device, agree to be a test subject and have the device implanted.

"When you were first brought into the hospital and in surgery."

"You've been chipped for 10 days, and you didn't tell me?!"

"Anders presented the option, and I agreed. We didn't want you to worry unless we were actually going to use it."

I turned to Anders. "You knew about this?"

He nodded. "I'm the only person who has the GPS locator matched to his chip. Even the lab can't tell where he is."

"So, what's the plan? Send Conner into the mouth of hell and hope he doesn't get found out or killed? How will you know if Conner's safe or even if Mitchell is in the building?"

"The only way to communicate through the chip is when the signal disappears," Captain Oliveri answered. "So, if Conner needs to communicate for us to move in, he has to remove the chip and destroy it. That will be our signal."

I looked at all three of them in shock. "All three of you have already discussed this? Where the hell was I?!"

Captain Oliveri gave a firm nod. "I had this in the back of my mind ever since the Mitchell incident escalated when you came into the station that first night, and we found that girl in the box. It was always a last resort option, but when you were taken, and Kyle was shot, cutting our ties with the RCMP and their ERT unit, I knew we needed to act on it. Mitchell wasn't just going to let you two go. I made the suggestion to Anders, and he passed the idea on to Conner.

This is the first time we've been together to hash out the details."

I couldn't believe what I was hearing. The best option, the best plan that a police force Captain, an Inspector on the case for over 15 years and Conner came up with was that Conner was to sacrifice himself to Mitchell and hope everything worked out and they caught him? Unbelievable.

"Okay, so let's hash this out." I was so hurt that this had all been discussed behind my back while I was in the hospital after being tortured for Mitchell's amusement. "Question one - how is Conner supposed to cut this thing out of him without someone noticing him doing it or that he's bleeding all over the place?" Captain Oliveri went to answer, but I moved on. "Two – what if he removes it, smashes it, and by the time your guys move in, Mitchell is gone?"

"We'll have an undercover team within a couple blocks of his location at all times, waiting for my signal to move in." Anders jumped in before I got to number three.

"Okay, three – what if Mitchell lawyers up again and gets off? Then we'll have an even bigger target on our back, and that's IF Conner makes it out alive."

All three men looked at each other for a good two minutes. It seemed that I had reached the point in their plan where they were stuck. The silence in the room was suffocating.

"I'll have to get my hands dirty." My head whipped to Conner, and a yelp ripped from my mouth as the jerking motion twisted the sutures in my neck.

"No," I shook my head as I took in the resigned look on Conner's face.

"It's the only way to get the charges to stick. If I do the job and then cut a plea deal or confess in the trial, they won't be able to throw out my testimony."

"But you'll end up getting arrested and serve time."

"Not if Superintendent Harper is involved." Anders, Conner and I all looked at Captain Oliveri. "He's the only way to get inside Mitchell's ring. Toronto PD isn't allowed to touch the case, so that means we can't help. We can't be involved, at least on the books. But if this goes through Harper, he can put you in as an informant, and you'll be clear of all possible charges."

"But we can't trust him," I pressed. "He'd kill both Conner and me if it got him the arrest on Mitchell's case. He's already said he wants to use us as bait."

"So, then that's what we do." Conner's voice had more confidence in it. "We tell Harper that it's getting to be too much, especially after your mom's death, which is true. I don't want to risk anyone else's life, especially not yours. We tell Harper I'm willing to be his bait like he originally wanted, but we don't tell him about the tracker. That remains with you guys. At least then, we'll have people on our side that we know we can trust and will have my back. It's the best hope for the charges to stick for Mitchell and for me to get out alive."

We all looked around the kitchen table at each other, the silence allowing us the chance to voice any more concerns. It was clear none of us liked this, but after talking it out for hours already, this seemed like the only possible option.

"Well," Captain Oliveri said as he looked at Conner. "I think it's time you give Harper a call."

Chapter 49

The audacity and self-righteousness that Harper demonstrated when he walked right into our home when he arrived shouldn't have surprised me, but it did. His unprofessionalism was astounding.

"What are you doing here?" Harper barked as his eyes took in Conner, Anders and myself at the kitchen table. He slammed our front door behind him, marched over to the table and pulled out his cell phone. "I'm calling your Chief of Police, and your ass is going to be canned for interfering. AGAIN."

"Too late," Anders said as he slid a manila envelope across the table towards Harper. "Termination papers from Chief Oliveri."

Conner had called Harper as soon as Oliveri left, ensuring Oliveri's plausible deniability where Toronto PD was concerned, but not before Oliveri handed over the forged termination papers to Anders.

Harper opened them up with a satisfied smirk on his face and read over the documents. "Serves you right," he huffed as he tossed the paperwork back on the table, "but that doesn't explain why you're here."

"We've hired him as personal security," Conner jumped in. "You know, since you pretty much left us out to dry and fend for ourselves."

"Well, what did you expect?" Harper taunted. "I'm not here to babysit you. I'm here to catch the Devil. If you had just listened to me from the beginning, none of this would have happened. It's your own fault you're so deep in this situation."

My gasp was audible as tears immediately filled my eyes.

"What the fuck did you just say?" Conner demanded as both he and Anders stood up from their seats and leaned across the table towards Harper. That moment of interruption gave Harper the opportunity to really look at the three of us.

The immediate shame in his eyes was probably due to seeing all three of us there in our black funeral clothing for the first time. "Sorry," he pushed out, a look of remorse and regret in his eyes. "I'm so sorry. I shouldn't have said that. I heard about your mother. My condolences."

"Not good enough," Conner seethed as I put my hand over his in an attempt to calm him down.

"Conner," I pled, "we don't have time for this."

"Addy, he just said —"

"I know what he said." I pulled Conner down to sit back beside me. "It was hurtful, unprofessional, and he's an ass," I sent a glare towards Harper, who was looking down at the floor, looking genuinely contrite, "but Mitchell is waiting for an answer and time is running out."

Harper cleared his throat. "Apologies, but she's right. Mr. Erbing is waiting, and we don't want to run out the clock. We need to solidify the plan."

"Okay," Anders pushed, "so what's this plan?"

Harper looked at me, looked at the chair in front of him and raised an eyebrow. At my nod, he sat and joined us at the table. "We leave you out as bait. You call Mr. Erbing and tell him you're turning yourself over to him and will be waiting at his warehouse for him."

"You know where his warehouse is and still don't have enough to hold him? Couldn't you raid the place and get all the evidence you need?" I was shocked, although I guess I shouldn't have been.

"Yes, Ms. Peters, we know all his crew, all his locations and his timetable. If we leave now and head right to Toronto, we should arrive right as he's leaving the warehouse and heading home to his wife and kids."

My stomach churned, and I almost threw up on the table. "He has a family?"

"Yes," Harper replied, a look of disgust on his face. "His wife is the den mother who is in charge of making sure all the girls are prepped, trained and ready for their transfers. His boys…" Harper shook his head but didn't finish his sentence.

"My God," I whispered, "he has kids and yet he still does what he does?"

"I know," Harper nodded, "that's why it's so important to catch him and take down his entire operation. He's already grooming his boys to take over, and they're only 10 and 13 years old. That'll also be part of your job while you're in there," he said to Conner. "We need to keep track of the boys and see how engrained in the process they already are."

"So, how will this whole thing work?" Conner asked. "You want me to call Mitchell, tell him I'm in, and then you'll just leave me to the wolves?"

"Not exactly," Harper answered as he pulled a silver men's chain out of his coat pocket. "We've put a micro audio recorder on this chain. It can record up to 100 feet away, so even if he has you take it off, it'll keep recording everything around it."

"But what if they find it and I'm caught?"

Harper shrugged his shoulders. "Don't get caught."

"This is the best option I have?" The disgust in Conner's voice echoed the disgust in my thoughts. Harper really didn't give a shit about Conner's safety at all.

"It's the *only* option with this short notice. We have to leave now if we're going to make it in time. You'll have to call Mitchell on the way and tell him you're on your way to Toronto to meet him."

With a deep breath, Conner looked at me, cradled my face in his hands and gave me a deep kiss. "I love you," he said against my lips before he moved his mouth up to whisper in my ear. "Listen to Anders, please. As long as I know you're safe, I'll be fine."

"Wait," I pulled back, panic taking over. "This can't be it. Doesn't Conner have to sign paperwork or something to prove he's an informant and doesn't end up getting arrested or charged? Doesn't he get any kind of safe word to get him extracted if he's in danger? This can't be all the prep he gets?!"

"Ms. Peters," Harper said as he stood and made his way to the door, "we have to move now. If we wait any longer, we'll miss this window. I'll go over more with Mr. Jensen on the way."

"He's right," Conner said, kissing me one more time before he got up and made his way to follow Harper. "I have to go."

I got up too fast, my stitches screaming in protest and crutched to the front door. This could very well be the last time I ever saw Conner, and I wasn't ready. I wasn't prepared.

"I love you," I whimpered as he wrapped his arms around me and held me tight. I kissed him like it was our last kiss because it very well could be, before Conner abruptly pulled away and walked out of the house.

Anders pulled out his laptop as soon as Conner and Harper disappeared down the laneway.

"Can you turn the TV on, please?" he asked as I stood at the window, watching the love of my life drive away. I had to believe that Conner was tougher than this and could and would survive.

"Sure," I mumbled as I hobbled to the couch and flopped down. Anders joined me as he continued to fiddle with his computer. "He'll be okay, Adeline."

I looked into his fatherly face and had never been so glad this man was in our lives. All I could do was nod in reply, not wanting to break down. If Conner was strong enough to put his life on the line, I was strong enough to support him and not break down.

After a few minutes, Anders got up and plugged his computer into the TV. Within seconds, we were looking at a live stream of a digital map with a blinking red light moving down the road. It took me a second to realize that it was a map of our area, much like Google Maps but completely black and green, and the red dot was Conner's GPS tracker.

"There's no delay in this," Anders said as he joined me back on the couch. "This is live to the second."

That was a relief I wasn't even aware I should have been concerned about. I didn't even want to think what the repercussions could have been if there was a five-second delay and we were five seconds too late in getting to Conner.

"We'll have this playing 24/7, and we'll have to take shifts to monitor what's going on. If Conner's light goes out, you press this button." Anders moved the computer mouse to the bottom left corner, where a white circle was. "It'll send an automatic notice to our operation's leader to move in."

All I could do was nod. This was real. This was really happening. Conner was on his way into the belly of the beast, and his life depended on me pressing a button on a computer screen.

"I...I just need a minute." I got up off the couch and made my way into the bedroom. This was too much. I just needed a moment alone to think and process everything. I hadn't even been able to process my mom's funeral, and here I was in another life-or-death situation for someone I loved. I barely had a moment to breathe.

I gave myself 30 seconds. 30 seconds to breathe, to mourn my mother, to worry about my father, to feel scared for Conner and to try and find my own strength. That was all the time I could afford. I had to be ready for this. I couldn't be distracted or second-guess anything.

I gingerly lowered my black dress over my hips and slid into a pair of Conner's sweatpants and one of his T-shirts. The smell of him was what I needed, but at the same time, it was almost too much. But I shook my head and made my way back out to go over details with Anders.

"I thought you might be hungry," Anders said from the kitchen island where he was slicing up cheese and meat and putting it on a plate that had crackers, apple slices and pickles on it.

"Thank you."

"So, I can take the first shift if you want," he said as he joined me on the couch and put the plate of food on the table in front of us. "We can do eight-hour shifts so that it's not too long and tedious. I have updated Chief Oliveri, and he's notified the team leader that Conner's on the move. He managed to call in favours from three guys he knows, and they'll be waiting at the warehouse for Conner's arrival. They'll keep an eye on the warehouse and will be waiting on my word to relocate if Conner is moved outside of a three-block radius or to move in if the signal goes out."

"So, you have direct contact with the team lead?"

He picked up what looked like an old cellphone. "This is a secure two-way radio. No one else can access this frequency. The only people this connects are me and the team lead."

I just nodded my head and looked back to the TV to watch Conner's blinking light move farther and farther away from home and closer to danger.

"He'll be okay," Anders encouraged again. "He has Harper's tracker, our tracker and Chief Oliveri's crew on standby, ready to move in. We have him covered."

"But what if Conner walks in and Mitchell shoots him on site? Nothing we have can protect him from that."

"If Mitchell wanted Conner dead, Conner would be dead. Mitchell wants to send a message not to mess with him, or you'll be his. He wants Conner back, and he wouldn't be sending you messages like the picture of your father if he just wanted to get Conner back to kill him."

He was right. Anders was making sense, but it didn't do much for the fear I felt and would be feeling until I saw Conner again.

"Why don't you head to bed," he said and put a gentle hand on my shoulder. "You've had a rough day and probably need to process life right now. I'll take the first watch and wake you in the morning."

With a grateful nod, I went to bed and let myself feel everything I'd been trying to suppress all day.

Conner hadn't moved outside of his three-block radius in the three days he'd been gone. His tracking chip was still blinking, and I took that as a good sign. Although the chip would still be blinking if he died, I was trying to focus on the fact that the blinking meant that nothing horrible was happening, and he didn't need the crew to move in yet.

I was just finishing my shift of watching Conner's movements on the TV and really needed to move. Sitting and watching the TV for eight hours was wreaking havoc on my back, especially with my already limited mobility. I was starting to walk a bit better, although I still needed the cane, and my cuts were starting to really heal nicely. The scars were now a rosy pink instead of the bright, angry red they originally were, and the sutures had already started to dissolve.

It had been the worst two weeks of my life, but I was hoping that as the wounds started to heal, my internal wounds would too. I still had nightmares every night and was still unable to look at myself in the mirror. I did, however, start to examine and look at my body in bits and pieces. I had to keep an eye on and continue to clean the cut and gunshot wound, but I had managed to compartmentalize the task and only see one inch of damage at a time.

"So, what do you have planned for the day?" Anders asked as he put his mug of coffee on the table in front of him and pulled my laptop onto his lap. Since his computer was connected to the GPS, I suggested he use mine to do any work he needed. Chief Oliveri had checked in sporadically over the phone, but Anders seemed to be a sleuthing master, digging up any and all new information about Mitchell that he could. The last update he found was that one of Mitchell's lesser-known associates had been arrested yesterday on child pornography charges.

"Not too sure. My back is killing me from all this sitting. I would love to go for a walk outside, but this cane is a pain in the ass in the trees and gravel." Anders huffed and gave me a small chuckle as I shook the stupid but necessary cane around. "I may just do some baking. How do you feel about banana bread?"

"Sounds delicious," he replied with a gentle smile.

The three days we had spent together had really shown me what a sweet and kind man Anders was. I knew he missed his family terribly. I had heard him talking to his wife and kids every night at bedtime, but when he hung up, he never brought it up and never made me feel like I was a bother or a burden.

His phone rang just as I was mixing the dry and wet ingredients, and the worry in his voice as he picked up immediately had me on alert.

"What's the matter?" he asked for a second time, and all I could hear on the other end was panic and crying. "Hold…hold on." He put the phone on his shoulder and nodded his head towards the front porch. I gave him a nod, telling him I'd watch the screen for him.

Poor man. How he managed this job and a family, I'd never know. He must have been so concerned about them, especially after what happened to my family because of my involvement with Mitchell. He told me this morning that his wife called him at 2 a.m. saying she heard a noise downstairs, only to find their 15-year-old daughter in the kitchen looking for a knife to sleep with under her mattress. Everyone was on edge, and it looked like the security Anders had put at his own house was causing more anxiety than it was helping.

I knew the feeling. I was constantly checking the house when Anders was getting sleep and I was on watch. Every crack and creek had me looking around. We left all exterior lights on at all times so that we could always see our surroundings clearly. But it didn't stop the feeling that we needed to constantly be on alert.

And clearly, I was failing at that since I hadn't even noticed how long Anders was gone until the oven dinged, notifying me it was at temperature. I had done all the prep and heated the oven in the time Anders had been outside on the phone. That had been at least ten minutes. I didn't want to intrude, but I wanted to make sure all was okay.

I grabbed my cane and went to the front window to see if I could see Anders pacing on the porch as he so often did. But I didn't see anything. I went to the door and stuck my head out, but I still couldn't see him. It wasn't until I rounded the wrap-around porch that I saw him leaning over the railing at the side of the house.

"But the pregnancy test was negative?" I heard him ask. "And you asked her why there was a need for a pregnancy test to begin with?"

Ooooooh, poor man. Anders, I had learned, had three kids. Twin 17-year-old boys who were both prepping to join the police force when they were done high school and a 15-year-old daughter who, by the sounds of it, was a handful and in a lot of trouble.

I didn't want to invade his privacy any more than I already had, so I quietly crept back into the house and sat on the couch as the smell of banana bread filled the space. I pulled out my cellphone, like I did a hundred times a day, and just looked at the screen.

Conner: I love you

I looked at the text message whenever my thoughts started to wander. Conner had sent the text while he was in the car with Harper on his way to meet Mitchell. It was the last communication I had had with him. And every time I looked at it, I struggled to figure out if it had been a goodbye or a reminder that he would fight for us.

The phone vibrated in my hand before the screen lit up with a picture of Conner and his name.

"Conner?!" I hadn't even let one full ring go by before I answered the phone in a panic.

"Not quite."

Chapter 50

Mitchell's voice on the other end of the line sent shivers down my spine. "But he's here if you'd like to talk to him."

There was a shuffle and a grunt through the phone line before Conner's full, deep voice came through the phone. "Addy, listen to me. Stay where you are. Don't –"

There was a dull thud in the background before more shuffling and Mitchell's sneering voice came back.

"I just have one question for you, Ms. Peters. Did you think I was stupid?" Mitchell's voice was full of venom, something I had never heard before. He was always so calm, eloquent and polished. The bite in his voice was new and unnerving.

"Did you think I wouldn't notice this whole situation has Superintendent Harper written all over it? Conner would never leave you if he had the choice. And for him to meet me at my warehouse? How the FUCK would he know where my warehouse was if it wasn't for Harper? And the necklace with the transmitter? Really? I swear, Harper is the dumbest smart person I have ever met. I bet he doesn't even know that I have one of my men planted in the RCMP."

I was already halfway to the door to get Anders before he continued.

"Honestly, I expected more from both of you. Trying to pull one over on me? Don't you know by now I'm smarter than you? More powerful than you? I'm always one step ahead and have more resources than you could ever imagine."

My concentration was divided between not tripping as I hobbled with my cane out the front door and listening to what Mitchell was saying. I had just rounded to the side of the house when Anders turned the corner, almost knocking right into me. He took one look at my face before he grabbed the phone from my hand and put it on speakerphone.

"I don't know what I'm going to do with you two," Mitchell continued. "It would be such a waste to just kill you both. With Conner's skill with investing and the stock market, he could make me a billionaire multiple times over. And to have you in my ring, you could do so much for me. With your body and brains, I could use you to fuck information out of my competition, be my little honeytrap."

The sounds on the other line of the phone escalated as if there was a fight. Anders ran ahead of me into the house and right over to the TV. I followed as quickly as I could to the sounds of Conner's cursing and cries of pain and more muted thudding and grunts through the background of the call. Until, all at once, I heard Conner scream, the blinking light went out on the TV screen, and an alarm rang out through Anders' computer and the TV, alerting us that the tracker was destroyed.

"CONNER!" I yelled into the phone.

"Now, now, Ms. Peters," Mitchell puffed out, trying to catch his breath, "let's not bother focusing on things we can no longer change and worry about the things we can. You will come to me. You will work for me. You will do whatever I ask of you, or I will destroy everyone you and Conner know until there is no one left in this world for you to turn to. I WILL have both of you. The only choice you have to make is how many people you're willing to sacrifice before you turn yourself over."

Anders dropped his cell phone that he was texting away on and picked up the radio that connected him to the team lead and ordered them to move in.

"Is that Inspector Anders I hear in the background?" Mitchell laughed. "Did he really just give the order for someone to move in? My dear Ms. Peters, we're nowhere near where Superintendent Harper's men are staked out."

Superintendent Harper's men? That must have meant that he didn't know about the tracker Conner had or Chief Oliveri's men. He must have been so focused on tracking Harper's men that he hadn't realized that there was another group watching him.

"You have one hour, Ms. Peters. One hour to leave your home and come to me or someone you know will die the most painful death imaginable. I think maybe I'll start with your father."

"NO!" I yelled. "I'll meet you. Where? Just tell me where."

"Well, why don't you ask Superintendent Harper where I am since he thinks he knows. One hour, Ms. Peters."

At the click of the phone, I grabbed my purse, turned off the oven and headed for the truck.

"Wait!" Anders called as he ran in front of me and blocked me from going down the porch steps. "Just wait."

"How can you say that?!" I cried as I tried to sidestep him but wasn't fast enough because of the cane. "The drive to Toronto is 50 minutes, and that's when I know where I'm going. I don't know where I'm going, and if I don't get there, he's going to kill my father."

"No, he won't. Your father will be fine. We have the cop still stationed outside of his hospital room."

"But —"

"We know where Erbing is. We're right around the corner. The locator chip we implanted on Conner went dead, so that means it got destroyed. Either Conner did it himself because it's time to move in, or it got damaged while Conner was getting knocked around."

I looked at Anders with tears in my eyes, not understanding why this man was waiting and preventing me from going to Conner.

"Think about what Erbing just said," he continued. "He said he will have BOTH of you, which means Conner is still alive. Erbing's not going to kill Conner. He wants Conner to work for him. He won't just throw that away. The chip is implanted in the skin between his thumb and his forefinger, so my guess is someone stepped on his hand and crushed it."

"WHAT?!"

"That's a good thing, Adeline. It means that someone is with Conner, and by how unhinged he sounded, I'd put my money on it, it's Erbing himself. This is personal to him. He won't leave Conner's torture to anyone else. He wants Conner's bruises to be made by his hands." I had to put my hand up for him to stop. The image of Conner, his strong, muscular, solid body being tossed around by Mitchell, just didn't compute. The only way that could happen was if something was already wrong with Conner and he was weakened. He was hurt.

"The call I placed to the ops lead was code for them to tighten up, not to move in. I wanted to make sure that Erbing wasn't on our trail. We know Superintendent

Harper's men are staked out by the waterfront industrial area, but our men are at Conner's actual location, ten blocks away from Harper's. Erbing doesn't know that we have a second team on him and waiting for my code word to move in."

"Well, why aren't they moving in?! If you know where Mitchell is and you heard what's going on, why aren't you moving in?"

"We need Superintendent Harper's men." Anders put his hands on my shoulders and bent down to look me in the eyes. "This is our one shot, Adeline. Chief Oliveri was only able to secure three of his contacts to help with his op, but Harper's men are only ten blocks away. And there's a helluva lot more of them."

Anders took the keys from my hand. "We have to wait for Chief Oliveri to connect with Superintendent Harper and convince him to move to the location we know. It's a tricky situation. We know Superintendent Harper won't like the fact that we're involved and might rush in to prove a point. Or ignore us all together. If we jump the gun, Mitchell could get wind of it, run, and we will never see Conner again. We need to work together to make this takedown happen as smoothly and as effectively as possible."

He was right. I was doing exactly what Conner had asked me not to do. I was thinking with my heart and not my head. But the clock was still running down.

"So, what do we do? Mitchell still gave me an hour's time frame to get to him before he started killing people I know."

"I know, and I've already messaged Chief Oliveri with Conner's coordinates and instructions to reach out to Superintendent Harper. We'll head to Toronto in case Chief Oliveri can't get a hold of Harper, but you're not going in. We have to trust the men we have on this and can't interfere. This is up to Oliveri and Harper now."

It only took Anders and me 32 minutes to reach the Toronto border. Anders drove and spoke to Chief Oliveri the entire way, the sirens blaring and a single red light flashing from the roof as he sped towards town.

Chief Oliveri had said that Superintendent Harper refused to believe that his men were in the wrong location. That was until he checked in with his men and heard that the location they were scouting was abnormally quiet and inactive.

The two teams were merging on site just as we pulled up to the Toronto PD Headquarters. I could hear yelling through Anders's phone and crackling over the two-way radio he and the ops lead had.

"We have movement."

Both Anders and I stopped at the entrance to Toronto PD Headquarters, blocking their doorways as his radio went off.

"Eight men, twelve girls and Erbing are on the move."

"Where are they heading?" Anders instantly ran through the doors and headed straight towards Chief Oliveri's office.

I hobbled as quickly as I could before one of the officers noticed me struggling to keep up and came rushing around with one of their wheelie office chairs. I recognized the officer as the one who had stood outside my hospital room.

"Here, Ms. Peters." He said as he helped lower me into the chair and then quickly pushed me after Anders. We caught up to him quickly and saw him and Chief Oliveri huddled over the radio.

"…keeps checking his watch while he talks on his cell. Some of the girls are making movements with their hands. They're putting their thumbs across their palms and closing their fingers over it." The radio crackled as the ops lead continued. "The doors of the loading bay across the street just opened, and they're heading that way. No one is looking around, no weapons visible, but at least five of the girls keep making that movement with their hands."

"That's a sign for help," I jumped in. "Girls are being taught in school to use it when they're taken or trapped in a dangerous situation. They're signalling for help."

Twelve girls. Mitchell had twelve girls on the move. Twelve girls' lives were on the line. They needed to be saved, but if we tried to save them, what would the consequences be? Anders and Chief Oliveri exchanged a look before looking back at me.

"If they're not looking around or screaming for help," I continued, "there has to be a reason. Just because the ops lead can't see any weapons doesn't mean that there aren't any. The girls could be strapped with bombs, or the men walking around with them could have knives or guns under their shirts and jackets. The girls are quiet because they were threatened, and they took the threat seriously because they probably already saw the consequences if they didn't comply."

"If we move early, we could tip Mitchell off, and he could bolt. A hand signal isn't enough to move in on. If we move in and Mitchell gets away or if he uses the girls as shields…" Anders wasn't questioning my judgment. He just wanted to make sure I was certain before he made the call. He trusted me.

But was I sure? Was I sure that we should risk the operation, risk the lives of the ops and Harper's men to save these girls? Was I really in a position to determine whose life was more important? And what about Conner's life? Was I really debating giving up Conner's life to save these girls? Risking his life, his future and our potential happiness?

I felt like I was playing God.

And I was being selfish. I had been so lucky to find Conner after my divorce and fall in love for a second time, against all the odds. There was no way I'd ever get over losing Conner. Tears burned behind my eyes as I thought of the possibility of that devastating loss. He was a part of me. If I lost Conner, I would be losing a part of myself as well. It wasn't even a question.

But it felt like it was already too late. The ops lead said that there were eight men escorting the girls…was Conner one of those eight? Was he going to be in the crossfire regardless? But this was so much bigger than Conner and I. This was so much bigger than me.

Perspective slapped me in the face. *This is so much bigger than me!* This was a sacrifice I had to make. I couldn't risk the lives of 12 girls so that I could potentially get Conner back and get a happy ending. I wouldn't be able to live with myself if I sacrificed those girls for that possibility. I had to realize that life didn't always end up the way I wanted it to, that life was messy, dirty, unfair, and just plain sucked. I didn't always get what I wanted. Reality wasn't the storybook ending, and reality meant that in order to do what was right, I had to give Conner up, and we had to put the lives of the girls first.

I knew in my heart that Conner would agree. He would give his life up in a second if it meant we would save twelve innocent children. I didn't know the ages of the girls, but if the ops lead was saying "girls" and not "teens" or "women," I had to assume they were young. They probably hadn't even started living yet. They had their whole lives ahead of them, and we were hesitating to save them because we didn't want to spook Mitchell? What the hell was wrong with us?

"Is capturing Mitchell more important than saving the lives of twelve girls?" I asked back. "Are you willing to risk their lives *hoping* that you capture Mitchell and the girls are still in his possession and alive? Who knows if those girls will ever see outside again. This is their only chance."

"Whoa," the ops lead crackled over the radio. "Sir, it looks like something is going down. Three of Erbing's higher-ups just entered the loading bay where Erbing is herding the girls, and two more blacked-out SUVs just pulled up." The radio cut out before the lead voice came back in. "…en more men just came out of the warehouse and are following Erbing's group across the street but keeping their distance. It seems like everyone who's anyone is here. Erbing is about 50 feet away from the loading bay. Ms. Peters might be right. If they get inside, we might never see them again, and with the number of heavy hitters showing up, those girls will disappear in the wind."

"Even if we don't get Erbing, we need to save those girls." I looked at both men, pleading with everything in me. At that point, Erbing and his men didn't matter. "Even Conner would say to forget about himself and save the girls. They should be your priority right now, especially since this might be your one and only shot to help them." *God, I hope we're making the right call. If Mitchell gets away again and we just cost him twelve girls… both mine and Conner's lives will be over. We'll be killed for sure. But not before Mitchell will go after everyone we know and torture them just to get back at us.*

With a nod to each other, Anders picked up the radio and gave the order.

"Breach! Breach! Breach!"

Silence filled the room as the radio went dead. It looked like Anders used the code word for the team to move in. The noises outside in the police station were silenced as well, and everyone was tuned into what was taking place in the Chief's office. You could hear office phones ringing and noises from the back cells, but the workstations and open area around Chief Oliveri's office were dead silent. Everyone was holding their breath.

Everyone must have known. As much as Chief Oliveri said that this was all off the books, everyone must have known that this was a movement against Mitchell.

The silence went on and on. Neither Anders nor Chief Oliveri radioed back for an update. We all just sat in silence, hoping for good news once the takedown was over.

My heart was in my throat thinking about everything that was on the line. The lives of the twelve girls. Oliveri's men who volunteered to help us out. Mitchell getting away. The consequences we'll face when Harper finds everything out. My life…Conner's life.

I could hear my heartbeat and the sound of my blood rushing in my ears. My hands shook, and the silence stretched on. The tension was so thick that it was hard to breathe. No one said a word until we heard the smallest crackle on the radio.

"Erbing's – ow –" the radio crackled and cut out, "… girls – secured."

"Repeat, is Erbing down or out?" Chief Oliveri responded.

There was more cracking on the radio before the ops lead voice came through clearly. "Erbing has been taken out." Noise erupted throughout the police station, but neither Anders nor Chief Oliveri joined in.

"And the rest of Erbing's men?" Anders asked.

"Taken care of. Some are out, and some are down and being handled by the ERT."

Both Anders and Chief Oliveri shared a look, their shoulders lowered in relief, and they patted each other on the back. Mitchell was dead, and his men were either dead or captured.

But I couldn't celebrate. The other half of me was still missing. Was he part of the dead or part of the group that was being handled by Harper's men? Or was he not even there at all? Tears ran down my cheek as I remembered the sound of Conner's scream over the phone before his tracker went dead. What if they had found the tracker and killed him? What if Mitchell wasn't as greedy as he had let on and just got rid of Conner anyway?

Anders looked over to me, taking in my tears and shaking frame, and grabbed the radio.

"What's the 20 on Conner Jensen?"

There was dead air for at least a minute before the radio crackled in response. "Jensen's M.I.A."

The silence that followed was deafening, as if a bomb exploded in the room, and all you heard was nothingness while chaos erupted around you. I slumped back in the chair as the world around me started to crumble. The sound of Conner being tortured when Mitchell had called me an hour ago was replaying over and over. The sound of grunts and cries of pain, the echo of kicks and punches…and now they couldn't locate him. Had Mitchell actually killed him? If he wasn't with the rest of the men moving the girls, and the ops lead was taking this long to find him…

I started to hyperventilate, my world spinning as I pictured Conner's big body beaten, bruised and bloody on some dingy cement floor, his eyes staring blankly up to the ceiling.

"Adeline," a soft voice murmured, "Breathe, Adeline."

I looked up to see Anders beside me, gently stroking my back in an attempt to calm me down, but nothing was working.

"What … if …he's gone?" I asked between gasps. My entire body was shaking in an attempt to hold it together. My brain was firing with so many different scenarios, one worse than the next, and all of them gruesome and horrifying.

"We can't think like that," Anders reassured. "We have to wait and hope for the best."

The radio crackled on the desk before the ops leader's voice broke the Sand Trap I was spiralling down.

"Jensen's been located, but he's down. Send an ambulance right away."

Chapter 51

Turned out that Harper was good at his job, just really bad at the people aspect of it. When the ERT walked into the Toronto Police Department Headquarters after everything went down, they brought in around twenty of Mitchell's men on top of the remaining five that had been moving the girls. And amongst those men were Mitchell's second in command, his advisors, his enforcers, his banker, his lawyer, all of his higher-ups, and his wife. Harper had had his men stationed around the city, poised for a unified strike. When Mitchell was on the move, that was when everything went down at once. Harper had managed to pretty much bring Mitchell's entire operation in.

"And Harper's not there?" I asked Anders as I sat in the waiting room of the hospital, waiting for an update. He and Chief Oliveri were at Toronto Headquarters trying to help the girls that were brought in while the ERT took over the interrogation rooms and started questioning everyone they brought in.

"No," his voice answered through the phone, "I'm assuming Superintendent Harper is updating his Chief on the take-down. Any news on Conner?"

"No," I sighed, wiping away another silent tear. "Not a peep. I was here before he arrived and saw when they brought him in. He looked completely broken, Patrick. He was unconscious with cuts and bruises all over his face, and his hand was wrapped in a Tensor. And they had him handcuffed to the gurney with two RCMPs at his side. I don't get it. Why is he handcuffed?"

"I don't know, Adeline. He was an informant. I get putting a protective watch on him, but I don't get –"

"Patrick Anders and Antonio Oliveri. You're under arrest for Obstruction of Justice. You have the right to rem –" The background voices cut out just before silence filled the phone line.

"Patrick?" I pulled the phone away and saw the call had been disconnected.

There was no way this was happening. There was no way Harper would arrest Anders and Chief Oliveri on Obstruction of Justice charges when it was because of *their* help that Harper's men got moved to the proper location to take down Mitchell.

I tried calling Anders back on his cell, as well as calling Toronto PD Headquarters to speak to Chief Oliveri, but there was no answer on either call.

I went back up to the nurses' station, now more panicked than ever. It felt like Harper wasn't done yet and was making some kind of final move. And with Conner being handcuffed to the bed and followed by two RCMPs, worry and fear settled in my stomach worse than before.

"Excuse me?" I asked the nurse whom I had bothered twice already. "Can you *please* tell me if there is any update on Conner Jensen?"

"I'm sorry, ma'am," she answered with clear annoyance in her voice, "but as I told you, I can't update you on anything until the doctor comes out."

"That's not good enough!" I was losing it. I had been at the hospital for three hours already, not allowed to see him and not given any update. "He was brought in here unconscious almost three hours ago, handcuffed to the bed! I want answers!"

My body was shaking, not only from my fear and frustration but from the fatigue my body had gone through today. The entire length of my cut stung, and the gunshot wound pulsed in pain. I was leaning heavily on my cane and honestly felt like I was about to fall over.

"Ma'am," the nurse scolded, "if you don't calm down, I'll have to call security."

"FINE! Call security. I'd love to talk to them. Maybe they could get me some answers."

SECURITY! NURSES STATION 4.
SECURITY! NURSES STATION 4.

The page through the system rang loudly in the area, but I refused to move. It was only seconds later that two men came into the nurses' station and quickly took in their surroundings. All the nurse did was point to me and go back to typing on her computer.

"What seems to be the problem?" The first security guard seemed serious but kind, taking in the state of my body and how heavily I was leaning on my cane. The second security guard I recognized from when I was in the hospital. He was one of the guys who tried to throw Conner out of my room before Anders stepped in and updated the team on our situation. I only prayed he recognized me.

"Do you remember me?" I asked him, ignoring the question of the first security guard.

"Maybe…you do look familiar." He squinted at me before his eyes took in the cut down my chin and neck and lit up with recognition. "You were the woman who was kidnapped and had the cop stationed outside your room."

"Yes, Adeline," I said and extended my hand to his. I tried to be as polite as I could as it seemed like this guy might be my only chance at getting somewhere.

He gave me a nod and shook my hand, confused as to why they were paged to the area when I was being cordial. "What can we do for you, Adeline?"

"Conner, my partner, was brought in three hours ago. He was brought in with two RCMP and was handcuffed to the bed, and I haven't been able to speak to anyone, get an update from any of the doctors or tell the RCMP there's been a mistake."

"What do you mean a mistake?"

"You know how we had the guard outside our room when I was here?" At his nod, I continued, "It was for our protection because we were being hunted by someone. Conner has been working with the police and was undercover when the raid happened, and the RCMP have taken him in, thinking he's a bad guy."

The first security guard quirked an eyebrow in disbelief as he continued to size me up, probably assuming I was an escaped patient from the psych ward with my story about being hunted and going undercover.

"Was this the Mitchell Erbing takedown?"

"You heard about it?" I was completely floored. I wouldn't have thought word would have gotten out yet.

"About two hours ago. Our boss briefed us that a couple of his men were being brought in for treatment and were high flight risks."

"But Conner's not!" I pleaded. "Can you please see if you can get one of the RCMPs to come out here and speak with me? You know what we went through when I first got brought in. You know we were under protection. Please?"

He cocked his head to the side, signalling for the other security guard to join him as they both walked to the nurse's station and spoke to the nurse there. I swayed back and forth in exhaustion as I waited.

The nurse picked up her phone and made a call before she passed it over to the security guard who I somewhat knew. After a few words that I couldn't hear, he handed the phone back to the nurse and made his way back over to me.

"Here," he said as he grabbed one of the hospital wheelchairs for me. "You look like you're about to fall over."

A traitorous tear left my eye at my exhaustion and stress. "I am."

As soon as I sat down, he started to push me down the hall. The other security guard didn't follow but left down a different corridor. "I don't have an update for you," the guard said, "but I convinced one of the RCMP to at least hear me out and maybe speak with you."

"Thank you," I sighed. "That's all I've wanted all night."

We were silent as we made our way through the halls until we came to a door with an RCMP in black tactical gear standing guard.

"Are you Corporal Eng?"

The Corporal nodded. "You have two minutes. Start talking."

The security guard quickly told him about when Conner and I had first come to the hospital and how Inspector Anders put a guard at our door. Corporal Eng looked at me skeptically, clearly not believing the security guard's story about me surviving being cut in two and put under police protection. *Clearly, this guy got his people skills training from Harper.* It wasn't until I cleared my throat, got both men's attention and traced my finger from chin to chest, showing Corporal Eng the cut, that he quirked his brow and nodded for the security guard to continue.

When the guard started to tell Corporal Eng that he believed there was a mistake, the Corporal interrupted the security guard and turned to me with resolution on his face. "Mr. Jensen is a known associate of Mr. Erbing. We have records of his involvement going back over 15 years."

"I know," I agreed and wheeled myself over to the men. I was tired of them talking *about* me instead of talking *to* me. "That's why Mitchell was after him again. He wanted Conner back in his circle. Harper put Con –"

"*Superintendent* Harper," Corporal Eng corrected with a sneer.

I took a breath and gave Harper the title his associate clearly thought he deserved. "Superintendent Harper put Conner in as an informant since Mitchell wanted him back so much. He told Conner and I we needed to be bait."

"There's no record of an informant in Mr. Erbing's circle in any of Superintendent Harper's paperwork. Unless

507

you can get a hold of Superintendent Harper and have him tell me otherwise, Mr. Jensen is being arrested and prosecuted with the rest of Mr. Erbing's associates."

"What about innocent until proven guilty?"

Corporal Eng had the balls to actually laugh at me. "Listen, lady, unless you have proof, innocent or not, he was in Erbing's warehouse at the time of the raid. He's an associate, no matter which way you look at it."

Fucking Harper. I knew we should have had Conner sign paperwork before he left, but Harper said he'd take care of everything on the drive to Mitchell's warehouse so that they didn't waste any more time. How such an untrustworthy man could be the Superintendent of the RCMP's Emergency Response Team made me fear for our country.

It was always about proof. There was no proof that Kyle broke into my house to install the cameras at the tri-plex, no proof that he had vandalized my car. Mitchell kept getting released after a 48-hour hold because there wasn't adequate proof. There wouldn't even have been any proof Kyle had kidnapped me if it hadn't been for the cameras…

"My cell!" I grabbed my cell phone out of my purse and opened the app for the video cameras around the house. "Harp…Superintendent Harper came to our house and made the deal. I might be able to pick up the conversation on our security cameras. That would prove a verbal agreement."

Corporal Eng clenched his jaw as he watched me scroll through my phone. I pulled up the playback for the date I would never forget. The date my mom died and Conner sacrificed himself for me. I sped up the time on the video until I saw Harper push through our front door.

"Here!" I rushed as I showed Corporal Eng my cell phone. "Just turn the volume up."

All three of us crowded around the cell phone as we watched the front door camera. We watched Harper come onto the deck, push his way into the house without knocking and could hear him yelling at Anders before he slammed the door. The voices immediately muffled, but you could hear murmurs through the dining room window that was right below the camera. And although it was faint, you could hear Harper's informant deal.

Without a word, Corporal Eng opened the door to Conner's room and disappeared, slamming the door behind himself.

"Is that a good sign or a bad sign?" I asked the security guard as we both watched the door to see what happened next.

"No clue," he answered as the door opened, and both RCMP walked out. The one we had been talking to was putting a pair of handcuffs in his jacket pocket.

"You can go in."

I nodded a thank you to Corporal Eng as he handed me my cell phone back and had the security guard wheel me into the room.

And there was the most beautiful and gruesome sight I had ever seen. Conner was sitting up in the hospital bed, his shirt off and his torso completely wrapped in a dressing. His left hand was in a cast with pins and screws sticking out of it, and his face was swollen with cuts and bruises.

"Oh, Conner," I cried as I got out of the chair and hobbled over to the bed.

"Hey, Cricket."

Chapter 52

"Mitchell was on to me before I even stepped foot in his warehouse. I had barely even knocked on the door before it was opened, I was pulled inside, and four men had their guns pointed at me."

I gripped Conner's good hand as we sat in his hospital room. He was providing an official statement for the first time. Conner had been smart and refused to tell the RCMP anything until they documented that he was an informant or until he had a lawyer present.

When he had woken up, handcuffed to the bed, and questioned why he was being restrained, the RCMP immediately went on the attack. Conner had said they had come in, guns blazing and attitudes high, barking at him about his involvement in Mitchell's drug and sex trade rings. They were trying to get him to admit guilt, trying to trap him through coercion and putting words in his mouth. They even refused to attempt to contact Harper when Conner had told them about the deal he and Harper had made.

Now, after I had shown both RCMP our security video where you could hear Harper tell Conner he was going to be an informant, their attitudes drastically changed. That didn't mean that we still didn't obtain a lawyer and record the entire conversation.

"They threw me in a room in the basement and beat the shit out of me. They scanned me while I was on the ground, found Harper's recorder in the chain, and beat me again. Mitchell immediately put me on collection duty and told me if I didn't bring him any 'fresh meat' within 24 hours, he'd kill Adeline." He squeezed my hand and looked at me before he continued.

"They had a guard follow me everywhere I went. I found a young homeless woman who was digging around the dumpsters behind the warehouse. When I approached her and asked her what she was doing, she panicked and asked me to help her. She said she'd do anything as long as I could help her get off the street and hide her from her ex. When I told her I could help her get off the street, but it wouldn't be pretty and would probably be worse, she said she didn't care. I brought her in and gave her to Mitchell and was forced to watch as a group of guys 'tested the merchandise.'"

"My question is, why didn't Superintendent Harper have a written contract or agreement for you to sign?" the lawyer piped in. He sat on Conner's other side and recorded the entire conversation on his own device. Since we still couldn't get a hold of Anders or Chief Oliveri, Conner ended up calling Thane, whose brother was a lawyer, and asked for some help. Within the hour, the lawyer was in Conner's hospital room, and Brie, Thane, Jess, Austin, Tasha, Josh, Kate, and Max were all sitting in the waiting room, not so patiently waiting for an update…or any information at all.

"Harper said that evidence had been going missing, and he was worried something was going on with his team, so he didn't want anything written for someone to find and leak. He didn't want a paper trail."

The lawyer nodded as he scribbled something down, and we turned back to the two RCMPs. The questioning went on for another hour, directed at both Conner and myself. I knew that I wasn't in trouble and didn't *need* to answer any of their questions, but I had clearly been connected to the investigation and takedown and was privy to the inner workings of Anders and Chief Oliveri's plans. Both RCMPs shook their heads when we told them about the chip and the GPS tracker and how it led the ERT to the proper location, uttering about obstruction of justice and playing with people's lives.

But I didn't care what they had to say. It didn't matter that Anders and Chief Oliveri had to operate off-book and interfere with a Special Op. If it weren't for them, Mitchell would still be alive, and I didn't even want to think about what would have happened to those girls. Both men were heroes.

"Superintendent Michael Harper, with the RCMP's elite Emergency Response Team, is set to receive The Order of Canada this Thursday for his outstanding dedication and achievement in bringing down Canada's largest drug trade and sex trafficking ring. The Governor General will present Superintendent Harper with the award during a ceremony at Parliament Hill where he will be recognized for infiltrating and dismantling Mitchell Erbing's entire operation in a single organized attack."

"I'm truly honoured to be recognized for my work. It took over five years of commitment, dedication, evidence, planning, gut instinct, and excellent detective work that allowed me and the RCMP to finally bring down Mr. Erbing's empire, and I couldn't have done it without the trust of my team."

Conner flicked off the TV and threw the remote on the couch beside us. "God, that's the same drivel he spouted off to us weeks ago. Man, that guy really does like the smell of his own bullshit."

It had been a week since everything had gone down and six days since Conner had officially been cleared of all possible charges and affiliations with Mitchell. He had been released from the hospital the day after he gave his statement. He was still very broken and bruised. His left hand was completely crushed and needed pins and screws to hold it together. The doctors said it would be about two months before the bones would fuse back together and they would be able to remove the screws, but he would always have the pins in his hand.

On top of that, he had three broken ribs, a ruptured ear drum from being punched in the ear multiple times, multiple cuts and bruises all over his face and body, and a dislocated hip. Most of his injuries would heal, but the doctors said he'd always have limited mobility and use of his left hand, and would probably have vertigo or balance issues from the damage to his inner ear. With lots of physical therapy, he may get to about 70% of what he used to be.

And frustratingly enough, it was Harper who saved the day and was the conquering hero. He was the one who took down Mitchell himself. After Anders and Chief Oliveri convinced him to have his team move locations, Harper booked it there to join his men. We were told it was already a shitshow and full-on gunfight by the time he showed up on the scene, but as soon as Mitchell saw him, Mitchell turned his gun on the girls and said he would shoot if Harper's men didn't back away. In return, Harper shot Mitchell right between the eyes.

Luckily, up until that point, both sides had wanted to save the girls. Sadly, Mitchell's side only cared because the girls were considered "valuable assets" which had already been sold to clients around the world.

In the end, Harper's Emergency Response Team saved all the girls and took down Mitchell's entire operation. Harper himself was deemed the hero and was being awarded by the country, while Conner and I received a formal thank you from the Toronto Police Commissioner; Conner for having the implant in his hand, which signalled the proper location, and me for telling Anders to order the takedown when I heard about the girls giving the hand signals. Because of the two of us, everyone moved in at the right time and place, resulting in Mitchell's death and the rescue of the girls.

Everything was pretty much wrapped up in a nice pink bow, but it didn't feel that way. Justice hadn't been served.

Mitchell didn't have to pay for his crimes. When the takedown was made public, and his list of crimes was out for everyone to see, the amount of evidence that Harper had, the detailed accounts of what Mitchell did or had his people do…death was too easy for him. He shouldn't have gotten off with a simple kill shot between the eyes and instant death. Mitchell had irrevocably changed both Conner and me, leaving permanent scars that would never fully heal or disappear and mental trauma that changed us to our core. I couldn't even imagine the trauma and horrors he had inflicted on anyone who had actually been taken and forced into his trade, into his world of pain and torture and slavery. Death had been a mercy he hadn't deserved.

And then there were the true heroes, the real people who saved the day. But because Anders and Chief Oliveri were both charged with obstruction of justice, there was zero recognition, not that either of them wanted it. It was because of Conner's official statement that the charges were dropped for both of them, and they were forced into early retirement, which neither one minded. But it still burned my ass that after everything they did, all the work that Anders had put in for over 15 years, the connections Chief Oliveri used to make a smart plan that worked flawlessly, they pretty much received the equivalent of a dishonourable discharge.

But there was nothing we could do. Neither Anders nor Chief Oliveri wanted to contest their forced retirement, and there was no getting through to Harper to try and convince him to give recognition where recognition was due. Not only was he a stubborn ass that thought he walked on water, but there was literally no getting through to him. He wouldn't answer our calls and eventually blocked us, so we couldn't even leave a message.

Officially, according to the news and public knowledge anyway, the case was closed. The bad guy was stopped, and the proverbial good guys won, even though not all the good guys received the recognition.

I looked over to see Conner, my good guy, my hero, lying down on the couch, on the verge of passing out. The pain meds they had him on were strong and knocked him out, but he was here. He was safe. We were together in a home that we both created, that was filled with a mixture of both our lives and a love that I never thought would be my reality.

This man, this beautiful, strong, stubborn man, had given me a love and a life I didn't know was possible. It was a life where I had a voice. A life where I was his partner, his equal. A life full of laughter and adventure and so much love. A life where someone thought I was worth loving and fighting for.

But it wasn't just because I now had Conner in my life that it was worth living. It was because this life, with all the struggles, the fighting, and the fear, changed who I was.

Going through all that trauma forced me to dig deep and find out what I was really made of, and this past year, I faced more trauma than I knew what to do with. Being stalked, videotaped, my home being broken into, my vehicle being vandalized, being kidnapped, assaulted, tortured, my mother's death, my father's hospitalization, and Conner's time in Mitchell's circle...my reality had been what nightmares were made of.

But those nightmares showed me what I was capable of. They were experiences that showed me that I did have a backbone, that I was strong and determined, and turned me into a person who wasn't afraid to speak their mind and stand their ground. I became a person who was seen and heard and saw the power that I had in me and the potential to live a life I *wanted* to live. A life the old me never thought

I deserved or would ever have. A life where I was able to come into my own and discover who I was down to the core and be unapologetic about it.

In a small town, in the middle of nowhere, I had finally found a life worth living, a life worth fighting for. Conner and I had a lot of work ahead of us, a lot of healing, both mentally and physically, but if I was ever sure of anything in this life, it was that the life Conner and I had built together was worth it. We were worth the work and the fight, and more importantly, I finally realized that *I* was worth the work and the fight. I was worth it. I was finally able to be myself, be who I wanted to be, other people's opinions be damned. I was honest with my feelings and transparent with my thoughts, and there had never been a time in my life when I felt more comfortable in my skin, more confident in who I was and that I was finally living life as the person I was always meant to be.

And for the first time in my life, I was able to say that I was happy with who I was. That I finally felt like I was enough. That I was finally me.

Epilogue

One year later

"Hello?" My voice was groggy as I answered my cell phone. A quick look at the alarm clock showed that it was just after 3 a.m.

"Hi, Adeline, it's Michele. Sorry to call you so early in the morning." It took me a second to realize I was talking to my placement worker at Child Services.

"Oh, uh, hi, Michele, it's no problem. What's up?"

I got out of bed, not wanting to wake up Conner as he had just got home two hours ago after his shift at *Ape Hangers*, and walked into the living room.

"Well, we've got a bit of an issue. It's Simone. Her mom was just arrested. Simone's being brought in tonight, and she asked that I give you a call."

Simone. She had to be the sweetest girl you'd ever met. And it was even more remarkable if you knew what she'd been through growing up. Her mom had been arrested multiple times for prostitution, and they had no idea who her dad was. She'd been around sex, alcohol, drugs, and God knows what else since the day she was born, and yet, she wasn't broken down. Yes, she had sass and attitude, but I wouldn't expect any different from someone who has had to raise and advocate for themselves their whole life. She was Tyler's girlfriend, and they were a good influence on each other.

"I know you'll want to talk this over with Tyler and Conner, and Simone's aunt is always an option, but I thought I'd try you first."

"Thanks, Michele." I looked out the side kitchen window and saw the tiny house where Tyler was sleeping. "Can you give me an hour? Is Simone safe for now?"

"Yes, she's safe; she's at her neighbour's right now."

"Okay," I answered, immediately knowing a family meeting was needed. "Give me an hour. I'll chat with Conner and Tyler and get back to you ASAP."

The role of Emergency Relief Foster Parent was tough. You didn't always know who was walking in your door or what traumas they carried with them, but when you saw the relief on the child's face at having a bedroom to themselves, clean clothes, warm food and trusting adults there to help, it was worth it.

We had been in the role for about eight months now and had had three placements. But when Tyler arrived on an emergency placement six months ago, we knew we couldn't just be emergency relief for him.

Tyler's childhood had been rough. He lived in the old, run-down part of Hennington, sandwiched between a halfway house and a crack house. Hennington OPP was there all the time doing raids and arresting people, and as impressionable youths will do, he got involved in their crap too. His neighbours had talked him into helping with drops and pick-ups, and once the school found drugs on him and hundreds of dollars in his locker, Child Services became involved.

Tyler had been fifteen when he showed up at our door with Michele. His teacher had called the police when he had shown up to class with round cigarette burn marks on his arms and had a hard time sitting down. He was taken to the hospital immediately for an assessment. His parents were charged with child abuse and stated that they didn't want him back. We took him in and immediately wanted to keep him forever.

Conner saw a bit of himself in Tyler and didn't want to see him fall into anyone else's trap like Conner had with Mitchell. The next morning, Conner called Michele and asked what steps needed to be taken if we wanted to pursue custody of Tyler.

Over the next six months, Tyler stayed with us under a court order while we took whatever steps were required of us to legally adopt him. Of course, we had asked Tyler if this was something he wanted, and when the tears came to his sad brown eyes, and he nodded his head, thanking us for being the first people to actually want him, we knew he was home.

Conner took him under his wing right away, talked to him about right and wrong and got him into the gym to help channel his anger. And just this past summer, they worked together to build the tiny home that sat beside the creek in the backyard. It was Conner's way of helping Tyler learn life skills, much like Matthew did for Conner.

"Who was that?" I turned around to see Conner walking into the kitchen to get a glass of water.

"It was Michele. It's Simone."

Conner dropped his head and shook it slightly back and forth. He felt the same way about that girl that I did.

We had both met Simone multiple times and even took care of her when her mom had 'friends' over, and Simone just needed to get away. She even stayed with us for one week when she had the flu and needed someone to take care of her.

"Why don't you go get Tyler, and I'll make some coffee?"

I just nodded, grabbed my housecoat and outdoor sandals, and made my way to Tyler's house.

He was 16 now but still suffered from night terrors and had trust issues. His parents would always steal from him and abuse him when something didn't go their way, so he was always on guard. We realized after the first week that unless he was locked in his room, he wouldn't sleep. He would even lock his bedroom while he was at school so that nothing would be taken. It was a hard habit that he was still working on breaking. He apologized profusely when we questioned him about it. He said it wasn't that he didn't trust us, just that he *couldn't* trust anyone. We thought his own place for his own stuff might be the best answer, and quickly, that tiny home became his safe space.

I walked up to the navy blue home with white trim and knocked on the door.

"Tyler? Wake up, bud. Family meeting."

I had to knock two more times before he answered.

"Madds?" he asked, using the name he created for me, a short version of Mama Addy. "What's going on?"

"Michele called. It's Simone."

"Fuck." He breathed out the curse, grabbed the sweater that hung by the door, and followed me back to the main house. "Her mom got arrested again, didn't she."

"Yup. She's at the neighbours right now, but Simone asked Michele to give us a call."

"Smart girl. I knew I liked her for a reason." I couldn't hide my smirk as I looked up at the kid who towered over me at 6 foot 2 and rubbed my hand up and down his back as I led him into the house.

Conner was at the dining room table with three cups of coffee and a box of cookies laid out.

"Hey, kid," Conner greeted with a slap on the shoulder as Tyler sat down. "You good?"

"Yeah," Tyler drawled as he took a sip of his black coffee, "I just worry about Simone. I wish her mom would just fuck off already or that Simone would just get emancipated. She just keeps getting her hopes up every time her mom shows any type of improvement, and then boom, the bomb drops, and she's cleaning up her mom's mess again."

"That's not up to us, Ty," Conner offered. "All we can do is be there when the people in our lives need us and not judge them for needing help."

"I know."

The relationship between Conner and Tyler often reminded me of the relationship between Lorelei and Rory from *Gilmore Girls*. Although technically one was the guardian and the other the child, it was more of a sibling/friend/mentor relationship. We tried to be there for Tyler as much as possible and provide structure, guidance and security, but he was sixteen now. He was already grown. We didn't need to parent him. We needed to help him, shape him, and guide him in a direction that would lead to a better life. And although we had to put our foot down and set rules and boundaries, we respected that he was his own person who knew what he could and couldn't handle and knew when to ask for help.

"So here's the situation," I started. "Michele called, and Simone's mom got arrested, and Simone asked her to call us for an emergency placement. You know we love Simone, and she's always welcome here, but we need to talk about this."

"What are your thoughts?" Conner asked as he looked at Tyler.

"I want her out of that house," Tyler said, anger evident in his voice. "She feels safe here. She's told me so before. I'd love for her to be here and to get to see her all the time. You guys know that."

"Yes, we do," I answered, "but if she's here, it means she's here. In this house, upstairs. It doesn't mean you two are living together in the tiny house."

Tyler nodded his understanding, but Conner pressed on.

"We're serious here. The only reason you're out there is because of your situation. Simone's situation is not the same. In fact, it's probably the exact opposite. She's been fending for herself for so long that she'd probably love having someone else take care of her and watch over her. You're both healing, Tyler, and that's more important than hormones."

"I know," Tyler said, this time looking at both of us. "I love her, but I'm scared for her." That was the first time he had admitted it to us, although we both already knew he did. The boy was crazy about Simone. "I worry about her. Every day. Whenever I'm not with her at school, I worry about what she's walking into when she gets home or who and what she'll find in her house when she wakes up. I...I need her here."

We had a rule in the house that no matter what, there was no lying. It didn't matter if you knew it was something we didn't want to hear or something that would get you in trouble. In this family, you didn't lie. And when Tyler said that he needed something, we knew it was true. He rarely showed weakness, and to him, asking for help was just that. So when he said he worried about Simone and needed her here to make sure she was safe, I instantly knew he meant it.

Conner and I shared a look before Conner nodded at me. "Okay," he said. "Addy will call Michele back, and you and I can talk out some details on the way back to your place."

The guys grabbed their coffee cups and made their way back outside. I watched as they went out the front door, around the deck and down the back steps to Tyler's little home. They were both talking and nodding as they stopped at Tyler's doorway. It wasn't long before Conner grabbed Tyler from behind the neck, looked him in the eye and gave him a man hug.

I grabbed my cell and called Michele back.

"Hi Michele, it's Adeline Jensen. When can you drop Simone over?"

As it was a warm May evening, I decided to sit on the front porch while I waited for Simone to be dropped off. Conner and Tyler were still out back, now in Tyler's home, either playing video games or discussing their workout programs.

The bond those two had made my heart melt. Conner was such an amazing father figure. I couldn't count the times that just watching him in a fatherly role made me wet for him. And he didn't hold anything back, either. He was a straight shooter, telling Tyler how things were, no sugarcoating or pretending they weren't what they were.

When Conner told me a condom had fallen out of Tyler's gym bag one day while they were working out in the garage, I was worried about how we were going to deal with it. But in true Conner fashion, he called a family meeting and put it out there that the tiny house wasn't made for Tyler to use as a sex house but that he was glad he was at least using condoms. He told Tyler that if he and Simone were going to have sex, he'd rather they be safe and use the house than be all over town doing God knows what. But if his grades started to slip, or he noticed Simone over more than usual, coming and going at all hours of the day and night, they'd be having a much different discussion.

I, on the other hand, tried to focus on the consequences. No matter how careful people were, accidents happened, and neither of them was in a position for an accident to happen.

Tyler had been embarrassed and defensive and stormed back to his home, swearing at us to mind our own fucking business. But an hour later, he came back out, apologized and asked if he could talk to Conner about some "guy stuff."

I couldn't help the smile that came when I thought about how awkward Tyler had been or the "what the fuck do I do" look Conner had sent me when Tyler asked for a "guy talk." But the two of them just always seemed to just get each other. Not to say that the two of them didn't yell, swear and fight with each other because they did, but that was what the gym was for – to work out their aggression and differences. You couldn't stay mad and angry at someone when you were trusting them to spot you when you were squatting 500 pounds.

The gym came into view as I walked around the wrap-around deck, taking in the warm wind through the trees, the chirping of crickets in the surrounding woods and the soft sound of the creek.

Conner and I had gotten married in our backyard by the creek one month after the Mitchell fiasco went down. We figured, after everything we had been through, what was the point in waiting. We had already fought and risked our lives for each other; what else were we waiting for?

It had just been Kate and Max, Jess and Austin, Brie and Thane, Tasha and Josh, Phil and Ian from *Ape Hangers*, Conner's parents, and Antonio Oliveri. Patrick Anders gave us the honour of officiating the ceremony. Both Conner and I had limped out to the creek; thankfully, I had been able to go without the cane by then. We had a five-minute ceremony, and then we all just gathered in the backyard for a BBQ and drinks.

That's how most of the summer had passed, with friends out in our backyard.

By Christmas, we had already contacted Child Protective Services and inquired about becoming Foster Parents. The fact that Mitchell had had two boys who were now in the system had stuck with Conner and me as the multiple trials and arrests took place over the months. Those two boys were completely innocent in the matter, and yet, because of the decisions of their parents, their lives would be so much harder than necessary.

Conner and I briefly talked about taking the boys in ourselves as we knew what they had been through, but we couldn't. It was too close to home. The boys were too connected to what had happened to us and of no fault of their own. We couldn't do it, but it didn't stop us from helping other kids when the situation arose.

On New Year's Eve, the one-year anniversary of when Conner and I had our first kiss, I was working on my second novel. The first one was with my old boss at the publishing firm getting edited when I found the list. The list of ten things I had wanted to accomplish my first year after being divorced.

I had read it over with a huge smile on my face. I could proudly say I had crossed everything off that list, but I quickly realized that it didn't matter. It didn't matter that I now worked out in the gym with Conner and Tyler or that I had been able to grow a garden at the side of the house and keep the flowers alive all season. It didn't matter that I was able to cook all the dishes on my list or that I volunteered at the local animal rescue Monday nights.

All that mattered were numbers 6 and 10; #6 – do something brave just for you, and #10 – look into becoming a foster parent or adoption.

I had been brave this past year and fought for myself and Conner. I had been brave in fighting for the relationship I wanted, brave in fighting for the life I wanted. I was brave in standing up to Kyle and Mitchell and, most importantly, brave in finally allowing myself to be me.

And the bravest part was opening my heart, my home…and myself to someone in need. I looked over at Tyler's little home and smiled. Adopting Tyler had been a no-brainer. I still struggled if I was a good mother figure and if I was the best person to give advice, but no one would ever care for that boy more than Conner and I would.

I looked at the life around me and thought about the two men in my life who completely filled my soul: Tyler, who challenged me but gave my life purpose and meaning, and Conner, my beautiful husband and partner who not only accepted my quirks and insecurities but constantly encouraged me to "just do you."

I sat out on the back deck and took it all in. The clear night sky with the millions of shining stars, the fireflies that flashed in the trees and the moonlight that glimmered off the creek. I listened to the noises around me: the crickets that were a constant soundtrack to the night, the gentle breeze moving through the leaves and the faint sound of laughing from Tyler's tiny house. If I had never moved to Hennington, I would have never found this peace and all the possibilities that it had presented and still had to offer.

This town taught me how to be brave, be fearless, and how to be me. Hennington wasn't just a small town in the middle of nowhere Ontario. It was the place where I got to start over, begin my life again and face my fears head-on. It was where I had to learn to trust myself and be strong, where I discovered that there was true evil in the world and had to face it head-on. I had experienced growth and adventures that I never would have had if I hadn't moved and stayed here.

Just a simple decision had completely changed my life, and I couldn't wait to see what adventures this new life brought me next.

The End

Acknowledgements

I can't believe I'm here.

Never in a million years would I have imagined that my thoughts would have turned into words, and those words would have created a story that people are actually wanting to read. I cannot thank all of you enough for taking a chance on my story and actually making it to the end.

To Michelle and Kelley: You were amazing Beta readers. The entire time, you showed me kindness, encouragement and honesty. It's because of you two, that I was able to finally see this story as something worth publishing, and not the complete dumpster fire I was worried it was. Thank you for not holding back with your thoughts and for your many check-ins.

To Ava: Thank you for reaching out and offering your guidance and direction. You were an amazing sounding board, and without you, I would have been completely lost.

To the wonderful Cygnets: I've never met such an encouraging, motivational and open group of women, who were able to help, answer all my many questions, provide tips and tricks, and were there with encouragement the entire way. The amount of love and support you have for each other is truly heartening. You showed me that anyone could publish a book, and that it wasn't the far-off dream that I thought it was.

To TL Swan: You'll probably never read this, but thank you for being so grounded, down to earth, and honest about the publishing process and the struggle of taking an idea and transforming it into something you can present to the world. If I hadn't found your books, your groups, and videos, I would never have found the courage to do this. If we had more people like you in the world, more people would be following their dreams and finding the courage to try something new.

Michele – You are one of my dearest friends and were the first people who got introduced to Adeline and Conner. You had the most enthusiastic response when I told you I was writing a book, and have been there for every step of the publishing process. You have been an amazing cheerleader. Thank you.

And finally, my husband. I could not have done this without your support and encouragement. No matter how many times you've teased me for reading my smut books, you enthusiastically encouraged me to write my own story and get it published. You are the reason I know what love is and am able to write amazing, honest and realistic men like Conner. Thank you for always being my best friend and for constantly telling me I'm enough.

About the Author

Jenn grew up in Ontario, Canada, where she continues to live with her husband, her dog, her piles of books, and her numerous fake plants.

She is an avid romance reader, an animal lover and dreams of one day seeing her name in lights.

This is her debut book, with more planned in the future.

Printed in Great Britain
by Amazon

47711125R00304